MORE ADVANCE PRAISE FOR *RESTRIKE*

"There's a major new presence on the crime scene . . . Reba White Williams. *Restrike* will strike a big hit with sophisticated readers who love culture, uncommon criminals, and terrific writing. You won't be able to put this book down!"

—ALEXANDRA PENNEY,
the bestselling author of *How to Make Love to a Man*,
former editor-in-chief of *SELF* Magazine

"*Restrike* is a thrilling and compelling story of murder and treachery. Reba Williams kept me spellbound."

—FRANCESCA ZAMBELLO,
Director of the Glimmerglass Festival,
director of opera and musicals,
including *The Little Mermaid*

"For art lover and mystery fan alike, *Restrike* is a feast."

—SUSAN LARKIN,
author of *Top Cats: The Life and Times of the New York Public Library Lions*, *American Impressionism*, and other books

"A novel that does what the best fiction should always do: it fully inhabits a fascinating subculture. The investigation at the heart of this novel is not just into murder, but into the nature of fraud, forgery, and the secret selves that often rise up unexpectedly to ambush us."

—K. L. COOK,
author of *Love Songs for the Quarantined*
and *The Girl from Charnelle*

Cousins Coleman and Dinah Greene moved to New York City after college to make their mark on the art world, and they have—Coleman as the editor of an influential arts magazine, and Dinah as the owner of a print gallery in Greenwich Village. But challenges mount as Coleman discovers a staff writer selling story ideas to a competitor, while Dinah's Greene Gallery slips into the red. When billionaire Heyward Bain arrives announcing plans to fund a fine print museum, Coleman is intrigued and plans to publish an article about him, and Dinah hopes to sell him prints. Then, unexpectedly, swindlers invade the art world to grab some of Bain's money, and a print dealer dies under mysterious circumstances. Risking her own life, Coleman sets out to unravel the last deception threatening her, her friends, and the once-tranquil world of fine art prints.

Restrike

Restrike

Coleman and Dinah Greene Mystery No. 1

Reba White Williams

All characters appearing in this work are fictitious.
Any resemblance to real persons, living or dead,
is purely coincidental.

Delos
P.O. Box 457
Edinburg, VA 22824
888.542.9467   info@Delosfiction.com

Library of Congress Control Number: 2012954891

Restrike

1. Verb: To hit again.
2. Noun: A fine art print made later than the first edition, usually inferior, and often made after the artist's death.

—— Prologue ——

NORA TIMOTHY SAT up, her heart racing.

Something had frightened her. There! Bangs, crashes. A shriek, cut off. That was the sound that had woken her.

Mrs. Timothy was eighty-four and a widow. She read the newspapers and knew what could happen to old ladies who lived alone. She lay down, holding her breath, trying not to make the bed creak or the sheets rustle. Twice she reached for the telephone; twice she pulled back. What if they heard her calling for help? The walls were thin and the door was flimsy.

The crashes grew louder. Surely someone in the building would call the police.

She pulled the quilt over her head, closed her eyes, and prayed for the boy across the hall, and for the Blessed Lord to protect her. The church clock struck one and she heard the shriek again. She folded the pillow around her head to shut out the sound. Someone would call the police, she was sure of it.

TUESDAY, 2:10 AM

Bethany turned on her bedside light, looked at the clock, and groaned. She rolled out of the narrow bed and slipped her faded cotton flannel robe over her naked body. Her toes curled with the shock of the icy linoleum. She ran to the kitchen and switched on the electric kettle. More and more lately she fell asleep as soon as her head touched the pillow, only to wake a few hours later. Her mind searched for problems to worry over, and not until six or seven or even eight in the morning would sleep return. Sometimes a cup of Sleepytime tea helped.

She pulled the blanket off the bed and settled in the big stuffed chair by the window, wrapping the blanket around her. The radiators wouldn't produce heat again until six when their clanging would wake her, if she were lucky enough to be asleep.

Bethany read anything she could find on insomnia, and she'd tried every remedy she'd ever heard of. She knew not to lie in bed fretting; it was best to get up and read something boring. She was working her way through the New York Public Library's career guide section. She'd soon be looking for work, and if she couldn't find another job in the art world, she'd have to find one somewhere else.

When the kettle whistled she made her tea, staring down at the empty street two floors below. The only sign of life was a skinny gray cat slinking around the garbage cans near the streetlight.

She was watching the cat, feeling sorry for the miserable creature, when a figure turned the corner off Seventh

Avenue and strode west on Charles Street. Who would be out at—she glanced at the clock again—2:20? The figure had a dark beard, and wore whites—probably a doctor from the clinic on Sixth Avenue. He wore a raincoat and a knit hat pulled down low, and carried a doctor's bag in his gloved hand. Strange combination—a coat too light for this clear and crisp October night, and a woolly hat and gloves, more suitable for January. He disappeared into a tenement across the street. A house call? Maybe he lived there. She picked up her notebook and made a note of the doctor's arrival time, just as instructed in *Everything You Need to Know About Being a Detective*; the best career guide she'd read, although still tedious. So far, it was not sleep-making.

She glanced longingly at P. D. James's *Death Comes to Pemberley* lying on her bedside table. Jane Austen was a favorite writer, and she loved "After Jane" books, especially when written by such a talented writer. But she knew better than to read anything exciting. Maybe when she finished the latest how-to she'd get a job as a detective, like Kinsey Millhone. Or maybe she could become a bounty hunter like Stephanie Plum. Yeah, right. Z was for zero chance.

Movement in the street again caught her eye; the doctor was walking east. If he'd made a house call, it was a quick one; it was only 2:40. She noted his departure time and returned to the book.

Oh, misery, Bethany thought. Time passes slowly when you're awake, and nearly everyone in New York is asleep.

TUESDAY, 6:00 AM

Mrs. Timothy woke at her usual time. She remembered the commotion in apartment 3B, but with the arrival of a new day, the noises she'd heard didn't seem so alarming. She listened, cocking her head towards the door. Silence, thanks be to Heaven.

She pushed her feet into fuzzy slippers and pulled on her navy wool robe. She lit the gas burner under the percolator and shuffled into the bathroom. When she'd washed the sleep from her eyes, she pressed her ear against the hall door. Not a sound.

She opened the door a crack and peered out. The hall was empty, but the boy's door was ajar.

Oh dear, he wouldn't want someone to walk in. He'd given her his number in case of an emergency; she'd call him. She let the telephone ring ten times, but nobody answered. He must be out, or asleep. With that door open, if he hadn't been robbed already, he soon would be. Greenwich Village wasn't as safe as it used to be.

She poured coffee into her yellow mug decorated with smiley faces, and added milk and sugar. After a few sips for strength, she locked the door behind her, and crossed the hall to 3B.

Just inside the entry was a life-size photograph of the boy, looking like a laughing angel, his fair hair blowing in a heavenly breeze. He'd told her he'd modeled for photographers. This must be one of the pictures. Such a lovely boy.

She frowned at the mess: chairs turned over, one broken. That's what she'd heard last night—a wild party. Maybe too much to drink. Avoiding the shards of broken glass, she tiptoed to the bedroom: if the boy was sleeping, she didn't want to startle him.

At first, she couldn't make sense of what she saw. She closed her eyes and shook her head to clear it. But when she looked again, nothing had changed. The white walls were splashed with red.

She stared at the body on the bed. The boy's beautiful blond hair was red with blood. She screamed. Even when people surrounded her, even when somebody put his arm around her, she couldn't stop screaming.

── One ──

Coleman Greene paused just inside the entrance to Killington's auction room to look at a group nearby. The central figure, a dark-haired fortyish man, was only a few inches over five feet tall—about Coleman's height in the three-inch heels she always wore—but like Napoleon, he exuded power. This had to be Heyward Bain, the man she wanted to meet. He was flanked by an enormous hulk—probably a bodyguard—and a voluptuous redhead in a pink Chanel suit, dripping gold chains.

Coleman stared at him as long as she felt she decently could, memorizing his tanned face. She was close enough to see that his eyes were a light gray, and his black eyelashes were so long they looked false. She'd have liked to speak to him, but there wasn't time. The auction was about to begin.

She was looking around for an empty seat when her cousin Dinah touched her arm. "I saved you a seat down front—all that was left when I got here," Dinah said.

9

"Before we sit down, check out the trio to my left," Coleman said in a low voice.

Dinah's blue eyes widened. "Who are they? I've never seen them before. I'd remember."

Coleman nodded. "Anyone would—they're definitely distinctive. They're new in town. Debbi Diamondstein called me late last night to tell me that Heyward Bain has come to New York to open a print museum; she said he'd be here and I should introduce myself. She's handling his press, and she wants me to interview him for *ArtSmart*. That's Bain."

Dinah was still staring. "A print museum!"

It figured that Dinah, newly married and a print dealer, would be more interested in Bain's plans for a museum than his looks or his fortune. Coleman, on the other hand, was thrilled to see a handsome new bachelor in town.

"Is he here to buy? Or is he just sightseeing?" Dinah asked.

Coleman shrugged. She was scanning the room for celebrities to mention in her article, but Bain was still on her mind. "Who knows? If he buys, I'm sure he'll have someone bid for him like all the other big-deal collectors."

Dinah was still staring at Bain and his entourage. "Who's the redheaded woman?"

"It must be his assistant," Coleman said. "Debbi told me her name—Ellen Carswell. She's expensively dressed—that outfit costs thousands, and her jewelry looks real. I wonder if she's more than an assistant? I'd hate to learn that Bain was already spoken for."

At ten o'clock Killington's top auctioneer, a tall brunette in a trim black pantsuit, stepped into place at the podium. She'd move the auction along rapidly, with one lot sold every forty seconds. A lot might include only one print, or several. If all went well, two hundred lots of about three hundred prints would have been sold shortly after noon. Coleman planned to stay till the end of the auction, or until she saw Bain leaving. She could get the auction details from Dinah. Bain was the news.

She craned her neck for another look around. The room was packed with dealers, collectors, artists, art press, and an unusual number of spectators—who, unlike those who planned to bid, didn't have paddles— and it buzzed. The crowd looked expensive—designer clothes, coiffed hair, even furs, unnecessary on this beautiful October morning. The room even smelled rich: perfume, a hint of tobacco, and the odor of new leather.

Killington's, the largest and grandest of the auction houses that had opened in the years since the price-fixing scandal at Sotheby's and Christie's, was holding its first auction of the season. After more than a month of pre-opening festivities—benefits for the New York Public Library, the New York Botanical Garden, and the Central Park Conservancy—Killington's was launching its autumn season with a print auction.

A surprising choice. Prints weren't as glamorous as many other art objects. Nevertheless, Killington's had rounded up some outstanding works and attracted a stellar crowd.

But if not for Heyward Bain, Coleman wouldn't have covered the auction; she'd have sent one of the writers. Since she'd bought *ArtSmart* three years ago, she wrote only a monthly column and a few important articles a year. Bain was her kind of story.

Still, since she was there, she would pay attention to the auction. Of the many interesting and unusual works on sale, the biggest draw was a rare print by Winslow Homer, *Skating Girl*, from about 1890. Homer had used the image several times—a long-skirted girl on ice skates holding a muff and smiling flirtatiously at the viewer—but no one had ever seen this print. The ice in the print glistened in sunlight, an effect achieved with flecks of white ink or paint—added, according to the experts, by Homer himself, greatly increasing the print's value.

The crowd held its breath as the bidding soared swiftly past the high estimate of $150,000. *Skating Girl* sold for an astonishing $500,000. Coleman strained with everyone else to spot the person with the winning bid, paddle number 132.

"Who's he? I don't seem to know a soul today," Dinah said, watching the tall, slightly stooped man in a modish English-cut suit stroll toward the back of the room.

"Simon Fanshawe-Davies. He's an Old Master paintings dealer, works for the Ransome Gallery in London. Look, he's talking to Heyward Bain—he must have been bidding for him. Why else would an Old Master dealer buy an American print?"

Dinah shook her head. "I haven't a clue. I've never heard of him, let alone seen him at a print auction. Usually when a collector asks somebody to bid for a print, he chooses someone who knows something about them. If I were a collector instead of a dealer in not-very-expensive American prints, I'd have asked David Tunick to bid for me. I've heard he even handled a Homer with that same type of enhancement."

"I agree, he'd have been the logical choice. Maybe Bain and Fanshawe-Davies are friends. I'll find out. I'm going to interview them both. I'll call you later."

RESTRIKE

But by the time Coleman forced her way through the crowd to the back of the room, Bain and his companions had disappeared. She wandered around looking for Bold Face names, but a number of bidders and most of the sightseers had left after the Homer sale. She couldn't spot a single celebrity.

Maybe she could find a Killington's source who would tell her something about *Skating Girl*'s provenance. The auction catalog contained almost nothing about the print's history, not even the identity of the seller, usually a matter of public record when the object was rare and expensive.

Coleman glimpsed the lanky figure of an old friend, Zeke Tolmach, across the room and waved. She'd have enjoyed a chat with Zeke, but she'd spotted a bespectacled junior assistant in Killington's public relations department. He'd been known to spill secrets when he'd worked at Brown's Auction House in Dallas. Maybe he'd be as indiscreet today.

Nearly two hours later, Coleman abandoned the exhausted young man in the Third Avenue luncheonette where she'd plied him with coffee and doughnuts. After a lot of coaxing and some not-so-gentle bullying, he'd revealed the name and telephone number of the seller of *Skating Girl*—Jimmy La Grange, a small-time dealer she'd never heard of. Odd. Anyone with the money to acquire art that valuable should be in her Rolodex.

Back in her office she tried the number, but La Grange's answering machine picked up. She left a message, but she'd also try again later. Persistence might be required to get this guy to talk. How had an unknown dealer acquired such a valuable print? La Grange had some explaining to do.

Meanwhile, she needed to interview Simon Fanshawe-Davies and Bain. Coleman decided to ask Debbi to set up meetings with both of them. Debbi would do all she could; she was *ArtSmart's* press agent as well as Bain's. She was also one of Coleman's best friends.

Fifteen minutes later, she had a dinner date Wednesday evening with Bain, and breakfast with Simon Wednesday morning before the Grendle's auction. She entered the appointments in her diary and turned to her messages. Nothing important except that her friend Clancy from the *New York Times* wanted her to call him. Urgent.

"Clancy? What's up?"

"A suspicious death early this morning of a guy connected to the art world. Jimmy La Grange. Do you know him?"

"What? I can't believe it. I've never met him, but I've been trying to reach him. A print he owned sold at Killington's this morning for half a million dollars."

"You have to be kidding. The police say he's a part-time art dealer, part-time model, part-time actor, maybe a small-time hooker. They sure don't think he had any money—he lived in a run-down tenement in the West Village. They think his death was a sex-gone-bad crime—he wanted it rough, and it got *too* rough," Clancy said.

Coleman was taking notes. "Tell me everything you know, then I'll fill you in on the auction and the print."

"Okay, but can you get me background on this guy? It might not be a story for the *Times*, but if it is, I've gotta be prepared."

"I'll find out what I can. Dinah probably knows him. Now, tell."

"The police say he picked up a couple of biker types and took 'em to his apartment. A neighbor on the way home after a late night out saw two gorillas leaving La Grange's building about one this morning. The police think La Grange was probably dead or dying by then. They'll know more after the autopsy, but they already know he was battered to death. Did you know he was into rough stuff?"

Coleman grimaced. "Yuck. No, I never even heard of him till today. I don't know anything about him but what I've told you. Who discovered the body?"

"An old lady who lived across the hall noticed his door was open, and went in to see if he was all right. She'd heard a lot of noise the night before, but didn't see anyone. But the one witness they have is sure he'd recognize the men he saw."

"Too bad about La Grange. Young, on the verge of getting all this money, and dying in such a terrible way," Coleman said.

"Yeah, he got a bad deal. Of course, if it was an accident, a consensual sex death, it's nothing to do with the *Times*. But if there's an art angle, I have to look into it. What do you think?"

"There's a *big* art angle. Have you heard the Heyward Bain story?" She reported what she knew about Bain, the purchase of *Skating Girl*, and Jimmy La Grange.

"I'd heard about Bain and the museum, but I had no idea of a connection with La Grange. I'll talk to my police sources, see what they know. Call me if you learn anything from Dinah."

Coleman fetched a cup of coffee from the conference room, sat back down at her desk, and pondered Jimmy La Grange's death. The poor guy finally gets a big financial break, and is immediately killed. That couldn't be a coincidence. But neither could it have been somebody trying to steal the money he got for *Skating Girl*: Killington's wouldn't send out the check for weeks. But what was the link between the print and Jimmy La Grange's death, if not money?

She telephoned Dinah, but Dinah knew almost nothing about La Grange. She'd met him a few times when he'd visited the gallery, offering prints for sale, but that was the extent of their acquaintance.

"He sold prints he picked up at garage sales, places like that. He was a runner—didn't have a gallery—carried everything he had for sale in a portfolio. I liked him. He was shy, sweet, quiet. I bet *Skating Girl* was supposed to be his big break," Dinah said.

"Yes, but it may have turned out to be a curse. His selling that print for so much money almost certainly caused his death."

"Do you know anything about his personal life?" Coleman asked.

"No, I didn't know him that well, and I never heard any gossip about him. But I don't think that looking-to-be-beat-up story makes sense. He told me he made more money modeling than selling prints. His face was his fortune—he was gorgeous," Dinah said.

"Maybe he *wasn't* seeking sex—maybe it was a gay bashing," Coleman said.

"It's awful no matter how it happened. Let's don't talk about it anymore. Are you going to Grendle's auction tomorrow? They have a lot of junk, a few nice things, and one fabulous print—a rare Toulouse-Lautrec. It has to be on Bain's list," Dinah said.

"I'm going in the hope Bain'll turn up. But before the auction, I'm meeting Simon Fanshawe-Davies. I wish I knew more about him. Do you know a Renaissance art expert who could fill me in on Simon's background, and his relationship with the Ransome Gallery? I don't know if he's a partner, or what he does there."

"Several of my graduate school classmates specialized in the Renaissance, but they mostly work in Europe. I'll see who I can find. Do you want to have lunch after the auction?"

"Sure, what about the Red Dragon? I'll make a reservation."

"Okay, see you at Grendle's."

— Two —

D INAH HUNG UP and turned to Bethany, filing in the back of the gallery. "You know Jimmy La Grange? That runner who comes in once in a while? Coleman says he was killed last night, maybe by gaybashers, maybe rough sex."

Bethany frowned. "That's awful. He seemed like a nice kid—he couldn't have been more than twenty or twenty-five. I'm sorry he's dead."

Dinah returned to the stack of bills she was studying, but looked up again when Bethany sat down in the chair across the desk.

"Dinah, I have to find another job. I'm not earnin' commissions, I can't live on my base salary, and you know I have to send money home. I sit here all day doin' nothin,' and no one ever comes in—there's no drop-in business. Most of the time I read. Maybe some people would like gettin' paid to read mysteries, but I hate it. And I'm losin' sleep worryin'—I was awake nearly all last night."

19

Dinah groaned. "I've been halfway expecting this. Will you at least stay until the end of the year? The Luigi Rist show should be successful, his color woodcuts are beautiful, and our Christmas business should do pretty well. I promise I'll make it up to you financially if you'll stay. We'll work out what your commissions might have been if we were in a better location and open weekends, and I'll guarantee them, plus a Christmas bonus."

"Okay. But that's it, Dinah. I'd love to stay with you long-term if the gallery were in a better location. You need to be in an art neighborhood with other galleries to get the business."

Dinah sighed. "I know. I'll talk to Jonathan about it again tonight."

———

When Coleman had done all she could think of to pursue the Skating Girl story, she was forced to return to a problem she'd mentally shelved.

The latest issue of the *Artful Californian*, a new magazine published in Los Angeles, lay on her desk. The cover story, about paintings by Georgia O'Keeffe in New York collections, was one she'd planned to run in the January issue of *ArtSmart*. Even the illustration on the cover, an O'Keeffe painting featuring a great sheaf of calla lilies, was the image she'd have put on the cover of *ArtSmart*.

For three months in a row, the *Artful Californian* had published stories that Coleman's staffers were working on, printing them before they could appear in *ArtSmart*. Some of the articles showed up in the magazine proper, which was, like *ArtSmart*, a monthly. Others were featured in the *Artful Californian Online*, an e-newsletter published every Tuesday. None of them had been as well-written or as thoroughly researched as an *ArtSmart* article, but Coleman could no longer use the features she'd planned; she'd look as if she were copying the California magazine. Worse, she was sure one of her employees—all of whom she thought of as friends—was selling her ideas.

She looked around the cream-colored walls of her office, hung with framed *ArtSmart* covers. After Coleman bought the failing magazine, she'd redesigned it and built up its circulation and advertising revenues with what had turned out to be an instinct for the next art trend. But if another magazine got there first with her best ideas, its management could beat her out with subscribers and her advertisers would disappear. The proprietor of the Zabriskie Gallery, her largest and most profitable advertiser, had warned her about the rise of the *Artful Californian*, and advised her to make sure she stayed on top of the art market, if she wanted to continue to be their leading advertising outlet. Coleman was worried. She'd staked her career and a lot of borrowed money on the future of *ArtSmart*.

She rose and paced the room, Dolly at her heels, pausing first at one, then another of the framed magazine covers. She picked up the little Maltese and cuddled her while she looked at what she thought of as Dolly's cover, a Christmas tree with dog-shaped ornaments. The story was about a Soho restaurant where, in defiance of a city ordinance, the art world took their dogs. This occasion was a Christmas party attended by some of New York's most prominent art collectors and their pets. The host of the party was ostensibly Dolly's chum Thomas, an aging pug, frequently photographed with his glamorous socialite owner. In the article, told from Dolly's point of view, the guests were the dogs and their owners were attendants. The name of the restaurant was never mentioned, but many *ArtSmart* readers recognized it and its patrons. Those in the know ran up social mileage informing the less knowledgeable.

She stroked Dolly's head. "You liked that party, didn't you, Dolly?" she said, and the little white dog wagged her tail, her pink tongue slightly visible in what Coleman thought of as a smile.

Some of Coleman's favorite cover stories were about collectors in action. She'd traveled to Israel with Shelby White and her husband, the late Leon Levy, famous for their antiquities collection. That cover featured photographs of the couple's faces imposed on cartoon figures astride camels, a Hollywood desert in the background.

When she'd interviewed the Wall Street mogul and house collector Dick Jenrette in St. Croix, Coleman persuaded Jenrette to guide her and the *ArtSmart* photographer through his sugar plantation house while its restoration was underway. On that cover, Jenrette, who usually appeared in a dark suit in one of his perfected houses, climbed through what could have been a bombsite wearing a casual shirt and khakis.

Coleman had been confident she could generate enough ideas to keep *ArtSmart* the talk of the town for years—but not if they were stolen before she could use them. She didn't know what to do, or where to turn. She couldn't discuss her problem with anyone at the magazine, since she didn't know whom she could trust. Worse, she couldn't talk about her problem with Dinah.

Coleman was a raggedy five-year-old orphan when she went to live in North Carolina with her seven-year-old cousin Dinah and their grandmother and great-aunt. Since then, for more than twenty-five years, Coleman had confided every problem, every plan, and nearly every thought to Dinah. But Dinah's investment-banker husband, Jonathan Hathaway, had arranged the financing that enabled Coleman to buy *ArtSmart*. He'd devised a complicated deal Coleman barely understood, but she knew that as long as profits grew, she remained in charge. If profits fell, her backers could take over. If they dropped enough, she could lose the magazine.

If she told Dinah about the leak, Dinah would tell Jonathan; Coleman wouldn't dream of asking her not to. But Jonathan might take *ArtSmart* away from her.

She needed to discuss the problem with someone she trusted. She hadn't thought of confiding in Zeke until she'd glimpsed him at the auction. She'd last seen him at Dinah's wedding in June. Their paths rarely crossed these days. But they'd been friends since they met as undergraduates at Duke. He'd majored in art history, as had Dinah and Coleman. Because they were in classes together, they saw a lot of him.

After Duke, Zeke, whose family lived on Long Island, had returned to New York. He'd graduated from Columbia Journalism School with Coleman and Clancy, but unable to find a good job with an art publication, had worked at *Business Week* for several years. He tried hard, but he hadn't liked being with a big magazine and just couldn't stay interested in business. He resigned, and freelanced for *Art News* and other art magazines until he bought *Print Journal*, a newsletter that he still ran. He was the perfect confidant. He knew enough about publishing and the art world to be helpful. He was acquainted with the *ArtSmart* writers, and most important, he'd been Coleman's friend for more than fifteen years. She trusted him.

She punched in his number. He answered on the second ring.

"Zeke, it's Coleman."

"Coleman, what a surprise! I was thinking about you."

"You were? Why?"

"I saw you at the auction today, and after the auction, I had lunch with Dinah, and we talked about you. I mentioned how rarely I see you."

"Well, that's about to change. I have a problem, and I need your help. I know you're busy covering the print auctions, but if you possibly can, I'd like to see you this afternoon or evening. It's urgent, or I wouldn't ask."

"Sure. I can be free by six thirty. Shall I come to your office?"

"No, I'll meet you at the Creedmore Club."

Coleman and Zeke sat side by side on a worn brown leather couch at the rear of the library of the Creedmore Club, one of New York's three women's clubs. Except for the two of them (and Dolly, snug in Coleman's carryall), the comfortable room—lined with brightly colored book-jacketed volumes by the large number of club members who were writers—was empty. At this hour, everyone was sipping tea in the drawing room or cocktails in the bar.

Coleman described her problem with the *Artful Californian*, and explained that she believed one of the staff was responsible. "So that's the story," she said. "What do you think I should do?"

Zeke's mobile monkey face, usually cheerful, reflected her distress. "Are you positive that's how it's happening?

You've known the writers for years. It's hard to believe they'd sabotage the magazine or risk their jobs. They seem so proud of *ArtSmart*," he said.

"I know. It must be someone who's desperate for money."

"Does anyone have a drug problem?"

Coleman didn't drink or smoke, let alone use drugs, and she was pretty sure everyone at the magazine shared her values. "That seems to be why people steal these days, but I'd swear no one at the magazine is on drugs."

"Could the leak be your printer or somebody like that?"

Coleman rubbed her forehead. Just talking about the problem gave her a headache. "Don't I wish. No, these are ideas we've discussed at editorial meetings, and I've assigned them to someone, but before we can get the story completed, it's in print in the *Artful Californian*. No one but the writers could have known what was said in our meetings."

"Give me some examples."

"We planned a story about that couple who built a replica of Tara in Bedford—at least on the outside it's Tara-like. Inside, it's a series of lofts, crammed with Schnabels and Lichtensteins and Twomblys. It's a bad match—the house is ghastly—but it's a good story."

"Couldn't that have been coincidence? They're pretty conspicuous people."

"Possibly, I guess, but look at this." She handed him the current issue of the *Artful Californian*, and described the article she'd planned on Georgia O'Keeffe paintings in private collections, including her cover design. But when she'd tried to make appointments with the collectors, her California competitor had set up meetings with everyone on Coleman's list.

Zeke nodded. "I'm beginning to agree with you. That can't be a coincidence. Anything else?"

"Yes. We were doing a story on the best and worst food in museums, both in the restaurants and the catering at their benefits. We hadn't even decided which the best and worst were, and they printed it."

"That settles it. The food story isn't even newsy. Fun, but not news. Have you narrowed it down?"

Coleman sighed. "Yes, unfortunately. I've eliminated everyone but my two longest-term writers—Tammy Isaacs and Chick O'Reilly."

"I know Chick, and I dated Tammy a few times," he said.

Coleman raised her eyebrows. "You did? I wouldn't have thought Tammy was your type."

"You got that right. It had a bad ending."

Coleman waited for Zeke to continue, but when she could see he wasn't going to elaborate, she said, "I've worked with them both for years, and I thought I knew them, and could trust them. But they're the only ones who had access to all the information."

"Has either one been acting odd?"

"It may just be in my mind, but I think they're both acting strange. Tammy avoids me. We used to get together for lunch occasionally and chat about girl stuff: clothes, movies, diets. But I've tried several times in the last month or so to have lunch with her, and she's always busy."

"And Chick?"

"I know him better than anyone else at the magazine. He has a partner, David Edwards, a paper salesman. I've been there for dinner with the two of them many times. Chick's the closest person at *ArtSmart* to being a real friend, not just a workmate. He usually wants to talk to me too much—he's a gossipy, friendly guy. But lately, he seems uncomfortable around me. I think he's avoiding me, too."

"You have to insist on getting together with both Chick and Tammy," Zeke said. "You don't have to accuse anybody or mention the leaks, just meet with each one and draw them out about what's going on in their lives. You do it all the time for articles."

"You're absolutely right," Coleman said. "I kept thinking there was no alternative except confrontation. I guess I haven't been thinking straight. I usually discuss everything with Dinah—" she broke off.

Zeke nodded. "Dinah would tell your money man, right?"

Coleman didn't reply. She'd never discuss Dinah with anyone, and anyway, there was more to it than that. Dinah was another person who hadn't seemed herself lately. Not happy the way she'd been while she and Jonathan were dating, certainly not the joyful bride she'd been in June. Coleman didn't know what had changed, or why, but she wasn't about to add to Dinah's problems. Aware of the long silence between them, she glanced at Zeke. He was staring into space.

"Hello?" Coleman said. "Anyone home?"

"I don't think I like what marriage has done to Dinah. She told me today she still wants to be a big-time dealer, but she knows she's never going to make it on Cornelia Street. She says business is terrible, and I'm not surprised. All that neighborhood is good for is great restaurants and Jonathan's commute to Wall Street. It's definitely bad for an art gallery. She knows she should be in Chelsea or at least midtown, but she seems powerless to do anything about it. I think she wants to move, and Jonathan won't let her."

Coleman hoped her expression didn't reveal that this was the first she'd heard about Dinah's problems with the gallery—and Jonathan. Coleman now knew why Dinah was worried, but she couldn't immediately see how to help. She'd have to give that some serious thought. Meanwhile, she wouldn't discuss Jonathan with Zeke either. Jonathan was family, for better or worse. "I think Jonathan sees Cornelia Street as a convenient commute, but also as a safe spot for Dinah. He adores her," she said.

"Maybe so, but I bet he's making sure she doesn't do anything except what he says. He acts like he's used to getting his way. Back to your leak: Get busy. You're a great interviewer. You can get it out of the guilty one." He glanced at his watch. "I've got to go—I'm meeting people for dinner. Keep me posted on your problem. Is there anything I can do to help?"

"Yes, please. Could you see what you can find out about the *Artful Californian*? Who owns it, that kind of thing? I could make some calls, but I don't want anyone to know I'm checking."

"Sure. I'll look into it right away." He kissed the air near her cheek, and headed for the elevator.

Coleman picked up Dolly's pouch and followed Zeke out. Talking to him had been a relief, and she had a plan of sorts. Even more important, while they talked her thoughts had clarified. She was convinced that someone at the *Artful Californian* must have figured out a way to make some real money with this spying, although she couldn't see how. They could ruin *ArtSmart* and increase their advertising revenue, but after *ArtSmart* was destroyed, where would they get their ideas? And the two writers she suspected wouldn't risk their jobs for chickenfeed. Bribing either one of them would come high. Something had to be going on that she didn't understand. How could she learn what was behind the attack on *ArtSmart*?

And how could she help Dinah? Coleman had had reservations about Jonathan from the beginning. He *did* adore Dinah, but he was so possessive, so jealous. He even resented Dinah's close relationships with Bethany and Coleman. Coleman was sure that possessiveness was the basis of his not wanting Dinah to move her gallery. He wanted all of her attention for himself. But why hadn't Dinah told her what was going on?

When she reached the sidewalk, Coleman took Dolly out of her pouch, snapped on her leash, and with Dolly leading the way, headed for home. When they got there, after feeding Dolly and giving the little dog another walk, Coleman planned to spend an hour in her sewing room, which always absorbed her. It was her favorite recreation, a different kind of creativity from her work on the magazine. After that, she'd soak in a hot tub and think about everything, including her bleak social life. She did some of her best thinking in a tub full of hot water.

—— Three ——

TUESDAY NIGHT

IN THE APARTMENT above the Greene Gallery, Dinah changed into jeans and an old shirt of Jonathan's. She pushed the sordid story of Jimmy La Grange's death to the back of her mind—Jonathan wouldn't want to hear about *that*—and turned to cooking, a task that always relaxed her. When she cooked, she found herself back in the kitchen with her beloved grandmother, learning the craft that had helped support their little family, and helped pay her way through college. Cooking was for her what sewing was for Coleman—a lifesaver then, comforting these days. The family—her grandmother, her great Aunt, and Coleman—had been poor, but the warmth and love they had shared had made her childhood so very happy. She wished her grandmother or Aunt Polly was still alive. She wanted to talk to someone about her feelings about Jonathan and the gallery, but she didn't want to tell Coleman. Jonathan and Coleman didn't get along very well, and this would make matters worse. She sighed and concentrated on her cooking.

Hoping to put her husband in a mellow mood, she prepared one of his favorite dinners: gumbo, crammed with tomatoes, garlic, okra, and baby shrimp, accompanied by tiny corn muffins, and followed by a spinach salad. She set the table, and when all was ready, showered and changed again, this time into a gray-blue silk caftan Jonathan had given her; he said it was the exact color of her eyes. She piled her long dark hair on her head the way he liked her to wear it, and added big silver earrings. When she'd put on fresh lipstick and mascara, she sat on the sofa in front of the fire to wait for his arrival. Baker, Jonathan's ancient golden retriever, snored on the floor nearby.

She was leafing through *Vogue* when she heard the street door open, and Jonathan's steps on the stairs. She glanced around once more to make sure everything was the way he'd want it. The brick-walled, loft-like apartment was filled with appetizing smells, and the flickering candles and soft glow of the fire created a warm and soothing ambience. She rose to greet him, Baker at her side.

As he so often did, Jonathan had brought her flowers, tonight her favorite freesias. The perfume she wore, which he had especially made for her by a woman in Los Angeles, was based on their delicate scent. She kissed him, then put the flowers in water in a vase on the coffee table. Jonathan was mindful of the things she'd heard so many men forgot—flowers, gifts, private anniversaries. And he was a wonderful lover. The honeymoon continued—at least until the topic of the gallery came up.

They sat down to dinner at the kitchen end of the big table in the living-dining room, and Dinah drew him out on his day. She was proud of Jonathan's success as an investment banker, and fascinated by his deals. She also liked his looks—his narrow head, his bony, aristocratic face, his dark eyes bright with enthusiasm, his soft brown neatly combed hair. Tenderness welled up in her.

After dinner, Jonathan settled in his favorite chair by the fire, his long legs stretched out in front of him, Baker asleep with his head on Jonathan's feet. Dinah poured his coffee, handed it to him, and sat down opposite him.

"What kind of day did you have? I've done all the talking," he said, leaning over to scratch Baker's head.

"Exciting! I bought a beautiful Rist print—*Red Roses*—for the show—and Jonathan, guess what!" She described the bizarre trio at the auction, the sale of the Homer, and Heyward Bain's plans for a print museum. "Coleman plans to publish a prints issue in May to coincide with the next print auctions. She says the Print Museum is the biggest art news in a long time."

Jonathan removed his horn-rimmed glasses and cleaned the lenses with his handkerchief. He put them on again and said, "I bet the whole thing never comes off. So many phonies come to New York, announce grandiose plans, and disappear. Like that French guy sent over to head up the big multinational, who promised all those nonprofits millions of dollars, and then got fired and skulked home to France, leaving the charities in the lurch. Don't bank on sales you'll never make."

Dinah shook her head. "I just like the idea of a print museum. I haven't given any serious thought to selling to it—I don't think the museum will make any difference to me or the gallery. Why would Heyward Bain care about American color woodcuts? Or early screenprints? They'd be way down on his list of priorities for a museum. But I'd love to know why he decided to do what he's doing. I'd like to meet him, but I probably never will." As soon as she'd said it, she wished she hadn't. Even saying she'd like to meet another man could make Jonathan flare up with jealousy.

"Well, who cares if you sell him anything? We don't need the money. And why do you want to meet some parvenu from nowhere?" Jonathan slammed his coffee cup onto the saucer.

Dinah winced. So much for the mood she'd tried to create. He crossed the room, refilled his wineglass, and brought the half-full bottle to the coffee table. Not a good sign. In for a penny, she might as well go ahead. "Since you ask, I care about selling to him or anyone, and as to why, I'll tell you—again," Dinah said. "I've worked for years to build a reputation in the print world. When we decided to get married, you said you'd help me realize my ambitions, my dreams. We agreed I'd devote a minimum of two years to being a full-time dealer. But Jonathan, I'm not a d-dealer: I'm a housewife with a h-hobby."

She felt like a broken record. She'd said these same things to him over and over since she opened the gallery in July. Horrors, she was stuttering. She'd stuttered as a child when she was frightened or upset, but rarely since.

"Don't be absurd. Obviously you're a dealer—you have your own gallery—that's everybody's dream, including yours. At least, that's what you said before we got married." Jonathan's voice had risen, and Baker sat up and whimpered. Jonathan refilled his glass, but his hand shook, and he spilled wine on the table.

"No one c-comes to the g-gallery. A Greenwich Village side street is a t-terrible location for an art g-gallery. I don't do anything but p-play with p-prints, and now Bethany's going to quit."

"Good riddance. That girl is no asset. She's politically to the left of Nancy Pelosi, and I can't stand her ethnic look. Why can't she wear more conventional clothing? She probably frightens the customers." Jonathan stood up and started to pace. Baker struggled to his feet and limped behind him.

"But I n-need somebody in the g-gallery while I'm at auctions or visiting artists. And Bethany's g-good at selling p-prints and managing on her own. And she's from North C-Carolina, from home. She's my b-best friend after C-Coleman. I don't c-care about her politics, and I don't agree with you about her looks. I love her c-clothes, and I think she's g-gorgeous."

A muscle in Jonathan's cheek twitched. "You should see customers only by appointment. It's much safer than dealing with any Tom, Dick, or Harry who walks in off the street. I've repeatedly suggested that, and I cannot see why you won't do it."

Dinah stared at the wine he'd spilled on the table. She reached out to the coffee tray for a napkin. "I've told you: seeing by appointment is for retired people. I'm young and energetic. If I only see customers by appointment, I may as well c-close the g-gallery. Why c-can't you understand this is important to me? Why c-can't we move to Chelsea or midtown, or at least let me m-move the g-gallery, if you want to l-live in the Village? We c-could let the space d-downstairs." She dabbed at the spilled wine with the napkin, and the red soaked into the heavy linen.

"That's ridiculous. The economics would be terrible, and besides, it's convenient having you live above the gallery. For God's sake, Dinah, leave the table alone. The wine won't hurt the glass tabletop, and you're ruining that napkin."

Dinah twisted the wine-stained napkin, staring at it. A wedding present, it was monogrammed, one of a set of a dozen, and unless she put salt on it right away, it probably *was* ruined. She couldn't bring herself to care. "Jonathan, don't p-pretend this is about m-money. You j-just want me to be a full-time wife. But I will *not* g-give up my work with prints, even if I have to forget about being on my own and g-get a job somewhere. Which I will do, if the g-gallery keeps losing money."

"Don't be silly. Don't you think having your own gallery, no matter how small, is better than working for someone else? Anyway, we bought this place for the space downstairs, and you agreed to it." Jonathan was nearly shouting, and Baker whined again. "I'm taking Baker for a walk," Jonathan said, grabbing his coat and Baker's leash from the closet. The door crashed behind him.

Dinah cleared the table and loaded the dishwasher. She poured salt on the stained napkin. She cleaned the kitchen, tidied the sitting area near the fireplace, and left the napkin in cold water to soak overnight.

When Jonathan returned, she pretended to be asleep. She was thinking about Jimmy La Grange, and Coleman's speculation that his death might have something to do with *Skating Girl*. She hoped not. She'd hate to learn that the print was connected to anything so awful. She liked thinking of the image. She imagined herself the girl on skates, flying across the ice—happy, carefree . . .

—— Four ——

WEDNESDAY MORNING, 8:20 AM

BEFORE SHE WENT to bed Tuesday night, Coleman had decided what she was going to do about the leak at *ArtSmart*, but she couldn't begin to put her plan into effect until after lunch with Dinah on Wednesday. She left a voicemail for Tammy to meet her at the Starbucks in the *ArtSmart* building at two, and raced off to the Regency Hotel. Trust Simon to choose *the* spot to see and be seen at breakfast.

She was drinking her second cup of coffee and working on the *New York Times* crossword puzzle when Simon slouched in, twenty minutes late. He glanced around the room to see who was there, nodded to Donald Trump two tables away, and blew a kiss to fashion designer Nicole Miller, who looked surprised at an intimate greeting from a man she obviously didn't recognize. He made sure everyone in the room observed his arrival before joining Coleman.

"What a wonderful way to start the day, meeting a beautiful lady for breakfast. I've been looking forward to this." Simon smiled and brushed his fair hair back from his forehead. He was nice looking, she supposed, but when he bared his big teeth, Coleman felt like Red Riding Hood encountering the wolf. Or maybe Clarice Starling face-to-face with Hannibal Lecter. She recognized the caps. A bi-coastal dentist catering to the stars mass-produced that smile, but on Simon, it seemed threatening.

When he slid into the chair across from Coleman, his leg moved against hers. Coleman was sure it was deliberate. She'd eaten in this room many times, sometimes at this very table, and it had never happened before. She moved her legs to the side, and nodded to the hovering waiter.

Simon ordered eggs Benedict. Coleman chose grapefruit juice and the egg-white omelette. She tried to ignore the woman at the next table devouring bacon and brioche French toast. Just smelling the bacon, Coleman would probably gain two pounds.

As soon as they'd ordered, she took out her pen. "Congratulations on acquiring *Skating Girl*," she said.

Simon's grin widened. "Thank you! A milestone: the first of many purchases for the Print Museum. Heyward has asked me to do all his auction buying."

Wow, that was a good deal for Simon, especially since he had no background in prints. "Is Heyward an old friend?"

He looked amused. "No, but it was old friends at first sight."

"Then maybe you can tell me about him. I'm having dinner with him tonight, and I'd like to know more before we meet. Where's he from?"

Simon's oleaginous veneer disappeared. "You'll have to ask him, but I don't think he'll tell you. Heyward and I think that the world is too preoccupied with the past. We believe in living in the present."

His tone was patronizing, infuriating. She felt a rush of heat to her face and neck.

The waiter arrived with their orders, and she waited until he finished serving before she spoke. The delay gave her time to cool off. "Well! That's an interesting point of view. Do you feel the same way about the history of works of art? Aren't you concerned that Killington's didn't provide *Skating Girl's* background?

Simon took a big bite of his eggs, and shook his head. "Not at all. It's so unmistakably a Homer, the image is so well known, neither Heyward nor I thought provenance was an issue. We feel the same way about the Lautrec coming up at Grendle's—it's a superb impression, and very rare. We don't care where it's been, or who owned it."

Strange. Most museums were sticklers about an object's history, and wouldn't touch a work of art unless its pedigree was sound. Ethical Renaissance art dealers were usually pretty picky, too. Wonder how Rachel Ransome felt about Simon's attitude? "Don't you think it's peculiar that such a rare Lautrec is being sold at a second-rate auction house?" she asked.

Simon shrugged. "Grendle's could have charged the seller nothing, knowing they'd get a big fee from the buyer. And the Lautrec will bring in a lot of people, and get Grendle's a lot of publicity."

Maybe he was right, but she still thought it was odd. "Do you plan to bid for *The Midget* for the Print Museum?"

He looked down his nose. "I intend to buy *The Midget* for the Print Museum."

What a jerk he was. "Oh, I see—no matter what the cost?"

"Of course. Heyward can and will pay whatever it takes to get the best."

Why were Heyward Bain and Simon on such good terms? Maybe Bain was a creep, too, despite being so gorgeous. "How'd you and Bain meet?"

"A mutual friend introduced us, and I was intrigued by Heyward's project. I decided to put Ransome's into the print business. It's my own personal baby, and certain of success: Heyward and I are acting virtually in partnership. Now, that's enough about me. How did an enchanting little girl like you become the owner and editor of an art magazine?" He rubbed his leg against hers again.

When she moved her legs this time, she kicked him in the shin with the very pointed toe of her Jimmy Choo. He raised his eyebrows again and took another bite of eggy muffin, dripping with hollandaise. A blob of the sauce fell on his Sulka tie. If she'd liked him even a little, she'd have mentioned it so he could remove the stain before the tie was ruined.

"Sorry, this table must be smaller than usual. I keep bumping into your legs," she said. "By the way, I heard some shocking news this morning. Jimmy La Grange, you may know him—he was the seller of *Skating Girl*—was killed last night."

An odd expression passed over Simon's face. She'd swear it was anger. What could that mean?

"What a pity," he said, his voice flat. His plate clean, he looked at his watch, and frowned. "Oh dear, I fear I must move on. I have a thing or two to do before the auction. It's been absolutely marvelous."

When he rose, Coleman caught a whiff of a strange odor: hay or dried grass, barnish—horsey for such a citified guy. Had he been pitching hay? More likely rolling in it, like the ass he was.

She'd picked up a few good quotes, but she was leaving their meeting with more questions than answers. Who was the friend who'd introduced Simon to Bain? Why in the world was Bain letting this creep do all his buying? *Had* Simon known Jimmy La Grange? And why would Simon be angry about La Grange's death?

—— Five ——

FIFTEEN MINUTES BEFORE the bidding would begin, Dinah was in her seat, paddle in hand. Grendle's, the ancient auction house on First Avenue in the Fifties, was smaller and shabbier than Killington's. The auction room was painted a muddy beige, and smelled of damp and mice. But it was jammed with people. The number of reporters and curators was even larger than it had been yesterday; the press wanted to see Bain, and the museum crowd wanted to look at Toulouse-Lautrec's *The Midget*.

Dinah had seen the print at Grendle's preview. It featured a cabaret actor, a tiny man in a top hat, white tie and tails, not an image the dwarf Lautrec might have been expected to find appealing. But the little man had great charm and the print was brilliant with splashes of scarlet against the vivid yellow background, sharply contrasting with the black and white of the figure's apparel. It was an outstanding example of Lautrec's Parisian nightlife series.

According to the auction catalog, only three impressions were believed to exist until this one—the fourth—emerged. No one seemed to know who was selling it. But even without a decent provenance, *The Midget* should fetch a great deal of money. She assumed Heyward Bain would buy it, but he'd have a lot of competition.

Coleman, in an olive green shift and matching red-trimmed coat Dinah knew she'd designed and made, appeared minutes before *The Midget* was to come up. Her short blonde curls were carefully arranged in disarray, and she wore huge gold hoops in her ears. Dinah had never seen her looking better. She was sure Coleman had dressed to impress Bain.

Coleman sat down beside Dinah, and speaking in a low voice, said, "Fanshawe-Davies says he's going to buy the Lautrec for Bain—price no object. Look, there he is now. But Debbi called just as I was leaving the office to say Bain won't be here, damn it." She was already scribbling in her notebook.

The early bidding had been desultory, with prices near the lower end of their estimates, and the crowd was restless and noisy. But the room became silent and tense when a Grendle employee brought out the Lautrec. The crowd sighed in near unison, while dozens of covetous curatorial eyes stared at the work.

Simon held his paddle up ostentatiously throughout the bidding. One after another the bidders dropped out, until only Simon and a telephone bidder remained. When the phone bidder faded, Simon bought *The Midget* for $1.2 million, a record. Most of the people in the room, including disappointed bidders from both the Museum of Modern Art and the Metropolitan Museum of Art, left when the hammer went down on the Lautrec. Coleman raced after the departing curators to get their reactions to the price, while Dinah successfully bid with little competition on two prints that interested her.

Both went for a song because they were miscataloged, not unusual at a small, poorly financed auction house like Grendle's. They couldn't afford the large number of necessary experts to research and identify works correctly and completely. As Dinah had hoped, the museum curators who might have recognized the works were so distracted by the Lautrec, they didn't see what she had spotted.

One of the prints was a lithograph of St. Basil's Cathedral in Moscow, with an illegible signature. Dinah knew it was by a woman, Jolán Gross-Bettelheim, a Hungarian immigrant who had worked for the WPA in Cleveland. In 1933, she'd apparently made no prints, but she must have visited Russia. By 1934 she was back in Cleveland, and most of her work that year depicted Russian scenes. She'd eventually returned to Hungary and died there, a committed communist, as were so many artists of the 1930s. Dinah wanted the print for its historical value, as a symbol of a particular time. She knew several collectors who would buy it from her.

The other print, a colorful still life with flowers, was described in the catalog as a watercolor, but Dinah knew it was a woodcut. Grendle's had attributed it to Blanche Lazzell. If it were a Lazzell, it would have been a poor example of the artist's polished work. But it was by Cora Boone, a 1920s–1930s California printmaker. Dinah was familiar with Boone's primitive style, but she had never seen this image. This print, too, would be an easy sell.

Dinah should have been thrilled about her purchases, but she couldn't get her problems with the gallery and Jonathan, or Jimmy La Grange's death, out of her mind. She tried to think of something cheerful, and remembered her surprise for Coleman.

"I have a present for you," she said on the short walk to the restaurant. "You'll get it at the Red Dragon."

Coleman smiled. "Well, that's something to look forward to—and it's not even my birthday. What did you think of the Lautrec price?"

"Incredible. I don't like what's happening in the print world: Heyward Bain comes to town and starts throwing money around, and print prices soar. I'm afraid all that money is going to open Pandora's box, and let greed out to ruin everything. It's a world I love, and I hate to see it change."

Coleman nodded. "I know what you mean. I'm sure money must have something to do with Jimmy La Grange's death, but I can't figure out what. Anyway, if there *are* changes in the art world because of Bain, at least they'll be interesting to write about."

"I guess it'll be okay from your point of view, but not mine. I have a feeling of dread. Maybe it's Grendle's. The place looks and smells like a mausoleum."

They descended the steps into the restaurant, sparkling with glass, mirrors, and red lacquer, and were seated at their usual table. Dinah ordered a glass of white wine, Coleman a Diet Coke, and they chose a selection of appetizers instead of a main course.

Dinah looked around for familiar faces. Famous artists frequented the Red Dragon. "Do you see anyone interesting?"

Coleman, who was seated facing the room, nodded. "Fanshawe-Davies and Carswell are here."

Dinah glanced at them over her shoulder. There was no reason why the two shouldn't have lunch together. Simon had just bought the Lautrec for Bain, and the Red Dragon was conveniently near Grendle's. They could be talking about Bain's business. Still, they looked—what?—conspiratorial. She turned back to Coleman.

"What do you think?"

"She's in Chanel again—that suit is unmistakable. I wouldn't have thought burgundy was her color, with that hair, but it looks good. Can those be rubies she's wearing?"

Dinah shared Coleman's interest in clothes, but sometimes it was annoying. Like now. "Coleman, I didn't ask what she's *wearing*," said Dinah. "What do you think they're up to?"

Coleman shrugged. "Who cares? He's a creep, and she's an empty expensive suit. They're welcome to each other, whatever their relationship."

Their food came, and Dinah served herself and Coleman. "Do you know anything about Simon's love life?"

Coleman shook her head. "Nothing. I've seen him at art events for years, always with different women. He's not my type, but other women seem to find him attractive."

Dinah spooned minced chicken onto a lettuce leaf and passed it to Coleman. "What *do* you know about Simon?"

"Almost nothing. That's why I want to talk to a Renaissance expert, to learn more about him and the Ransome Gallery. Breakfast was a waste of time—he spent every minute bragging about how important he is to Bain and the Print Museum, and trying to play kneesy—" she broke off, staring. "Wow, who's that?"

Dinah looked up. "Oh, that's your present. Hi, Marise," she called, waving to the striking young woman at the top of the steps. Her short beige dress matched her tights and suede boots. Even her hair was beige, a shiny mane that hung straight to her shoulders, and her skin was a slightly lighter hue. She'd have looked monochromatic, but even across the room her slightly slanted eyes gleamed turquoise, and she wore a magnificent turquoise necklace.

"She looks like a Siamese cat," Coleman murmured. "Did I want one?"

"You want *this* one. She's your Renaissance expert," Dinah said, standing to greet her friend. "Marise Von Clemmer, this is my cousin, Coleman Greene, editor of *ArtSmart*." Dinah turned to Coleman. "Marise and I were classmates at the Institute of Fine Arts, and she got her PhD at Harvard. She's writing a book on Catherine de Medici."

When Marise had been brought a glass of Perrier— she said she wasn't hungry and couldn't stay long— Dinah said, "I really appreciate your coming, Marise. As I told you on the phone, Coleman needs background on the Ransome Gallery for a story she's working on. Can you help?"

"Of course. Therein lies a tale," Marise said in a soft, silky voice with an indefinable accent. "The Ransome Gallery—Rachel the heiress, and Simon the shill. Rachel was Henry Ransome's assistant. You know who Ransome was, of course? Besides being the outstanding Renaissance scholar of his generation, he collected art, and he had millions, family money, plus what he got from book sales, lecturing, and authenticating works of art.

48

"When he died, he left everything to Rachel. I don't remember her original last name, if I ever knew it. She changed her name to Ransome when she inherited, before she moved to London, and opened the gallery."

According to Marise, everyone had expected Ransome's estate to go to Harvard, but Ransome's executor supported the will, and no one contested it. All of Ransome's students and friends rushed to stand by Rachel. She'd been amazingly successful, producing brilliant catalogs, and dealing in some astonishing objects, including the Bronzino the National Gallery in London had recently acquired.

Coleman nodded towards the couple in the corner. "What about Simon? What's his role?"

"Oh, he's a salesman. No one knows where Rachel found him, or understands why she keeps him around, except he's good with old ladies of both sexes, and she prefers to deal with scholars. Some people say he's Rachel's lover, but I doubt it. I can't imagine her in love with *him*. She's older than he is, and much smarter. He knows almost nothing about art, but he can bone up when he has to. He claims to have gone to Harvard, but no one I know believes it. I keep meaning to check him out."

"What's Rachel like?" Dinah asked.

"She's reserved, reclusive, and what? Old-fashioned, perhaps. Because of her, the gallery has a superb reputation. Her track record is spotless in a field where there's a lot of greed, and some skullduggery—fakes, bad attributions, and the like. People say Rachel keeps Simon honest, probably with a big carrot and a bigger stick. Make no mistake, it is she who runs the gallery. I suspect she'd be a powerful enemy. She's very elegant, imposing.

She reminds me of a Medici." Marise's teeth gleamed in a slightly crooked smile. She sipped her Perrier, and glanced around the room.

"Thanks, Marise. I owe you," Coleman said.

"Anything for a friend of Dinah's, even more for a relative. Now, tell me about Heyward Bain."

Coleman tried to tell her the little she knew, explaining that she knew almost nothing about Bain, and wished she knew more. But they were interrupted by men coming over to pay homage to Marise. Simon was first, but Marise was icy, and he retreated. The last of the greeters was Mayor Bloomberg, who appeared out of nowhere, apparently to collect Marise. She stood up.

"I must get back to work," she purred. "Thank you for lunch, Dinah. So nice to meet you, Coleman. Perhaps I will know more about Mr. Bain and the loathsome Simon when next we meet." She disappeared up the stairs, the mayor at her side.

Coleman stared after Marise. "Who *is* she?"

"You know almost as much as I do. She was the Renaissance star in my class, and she knows everyone in her field. All I know about her personal life—and this won't surprise you—is that she has two Siamese cats. She and the cats travel to and from Florence, where Marise has a flat. Changing the subject: when are you going to meet Bain?"

Coleman shrugged. "We're having dinner tonight, an intimate affair: just me, Bain, the bodyguards, his secretary or assistant or whatever she is, and Debbi. He won't talk to the press without Debbi and Carswell present." She looked at her watch. "Will you take care of the check? I'll pay you back. I've got to rush off. I have a date with one of the writers, and it's probably going to be unpleasant. Thanks for setting up the meeting with Marise. The more I hear about Simon Fanshawe-Davies, the less I like the sound of him. And I don't like him in person, either."

"He does sound awful, but if Marise is right, Rachel Ransome keeps him under control," Dinah pointed out.

"I doubt it. I think he's a bad guy, and he may have escaped her when he came here," Coleman said.

— Six —

WEDNESDAY AFTERNOON

COLEMAN, RUSHING TO her date with Tammy, still hadn't decided exactly how to approach her. It wouldn't be easy; the woman had a sequoia-sized chip on her shoulder. She was in her mid-thirties and overweight. She could have looked voluptuous instead of fat if she'd dressed well, but she wore her clothes too tight, her skirts too short, and her blouses too low cut. Her dark hair was thin—too much color and teasing—and unbecomingly hennaed, and she'd had her eyebrows plucked into near nonexistence. Coleman wished there was a tactful way to suggest a week or two at the Golden Door for weight loss, followed by a new hairstyle and makeup, and then a clothes conference with Emily Cho, the best of the famous personal shoppers. It would never happen, but it was good to think about. Maybe it was because of designing and making clothes, which had helped pay her way through boarding school and college, that Coleman fantasized about makeovers. She'd spent a lot of time talking women into buying clothes that became them rather than the ones they coveted.

Coleman had hired Tammy from a public relations firm where she'd written press releases. She had little creativity and she wasn't a great researcher, but she was energetic, hard-working, and ambitious. After a lot of training, she'd come a long way. Most important, she was dependable. She met deadlines and didn't make mistakes. Those characteristics alone made her valuable, no matter how difficult her personality. She'd been grateful to Coleman initially, but recently she'd developed an unrealistic view of herself. She thought she deserved more—fame, money, men, everything. She complained that Coleman treated other writers better than she was being treated, and she snooped, trying to find out how much money others made. Her dissatisfaction with her role at *ArtSmart* might have led to betrayal. She was Coleman's pick for the leak.

When Coleman arrived at Starbucks, she paid for and picked up two cups of black coffee, then sat down at one of the small tables. She was still thinking about how to raise the subject of the leak when Tammy bustled in, radiating Arpége. As soon as she sat down, Tammy announced, "I have big news—I'm engaged!" She extended her left hand to show off an enormous diamond.

Coleman was surprised. This was the first she'd heard of a boyfriend, let alone a fiancé. "That's terrific. Who's the lucky man?" she asked.

"He's a very successful dentist in Chicago, where my family lives. We're getting married in April, and I'll move out there," Tammy said.

Coleman tried hard to be pleased for Tammy, but unless the bride-to-be was the spy, the Chicago move was a nuisance. Either way, Coleman would have to replace her.

"It's all been very sudden," Tammy continued. "We just finalized our plans. At first I thought I'd get a job out there, but I've decided I'd miss *ArtSmart* and working with you, so I'd like to stay on, and write from Chicago."

Tammy was acting uncharacteristically smarmy. Maybe she was just trying to make sure Coleman would let her work out of Chicago. "Well, your intended is a lucky man, and I don't see why you can't work part-time from Chicago," Coleman said.

"Thanks, Coleman. You're a pal."

For the next ten minutes Tammy babbled about her wedding plans, the reception—the live doves they'd release—and future babies. Coleman repressed a yawn, imagining infants with fat legs and bad hair.

Tammy and Coleman rode up together in the elevator to *ArtSmart*'s floor. Coleman had switched gears and was thinking about the afternoon and evening ahead, when Tammy, who'd been silent for at least thirty seconds, said, "How's Zeke?"

Coleman stared at her. "Zeke Tolmach? He's fine. Why?"

"Oh, we were an item once," Tammy said, her tone airy. "I broke it off, though—I wasn't ready to get serious, and he wanted to get married."

Coleman didn't comment, although she'd heard a different description of their relationship from Zeke. In the reception room, Coleman paused to let Dolly out of the pouch, and watched her stretch and shake herself.

Tammy picked up the topic again. "Didn't you go out with him?" she asked.

"Who? Oh, Zeke? A few times in college, but that was a long time ago," Coleman said. Why was Tammy bringing this up? And how did she know Coleman had dated Zeke? Their few dates hadn't amounted to anything.

"And you've never dated him since?"

"No, why do you ask?" Coleman said, tapping her foot. She was bored with the subject, and she had work to do.

"I heard he was in love with you, and you were stringing him along," Tammy said.

"Please. I hadn't seen Zeke since Dinah's wedding until yesterday at the auction—and before the wedding—when? Maybe last Christmas at a party."

"Was he your date for Dinah's wedding?"

Coleman frowned. "Of course not. I was maid of honor. My escort was Jonathan's best man, and I told you, I haven't dated Zeke since college. What *is* this?"

"Oh, never mind," Tammy said. "I wondered why he was still so crazy about you if you aren't going out together."

"Oh, Zeke's just never met the right girl," Coleman said, her head crammed with the problem of the spy, and with Chick, Heyward Bain, Dinah's difficulties, and all the work waiting for her.

"Well, that's insulting," Tammy huffed, and stalked down the corridor.

Coleman, startled, had no idea why Tammy was offended, but she knew she had to apologize or the woman would sulk for days. "Sorry if I misspoke," she called after her.

She could almost certainly eliminate Tammy as a suspect. Tammy's family must be well off; the wedding she'd described would cost a fortune. The size of the diamond suggested the groom was doing all right, too. How could she have money problems? Anyway, would someone so preoccupied with wedding plans and rug rats have the time and inclination for spying? But Coleman still didn't believe Chick could have done it. She intended to put him to the test. She'd try again to talk to him.

── Seven ──

Cнick was in his office, pounding away on his computer. His orange-red hair was rumpled and he had ink smudges on his hands and his nose. The fax machine on his credenza whirred away. His office smelled like the peppermints in the bowl on his desk.

When Coleman paused in his doorway, he looked up and grinned. His slightly buck teeth and his freckled face always made her see him as the poster child of the boy next door, or maybe appearing in a TV ad for something wholesome, like Cheerios. How could anyone who looked the way he did be a bad guy?

"How is everything?" Coleman asked.

"Fine, but busy, as you see," he said, gesturing at the piles of paper and the computer on his desk.

"Too busy to have lunch with me tomorrow?"

"Uh—sorry. I've got a date for lunch," he said.

"Then how about a drink tomorrow after work?" she persisted.

He shook his head. "Can't. I have to get home early. David and I have company coming for dinner."

His brow wrinkled in a worried frown, and his tone was evasive. She was sure he was lying, and her heart sank. "Okay," she said. "We'll talk now. This is about work, and it can't wait."

She sat down in his guest chair, and filled him in on Jimmy La Grange's death, what the police thought, and the tangential relationship with Heyward Bain.

"Whoa. What a story!" he said.

"Yes, it's fascinating. I hope you'll write it. If anyone can find out what it's all about you can. But it has its sordid aspects—the way La Grange died is pretty grim. I wouldn't normally publish something like this in *ArtSmart*, if it weren't for the link with the Winslow Homer print and Heyward Bain—that's big art news. Can you handle the gay bashing, rough sex, whatever it turns out to be?"

"Sure. I want the story. I know I can do it. But why aren't you writing it?"

"I'm going to concentrate on Heyward Bain, the Print Museum, and this creepy guy, Simon Fanshawe-Davies, who's helping Bain buy prints. The two stories connect, but each is a big piece by itself. It will take both of us to get them done. I'm looking for background on Bain and his cohort, and making sure everything they buy for the museum is kosher. The lack of provenance of the two prints Bain has so far acquired concerns me. While I'm doing that, you're going to find out everything you can about La Grange. How'd he get that Homer? He must have had a financial backer. Who? Where did he hang out? Did he have a history of the kind of thing the police think got him killed? Who inherits his money? We'll stay closely in touch. If I learn anything about La Grange, I'll pass it on. If you hear anything I should know for the Bain story, tell me. And keep me posted on how you're doing."

She could see that Chick was nearly jumping out of his seat with excitement. "I'll get on it right away," he said.

"Good. And Chick? This story is our secret. Don't talk to anybody in the office about it. If it's as big as I think it is, we don't want any leaks." She watched him carefully when she used the toxic word.

Chick nodded. He didn't seem to think her request was strange. Maybe he'd noticed what was going on with the *Artful Californian*. Or maybe he was the leak.

Coleman left his office knowing he'd write a great article. No one else at *ArtSmart* came close to having his ability to dig up information. Of course, there was the risk she'd read it in the *Artful Californian* instead of *ArtSmart*. But she didn't believe it. Only there was no one else. Could she have missed something? She sighed. She'd have to go over everything again—the meetings when ideas were discussed and stories were assigned. Who was present, who could and couldn't have had the relevant information at the time it was passed on. But not tonight. Tonight she was having dinner with Hayward Bain. She showered and put on the olive green and red outfit Bain hadn't seen when he didn't turn up at the auction. "If at first you don't succeed . . ." she told Dolly, who jumped into her pouch, happy that she didn't have to stay home alone.

In the taxi to the restaurant, she thought about Bain. She was ready for a new romance. She'd enjoyed a fabulous summer with a marvelous man—they'd shared his house in Sag Harbor on weekends—sailing, swimming, fireworks, sunshine, moonlight. But after Labor Day, they'd mutually agreed it was time to part. No acrimony, no regrets. But she'd like to meet an autumn companion. Walks in Central Park, while the crimson and golden leaves fell. New plays on Broadway. Fires in the fireplace. Halloween. Thanksgiving. Christmas. Snow. Could Bain be the one?

—— Eight ——

WEDNESDAY NIGHT

BAIN'S DINNER WAS in a private dining room at Brasserie 8½, famous for its elegant sweeping staircase and stunning modern design, the creation of the eminent architect, Hugh Hardy. Like the Red Dragon, the restaurant was below street level and popular with the art crowd, partly because it featured signed Matisse lithographs in the lounge, and a stained glass mural by Léger separating the kitchen from the dining room.

Coleman left thoughts of *ArtSmart*, the spy, and Jimmy La Grange outside the door of the dining room. She needed to concentrate on her interview, and on Bain. This was the first time she'd seen Bain up close. She had rarely met a better-looking man—those intense gray eyes, with their heavy fringe of black lashes, the brilliant smile in his tanned face, his high cheekbones. She admired his clothes, too; he was perfectly dressed. Artists tended to wear messy, bohemian clothes, or like Zeke, they were tweedy and academic-looking. Heyward Bain's suits were a work of art, as were his handmade shoes.

Even his height suited her—she didn't like big men. They towered over her, reminding her of bears, and bullies she'd encountered as a child. Bain had something else she couldn't quite define. She hadn't exchanged a word with him, but she felt a kind of recognition, a sense that she'd met him somewhere, although she knew she hadn't. Her New Age friends would say she'd known him in another life. Whatever.

She toyed with her veal, nibbled her salad, refused dessert, struggled to take notes—eating and writing at the same time was almost impossible. She exercised all of her charm, hoping to make a connection that would at least lead to a good story, if not a social relationship. But it wasn't working. Maybe he was distracted by his audience? She wished they were alone instead of in a room full of people, all of whom were listening to every word she and Bain spoke.

Debbi was uncharacteristically silent. Ellen Carswell was also quiet, and seemed to be effacing herself, although with her sumptuous looks and striking clothes she could never be inconspicuous. Tonight she wore an Issey Miyake white silk pantsuit and magnificent pearls. Everything about her screamed money, even the Mont Blanc she used for note-taking. But if a lover were supporting her, Coleman didn't think it was Bain. Their relationship seemed businesslike, even distant.

The elephantine bodyguards were also trying to be invisible, as if anyone that big could disappear. Why did Bain need those ever-present guards? Lots of rich people—even billionaires—in New York managed without hired muscle. Maybe his size made him feel vulnerable. More likely, he'd made enemies in the world he came from. Was that why he wouldn't discuss his past?

She tried to persuade him to talk about his background, but he never let the conversation become personal, at least about himself. When she asked him about his family, where he grew up, he shook his head and smiled. "I prefer that your readers evaluate the Print Museum on its merits, not on anything I may have done before I came to New York."

"Won't you at least tell me where you went to college?" Any scrap of information might lead to more.

He laughed. "I'm self-taught about art. I've never taken a single art history class."

But if he wouldn't talk, he sure could listen. He seemed fascinated by everything she said. In response to his interest, she babbled like an idiot about her career, her childhood in North Carolina, college and graduate school.

At the end of dinner he knew a lot about her, but she didn't know him one bit better. At this rate her article about him would be as bland and colorless as blancmange, her least favorite dessert at boarding school. But all that mystery made him even more fascinating. When he offered her a ride home—Debbi had her own car, and was driving Carswell—she hoped he'd warm up.

But when Bain's driver stopped the inconspicuous gray Lincoln Town Car outside her building, and Bain said a pleasant goodnight on the sidewalk, nothing had changed. He remained impenetrable. Still, when she glanced back at him from the lobby, she thought he looked after her longingly. But perhaps he was just watching to make sure she got in safely. She'd have to wait and see. She sighed. She hated waiting. If he didn't call her, she'd try to get Debbi to set up another appointment with him. She wanted to know this man. She must somehow get through to him, if only for the sake of her article.

—— Nine ——

Robert Mondelli hung up the phone and read his notes. His contact at the NYPD had asked him to look into a case that might or might not be his kind of thing. It probably wasn't. Despite Jimmy La Grange's occupation, the runner's death almost certainly had nothing to do with art. Still, Mondelli would spend a day or so to prove it either way.

Mondelli was in law school when his dad, a cop, had been shot and killed by a drug addict trying to break into a doctor's office. Mondelli dropped out of school and joined the NYPD to support his mother. He'd studied law at night and passed the bar exam, and considered joining a friend's law practice, but art crimes had fascinated him, and he'd stayed on the Job and made them his specialty. He took art history courses and haunted museums on weekends—still did. Three years ago, he'd resigned from the Department to set up his own agency specializing in the recovery of stolen art, and other art crimes. He'd been able to use his knowledge of the law and his experience with the NYPD, and he'd never regretted his decision.

The NYPD or City Hall often called Rob in as a consultant, mostly unpaid, but their referrals led to lucrative private-sector cases. He'd become famous in a small way, and the quality of both his life and his finances had improved. He wondered if he'd still be married if he'd left the police force earlier. The NYPD was notoriously tough on marriages, and many cops were divorced, sometimes more than once. After his own brief marriage ended badly, he had decided he wouldn't try again.

When the faxes on the La Grange case arrived, he flipped through them, looking for art connections. An unconfirmed tip from a guy at the *New York Times* that La Grange was the seller of a high-priced Winslow Homer print at auction. Unlikely. La Grange had less than a thousand dollars in the bank, and the police had found no evidence linking him to big money, or to the fancy art crowd. Except for La Grange's answering machine tape containing three messages from Coleman Greene at *ArtSmart*. Why was the well-known owner of a successful magazine so anxious to speak to La Grange? There was also a message from Simon, no last name, reachable at the Carlyle Hotel. According to one of the faxes, the police had identified, interviewed, and cleared Simon. Whoever he was, he had a solid alibi.

No paperwork had turned up on the Homer print. In fact, the police hadn't found any of La Grange's financial records, except for an invoice for $1,000 from La Grange to the Greene Gallery dated last week, stamped "paid." The Greene Gallery. Any connection to Coleman Greene? Oh, yeah, Dinah and Coleman were cousins. Uh, oh—that asterisk by Dinah Greene's name meant "tread carefully." She was married to Jonathan Hathaway. The Hathaway family had a lot of clout. It was hard to see how Rob could offend the Greene cousins, but he'd keep in mind that he had to tread softly. Unless, of course, they were guilty of something.

Coleman was red-penciling a manuscript when a Robert Mondelli called. He said he was a consultant to the police on the art aspects of the La Grange case, and her name had come up. Could he come to see her? Coleman agreed to see Mondelli in half an hour. That would give her time to run downstairs and pick up an early lunch.

She stood in line at Starbucks—there was *always* a line at Starbucks—and collected and paid for her coffee and a turkey sandwich. But on her way to the elevators she slipped on a wet spot on the marble floor, and careened into a bulky man emerging from a telephone booth. If he hadn't grabbed her, she would have fallen. She managed to keep her balance, but her coffee spilled all over both of them.

"God, that's hot," he said, trying to clean himself up with his handkerchief. Coleman dabbed at him with the paper napkins she'd collected with her coffee. "I'm so sorry—" Oh hell, the napkins were drenched. She was making it worse, and, not only that, she was patting his crotch. She felt as if she were in an episode of *Sex and the City*. She snatched her hand back, and fled, calling "Sorry" over her shoulder.

After a futile attempt to remove the coffee stains from her beige silk pants, she collapsed in her desk chair and stared at the soggy sandwich and empty coffee cup. The man she'd run into was worse off. She'd probably ruined him for life. Could a man be sterilized or become impotent after being scalded? Coleman hoped he didn't work in the building. With luck, she'd never see him again.

She'd barely picked up her pencil when the receptionist called to say Mondelli had arrived. She sighed and went out to greet him, Dolly at her heels.

Good grief! It was the man she'd injured. Well, there was nothing for it but to tough it out.

He'd apparently decided on the same strategy—he didn't acknowledge their previous encounter by so much as a blink. God, he was even bigger than she remembered. She wouldn't meet with him in her little office, she'd feel too crowded. Not to mention uncomfortable about their earlier encounter.

Coleman stood aside to let him precede her into the conference room. He reeked of coffee—surprise, surprise—and his gray suit was stained. She probably should have offered him money for the dry cleaners. He was maybe forty-five; six feet, or even taller; and husky, nice-looking, if you liked ex-football types, which she didn't. But she couldn't fault his thick dark hair slightly graying at the temples, or his heavy-lidded brown eyes. He had a deep mellow voice and a good smile. Still, Coleman was sure she wouldn't like Mondelli—he was too big, too much a cop. He'd be bossy and overbearing.

She sat down across the table from him. "How can I help you?" she asked, hoping she sounded cool, not like a clumsy oaf—oafess?—who'd spilled boiling hot coffee on a man trying to prop her up.

He said he was investigating whether La Grange's death was art-connected, or, as the police thought, a date turned bad. The police had given him her name and number because she'd been trying to reach La Grange. "Why were you so anxious to talk to him? Was he a friend?" he asked.

"No, I never met him. I'm working on a story about a man named Heyward Bain who bought a Winslow Homer print at Killington's yesterday. Since La Grange was the seller, I wanted to interview him. But I never reached him, and then I heard he was dead."

Mondelli frowned. "What makes you think La Grange was the seller?"

"I heard it from someone inside Killington's."

He raised his eyebrows. "Isn't that information confidential?" His tone was neutral, but she sensed disapproval. Naturally he'd disapprove: he was a cop.

"Yes, but that kind of information often gets out," Coleman said.

Mondelli made a note. "But it's also often inaccurate, isn't it? Is there anything else you can tell me about La Grange?"

Why should she tell him anything? He'd made it clear that he thought she was wrong about Jimmy La Grange being the seller of the Homer. Arrogant know-it-all. He'd learn soon enough that she was right. She'd like to tell him to get lost, but maybe if she gave him a little more information, she'd learn something.

"I mentioned his death to Simon Fanshawe-Davies— he bought the Homer for the Print Museum—and it seemed to make him angry. I couldn't understand why. Maybe you can explain?"

"Yes, the police have talked to Mr. Fanshawe-Davies," Mondelli said, capping his pen, and standing up. "I don't think I need trouble you any further, Ms. Greene."

Coleman scowled. Not only had he ignored her question, he hadn't the slightest interest in what she thought. "But you don't believe there's an art link to La Grange's death?"

He looked down at her. "There's no evidence of an art motive or connection, and lots of indications that his death was something else. I gather you disagree?"

She stood as tall as she could, but he still dwarfed her. This guy was not only a hulk, he was as thick as a plank. "I certainly do, but I can see you wouldn't be interested. This is the first time I've ever had dealings with the New York City Police Department, and I have to tell you, I'm not impressed."

His face remained impassive. "I'm sorry to hear that. Thanks for your time."

She walked him to the reception room, but only to make sure he left. First Simon, now this guy. The case was crawling with creeps.

Back in her office, she considered what she should do next. Before talking to Mondelli, she had assumed that when the police learned about Jimmy and the Homer, they'd investigate the connection, and figure out that there was more going on than the sordid story they'd decided to believe. She'd planned to learn whatever they turned up from Clancy, and pass it on to Chick. But it sounded as if the police were going to bury the art part of La Grange's story.

That was a problem. She couldn't publish an article telling readers that Jimmy La Grange, seller of the Homer, newly rich by about half a million dollars, was coincidentally killed almost at the same time he sold the print. Too many questions would remain unanswered. She'd look like an idiot. It was time to check in with Clancy.

"Clancy? I talked to Mondelli, the art cop. He seems sure La Grange's death isn't art-related. He's sticking with the cop theory about the sex thing."

"He'll have to reconsider. Not only was Jimmy La Grange the seller of the Homer, he was also the seller of *The Midget.*"

Coleman sat up straight, her eyes wide. "Wow, are you serious? How'd you find out?"

Clancy laughed. "You're not the only one with contacts. I got it from someone who works at Grendle's. What did you think of Mondelli?"

"Not much. A lot of muscle and a closed mind."

"Don't underestimate him—he's plenty smart—but so far, the police haven't found any evidence of an art link to La Grange's death, except what you and I've turned up. They have lots of physical evidence from La Grange's apartment of what happened. When they pick up the guys who were there, they can nail 'em easily. As far as they're concerned, even if we're right, Jimmy somehow found the money—maybe borrowed it—to buy those two prints, and that's the end of it. His death was something else entirely."

"But Clancy, there's no way that poor obscure little dealer could have 'found' or 'borrowed' the money to buy those two prints. We're talking hundreds of thousands of dollars here."

"I know. La Grange must have fronted for somebody who didn't want anyone to know he was connected to those prints. But why? They can't be stolen. There's been so much publicity about them, we'd know it by now."

"If La Grange was fronting for somebody, the real owner of the print is out of luck. Whoever he is, he'll never get his money now," Coleman said.

"Yeah, and if you weren't on the case, the seller of *Skating Girl* might *not* be out of luck. I bet the auction house checks were supposed to go to a PO Box, where the seller has access. But since you discovered that La Grange consigned *Skating Girl*, and the information got to the police, the check will go to Jimmy's estate instead. And thanks to me, so will the money for *The Midget*."

"Somebody's bound to be furious," Coleman said, remembering the expression on Simon's face when she'd told him La Grange was dead.

—— Ten ——

FRIDAY

COLEMAN'S CALENDAR WAS jammed: gallery and museum openings, book launches, auctions, interviews with artists and collectors, breakfasts, lunches, cocktail parties, and dinners. Much of what she did, saw, and heard had to be recorded for *ArtSmart*. When she wasn't attending an event, she was writing about one, or editing an article someone else had written about it. Coleman loved New York in the fall—exciting, stimulating, full of new ideas, new art, new people.

But while only a week had passed since Bain's appearance at Killington's and La Grange's death, she felt as if it had been months. Despite the brisk pace of her life, much of what interested her appeared to be bogged down. According to Clancy, the police remained confident that they knew how and why La Grange died, and saw no reason to look further. She hadn't identified or plugged the leak at *ArtSmart*. Heyward Bain hadn't called her, and Coleman had failed to learn anything about him despite dozens of phone calls, and hours on the Internet.

She'd pestered Debbi for information on Bain, but Debbi either didn't know anything, or wasn't talking. She dropped a few crumbs about the museum—Bain was hosting a series of group lunches for dealers, and Debbi had invited Dinah to the first one. Simon was selling contemporary prints acquired from artists or from other print dealers to Bain. He continued to buy older prints for Bain in cities outside New York, and at lesser-known auction houses. The most publicized purchases were four Dürers in Cleveland, and a Rembrandt in Boston, all for record prices. Inexplicably, Bain continued to rely on Simon the creep.

The day of Dinah's group lunch with Heyward Bain arrived, and at breakfast Jonathan was still trying to persuade her not to go. "I can't imagine why you want to see this guy. God knows, we've met enough new-money people in New York in the last few years."

"Oh, come on, Jonathan. Part of it's the mystery: who is this man? Where did he come from? He must love prints. He wouldn't be willing to commit so much time and money to them if he didn't."

"I don't agree. I keep telling you, he's using art to open doors otherwise closed to him. And as for who he is, I'm sure 'Bain' used to be an unpronounceable six-syllable name, and his money came from the entertainment industry, or real estate, or something illegal. After all, why should he try to hide his background if he isn't ashamed of it?"

Dinah picked up their empty plates and took them into the kitchen. He followed her, and she couldn't resist replying. "You're boring when you're so snobbish. Who cares how he made his money, unless it was illegally? Everyone can't be a doctor or a lawyer, and some people think investment bankers are infra dig. Coleman says he's fascinating."

"Really? Well, tell me this: how is Bain going to acquire all these prints? Is he going to advertise what he wants? If so, he'll raise prices dramatically, wreck the market, set new highs. Anyone who overpays is a fool asking to be cheated."

She agreed with Jonathan about the impact of Bain's activities on the print market—she wished it weren't happening—but he was being insufferable. "How else? I mean, if he doesn't say what he wants, how will dealers know what to offer him? And he has to outbid others, or he won't get the prints."

"There's something suspicious about the whole project. Maybe he's laundering money."

Dinah, putting soap in the dishwasher, didn't turn around. "I disagree, and so does Coleman. She had dinner with him and talked to him for hours, and she doesn't think he's a criminal. You haven't even met him, and you think you know better?"

By the time Jonathan arrived at the offices of Hathaway and Associates at 140 Broadway he'd cooled off, and was thinking clearly. He was a trained analyst who understood complicated financial deals. Surely he could figure out what Bain was up to, discover who he was. The source of all that money—if it existed—shouldn't be a secret unless it *was* illegal.

Dinah was naïve, innocent. He had to shield her, to take care of her. Until she met Jonathan, Dinah had never had anything, and had never been anywhere except North Carolina, graduate school in New York, and that nowhere town in Connecticut where she worked before their marriage. She could get hurt dealing with a guy like Bain. No one was going to hurt Dinah. He would make sure of that.

He punched in the extension for the company library. "Hello, Jonathan Hathaway here. I'd like everything you can find about Heyward Bain, probably in his forties, probably American, around five feet tall, dark hair, gray eyes, and reputedly rich. I want family background, financial details, education, criminal record, anything. It's a priority, okay? Thanks."

That was a start, but not enough. He'd cancel his appointments and get on the telephone. He'd call the family lawyers, accountants, and money managers. If none of them knew anything about Bain, he'd go through his personal Rolodex and call all his friends.

***

Bain stood near the door of the private dining room at the Four Seasons Restaurant on Park Avenue, greeting his guests. His suit had to be Savile Row. He and Jonathan probably used the same tailor. He introduced Dinah to Ellen Carswell, today in navy blue, with a jade pin on the lapel, and matching earrings. The knit suit was sexy, outlining her opulent curves, but she was formal and distant, almost cold.

Dinah recognized the other guests, all print experts. The only person she hadn't met was Simon Fanshawe-Davies. When Bain introduced them, the dealer acknowledged Dinah with an unflattering lack of interest. Dinah liked nearly everyone, but she was put off by Fanshawe-Davies. He was rude, and he had a lean and hungry look.

She sat on Bain's right, and for the first time she got a close look at him. Coleman was right. He was extraordinarily handsome.

While the others ate their soup, Heyward Bain described his project. He was committed to building a great museum that would cover the history of printmaking, and include examples of the best prints ever made. "I'll need all the assistance I can get, both in deciding exactly what should be in the museum, and in finding the prints. I've invited each of you here to ask for your help." He looked around, waiting for responses.

Dinah was trying to think of something to say when Simon Fanshawe-Davies spoke. "Do you have a list of the prints you want?"

His tone was annoying even when he asked an innocuous question. Coleman was right again. Fanshawe-Davies was awful. Dinah knew she was being irrational—she was judging him by the pricking of her thumbs. Why did Fanshawe-Davies make her think of Shakespeare? She sneezed. Oh Lord, it was Fanshawe-Davies's aftershave. She could smell it across the table. Coleman had mentioned his peculiar scent—like the Straw Man in *The Wizard of Oz*—but who would have thought it would give Dinah hay fever? She reached in her bag for a tissue and an antihistamine pill. Her eyes were watering, too. She sneezed again.

"We have a preliminary list of the prints we want. When you leave, Ms. Carswell will give each of you a copy. It's a beginning—it includes a lot of obvious choices, but we don't want to confine ourselves to the obvious."

Bain turned to Dinah. "For example, we'll devote a large room to the history of US printmaking. We'll want relatively unknown artists as well as the big names. I hope you have some nominations for milestones in your field. I understand you specialize in the history of colored printmaking?"

Fanshawe-Davies barged in. "But surely the most important prints will be Old Masters?"

"And, of course, contemporary prints—Jasper Johns, naturally," another dealer said.

Fanshawe-Davies sneered at the Johns advocate. "Surely negligible in the total scheme of things? Johns's prints are important, of course, but when you consider them in the context of the total history of printmaking—well! Here's *my* list of recommendations for the museum," he said, handing a sheet of paper to Ms. Carswell. He launched into what turned out to be a long monologue. He discoursed on quality, availability, auction prices, and priorities. He was articulate and well-informed and he never referred to notes. He didn't pause in his speech through the service of swordfish, salad, poached pears, and coffee. When anyone else tried to speak, he overrode them, and Bain, who seemed mesmerized, did nothing to stop the flow.

Fanshawe-Davies ended his remarks just as Ms. Carswell looked at her watch, put down her coffee cup, and stood. Bain rose when she did, thanked them for coming, and Ms. Carswell ushered them out. Fanshawe-Davies was the only guest who'd said more than hello and goodbye. His timing was impeccable. He'd filled the available time exactly.

Dinah walked downstairs to the ladies' room to wash her face. She was dripping mascara and her nose was tomato-red. Worse, she felt like a fool. She hadn't said a word. Maybe the looming failure of the Greene Gallery, and hearing Jonathan tell her every day she was unsuited to running a big gallery, had sapped her confidence more than she had realized.

She blew her nose and powdered it, tidied her hair, put on fresh lipstick, and headed for the Fifty-Second Street door, looking forward to the haven of Cornelia Street, another antihistamine, and a long nap.

Before she reached the doors, someone grabbed her arm. She turned, ready to smile a greeting, and cringed.

"Maxwell Arnold! What are you doing here?"

The man smiled. "What are *you* doing here? I eat at the Four Seasons every time I come to New York on business. Whenever I'm here, I inquire about you and your adorable cousin Coleman. I've never lost interest in the two of you, my dear, and I never will."

"Let me g-go!" Dinah whispered. She wrenched her arm out of his grasp and ran for the door.

In the taxi she struggled for control, and by the time she reached Cornelia Street, she could talk to Coleman without stuttering. "I ran into Maxwell Arnold at the Four Seasons," she said when Coleman answered her cell phone.

Coleman didn't speak for a moment, then, "What did he say?"

"Nothing. Well, he said he came to New York on business and he always asks about us."

"Is that all?"

"Yes, but Coleman, it was the way he said it. He scared me."

"He's scary because he's crazy, but he can't hurt either of us unless he catches one of us alone in the dark, and even then he'd have to have some of his bully-boys with him," Coleman said. "What did he look like? Have his evil ways caught up with him? Or is he a Dorian Gray?"

"There's no justice—he looks pretty good. Still tall, of course, and not as heavy as lots of guys who played college football. He may have even lost weight since college. Sun and alcohol have roughed up his skin, but he still has good hair, and it's still black. And Satan still looks out of those crazy no-color eyes."

"I'm sure that couldn't change unless he was Born Again. And pigs might fly. How was your lunch?"

Dinah sneezed. "Oh, I came across like an idiot. I couldn't think of anything to say fast enough to get a word in. Simon Fanshawe-Davies talked the whole time, and his ghastly aftershave or whatever it is gave me hay fever. The only good news is that Bain wants me to offer the museum a group of my kind of prints."

"That's what counts—you're the expert in your field. You stand out wherever you are."

Dinah sighed. "I didn't today."

"Forget it—it doesn't matter. Did anyone mention Jimmy La Grange?"

Dinah blew her nose. "No, not a word. He died less than two weeks ago, but it's as if he never existed."

"I agree. No one seems to care how or why he died. It makes my blood boil. Speaking of blood boiling, are you going to tell Jonathan about Maxwell Arnold?"

"No. If he knew, he'd get me an armed guard, or two or three. I'd look like Heyward Bain."

"You've got a point. But if Maxwell turns up again, you *must* tell Jonathan. It was one thing to keep all that a secret when he stayed in the South, but if he's bringing his vendetta to New York—"

"We'll see," Dinah said.

—— Eleven ——

COLEMAN WAS SORRY Dinah had encountered Maxwell Arnold. She'd brought that hellhound into Dinah's life, and she wished she could undo it. She'd gone over and over it in her mind, but she couldn't see what she might have done differently—except, of course, never gone out with him. But that hadn't seemed like an issue at the time.

In the spring of her freshman year at Duke, Coleman's life was close to perfect. The weather in Durham was beautiful, and she was busy with school, with friends, and with her sewing. Boys lined up for dates, and she went out a lot—not just with Duke boys, but boys from North Carolina State College in Raleigh, and the University of North Carolina at Chapel Hill. She'd met Maxwell Arnold at a party. He was a Big Man On Campus at UNC, and he'd seemed okay. He'd asked her out several times, but she'd always been busy, until he'd invited her to have dinner with him on a Saturday night several weeks ahead. She was free, and accepted.

He'd told her they were going to Snyder's, a famous steakhouse, so she dressed up in a blue silk dress. But when Maxwell picked her up, he didn't take her to the restaurant. He drove her into the woods, where four of his fraternity brothers were waiting in a clearing. She'd dated all of them once or twice, and they'd been nice enough, so she was puzzled, but not frightened. They reeked of beer, but that wasn't unusual.

But Maxwell shoved her out of the car, and said, "Okay, Ice Maiden, which one of us do you want to do first? We've had enough of your cock-teasing shit. Who the hell do you think you are?"

Coleman had felt a flash of fear, but fear affected her as it always did: she became furiously angry. With her rage came the certainty that if she showed weakness, they'd rape her. Her only hope was attack. She stood as tall as she could, which wasn't very tall, and said in an ordinary conversational tone, "You're great big strong men, and I'm not a very big girl, and I'm alone. I can't stop anything you do to me. But hear me: if any one of you touches me, I'll walk back to campus, and I'll tell the world about you, and what you did. You'll have to kill me to stop me.

"And you, Tommy, will *not* go to medical school, I promise you that. Tonight will end your hopes of a medical career. And you, Buddy—you told me you plan on law and politics. But not in *this* state, not if you hurt me. I'm Miss Ida Slocumb's granddaughter, and don't forget it. You'll have to leave the Carolinas, maybe even the South, once people hear my story. And Henry, you're practically a neighbor. I know your sister and your mother, we're members of the same church. They think you're a devout Christian. I'd hate to hurt them by telling them what you really are, but I'll do it in a minute. Paul—your fiancée's in my Spanish class. She'll never marry you if she hears about tonight. She's a decent girl and deserves better than you—and believe me, she *will* hear about you.

"I know that if I tell the world about you, my reputation will be gone, and I'll have to leave Duke, and I'll be infamous as the person who ruined all your lives. But a lot of people will thank me for telling the world what you are. I bet this isn't the first time y'all have tried something like this. I promise every one of you: touch me, and your lives will be over starting tonight."

Coleman stared at the boys, who seemed paralyzed, their faces gleaming pale in the twilight. She turned to Maxwell Arnold and said, "A lot of people saw me leave the dorm with you tonight. Everyone will know what a monster you are. You probably don't care, and from what I know about your family, they probably wouldn't care either. But touch me, and you'll go to jail, so help me God.

"And that's not all. If you ever come near me—if you ever even speak to me again, I'll curse you such a mighty curse you'll wish you'd never been born. I'll devote the rest of my life to taking my revenge on you. I'll stay after you until I die, and after my death I'll haunt you."

That night was engraved in Coleman's mind forever—the words she spoke, the scent of the pinewoods and the honeysuckle, the soft night air, how the boys looked, and how she felt. Mostly she felt anger, but in the back of her mind was a tiny flicker of fear. They *could* have killed her, of course, and they were all drunk. Drunks were unpredictable.

But they got back in their cars, and she climbed in beside Henry. She knew his family best, and she certainly wouldn't get in a car with Maxwell Arnold. She looked back, and Maxwell Arnold was standing in the clearing by himself, staring after her. He shook his fist at her as the car pulled away. Neither she nor Henry spoke on the way back to campus.

If only that had been the end of it. The boys—Tommy, Buddy, Henry, and Paul—begged for an opportunity to apologize to her, but she wouldn't speak to them, so they turned to Dinah to plead for Coleman's mercy. They blamed everything on Maxwell. He'd told them she was "willing," it was a "party," Coleman "wanted it." After they sobered up, they knew how close they'd come to ruin, and that she still held their futures in the palm of her hand. But there was nothing they could do but get on with their lives, so that's what they did.

Except Maxwell Arnold. The way Maxwell saw it, Coleman had humiliated him in front of his buddies, and he was determined to make her pay for it. He kept his distance from Coleman, but he bugged Dinah. Every time he saw her, he told her how much he hated Coleman and Dinah, too, because she was Coleman's cousin. Coleman considered complaining to the authorities, but he never actually threatened her or Dinah, and she wasn't sure he was doing anything illegal.

Anyway, the Arnolds owned one of the biggest tobacco processing companies in the South. Even with the decline of smokers in the States, they made a ton of money exporting their products to the third world, and they contributed to all the right politicians. She didn't think anyone would do much about Maxwell, unless they caught him breaking the law. Even then, he'd probably get his hand slapped.

Arnold's little "party" had put her off college dating. She never knew what trap Maxwell Arnold might set for her. And as much as she'd tried to reassure Dinah, Coleman thought Maxwell was dangerous. She'd received notes and cards from him several times a year ever since that long-ago evening. The notes were never overtly threatening, but they were ugly. She could handle it, but she wished he'd stay away from Dinah. Coleman kept hoping he'd forget about her and Dinah but he hadn't changed, even after she'd read that he'd married. Seemed like he had some kind of grudge against her that was bigger than an episode in the pine woods outside Durham.

That evening in the King Cole Bar at the St. Regis Hotel, Coleman sipped a Diet Pepsi and told Zeke about her conversation with Tammy. "She's so wrapped up in wedding plans she's not thinking about anything else. And she doesn't seem to need money. I can't see why she'd do it."

"Well, if you're pretty sure it's not Tammy, then it's got to be Chick, right? What are you going to do?"

Coleman rattled the ice in her empty glass. "Talk to him, I guess. What else can I do? I'm writing the best stories myself, keeping my ideas secret so they won't be leaked. I'm exhausted, it's bad for morale, and time-wasting. I should be investigating Jimmy La Grange's death, or at least the history of the prints he's supposed to have owned, and how he got them. New subject: have you learned anything about the *Artful Californian?*"

"Damned little. I studied every issue, and I don't recognize a single name on the masthead, or a byline. The major editorial difference between *ArtSmart* and the *Artful Californian* is that *Artful* takes very strong critical positions on contemporary artists—unknown California artists, Australian artists, Russians. They push the work. They aren't touting the work of any East Coast artists, so they must not have staff here. I haven't ever met anyone who works there, have you?"

"No, not a soul. I've noticed they publish puff pieces on certain artists. We don't hype artists. I think it's unethical for a magazine to do it, and most people in the business agree. It's too easy to buy up paintings, run up the prices, and sell them. But if you'd stoop to stealing ideas from another magazine, what's a little more slimy dealing?"

She paused. "Wait a minute. I have an idea. Suppose they want to damage *ArtSmart* enough to be able to buy it cheap? They could merge the two magazines, and they'd have a great entry into the East Coast art world. With *ArtSmart*'s reputation for catching trends—if its reputation isn't ruined by then—they could buy art, and then push it—they could make a fortune. Double, triple, quadruple their investment."

Zeke leaned towards her. "Have you ever known anyone who did it?"

"Yes, a columnist for a now-defunct art magazine. He used to seek out little-known talented artists who were desperate for money. His secret partner bought up the artist's work for next to nothing, and put it away. A year or so later, the columnist would 'discover' the work, and write a glowing review, and the value of the artist's work would shoot up. Suddenly the artist was hot, and everybody was trying to buy his work," Coleman said.

"What kind of money was involved?"

"An artist told me the critic's partner bought five paintings from her for a thousand dollars. Two years later, he sold *one* of them for $50,000," Coleman said.

"Good God! If a lot of artists were involved, we're talking multimillions. How do you think *Artful* is working it?"

"Management might have several people buying art, several people writing rave reviews. That's probably what they're doing with the art they're touting now—Russian, Australian, whatever. But if they could get *ArtSmart*, and get an in with New York artists, they could go big-time. Before readers caught on, the people behind the magazine would make a fortune."

"I bet you're right, Coleman. That's got to be it," Zeke said.

"We may know why, but we're not any closer to knowing who. Who owns the *Artful Californian?*"

Zeke shook his head. "A holding company with an innocuous name—'Art-All.' I'm trying to learn more about it, but my lawyer says these holding company structures can be impossible to penetrate."

"Well, let me know if you learn anything," said Coleman. "Thanks for the drink, thanks for listening, and thanks for your help."

***

Jonathan stayed in his office until after nine, talking to the West Coast. But he learned nothing. Heyward Bain had no school records, no employment history, no telephone listing, no credit rating, no social security number. Jonathan wouldn't have dreamed it was possible to live forty years and leave no tracks. It was as if Bain didn't exist. He *must* be a criminal.

— Twelve —

AFTER SHE'D FED and walked Dolly, Coleman put on her nightgown and robe and settled down on the couch in the sitting room. She loved her little apartment on East Fifty-Fourth Street. Debbi and Dinah nagged her to buy something bigger and fancier, but even if she were as rich as Bill Gates, she wouldn't move. The kitchen was tiny, but who cared? She didn't cook. Her snug home office was a desk in the dining nook. The sitting room windows looked out at the Queens skyline beyond the East River, gorgeous at night. She'd installed bookshelves wherever she could fit them in, and the room was warm and inviting.

But the best part was the two bedrooms. Coleman slept in the smaller one—Dinah said its narrow bed and white walls reminded her of what she'd read about nuns' cells—and used the second bedroom as her sewing room, where she kept her sewing machine and the dressmakers' models she'd had made for herself and for Dinah. She hung many of her dresses and suits on a big clothes rod on one side of the room, instead of crushed in a tiny closet. The shelves on the other walls were stacked with brilliantly colored fabrics—bright green, turquoise, blue, red, hot pink—and fashion magazines. She'd designed it to look like the sewing room where she'd worked with Aunt Polly, except then the magazines hadn't been *Vogue* and *Bazaar*, but battered copies of *Ladies' Home Journal* and *Good Housekeeping*.

When she'd arrived at Slocumb Corners, a dirty, uncivilized five-year-old orphan, the household was desperately poor. Coleman had always been poor, but her grandmother, Miss Ida, Miss Ida's sister, her great-aunt Polly, and even seven-year-old Dinah *worked*. The people Coleman had lived with mostly drank and smoked dope. Coleman had never known people who worked the way her new family did.

Miss Ida baked—wedding and other cakes were her specialty—and catered for parties, and Dinah helped in the kitchen. Aunt Polly sewed. She made dresses, and anything else the local ladies wanted—curtains, slipcovers, baby clothes, whatever. She did alterations, too, and Coleman helped her. Coleman took to sewing, and by the time she was in sixth grade, she was making all her own clothes and Dinah's. She winced when she remembered those clumsy creations, but the clothes she'd designed and made for high school and college were much better-looking. When her classmates saw them, they, too, wanted "Coleman" labels. She'd sewed her way through college.

These days, she could afford to buy designer clothes, and sometimes she did. But most outfits for someone only five-feet-two-inches tall were designed to make the wearer look cute, and Coleman hated cute. She wanted clothes to make her look taller, slimmer, more sophisticated, and the best way to get them was to design them herself. Fashion wasn't easy if you were short, curvy, blonde, and dimpled. Anyway, playing with fabrics and patterns was fun. And relaxing. If she weren't so tired, she'd go in the sewing room and work out a new design, but she just didn't have the energy.

She picked up the *Daily News* from the stack of newspapers and skimmed through it, but she couldn't concentrate. Dolly climbed onto her lap and settled down for an after-supper nap. Coleman stroked the little dog's soft fur and picked up the TV remote. Maybe she could find an old movie—she loved fifties films—but before she could turn on the television, her phone rang.

It was Clancy. "Bad news, Coleman. The police have decided they were right from the beginning. They never found anything to tie Jimmy La Grange's death to the sale of those prints. If they ever find the guys Jimmy was seen with, they can easily make their case. But they're not looking very hard."

"Are you still working on it?"

"No. Unless something new turns up, it's over, at least for the *Times*. But I know there's an art connection. I can't figure out how La Grange could have bought those two prints, or why the real owner—or owners—are lying low, unless they have something to hide. Keep me posted, okay?"

"Sure. Thanks for calling, Clancy. Let's talk soon."

Coleman lay back down on the couch, Dolly on her chest. Clancy's throwing in the towel was a blow. He was her only link to the police. The *New York Times* had great sources. But she couldn't blame him.

All she had were questions: Who killed La Grange and why? Who *was* Bain? What about Simon?

—— Thirteen ——

FRIDAY
London

RACHEL RANSOME HAD not heard of Jimmy La Grange's murder, but she knew that he was ostensibly the seller of *The Midget*. That kind of information came readily to the owner of the Ransome Gallery. News of La Grange's sordid death was not important enough to make the London papers, but even if an item had appeared, Rachel would not have read it. She found the daily news at best boring, at worst distracting. She was immersed in the sixteenth century.

In the more than ten years since Rachel had established the Ransome Gallery, she had become successful. She did not seek publicity, and the passing years had made her even less interested in other people than she had been when she was young. Few members of the public knew the Ransome Gallery existed, but every important museum in Europe and the United States sent representatives to call on the gallery, and every private collector of Renaissance art knew Rachel. She met with clients by appointment. There was no walk-in business for the treasures found at the Ransome Gallery.

Many of the works Rachel sold were part of her inheritance from Ransome. She doled them out, since Renaissance connoisseurs coveted treasures from Ransome's collection. Other objects had come her way through *The Record*, the document Ransome left behind detailing locations of art all over the world—in museums, of course, but more important, in private collections. Nothing was more useful to a dealer than supply, and the owners of works of art tucked away in attics or dark corridors in freezing country houses were often willing to sell them when they learned of their value. Finally, some works came through those who had known Ransome, and honored Rachel as his heir.

She had no need for the wealth she had accumulated through the sale of art. Ransome had left her far more money than she could ever spend. Her life was patterned on that of Professor Ransome's. He had taught her to enjoy elegant simplicity. She had been so influenced by Ransome that she could not remember what her tastes had been before the many years she'd spent with him.

Because she lived such a secluded life, she might never have heard about Simon's purchases for Heyward Bain, had she not happened on an item about him in the art press. She had learned about the sale of *The Midget* from a story in *Art Journal* and had inquiries made as to its seller. She did not discuss these matters with Simon. She thought of him as a remittance man. She paid him handsomely to stay out of England, and away from the gallery.

Recently, however, a Dürer collector had come in to choose a piece of Renaissance jewelry as a gift for his wife. After he selected a handsome pendant and was waiting for it to be wrapped, he said, "I've never seen Dürers in more beautiful condition than the four woodcuts Simon bought for Heyward Bain—not even collector's stamps. Do you know anything about their provenance?"

"I haven't been involved in Simon's purchases for Bain. Which Dürers were they?"

"*The Holy Family with Three Hares, The Virgin Crowned by Two Angels, The Beheading of St. John the Baptist*, and *The Annunciation*. Would you ask him where they came from? They were sold at an auction house I never heard of, and the only provenance in the catalog was the Ransome Gallery. Nothing before that."

Rachel nodded. "I'll ask, and let you know."

Four Dürer woodcuts in exceptional condition? Where could Simon have found them? But she was preoccupied with a puzzling attribution, and put the subject aside.

She didn't think of the Dürers again until evening when she was sipping her pre-dinner sherry. A faint suspicion occurred to her, but she dismissed it as impossible, and turned to her grilled turbot and asparagus.

In her bedroom that night, however, she unlocked the closet where her furs and less valuable jewelry were kept, opened the safe secreted behind a panel, and took out the ancient Italian chest containing her more precious jewelry. Behind the chest and yet another panel, opened by a pressure point, a locked metal box housed the four notebooks in which she had written the information culled from *The Record* before storing the originals in the bank vault. She turned to the D's. There it was: "Dürer—four woodcuts in pristine condition. No collector stamps. Baldorean Collection. Keeper, Yeats."

The prints listed were the four that Simon had purchased for Bain. Simon had stolen those prints from the Baldorean Collection. There could not be an identical set of Dürers in existence, and they could not have come on the market in any other way.

He had gained access to *The Record*. Worse, he had used the gallery's name when selling stolen prints. He had dared to involve the Ransome Gallery in his petty schemes. She was angrier than she had been in many years, but this was not the time to waste energy on impotent rage. She would end Simon's schemes, but not tonight.

After she returned everything to the safe and secured the system, she put on one of the high-necked, long-sleeved white silk gowns she bought from a little shop near the Rue de Rivoli in Paris, unbraided her hair—still as heavy and thick as when she'd first met Ransome, but now streaked with gray—and brushed it. When she had settled down in her four-poster bed, propped up on the big white pillows and tucked under the white eiderdown, she sipped the hot chocolate that her housekeeper had left in a thermos on her bedside table.

Usually at this time she read a few pages from Jane Austen. She read and reread Austen's novels. She had never found anything to equal them for bedtime reading. But tonight she stared into space, thinking. When she finished her chocolate, she set the cup down and switched off the bedside lamp. She would put her worries aside for the weekend. Almost immediately she fell asleep.

On Monday, Rachel met her assistant downstairs at eight thirty. Miss Manning, sixtyish, small and prim, had been "made redundant" in her previous job and was grateful for her current employment, which included a number of perquisites—tickets to museum and gallery openings, a delicious lunch, and exquisite teas—in addition to a very good salary. For six years she'd assisted Rachel with both her personal affairs and the business of the Ransome Gallery. Rachel trusted her more than she'd trusted anyone since Ransome died.

"Miss Manning, I want you to assemble material on the Heyward Bain print purchases Simon has arranged in New York. Get me copies of everything about the Print Museum that has appeared in the press. As soon as they are awake over there, call New York and ask for press releases, lists of prints Bain wants or wanted, lists of prints bought, anything to do with his museum."

Miss Manning took notes rapidly, bobbing her untidy gray head. When she'd completed them she looked up, her bright brown eyes shining, her head cocked. Miss Manning resembled a West Highland terrier, and she was also temperamentally rather like one. She was fanatically loyal to Rachel, and took umbrage at anyone who slighted or abused her employer.

"Please ask Accounts to give me a list of everything the gallery has sold to Bain, with receipts, profits, and so on—they will know what I need. And call the solicitors' office, and see if Mr. Quincy can come to see me this afternoon, or if that is not possible, tomorrow afternoon.

"Please call a locksmith and the security people. I want all the locks changed today. We'll pay a bonus to get it done quickly. The lower floors should be on one key or set of keys, and re-issued to the staff. The locks on my private floors should have three sets of keys only—one for me, one for the housekeeper, and one for you."

Miss Manning's head bobbed, and Rachel continued. "I want both the big safe in the basement and the small one in my closet either replaced or the combinations changed, whatever security thinks best. Have them go over the whole place, check everything.

"I am going out on an errand. I shall go straight to the hairdresser afterwards, and be home for lunch at the usual time. If you should speak to Simon, do not mention any of this to him."

Rachel pulled on her mink-lined boots, slipped into her mink coat and settled a mink turban over her tightly braided coronet before she walked the few blocks to Simon's flat in Mount Street. Warmly dressed as she was, she shivered in the raw November air. Among her few extravagances were furs and cashmere. She suffered the cold more every year.

She let herself into the flat, and began her search.

The combination for his small safe was, predictably, his birth date, but it contained nothing but a few pieces of the less expensive jewelry she had given him for birthdays and Christmas presents in their early years. She dropped the cufflinks and tie bars into her alligator carryall. The room-sized bedroom closet was crammed with his clothes—suits and jackets and trousers on hangers, shelves of sweaters and shirts, boxes of shoes. The closet reeked of Simon's scent, but she found nothing unusual.

The sitting room was modern, comfortable, and brightly lit, but held little of value. She searched the desk, but she discovered nothing of interest except cancelled checks and unpaid bills, testaments to Simon's extravagance.

The entry area closet was locked. She selected a key from her ring and opened it. When the gallery had leased the flat, Rachel had obtained a set of keys. Simon had never noticed. He was too self-involved to pay much attention to what other people did.

She flipped through the magazines stacked on the shelves. Pornography. On the floor, a basket of sexual toys. Some of the clothes hanging on the bar were women's, including a nurse's uniform. They were all in large sizes. A trunk-like box full of cosmetics, makeup, hairpieces, and wigs.

A padlocked metal file box caught her eye. She took it into the kitchen and wrenched it open with pliers she found in a drawer.

There they were: photocopies of her summary of *The Record*. She dropped them in her bag, and opened a small file folder underneath the photocopies. It was empty except for two sheets of lined paper with "TO DO—LONDON" in capitals at the top. In Simon's neat handwriting was a list of planned tasks, and the dates by when he expected to complete them. "Make dentist appointment, March." "See tailor, April." Number six on the list was "Get rid of Rachel, June."

"Get rid of Rachel," indeed! Did the fool think he could wrest the gallery away from her? Or did he plan to murder her? Perhaps he did. Simon had no morals, but she had assumed that his sense of self-preservation would keep his behavior within reasonable bounds. She had been wrong.

She dropped the list in her bag, and using the telephone on the desk, dialed her private number. "Miss Manning? When the locksmith comes, please accompany him to the Mount Street flat. I want those locks changed as well. I shall leave the keys to the flat with the owner of the trattoria on the corner."

Rachel put the empty metal box inside a plastic trash can liner, and dropped the bag in a rubbish bin outside a construction site a few houses down the block. After she left the flat's keys with the obliging owner of the trattoria, she hailed a taxi. It was Monday morning, and on Mondays at eleven she had a standing appointment with Jean Claude at his hairdressing salon in Jermyn Street.

At half past one Rachel joined Miss Manning for lunch at a small table drawn up before the fire in the sitting room. Miss Manning reported on her morning's activities while they ate. "The locks have been changed. The keys are on your desk. The security man says there's no need to replace the safes, but you must choose new combinations. He recommended a few other minor security measures—bars on the first floor bathroom window and the ground floor powder room window, and a chain on the delivery door. I told him to proceed. He's recoding the alarms. You have only to choose the new codes."

"Were you able to get material on Bain and his museum?"

"Everything is on your desk with the accounts summary. Mr. Quincy can come this evening at six, if that's all right?"

"Yes, fine. Since Simon will spend most of his time in New York in the future, he will no longer need the flat or the country house. I have decided to sell them. You may know whom to call. If not, ask Mr. Quincy's office. The two cars Simon keeps in the country should also be sold, and the horses. Please ask someone in Quincy's office how best to dispose of everything. Move as quickly as possible.

"Also, I want to reduce staff to the minimum. Leave a caretaker in charge of the house and garden, and arrange for someone to take care of the horses until they are sold, but everyone else should go immediately. We should release everyone on the payroll who does not work for the gallery or for me personally. Get Accounts to work out settlements."

Rachel had declared war. She knew it would be vicious and bloody. She would do all she could to protect the name of the gallery, but secrets would emerge. Perhaps it was time, even past time, that the truth was revealed.

—— Fourteen ——

D INAH SCRAMBLED TO put together the portfolio of
colored woodcuts and screenprints she planned
to offer Bain. She wrote an essay explaining her choices,
and how they fit into the history of color printmaking in
the United States, and she enclosed color photocopies of
each of the images.

When she handed the package to the messenger who
would deliver it to Bain, she knew she'd done a good job.
Now all she had to do was to wait. That was the hardest
part. Luckily, she was busy with the Rist exhibition.

Dinah jumped every time the telephone rang, hoping
for a call from the Print Museum. When an envelope
bearing the museum's return address arrived, her heart
stopped, but it was an invitation to the opening of the
Print Museum for the first Sunday evening in January.

That was something to look forward to, but it didn't relieve her tension about the possible sale to the museum.

Dinah was also anxious about the Rist opening. Suppose no one—or just a few people—came? Coleman had promised to arrive early to support her during the first half hour or so, but Dinah wouldn't relax until the gallery was crammed with people, and she could see that they liked the prints. Maybe she'd sell some at the opening—maybe even a lot. She mentally crossed her fingers.

She was thrilled when she received a letter from Ellen Carswell, accepting the prints Dinah had offered for the museum, and enclosing a handsome check.

Bethany jumped up and down, shouting "Go girl!," and when Dinah called Coleman, her cousin said, "I told you it would be okay. You're good at what you do."

But Dinah didn't tell Jonathan. He'd only rant about Bain and the Print Museum, and she didn't want to spoil the moment.

—— Fifteen ——

Monday Evening
London

WHEN HER SOLICITOR arrived, Rachel offered him a drink, and put a tray of nuts, olives, and cheese straws on the table near his chair. She sat opposite him in front of the fire, her back erect, and her head held high.

"Mr. Quincy, I recently paid far too little for a Toulouse-Lautrec poster, and the gallery profited unduly from its sale. It was tantamount to cheating the client. I wish to reimburse the person from whom I bought it. The gallery will keep neither the profits nor a commission, and will absorb the auction commission on it as well as what we originally paid for it. I should like you to draw up an agreement that the woman who sold it to me will sign, accepting the money, and indemnifying the gallery. Can you do that?"

"Of course, Mrs. Ransome. When do you want it?"

"Immediately. As soon as I can arrange an appointment with the owner, I shall fly to Paris. But that is not all. I want to dismiss Simon. How can I do it?"

Quincy shook his head. "Mrs. Ransome, that would be almost impossible. Our firm drew up the agreement under the terms you specified. The only grounds you have for severing the partnership are criminal activities. You must prove he has done something illegal."

"I think I can, after I settle the Lautrec affair. Meanwhile, I may need cash. He has not deposited funds for works sold—the Lautrec, for instance—in the gallery account. I assume the money is in his personal account in the United States. There's a great deal of money missing for his expenses in the United States, far more than I authorized. I shall have to pay the seller for the Lautrec out of funds set aside to buy art objects. Luckily I keep a sizable amount in that account in case I have to act swiftly, but it will leave me short."

"If necessary, our firm will be glad to arrange bridge financing," he said.

"Thank you. I have already begun to liquidate assets used by Simon, which he said were necessary to generate sales—entertaining prospective clients, and so on. But selling everything will take time."

"If you're going to sever all connections with Simon, you should also change your will," Quincy said.

"I agree. I shall leave everything to Harvard. It is what Professor Ransome originally intended. Can you revise my will as soon as possible?"

"Certainly. Now, tell me what proof you have of Simon's criminal activities. If it's ironclad, he forfeits everything.

His twenty percent of the Ransome Gallery reverts to you. In any case, we can claim the money in his accounts in New York, but that, too, will take time."

"It began with the Lautrec. Last summer Simon told me an American named Bain was starting a print museum in New York. Simon said the gallery could make a great deal of money selling Bain prints for the museum. He wished to start the print business—Ransome's has never dealt in prints—and if he had an important print to offer Bain immediately, his success was assured."

"You helped him obtain such a work?"

"Yes. I knew of the whereabouts of a rare Lautrec poster—I had mentioned it to him long ago—and he asked me to see if the owner would sell it. He said he had researched the market, and he told me what I should pay for it. I spoke to the owner by telephone, she agreed to sell it, and I sent a courier to pick it up. I later read Simon had sold it at auction for more than ten times the amount I had given the owner. Simon arranged to have someone else sell it in that person's name, and Simon bought it for Bain, and charged Bain a fee for bidding for him. I'm not entirely sure of the legalities, but, of course, everything he did was unethical."

"I'm not certain that's sufficient for our purposes. It will require—"

She interrupted him. "I am also certain he has stolen four Dürers from an English museum. But before I pursue this, I must settle with the woman who sold the Lautrec to me. I called Simon when I read the story about the Lautrec, and I pointed out that both the seller and the buyer had been cheated. He replied that the gallery had made huge profits, and as I was the one who had paid so little for the print, if anyone were guilty of unethical conduct, it was I. Of course, since no money has been deposited to the gallery accounts, the gallery hasn't made any profit—but he was right. I had no idea of the value of the print, I know nothing about the print market, and I accepted what Simon said about its value. But I could never prove it, and I should not have been so naïve."

Rachel sipped her sherry, and continued. "I have brooded about the Lautrec for weeks. When I concluded that Simon had stolen the Dürers, I made up my mind: he has to go. His actions could ruin everything I have built. Nothing must touch the gallery, or in any way affect Professor Ransome's reputation. His integrity was unquestioned throughout his life. It must remain unimpeachable."

"Are you certain you can prove Simon has stolen art from a museum?"

Rachel understood his doubts. Art theft was notoriously difficult to prove. Once a work was removed from a museum, and had traded in the marketplace or had been bought by a secretive collector, it was difficult to tie the theft to an individual.

"Yes, you and I will prove the theft together, but first I must settle the Lautrec matter. If the former owner of the Lautrec learns what has occurred before I talk to her, she will take legal action against me and the gallery. She will seek publicity, and she will certainly get it. I cannot allow that to happen."

— Sixteen —

TUESDAY EVENING
New York

TRUE TO HER promise to arrive early, Coleman, chic in a leopard-print tunic over black leggings and black boots, was one of the first at Dinah's opening. A waiter handed her a glass of Perrier just as Marise Von Clemmer, exquisite in a turquoise long-sleeved wool dress and silver jewelry, appeared.

"Marise, so nice to see you," Coleman said.

"I'm glad to see you, too. I have information for you: no one named Simon Fanshawe-Davies ever attended Harvard," Marise said.

Coleman smiled. "So he really is a phony. It's a relief to be sure. I'd hate to think I was so wrong about him. Someday I'll have to go to press with the print issue of *ArtSmart*, and till now I haven't had anything about Simon, much less Heyward Bain."

"You now know everything I know about Simon. I also have a tidbit for you about Bain. A child prodigy named Heyward Bain worked with Professor William Laramie at MIT. Laramie's still there. I cannot promise that the child prodigy grew up to be the art billionaire, but it seems probable."

Coleman wrote Laramie's name in her notebook. "I bet that baby genius is my mystery man. Thanks, Marise. I really appreciate your help."

"I hope it is he. While we're speaking of mysteries, what does Dinah know about Jonathan Hathaway's first marriage?"

Coleman had questioned Dinah about Jonathan's former marriage and divorce, but Dinah'd been so starry-eyed, she apparently hadn't asked him anything about it, or if she had, Jonathan had ducked her questions. "As far as I know, absolutely nothing. Why?"

"Jonathan's dreadful sister Alice is talking about Jonathan's past, and Dinah shouldn't hear the gossip from a stranger. I think you should decide what to tell her. Jonathan's marriage and divorce were a scandal, widely known in Boston, but Boston is such a closed society, the news may not have traveled to New York.

"The woman's name was Judy something. She was a secretary at the Harvard Business School, and had a lover in every class for four or five years in a row. When she became frayed around the edges, she looked around for a husband, and chose Jonathan—rich, nice-looking, and naïve—and cut him out of the MBA herd like a sheepdog. He was wild about her. He married Judy while he was still at the business school because he thought she was pregnant. She wasn't, of course. Then, I guess she couldn't help herself and fell into bed with another MBA, and he caught her."

"Was the divorce scandalous, too?" Coleman asked.

Marise shook her head. "No, Jonathan moved to New York, and the Hathaways paid Judy off. I think she lives in California. Alice said he told his mother that any future bride would be young and innocent as Princess Diana was, and if necessary, he'd lock her up in a tower to make sure she stayed that way. He made a joke of it, but Alice thought he was halfway serious."

"Dinah fills the bill. Her nickname in college was Sleeping Beauty. She waited a long time for her prince. She said she'd know him when she saw him. She thought college boys were clumsy and crude. I agreed with her, but after we came to New York, I tried to persuade her to go out and have a little fun, and get to know some men as friends. But Jonathan was the first man she dated."

Coleman had been worried when Dinah decided to marry Jonathan. Dinah was so inexperienced, she had so little basis for comparison. How could she be sure Jonathan was right for her? Coleman felt responsible because she'd introduced Jonathan to Dinah. He had a great reputation as an investment banker, and she'd been thrilled when he'd backed her, but Coleman hadn't thought of him as a prospective date. He was too serious and too Wall Street for her—boring. But Dinah had come to the celebration dinner after the deal was finalized, and it had been love at first sight for both Dinah and Jonathan.

Coleman tried to check Jonathan out, but no one in New York seemed to know him. He'd been a loner after his move to New York until he met Dinah. Jonathan fit all of Dinah's specifications—gentlemanly, thoughtful, mature, adoring. He'd seemed perfect for her until recently, when, if Zeke was right, they'd begun to quarrel over the gallery. They'd had a long courtship—nearly three years—so Dinah had had lots of time to get to know Jonathan. But maybe you never knew a person till you'd lived with him. And theirs had been an old-fashioned and proper courtship. No living together before marriage for Dinah and Jonathan.

Marise was looking across the room at Dinah. "Well, it's a fairy story, but it may not be *Sleeping Beauty*, it might be *Rapunzel*. I think he *is* keeping her locked up, although it's obviously a gilded cage. She should be famous by now. She made the highest grades in our class at the Institute of Fine Arts, and she's very talented. This little out-of-the-way gallery is no place for her."

Coleman nodded. "Dinah was a star in high school and at Duke, too. She deserves a much bigger stage. But back to Jonathan: why is his sister talking about all this now? The divorce was years ago."

Marise made a tiny moue. "Something's got her stirred up. Maybe she's seen Judy recently. She'd hate anyone Jonathan married, but I think she has a sneaking admiration for Judy, who's said to be beautiful, and wicked. I went to Miss Porter's with Alice, and I saw her at a school function last week. Ordinarily, I wouldn't spend five minutes with her—she's ghastly—but I'm fond of Dinah, and I thought you should know what her sister-in-law is saying. She loved telling me all about Jonathan and Judy, and didn't care who heard. It's bound to reach Dinah eventually—Miss Porter's has lots of alumnae in New York."

Zeke Tolmach, color high, eyes sparkling, pushed through the crowd towards them. Marise saw him coming, and excused herself to look at the exhibition and to congratulate Dinah.

Marise was barely out of earshot when Zeke said, "I've found the link between *ArtSmart* and the *Artful Californian*. You were right—the spy is Chick O'Reilly!"

"Oh, hell. How do you know?" Coleman had continued to hope against reason that the leak wasn't Chick. She didn't want to lose him as a writer or a friend.

Zeke glowed with pride. "It's Chick's partner, David Edwards. You told me he sells paper, so I called the *Artful Californian*'s purchasing department, pretending to be a salesman with Great Mountains Paper. They said they buy their paper from Johnson and Gray, and I called J&G, and asked for Edwards, and he works there. He's bound to know everyone at *Artful*, and everything Chick knows."

"It's a link, but not proof that Chick's done anything wrong. Maybe Chick confides in David, and David is selling the information," Coleman argued.

"I'm afraid you'll never get proof, but if you ask Chick about it, you might be able to learn something from his reaction," Zeke said.

Coleman sighed. Zeke was determined to prove he was a great detective. Well, she'd asked for his help. It was irrational to be annoyed because she didn't like what he'd discovered.

"Oh, I'll talk to him. He should be here tonight. He's working on the Print Museum story, and Heyward Bain—" she broke off, and stared towards the door. Zeke followed her gaze to where Heyward Bain stood. Bain caught Coleman's eye, smiled, and moved through the crowd towards them.

"Hello. I hoped I'd see you here," he said.

"Hi," Coleman said. "You know Zeke Tolmach, don't you?"

"Of course." They shook hands, and Bain looked at the prints on the wall nearest them. "You know, these really are beautiful prints. I must look at them, and congratulate Dinah. Nice to see you both." He nodded, and moved away into the crowd.

"You've got it bad, haven't you?" Zeke said.

"I think he's very attractive. Does it show that much?"

"To me it does. But I've known you a long time. I doubt if anyone else has noticed. How does he feel about you?"

"He's never asked me out, and you saw how much he wanted to talk to me just now. Listen, Zeke, I've got the miseries because of this business about Chick. I think I'll turn in early. But I better look at the prints before I go, or Dinah will never forgive me."

When Bain completed his circuit of the gallery, he joined Dinah, who was still greeting newcomers. "Congratulations! It's a wonderful show, and the catalog is excellent," he said.

"Thank you! It's been great fun—I'm thrilled with the size of the crowd, and I'm so pleased you're buying the prints I proposed. Thank you again." She heard herself babbling. She wished Bain didn't make her nervous.

"Will you have lunch with me tomorrow or Thursday? I'd like to talk to you privately."

His brilliant gray eyes were fixed on hers, and she looked away. Why should he want to see her alone? If he wanted to talk about prints, why privately?

"Well, sure, I mean—I'd like that. Thursday would be best. Where would you like to m-meet?"

"How about Michael's at twelve thirty?"

"Yes, I know it—West Fifty-Fifth Street, right?"

"Good. I'll see you there!" He lifted her hand in his, kissed the air slightly above it, and was gone.

Dinah stared after him until she became aware that both Coleman and Jonathan were waiting to speak to her. Oh, God, had they overheard Bain inviting her to lunch?

"What was that about?" Coleman said.

"He was congratulating me on the proposal I put together for the museum, and on the show—polite platitudes. You're pale. Are you okay?"

"I'm just tired—I'm on my way to an early bed. Congratulations on the show—it's great. I'll call you tomorrow," Coleman said, and headed towards the door.

"We'll talk later," Jonathan said, his tone frigid. The muscle in his cheek twitched. Dinah had a horrible feeling he *had* heard her make the lunch date with Bain.

Bethany, smiling, took a break from working the room to whisper to Dinah. "We've sold more than half the prints already, and Ted Wolfe says he's goin' to review the show for the *New York Times*. We could sell out the show."

"That's great! Thanks, Bethany."

"Some of the clients are tellin' me they'd like to come in extra early tomorrow to look at the Rists that haven't sold. Can we open at eight?"

"Sure. We can't afford to miss any opportunity."

Bethany moved back into the fray, and Dinah greeted Zeke, hovering nearby. "Who's that?" he asked, staring at Bethany. Dinah followed his gaze. Bethany wore a long slender dress in a golden brown, a few shades darker than her skin. Her earrings were tinkly golden bells, and she wore armloads of thin gold bangles, and gold sandals.

She turned back to Zeke, who looked dazed. Dinah wasn't surprised. Men—except Jonathan—found Bethany devastatingly attractive. "That's my assistant, Bethany Byrd. Do you think she's pretty?"

"Gorgeous. Maybe I'll ask her out for supper."

"I think you'd enjoy it. She's great fun."

It would be wonderful if Bethany and Zeke hit it off. She was tired of Zeke mooning over Coleman. He'd had a crush on her since college, and it was time he got over it.

Coleman unlocked the door of her apartment, unzipped Dolly's pouch and set it on the floor. She kicked off her boots and flung herself on the sofa. Dolly scrambled out of the carrier and onto Coleman's chest. She licked Coleman's ear, and Coleman rubbed her head. "Oh, Dolly, Heyward Bain is the most attractive man I've met in years, and not only is he totally uninterested in me, I think he's fallen for Dinah, and Dinah for him."

Dinah must really like Bain. She not only hadn't told Coleman about Bain's invitation to lunch, she'd lied about it. And Dinah never lied to Coleman. Why would her lunch with Bain be a secret if it were business?

Coleman got up to look in the refrigerator, which, as usual, was empty of everything but vegetables and low-fat yogurt. Just as well. If there'd been anything tempting available, she'd have gobbled it down. She settled for a cup of diet cocoa, gave Dolly a dog biscuit, and went to run a hot bath. She needed to do some serious thinking.

—— Seventeen ——

TUESDAY NIGHT

W HEN THE LAST guest had departed, and Jonathan and Dinah had disappeared upstairs, Bethany and Zeke walked the few blocks to Sabor, a Cuban restaurant where Bethany said they'd be able to get a good meal without a long wait.

"I'm told the empanadas are the best appetizer here, but I'm havin' the *frituras*—they're all vegetable," she said.

"Are you a vegetarian?" Zeke didn't know many vegetarians, and those he knew disapproved if anyone else ordered meat. He didn't want to offend her.

"No, but I grew up in the South, and we were poor, so I'm used to not eatin' much meat. Meat was more like a condiment than a course."

"Uh—aren't you Indian? I mean isn't your family from India?" Zeke asked.

Bethany laughed. "Oh, no! I reckon the census classifies me as African American, but my family is a mixture of everything. We're not black, at least not to look at. We have Native American blood, white blood, and goodness knows what else."

"How'd you happen to come to work for Dinah?"

"My family's from the same part of North Carolina as the Greenes, and the head of our family, Aunt Mary Louise, was great friends with Dinah and Coleman's grandmother. We played together as children, went to the same school."

"But most of the time you don't talk the same way they do—and sometimes, like now, you sound like the BBC. What gives?"

She emphasized her crisp accent, "Oh, I can talk either way. I change according to what I'm talking about, or to whom I'm speaking. I had a teacher who told me everyone should be able to speak standard educated English, and Southern dialect. I use Southern dialect. When I talk to my family and friends, and sometimes in New York—it's a conversational stimulant. People always ask where I'm from, and before you know it, we're friends—and they're buyin' a print."

He laughed.

The food arrived and between bites he drew her out on her background. They ate sea bass in a garlicky green sauce, and a delicious coconut dessert. Bethany told him she studied commercial art at Eastern Carolina University, and after graduation worked for a printing company in Charlotte, but she'd been bored, and decided to come to New York. She'd fallen in love with the New York art scene, and had been with an East Village gallery when Dinah had offered her a fabulous deal to work with her.

"At least, it would be a fabulous deal if the gallery were in the right location, which it isn't, and if it had decent sales, which it doesn't. As it is, it's a disaster—I'm goin' to have to get another job, or starve," she said.

She scraped the last of her dessert from her plate and sat back with a contented sigh. Zeke smiled. She wouldn't starve tonight. He liked watching her eat. She was so full of—what? Gusto, that was it. Her enthusiasm was infectious.

He asked why Dinah didn't move the gallery to a better location. He was sure he knew the answer, but he wanted to hear what Bethany said.

"Jonathan writes the checks, and Jonathan doesn't want her to move—it's as simple as that. I think he's afraid if she's successful, she might leave him. God knows, I would, he's so bossy."

"If she moved to a better location, you're pretty sure she could make a go of it? And you'd stay with her?"

"Oh, yes. I'd rather do that than anything I can think of. If Dinah will just stiffen her backbone a little, it might happen. I'm keepin' my fingers crossed, 'cause it's not in her blood to let a man walk all over her."

"What do you mean?"

"Her grandmother was a Slocumb, and the Slocumb women are famous in the South. Seems like there's a Slocumb heroine in every war. There's a statue of one of them near where we live. Just as well those girls are strong—by the time they came along, the family had nothin'. They managed, but it was rough. Dinah knows how to work and to fight."

"And Coleman?"

"Coleman doesn't know the meanin' of words like 'surrender' or 'quit.' She's the toughest little thing you ever saw, and scared of no one and nothin', includin' the Devil himself. People say she met the Devil more than once, and the Devil ran away with his tail between his legs."

"Have you met Heyward Bain?" Zeke said.

Bethany grinned. "I saw him tonight, but I haven't met him. Why? Do you think he's the Devil?"

"I don't know. Maybe. I don't like him, but I think Coleman's got a thing for him. They make a good-looking couple. He even reminds me of her—I guess it's because they're both so small. Do most women find short men attractive?"

Bethany laughed. "I can't answer for most women. But *I* do—some men, anyway. Alan Ladd. Paul Newman. Humphrey Bogart. Steve McQueen. Tom Cruise. Heyward Bain is handsomer than any of them, except maybe Newman."

She looked at her watch. "Oh, drat. It's late. I've got to try to get some sleep."

He signaled for the check. "What do you mean, 'try'?"

"I'm a terrible sleeper, and since I've been worryin' about my job, it's been worse. I hardly ever sleep through the night."

"May I take you home?" Maybe if Bethany couldn't sleep, she'd like some company.

"You can walk me home. It's only a few blocks. But you can't come up. I'm exhausted."

But she let Zeke hold her hand, and when they said good night on the sidewalk outside her building, she kissed him back.

LATE TUESDAY NIGHT

Dinah sat at her dressing table brushing her hair, while Jonathan, the tic in his cheek worse than she'd ever seen it, paced the bedroom and harangued her about Heyward Bain.

"Are you going to have lunch with Bain?" he asked again.

"*Yes*, Jonathan, for the fifth time."

"Doesn't it matter to you that I don't want you to see that man?"

Dinah turned and faced him. "Jonathan, 'that man' is an important customer. He just b-bought a bunch of p-prints from the gallery—the p-portfolio I offered the P-Print Museum. I d-didn't tell you before, because I d-didn't want to have another row. He's a major f-figure in my f-field. 'That man' has asked me to have l-lunch in a p-public p-place. Why shouldn't I g-go?"

"Isn't the fact that I don't want you to go reason enough?"

"Jonathan, I d-do everything you ask that's reasonable, and a lot that isn't. I d-didn't promise to obey you when we g-got married. We t-took that phrase out of the ceremony—remember? And you must s-stop trying to tell me what to do about my b-business." She kept her voice level, and forced herself to hold back tears.

Jonathan stalked out. She supposed he'd sleep in the guest bedroom, as he'd done when he had a cold. She didn't care. She was sick of arguing. But she felt guilty, she wasn't sure her lunch with Bain *was* all business. She hated to admit it, but she found Bain attractive. She'd never have dreamed that only five months after her wedding she'd be having lunch with another man against Jonathan's wishes.

Jonathan started in again about Bain as soon as Dinah got up Wednesday morning. When he paused to breathe, she told him she had to go to the gallery early, and went in to shower. When she came out, he'd left for work. She dressed and hurried downstairs to the gallery. Customers poured in all morning.

Around noon, when no one was in the gallery but Bethany, Dinah ran upstairs to get leftovers from the opening for a quick lunch, and took Baker for a walk.

When she returned to the gallery with the tray, she said to Bethany, "Sorry about this, these sandwiches don't look too great. I didn't want to take the time to fix anything—someone will probably come in any minute."

"I'm so hungry I could eat anything that didn't bite back," Bethany said, gobbling a handful of tiny sandwiches with curled crusts. After she'd swallowed the last scrap, she said, "Dinah, why don't you quit arguin' with Jonathan, and just move the gallery? You can fight about it forever, but he's winnin' because you're still here."

Dinah stared at Bethany. "You know, you're absolutely right. Coleman doesn't argue with him, she ignores him, and does whatever she was going to do. I should learn from her."

"Yes, but don't just stop arguin'—act! Where would you rather be—midtown or Chelsea?"

"Chelsea's hot, but I'd rather be in midtown. Other areas come and go, but there'll always be galleries in midtown—and I don't want to have to move again," Dinah said.

"Last night I heard there's good space available in 20 West Fifty-Seventh Street. What do you think?"

"Oh, Bethany, that would be grand, I love that building. But what about the space here?"

"You can rent it—lots of small businesses would like it," Bethany said.

"But Jonathan won't like people being here on weekends—"

"Well, he can afford to leave it empty—he doesn't need the money. But it's not your problem, is it?"

"I guess not, but what about the cost of Fifty-Seventh Street? He won't pay for it."

"No, and you shouldn't let him. Didn't Miss Ida ever tell you, 'He who pays the piper, calls the tune?' If you want Jonathan to stop tellin' you what to do, don't take his money."

The gallery bell sounded, and Bethany pushed the buzzer to let two customers in. Dinah brushed away the crumbs, thinking about West Fifty-Seventh Street. Bethany was right. She would look at the space, and if she liked it, and could come up with the money, she'd take it. She'd had enough.

Bethany had arranged to meet Zeke at O'Malley's on Perry Street for supper after the gallery closed. He was at a table near the fire, reading the *New York Times*. His face lit up when he saw her.

They sipped beer and ate peanuts from the big barrel in the middle of the room while they waited for their hamburgers. The floor was littered with peanut shells, and a huge marmalade cat slept on a pillow near the fire. The room smelled of fried onions, beer, and wood smoke.

Bethany, as usual, was starving. When the burgers came she wolfed hers and ate a great pile of french fries. When she'd finished, she took a deep breath and let it out. The tension she'd felt all day while dealing with customers was draining away. "I nearly cancelled, I was so tired after the openin' last night and workin' today, but I'm glad I came," she said.

Zeke smiled at her. "Me, too."

Bethany tossed a peanut shell at the cat. It opened a drowsy yellow eye, and went back to sleep.

She'd heard a lot about Zeke from Dinah. She'd said he was unavailable because he'd been in love with Coleman since college. Maybe he *had* been, but she knew the signs. He was definitely interested in Bethany. She'd test him. "You've known Dinah and Coleman since college? You used to date Coleman?"

Zeke shook his head. "Oh, I took her out a few times. Nothing serious, just friends."

Bethany smiled. If that's the way he saw it, so much the better.

"What kind of a day did you have?" Zeke wanted to know.

"Busy. We sold a lot of the Rist prints, and some other stock, too. And, guess what? Dinah's goin' to look at a space on Fifty-Seventh Street. If she likes it, and can get the money, she's said she'll move, no matter what Jonathan says."

"Wow! That's big news. And I think it's the right thing to do. As for the money—maybe I can help."

"Really? It could get expensive. The space has been advertised so we know the rent, and it's pretty steep. Dinah and I worked on some numbers—"

"Oh, don't worry about that. I can handle it," Zeke said.

She stared at him. "You can make a commitment just like that, without even knowin' the cost?"

Zeke laughed. "Yes, ma'am. Only child, only grandchild. Lucky financially, but not so lucky in other ways. Neither my career nor my love life has gone too well."

Bethany smiled. "That could change."

— Eighteen —

COLEMAN KNEW THAT her interest in Heyward Bain had distracted her from what was most important to her: *ArtSmart*. She had a long list of things she should have done, some of them way overdue. She wasn't on top of the Print Museum story, and she hadn't confronted Chick.

She looked at Dolly, who was staring at her expectantly. "Dolly, I'm going to start a new chapter today—work, work, work. I'll forget all about Bain, I promise."

Coleman poked her head in Chick's office door, a Starbucks venti in her hand and Dolly at her heels. "Good morning! Have you got a minute?"

Chick looked up from his keyboard. "Hey, Coleman! Come in. I'm trying to clear my desk and calendar of everything else, so I can concentrate on the Print Museum story."

She sat down opposite him and opened her notebook. "How about catching me up on what you've learned?"

"Sure. It looks like La Grange not only was the seller of *Skating Girl* and *The Midget*, but also the four Dürers and Rembrandt's *Sleeping Kitten*."

"I hadn't heard about the Dürers or the Rembrandt, but I'm not surprised," Coleman said.

Chick, frowning, leaned back in his chair, his arms behind his head. "I can't understand how La Grange could have owned those prints. Where did he get the money? Why would any legitimate collector sell them to him? Why wouldn't the collector sell 'em at auction, or through an established dealer? Why were the Dürers and the Rembrandt auctioned in cities other than New York or London? And in second- or third-tier auction houses? They'd have done a lot better at one of the majors in a big auction city. Last: in every case the underbidder has been on the telephone. That's suspicious in itself."

Coleman, making notes, didn't look up. "I think so, too. Have you checked the lists that curators and dealers suggested for the Print Museum? To see who recommended those particular prints?"

Chick nodded. "Yep, *Sleeping Kitten* and *The Midget* were only on Simon Fanshawe-Davies's list. They're so rare no one else thought they could be bought. The Dürer prints were on several lists along with other Dürers—the print experts didn't agree about which ones Bain should own. The four he acquired aren't that rare, but they're in perfect condition, and getting the four together was unusual. They must have been in a collection somewhere, but no one knows where."

Coleman tapped her pencil on the desk. "Are there any other prints on Simon's list, and nowhere else? Prints Bain hasn't bought yet?"

Chick nodded again. "Two more Rembrandts, *Seashells* and *Winter Landscape*. Nobody thinks he'll find those—they're even rarer than *Kitten*. But no one's betting against Fanshawe-Davies. He's been amazingly successful at getting things for Bain."

Coleman leaned forward, her elbows on the desk, her head in her hands. "What do you think is going on?"

Chick offered her his bowl of mints, and when she shook her head, took one himself. "Jimmy must have been fronting for someone, maybe several people, but we don't know who or why. The lack of provenance for all those prints suggests some kind of illegal source, or sources, but nobody knows where they came from. I'm thinking the bidding was rigged; I think the telephone bidder was pushing up prices, probably in collusion with Simon."

"I agree. We have to try to find out everything we can about La Grange, including his death. We can't go to press with all these loose ends hanging, and if we don't tie 'em up, it looks like nobody will. But I'll understand if you don't want anything to do with this part of the story—La Grange's death was pretty ugly, and definitely not the kind of article you signed up to do when you joined *ArtSmart*."

Chick's freckled cheeks turned pink. "Oh, I want to do the whole thing. It's potentially big."

"Okay, it's yours. Keep me posted, will you?"

Coleman trusted Chick. She knew it wasn't rational—the evidence was against him—but her instincts kept telling her he was okay. And Chick's bulldog tenacity and his deep digging were exactly what were needed for the story.

Of course, if Chick *were* the leak, she might end up reading everything he discovered in the *Artful Californian*. It was a chance she was prepared to take. Coleman stood up, and started to leave Chick's office, but she paused near the door, and turned back to face him. She'd try again.

"Is there anything else?" Chick asked, his head cocked.

"You've seemed—I don't know—troubled in the past few months, not yourself. Is everything okay?"

He fidgeted in his seat. "Yes, fine. Certainly nothing wrong about the job. I'd tell you if I had a work problem, I promise."

Coleman returned to her office, and Dolly jumped into her lap. Coleman stroked her, thinking about what Chick had said. "Nothing wrong about the *job*?" Could he and David have personal problems? Or did he have another job offer, and didn't want to tell her until it was settled? It was possible.

When she'd first met Chick, he was writing for *Architectural Digest*. She'd thought he was wasted describing rooms he'd seen only in photographs, rooms by the same old decorators, the same contemporary art on the walls of the modern New York and California apartments, the same tacky details in the traditional houses. Imagine painting walls or woodwork to match a color in a featured work of art. Yuck. She'd even seen an entire room painted the bubblegum hue of a squirrel's genitalia in the painting by an Audubon wannabe over the mantle. Sick-making. Maybe someday she'd buy a decorating magazine and show everyone how it should be done. Yeah, and she'd wake up tomorrow looking like J.Lo.

Chick had taken to *ArtSmart* like a cat to cream, and his writing had improved remarkably. She still thought he was her friend no matter how bad it looked, but today he'd hinted he had a problem, and he wouldn't tell her about it. He was usually so open. In fact, he talked so much, it was hard to believe he could live a double life. Of course, as a gay man who had never told his family the nature of his relationship with his partner, he was doing just that. Oh, God, what a nuisance this leak was. It made her suspect everyone.

<hr />

Michael's was packed, and many of the customers were celebrities, but Dinah wasn't interested in the crowd. Even distracted as she was by her personal problems, and anxious about her lunch with Bain, she couldn't resist pausing to look at the prints that decorated the walls. They were by famous contemporary artists, including Jasper Johns, Frank Stella, and David Hockney. She promised herself she'd come in some day and seriously study them.

Bain stood up and held her chair for her. "Do you know this restaurant? Some people think the Cobb salad is the best in New York. Have you tried it? No? Then you must—how about a glass of white wine?" Dinah nodded, and Bain gave their orders to the hovering waiter. "I'm so glad you could join me today. I have two topics I want to talk to you about. The first is business. Why aren't you in a big gallery in a better location, with a much larger selection of prints?"

Dinah started to reply, but Bain continued. "I've read your articles on Jackson Pollock's and Lee Krasner's prints—brilliant. And your pieces on young printmakers—artists I don't know, but would like to—are really good. You should be handling more artists."

The waiter brought her wine and his iced tea. Dinah wanted to sip her wine—maybe it would relax her—but she didn't dare delay replying, given his tendency to override her. "Thank you, I'd like to, but—" she began, but he cut her off before she could complete the sentence.

"If it's money, I'll lend you whatever you need at current interest rates, with a bank as intermediary. As soon as the initial collection at the Print Museum is set up, I plan to give up an active role there, so it wouldn't be a conflict for me to back a gallery. What do you say?"

Dinah leaped in. "Well, it's a little . . . complicated. You see, Jonathan, my husband—he's my backer and—" Bain interrupted again. She wished he'd let her finish her sentences.

"He's a little short of capital? That's easy to fix. If you'd rather I deal directly with him, I'll call him."

Dinah winced. Jonathan would be furious if he knew Heyward Bain thought he needed money. "Oh, no, nothing like that! No, it's just he thinks I ought to stay small—"

"But wouldn't it help if I talked to him? *I'm* confident you're capable of handling a much bigger gallery."

Oh, God, Bain mustn't talk to Jonathan, things were bad enough already. But she might need Bain's backing, even though she didn't like the idea of being indebted to another overbearing man. Could he be nervous, his tank-like qualities temporary? Or would it be frying-pan-to-fire if she took his money?

"Thank you, but I don't think your talking to him would help. But I do plan to expand, and if Jonathan doesn't want to finance my expansion, I'll consider your offer. I appreciate your confidence in me."

Bain smiled. "Just let me know. The other matter I wanted to talk about is, well, more delicate."

Dinah braced herself. He was going to—what? Proposition her? Tell her he was in love with her?

Bain crumbled the roll on his bread plate. "It's about Coleman."

She looked up, startled. "Coleman?"

"I already know a great deal about her. How the two of you were brought up by your grandmother and your aunt. How you went to Miss Dabney's and then Duke—how Coleman made your clothes and hers out of old clothes—"

This man was way out of line. She didn't like being reminded of her poverty. "How in the name of goodness can you know that?"

Before Bain could reply, the waiter brought their food. Dinah tasted her Cobb salad, and put her fork down. It might as well have been shredded cardboard.

Bain had reduced his roll to stuffing mix. He looked up from the mess he was making, and his cheeks flushed. He must have read Dinah's expression, or noticed she wasn't eating. "I haven't been spying on you and Coleman. It's—well, I have my ways."

Dinah considered him. Who was this man? His prying was unmannerly; he was a strange person. But something about him was familiar. "Sometimes you sound almost Southern. It's not your accent—more the words you use: 'I have my ways.' Are you from the South?"

"I probably pick it up from you. Anyway, I know a lot about Coleman. When she first arrived at Duke, I understand she dated a lot but then she stopped dating, except for a few old friends. Did something happen?"

Dinah stiffened. Worse and worse. How dare he pry into their intimate affairs? His discussing their homemade

clothes was bad enough, but this was beyond imperti-
nent. "I think you know it did. I don't know how you
could possibly know, but if you do, you don't need me to
tell you."

"Dinah, I've heard the story, but I need to know how
it affected Coleman."

Dinah now knew he wasn't attracted to her, and in a
way, she was relieved. It certainly made her life less complicated. He *was* interested in Coleman, and that made
sense. Coleman was single, and she was the most attractive woman Dinah knew. "Are you in love with Coleman?"

He blushed, and shook his head. "I can't talk about
how I feel about Coleman—it's impossible to explain, at
least right now. But I promise you I wouldn't ask these
questions if it weren't important."

Dinah frowned. "I don't understand. Why don't you
ask her?"

"I can't. Please tell me. I swear my interest isn't frivolous."

"You're going to have to do better than that. How do
you know as much as you do?"

"I heard the story indirectly from one of the boys who
was there."

"I'm surprised you know that sort of person. Why do
you need to know more?"

Bain leaned forward. "I told you. I need to know what
it did to Coleman. Do you think it's because of what
happened that night that she's never married?"

Dinah shook her head. "No, I really don't. She quit
dating in college because she decided most of the boys
weren't worth her time. But she was around some awful
people before she came to Slocumb Corners. She'd
stopped trusting men by the time she was five years old.

With good reason. And we grew up in an all-woman household. She hardly knew any men after she came to Slocumb Corners—nothing happened to change her mind about men.

"It was different for me. I never met men, good or bad, so I dreamed about storybook men—I wanted a Prince Charming or a Mr. Darcy to come and rescue me. Anyway, I think Maxwell Arnold and his buddies only confirmed what Coleman already knew: there are some terrible people in the world."

Bain frowned. "You think she got over it? That—that episode didn't—I don't know—prevent her committing? Ruin her life?"

Dinah shook her head. "I don't think Coleman will ever marry. Not because of anything that happened at Duke, but because she has other priorities. She made up her mind a long time ago to dance to music only she can hear. Did she get over that little episode? Oh, yes. Coleman is the most resilient person I've ever met. She had to be, living through what she did. Some people are damaged by terrible childhood experiences, others are strengthened. Coleman is *very* strong."

"You keep mentioning the years before she came to live with your grandmother. What can you tell me about her life then?"

"Oh, if you want to know about that, Coleman will have to tell you. And lots of luck. She never talks about it."

They seemed to have nothing more to say, and neither of them wanted dessert or coffee. When they rose to leave, Dinah looked at her barely touched salad, and around the bright room, full of exciting art and people enjoying themselves. Some contrast with *her* lunch.

Oh well, it had been interesting. It would be even more interesting to tell Coleman about it, especially Bain's curiosity about her.

"I don't suppose I can persuade you not to tell Coleman what we talked about," Bain said, as if he'd read her mind.

Dinah shook her head. "No, you can't." She'd tell Coleman everything as soon as they had some private time. But she wouldn't confess that she'd thought Bain was attracted to her. She felt like a fool, and it would be too humiliating to tell anybody, even Coleman. He *must* be in love with Coleman. Why didn't he ask her out?

—— Nineteen ——

RACHEL RANSOME HAD finally reached Yvonne Jardin. Jardin, a famous actress since she was twenty and now in her sixties, was still beautiful, still imperious, and the former owner of *The Midget*. She was in great demand socially, but when Rachel hinted that the meeting she proposed would be financially advantageous, Jardin's calendar miraculously cleared.

They met for lunch in the dining room of the Bristol Hotel on the Rue du Faubourg. But before they ordered, Rachel explained why she was there. "Yvonne, I paid you far too little for that Lautrec poster. It sold at auction for $1.2 million."

"Why are you telling me this?" Yvonne asked, the famous velvet voice tight with fury. "Have you come to gloat? I am an actress, not an expert on these matters.

I trusted you to treat me fairly because you were Ransome's friend, and you paid me $30,000 for that print! So much for trust!" Even angry as she was, Yvonne was careful not to frown; Rachel was sure that injections kept her fair brow smooth. Yvonne was as mindful of her beauty as her bank account.

"I am here to make amends," Rachel said. "I have brought you a check. I had no idea the print would sell for so much, but you should not suffer for my ignorance."

Yvonne curled her lip. "And how much of your profit will you share? For what paltry amount is this check?"

"You misunderstand me. Ransome's is giving up its entire profit. We are not taking a commission. We regret that we erred so badly," Rachel said.

"Let me see this check."

Rachel held it out so that Yvonne could see the amount, but did not release it when the actress reached for it. "I would like you to sign a release. You will understand that I am concerned about the gallery's reputation. I do not wish anyone to think I would ever cheat a buyer or a seller. If I should unknowingly do so—as in this situation—I make restitution, as you see. I want you to trust me again."

Yvonne skimmed through the brief letter Rachel handed her. "Give me a pen," she said, and signed her name in big, sprawling letters, keeping one eye on the check.

Rachel and Yvonne did not remain to eat lunch. Yvonne, caressing her handbag where the precious check awaited her attention, made it obvious that she'd like to be alone with her money. Rachel wanted to get back to London.

In the car on the way to the airport, she lay back against the seat, drained. She longed to return to her studies, to leave the contemporary world to others. But a retreat into her beloved sixteenth century was not possible. The war with Simon had begun.

NEW YORK
Friday

Dinah and Bethany made an appointment to look at the space on West Fifty-Seventh, and when Dinah saw it, she fell in love. "It's perfect," she whispered, her cheeks flushed, her eyes starry. "But Bethany, where am I going to get the money?"

Bethany smiled. "Zeke says he'll lend it to you."

Dinah shook her head. "I wouldn't want to impose on Zeke, and anyway, I don't think he has that kind of money."

"It wouldn't be an imposition. He told me he'd like to help you. And he has the money. He said it wasn't a problem."

Dinah's face lit up again. "Really? I'd rather owe Zeke money than just about anybody I can think of—I've known him forever, and he's always been a good friend. What should I do?"

"Call him, and tell him you appreciate his offer to help."

Dinah made the call, and Zeke said he'd have the papers drawn up right away. He'd wire her the money to put a hold on the gallery space. She also called Coleman, who thoroughly approved of the new location, and the loan from Zeke. After talking to Coleman, Dinah was almost able to forget how Jonathan would react when he heard her plans.

~

Coleman worked her way through a pile of manuscripts awaiting final editing. Later, needing a change of pace, she looked at her to-do list. "I think it's time to call

MIT," she said to Dolly. "By noon even the most important professor should be in, right?" She spoke to a series of operators, but when she finally got the right extension, a machine answered: Professor William Laramie was on leave until early January, and couldn't be reached.

She cursed silently. She could eat six Snickers bars. She'd take Dolly for a walk, maybe the fresh air would clear her head, and she could forget her candy craving. But when she looked out the window, a mixture of rain and sleet was falling. Dolly would refuse to go out in this. She returned to her desk, and her calendar caught her eye. Oh hell, Thanksgiving was only a week away.

She preferred to ignore Thanksgiving. She refused all invitations for the feast. "Too much fattening food," she told Dinah. "I'll work, and if I eat turkey, it'll be in a sandwich at my desk." Holidays made her think about things she'd like to forget. Like eating Thanksgiving dinner in a church community hall, surrounded by the homeless.

———————

Zeke invited Bethany to his parents' house on Long Island for Thanksgiving weekend, or for the day if she'd prefer a shorter visit. But she'd said she had to go to North Carolina; everyone in her family came home for Thanksgiving. He'd settled for a dinner on the Tuesday night before Thanksgiving, and she'd requested Italian food. They went to Orso, and ate mushroom risotto, and drank red wine. While they were eating, he told her about the leak at *ArtSmart*.

"I've been trying to help Coleman figure it out. It's a secret from Jonathan, because he's Coleman's backer, so she hasn't told Dinah. But we're bogged down, and a fresh approach might be useful." He described the investigation that led to Chick. "But Coleman doesn't believe it's Chick, and I sort of agree with her. It just doesn't fit, somehow. In mystery books, things are black and white, not like this. I love mysteries, and I've always thought how great it would be to be Lord Peter Wimsey—"

"Oh, I do, too! I'd like to be Harriet Vane. I love Lord Peter, and I've always wanted to solve a mystery. But tell me again, slower. Maybe I can spot something you missed."

He repeated the story, adding details he'd omitted the first time.

Bethany leaned forward. "And the leaks stopped after Coleman stopped tellin' the group her ideas?"

Zeke nodded. "Yep, normally she'd discuss them with the writers—"

Bethany interrupted. "Could the office be bugged?"

"Bugged!"

"Yeah, well, I know it sounds silly, but I'm readin' this guide to bein' a detective—it says buggin' is illegal, but lots of people do it, and detectives should know how to check a place for bugs. And there've been a bunch of magazine articles lately about people scannin' offices for bugs, because there's so much industrial espionage going on."

"Bugged!"

Bethany laughed. "Oh, Zeke, get over it. It's not impossible. She could hire somebody to check for her, but wouldn't it be fun to get the equipment, and do it ourselves? If there's a bug, the listener is someone outside the office, and the leak isn't Chick."

Zeke shrugged. "Well, yeah, I suppose. But do you think we can persuade Coleman to let us do it?"

"I think so. She'd like it to be an outsider, somebody who's not a friend."

"Where do you get the equipment?" Zeke asked.

"Probably lots of places, but there's a store on West Fourth Street called 'The Spy Shop.' I've never been in it, but I've looked in the window, and they've got the stuff."

"Let's check it out when you come back."

She beamed at him. "Okay. What should we have for dessert?"

— Twenty —

DINAH AND JONATHAN spent Thanksgiving Day in Boston, where they shared an elaborate dinner in a private dining room at the Ritz Hotel with his cold, aloof father, his alcoholic mother, his acid-tongued sister, Alice, and a dozen more distant connections. Alice seemed especially vicious this year, and before they sat down to eat, Dinah kept moving around the room to avoid her.

But she couldn't avoid Jonathan's father. As the wife of the son and heir, on these occasions Dinah had to sit beside Father Hathaway. Talking to him was work. She started dreading a Hathaway family Christmas before she'd finished eating her Thanksgiving turkey.

———

Chick and David spent Thanksgiving Day with Chick's family in New Jersey, but before he left for the holiday, Chick wrote a long e-mail to Coleman describing his activities and discoveries in the days before Thanksgiving. He'd found Jimmy's accountant, who had Jimmy's financials, but they contained nothing of interest. The accountant said Jimmy had discovered *Skating Girl* in a thrift shop in Maine. It had been a bargain, but Jimmy had needed—and found—a backer to pay for it.

The accountant said that Jimmy was sure he was on his way to becoming a real dealer. He wouldn't tell his accountant who his backer was. He said Jimmy loved being mysterious, acting the big shot. Jimmy, according to the accountant, was just an overgrown kid.

Chick had tracked down some of Jimmy's neighbors, and now knew who he was looking for, or at least what they looked like. Several people described the two huge brutes who'd been with Jimmy the night he died. They said that the police thought they were prostitutes, hired through one of the bars; that the tough guys needed a place where they could connect with customers, a place where they could receive messages.

Chick had put together a list of Greenwich Village bars he planned to visit. He'd slog his way through them till he found someone who knew the men. He'd be in touch.

—— Twenty-One ——

DECEMBER

ONTHS EARLIER, DINAH and Jonathan had made reservations to go to Canyon Ranch in Arizona for Christmas. They'd invited Coleman to join them, and told her she could bring Dolly. Canyon Ranch welcomed dogs. But Coleman didn't want to be a third wheel, and she had a lot of work to do, so she decided to stay in New York. She would avoid Christmas parties and catch up at the office. If she had time, maybe she'd design some new clothes.

She'd made a few Christmas dates, including a holiday drink with Debbi before her friend left for a two-week stay in Florida. They always met at Bemelmans Bar in the Carlyle Hotel. Coleman was enjoying a Virgin Mary, and Debbi's vodka on the rocks was waiting on the table when Debbi arrived.

Coleman grinned, watching Debbi sashay towards the table. Debbi, who didn't mind being conspicuous, had style. Her orange Brillo hair stood out like a halo, and her big round glasses magnified her heavily made-up eyes. She bought her colorful and original outfits at vintage clothing stores. Tonight she wore a beautifully cut bright red suit in nubby wool, with the briefest of skirts, revealing an amazing amount of leg. Coleman reached out to finger the fabric, and raised her brows.

"Ancient Blass," Debbi said. "Happy Holidays." She took a swallow of her drink and put two small packages on the table. "These are from Heyward for you and for Dinah. You can deliver hers, can't you? You should open yours now." She looked at Coleman's black satin jump suit, nodded her approval. "Trendy."

"Thanks. I was strolling through Saks looking for ideas, and saw several jumpsuits. They inspired me to try something new."

Coleman opened her package. "Wow! They're fabulous." She held the big black enamel hoops studded with tiny multicolor stones against her ears. "How do they look?" Bain had probably given Dinah earrings, too, making the gifts seem impersonal business tokens. Oh, well, they were wonderful earrings. Debbi probably selected them.

"They're perfect with that outfit." Debbi searched for a cigarette, seemed to remember she couldn't smoke here, and reached for a handful of nuts from the bowl on the table. "Well, I'm out of here, thank God, but Simon, Ellen, and Heyward will all be in New York for the holidays. I've set Heyward up at dozens of parties. He'll be seen with models, starlets, all the usual tricks of the trade." She raised a finger to let the bartender know she was ready for a second drink.

Bain's presence in New York wouldn't make any difference to Coleman. She couldn't get another interview with him, and he obviously had no interest in seeing her socially. "Maybe I'll try to get together with Carswell or Simon over Christmas. How do I reach them?" Coleman asked.

"Simon's staying here at the Carlyle. You can reach Ellen at the office in Heyward's house, you have that number. You'd better hurry if you want to interview Ellen. She won't be around much longer. She plans to stay through the January opening of the museum, but after that, she'll go about her business."

Coleman frowned. "What business? I thought she was Bain's assistant."

"Yes, for getting the museum underway, but that's not her real job. She owns a company in Chicago called Computer Art Research Services. They did the research for Heyward that led to his establishing the Print Museum. She left an associate in charge of the company and came to New York to help Heyward get started."

Coleman's frown deepened. "You're kidding! Why didn't I know that?"

Debbi shrugged. "I don't know. It's not a secret."

"I guess I misjudged her. She's not exactly friendly, and she never says anything. I thought she was just a cold, efficient bimbo. I didn't see her as brainless, just boring. I never thought of interviewing her."

"Cool and efficient, yes, but she's also smart and interesting. You should talk to her. Here, I have a present for you. Open it, and then I've got to go. I have a few more stops to make tonight, and I can't go much longer without a cigarette," Debbi said.

"I appreciate your suffering for me as long as you have, but remember, every cigarette you skip probably prolongs your life."

Coleman ripped the gold paper, opened the box, and lifted out a filmy sea green scarf, glittering with pale green sequins. "God, this is lovely—thanks! This is for you." She handed Debbi a shiny green package.

Debbi tore open the package, and held up a vest made of red and gold brocade, patterned with small dragons. The label was Coleman's. "Fabulous! I've always wanted something you designed, and this will remind me of you. No one but you calls me Dragon Lady, thank God."

Coleman laughed. When they'd first met, she'd nicknamed Debbi the Dragon Lady because she constantly puffed smoke, and because she wore dark red polish on her long nails—dragon claws. "I didn't know at the time that your specialty is putting out fires," Coleman said.

Simon interpreted Coleman's call as an invitation to come on to her, and he bragged that he could get them into Le Cirque whenever she wanted to go, despite the crowded holiday calendar. Coleman was so sickened by the conversation, she claimed to be busy at the times he suggested. Fingers crossed, she promised to call him after New Year's. But Carswell was all business, and they arranged to meet for lunch at the Creedmore Club the following day.

When they'd ordered, Ellen said, "I'm very pleased that you invited me to lunch. I've heard so much about you." Her voice was low and husky.

Coleman smiled. "Nice of you to say so."

"Not at all. Even before I came to New York I read *ArtSmart* and admired what you did with the magazine."

Ellen's eyes were light brown, lavishly made up with thick black mascara and brownish eye shadow. Her suit was rust colored—a great color with her red hair—and she wore less jewelry than usual—just a simple gold E on her lapel, and plain gold earrings. Maybe she'd dressed down for lunch at a women's club—or lunch with a woman. She wasn't wearing perfume, and she didn't smoke, or if she did, not enough for the odor to cling to her hair and clothes. Seeing all that eye makeup, Coleman would have expected her to wear an old-fashioned and heavy scent. Tabu, maybe, or Shalimar.

Coleman gave silent thanks. She detested heavy perfume almost as much as second-hand smoke. "Tell me, how did you meet Heyward Bain?"

"Through my company in Chicago. Heyward asked us to look for a gap in the art world that he might fill. When he learned there isn't a print museum in the United States, he jumped at the idea, and his plans for the project sounded so interesting, I came along to help," Ellen said.

"But you're going back to Chicago to stay?"

"Yes. My business is there, and my mother lives there, and she's not very well. Incidentally, I introduced Simon Fanshawe-Davies to Heyward."

That was a useful tidbit. "How do you know Simon?"

"He was considering opening a Ransome Gallery branch in the United States, and trying to decide what its focus should be, so he consulted my company. I thought Simon and Heyward would get along."

Did Ellen look amused? At that moment the waitress served their grilled tuna, and Coleman was uncertain of exactly what she'd seen. "Yours is an unusual business.

How'd you get into it?" It was a clever concept, and Coleman suspected it had made Ellen rich, that the business—not a lover—paid for Ellen's clothes and jewelry.

Ellen said she'd joined a high school drama club, and became starstruck. After graduating, she'd moved to New York to study acting, but it hadn't worked out, she just didn't have the talent. She'd returned to Chicago, graduated from Northwestern, and then from the University of Chicago Business School. After a couple of computer-related jobs, she'd come into a small inheritance and used it to start her company. She lowered her eyes, toying with her food. "It's done pretty well," she said.

Coleman smiled to herself. Nice understatement, the antithesis of Simon the braggart. She liked Ellen more than she'd expected. "So I've heard. Back to the Print Museum: tell me how everything's going."

"Right on schedule. Heyward is organized and efficient, and the dealers, especially Simon, have been immensely helpful."

Ellen couldn't seem to resist bringing up Simon's name; she dropped it at every opportunity. Maybe they *were* an item. Coleman decided to push that button and see what reaction she got. "Yes, Debbi's filled me in on how helpful Simon's been. He's sold the most to the Print Museum, especially if you include the works that Bain has asked him to bid for. How do you account for that? Simon's a newcomer to the print world—he's moved ahead mighty fast."

"Well, he works hard, he's intelligent, and he's very attractive. Don't you agree?" She was watching Coleman like a chicken eyeing a June bug.

Coleman pressed harder. "Yes, very. He asked me to have dinner with him at Le Cirque next week."

Ellen's brown eyes narrowed. "How very nice for you. I understand it's a wonderful restaurant. I haven't been there."

Coleman teased Ellen a little more about Simon before getting back to business, but couldn't provoke any further reaction. Ellen's answers to questions about the Print Museum were interesting, though, especially her explanation of the Computer Art Research Services survey for Bain, how the research had been done, and Heyward's endorsement of the outcome.

"The only surprise was his decision to open the museum in New York. He could have located it anywhere in the United States, but he was determined to come here," Ellen said. She offered the information as if it should have special significance, but Coleman didn't get it: why shouldn't he come to New York? New York was the art center of the world.

———————

Bethany arrived at the gallery early every day in December, and settled down to drink her coffee and check out the tabloids until opening time, unless there was something pressing to be done.

Good Lord, the *Star* was running a reprise of the Jimmy La Grange story. It emphasized the gory way Jimmy died. It also contained startling new information: Jimmy had lived—and died—in one of the tenements almost directly across the street from Bethany's building on Charles Street. She shouldn't be surprised. A lot of people in the art world lived on her block. They couldn't afford anything better.

Something tugged at the back of her mind, and she pulled her detecting notebook out of her carryall.

There it was: her doctor sighting the early morning of Jimmy's death. Was the doctor visiting Jimmy's apartment? Had the old lady who found him called him? Or Jimmy himself?

~

Coleman tried to avoid a holiday lunch with Zeke and Bethany—too much time, too much food—but Zeke had pressed, and she'd agreed, mostly because she was grateful to him for what he'd done for Dinah. Anyway, the Sea Grill, overlooking the skating rink at Rockefeller Center, was special, and the stroll along Fifth Avenue to get there had been fun. Surrounded by tinkling bells, carols, the scent of roasting chestnuts and evergreens, and the cold clear air, even Coleman—dubbed Mrs. Scrooge by Dinah—had succumbed to the excitement of the season.

Today was a perfect day for the Sea Grill, with Rock Center's giant Christmas tree blazing outside the window, and the ice rink awhirl with skaters. The glistening ice reminded her of *Skating Girl*, and seeing Bain for the first time six weeks ago. She pushed away thoughts of Heyward Bain, and considered Zeke and Bethany.

They'd been going out together since the night of Dinah's opening of Luigi Rist's color woodcuts in early November. She was fond of Zeke, and glad he'd found someone, but she couldn't see a future for him with Bethany. Could a poor young woman of color from the rural South, whose family practiced an old-time religion and followed traditions that went back to Africa, be accepted by a rich and prominent Jewish family from Long Island? Especially when the groom—an only child—would be expected to take the bride's name? Had Bethany told him about this unusual family custom?

Oh well, they were adults, and their relationship was none of her business.

Coleman studied the menu while surreptitiously admiring Bethany. Her golden skin and elegant head were set off by her wool dress, an unusual shade of bronze. The topaz jewelry she wore with it was perfect. A Christmas gift from Zeke?

Coleman smiled at them. "Zeke, I want to thank you again for lending Dinah the money for the new gallery. You're a good friend."

"Isn't Zeke wonderful? Jonathan will be furious, but not nearly as angry as if Dinah had taken Bain's money," Bethany said.

Coleman was startled: Dinah hadn't told her *that* was a possibility. It had been far too long since she and Dinah had really talked.

"Coleman, Dinah told us you have Chick O'Reilly looking into Jimmy La Grange's death as part of the Print Museum story. The night Jimmy died, Bethany was awake for an hour or so around two AM She can't say for sure that she saw anyone go into Jimmy's building, but she—"

Coleman interrupted, and looked at Bethany. "Wait a minute. You live near Jimmy's building?"

"His address was in that follow-up story in the *Star* on Jimmy's death. Turns out his building is right across the street from mine. It's one of a line of similar buildings, and I don't know for sure which one the person I saw entered. But I saw a doctor going in one of the row at 2:20."

Coleman raised her eyebrows. "How can you be so exact on the time?"

"Oh, I'd been playing detective. When I can't sleep, I keep a diary of night sightings on Charles Street. Mostly cats." Bethany helped herself to the fried portobello mushrooms from the platter Zeke had ordered for the table.

Zeke passed the mushrooms to Coleman, who shook her head. "What do you think? Should Bethany contact the police? Didn't a policeman come to see you about Jimmy? Would he be the person to call?" he asked.

Coleman frowned. "I think the police have all but closed the case. They haven't made an arrest, but they claim they're looking for the guys they're sure did it. The cop *I* saw wouldn't give a hoot. He was sure he knew exactly why Jimmy died, and he didn't want to hear anything that might make him change his mind. I'll ask Clancy to pass on the information to one of his cop friends, and if anyone's interested, they'll call you." She made a note in her notebook.

Coleman and Dolly settled down on the sofa to enjoy Christmas Eve together. Coleman had rented several videos starring dogs so Dolly would enjoy them, too. They'd microwave popcorn later, and turn in early. Coleman would work at home on Christmas Day. She'd bought turkey meatloaf, wild rice salad, and Brussels sprouts from the takeout counter at Grace's on Third Avenue for their feast. When Lassie appeared on the screen, they both sighed with contentment.

—— Twenty-Two ——

DINAH AND JONATHAN were not enjoying their stay at Canyon Ranch. They avoided discussing the gallery, but the subject loomed between them like the proverbial elephant in the room. Jonathan was cold and distant, and Dinah felt guilty about having secretly leased the gallery on Fifty-Seventh Street. They went to church on Christmas morning, but even the beautiful music didn't soften the atmosphere.

On Christmas morning when Jonathan invited her to lunch at a nearby hotel, Dinah hoped he was calling a Christmas truce, that maybe he had even come to see the gallery her way. They were sipping glasses of pre-lunch champagne when he handed her a Tiffany box. "This is your six-month wedding anniversary present," he said.

Dinah had forgotten they'd been married six months ago today, but she wasn't about to say so. She opened the box. It contained a sapphire and diamond bracelet. "Oh, Jonathan, it's beautiful," she said, slipping it on her wrist.

"I've been thinking about you, and I finally understand you. You're bored. You don't have enough to do—that's why you want a big gallery. I have a better idea: we should have a child. You'll be so busy with a baby you won't want a gallery, but if you wanted to keep your hand in, you could see clients by appointment." He leaned back in his chair and smiled. He looked like the cat who'd finally eaten the canary.

Dinah dropped the bracelet on the table. "You must be out of your mind. You haven't listened to anything I've said. I have no intention of having a child any time soon. I've signed a lease on a Fifty-Seventh Street gallery, and when we get back to New York, I'm leaving you. You are so unbelievably obtuse, there's no point in discussing anything with you. I've had it."

She stalked out of the dining room, climbed in the nearest taxi, and headed back to Canyon Ranch. Luckily, their villa had two bedrooms. She'd move in the second room and call the Creedmore Club for a reservation. They wouldn't let members stay longer than two weeks, but that would give her time to make other arrangements. She'd check on commercial flights, and if they had nothing soon, she'd charter, and charge it to Jonathan. She'd never done anything like that, but this was an emergency.

—— Twenty-Three ——

JANUARY
Wednesday

AFTER JANUARY FIRST, New York began to function again. Life would soon be back to normal. Coleman's spirits soared, but they plunged when Dinah called to say that she'd left Jonathan, and was staying at the Creedmore Club. What could have happened that made Dinah do something so drastic?

Coleman took a cab to the club and the elevator to the fifth floor, where Dinah was unpacking in a pretty little room, all white paint and rose-patterned chintz. She hugged Dinah. "Are you sure you want to do this? I've never known anyone who wanted to be married as much as you, or anyone happier than you were on your wedding day."

Dinah was red-eyed and pale, but her voice was controlled. "I need some peace and quiet. We fight constantly, and Jonathan's decided we should have a child right away. You know how much I want children, but before we married, we agreed to wait a couple of years to give me a chance to get the gallery going, to prove myself. *He's* changed his mind. *He* wants a baby right away, and assumes it's entirely his decision to make. I don't even have a vote. After I told him I'd signed a lease on the Fifty-Seventh Street gallery, we had a big fight, and he accused me of getting money from Heyward Bain to finance it. We've barely spoken since, and I needed to get away from him, at least for a while.

"Whatever you do, I'm on your side," Coleman said.

Dinah tried to smile. "When I've caught up on my sleep and cooled off how about dinner later this week?"

"Absolutely. You're going to the Print Museum opening Sunday night, aren't you?" Coleman asked.

"Of course. Why don't we meet there? Go out for a bite after?"

"Great!"

Coleman left Dinah putting clothes away. She felt terrible for her cousin, but there was nothing she could do.

Meanwhile, Coleman's to-do list was growing. New tasks turned up, and a lot of the old items never seemed to get crossed off. Coleman still hadn't reached the elusive Professor Laramie at MIT. He was back on campus, but not returning her calls.

Coleman finally reached the professor's assistant, but when Coleman said who she was, and what she wanted, the woman was curt. "None of the people here talk to reporters, so I'm sure Professor Laramie won't call you back. You're wasting your time and ours with all these messages," she said, and hung up.

A young woman in the press office confirmed Laramie's assistant's statement. "The young people who come here to study are vulnerable. We have confidentiality agreements with them and their families," she said.

"Even after all these years?"

"Of course. The individual is free to talk about his experience here. But *we* can't. That would be an invasion of privacy."

Hell's bells. The only window on Bain's past that Coleman had found was barred. Now what?

—— Twenty-Four ——

COLEMAN HAD CLOSED the February issue of *ArtSmart* almost single-handedly while everyone else was at holiday parties. She didn't mind. She didn't like cocktail parties, and she enjoyed the February issue. The February cover was always a mischievous-looking Cupid, a *putto* with horns and tail, shooting "Art Darts" at the pretentious, the stuffy, or the vulgar in the previous year. Coleman never lacked for material.

But she had no time to rest, or congratulate herself. Chick was back, restored to health after a severe case of the flu, followed by Christmas in California with David. She'd asked for an update on the La Grange and Print Museum story, but he'd put her off. He said he had a few loose ends he wanted to tie up over the weekend. They set aside two hours Monday morning to talk about it.

Coleman was all but out the door on her way to the Print Museum opening when the telephone rang. She nearly ignored it, but curiosity won out, and she ran back.

"Coleman?" Clancy's voice sounded odd. "I hate to have to tell you this, but Chick is dead. His body has been found in the Village. It could be murder."

Coleman clutched the chair by the telephone table, afraid that she would faint. She was nauseated and icy cold. She couldn't speak.

"Coleman?"

She took a deep breath. "Yes, go ahead."

"He was beaten to death. The police say it happened Friday night, but his body was behind a dumpster in an alley, and only discovered a little while ago. His partner was away, or Chick would have been missed sooner. The police say Chick was cruising gay bars—they have lots of witnesses—and he was seen talking to two guys who match the description of the thugs they think killed Jimmy. They think he picked them up, and killed him the way they did Jimmy."

"Oh, that's nonsense—the cruising part, I mean," Coleman said, her voice stronger. "He was in those bars investigating Jimmy's death. He was on assignment for *ArtSmart*. Oh God, it's my fault he's dead." She gritted her teeth, determined not to cry.

"Calm down, and don't be silly. Chick was a grown man. He didn't have to accept the assignment and you didn't force him into that alley. You're a pro. This is a story and you should get on it right away. You're the only one who knows what Chick was doing and why. Incidentally, the police have already told his partner and his family. You don't have to break the news."

She took another deep breath. "Thank God for that. I *will* get on the story, but right now I've got to go to the Print Museum opening. I'm supposed to meet Dinah there, and if I don't turn up she'll worry. There's no way to reach her. There'll be a huge crowd, they could never find her, and it's black-tie. She won't have her cell phone with her. Thanks, Clancy. I'll call you later."

Coleman wrapped her evening cape around her, gave Dolly a second farewell cuddle, and went out into the falling snow.

The opening night of the Print Museum's Contemporary American Gallery was the most art-star-studded occasion Dinah had ever attended. The gallery was filled with curators, collectors, and artists. Everyone from the print world was here tonight, and lots of people from the general art world.

Jasper Johns was talking to a curator from MoMA, and Robert Kushner was chatting with dealer Matthew Marks. Dinah spoke to David Kiehl, the Whitney print curator, and waved at Alex Katz and his wife and favorite model, Ada, and to the Pace Gallery's Dick Solomon, chatting with artist Jim Dine.

The space was fully twenty-five-thousand square feet, with partitions arranged to allow vistas for viewing the large works. The dull-finished white-tile floors felt almost soft underfoot, promising relief from museum shin-splints. The walls were a soft off-white carpet-like material, illuminated by built-into-the-ceiling lights.

Dinah spotted the colorful Frank Stella *Circuits* series, named after famous auto racetracks, each roughly fifty-one inches by thirty-five—the complete set of sixteen. The two seven-foot tall Rauschenberg lithographs from his 1969 *Stoned Moon* series, commemorating the astronauts' first landing on the moon and late 1960s culture, were hung side by side at the end of a corridor. Rauschenberg's bright red and blue *Sky Garden* drew the eye away from his subtle black and white *Waves*. The galleries were crammed with treasures, and Dinah longed to spend time with them, but the rooms were so crowded that looking at the prints would be almost impossible. She vowed to return soon, and give them the attention they deserved.

She was astonished when Jonathan entered the gallery. She wouldn't have dreamed he'd have turned up here, given his hatred of Bain. Was he spying on her? She'd ignore him and talk to her friends. She was making her way towards Brooke Alexander, owner of New York's best known contemporary print gallery, when she heard Coleman speak her name. Dinah turned. Coleman was pale, her eyes sunken. "What in the world's the matter?" Dinah asked.

Coleman put a finger to her lips. "Shh, I don't want to spoil the opening. Chick O'Reilly has been found dead. Clancy says the police think Chick was cruising, and beaten to death by people he picked up. But Dinah, they're wrong—I know they're wrong."

Dinah put her arm around Coleman. She'd never known Coleman to faint, but she looked as if she might. Dinah glanced around the room for someone to help her get Coleman through the crowd and into the car, but Brooke had his back to her, and she couldn't see Bain.

Jonathan was talking to a gorgeous blonde, whose magnificent breasts were barely covered by a strapless red dress. Quick work, the snake: he'd been on the phone last night begging Dinah to come home. Well, he could go to the Devil. She'd manage on her own. She'd done all right for a lot of years before Jonathan Hathaway came along.

They pushed their way through the throng to the outside door. The street was jammed with cars, but Dinah spotted the limo she'd hired, and helped Coleman into its welcome warmth. The snow was falling harder, and the temperature had dropped into the teens. Coleman was still pale, and the hand that Dinah held was ice cold. Coleman opened the car window and let the fresh air blow on her face. When she closed it and turned to Dinah, she looked less ill. "Where are we going?"

"Is P. J. Clarke's okay? It's near here, you need food, and something hot to drink."

"No, I want to search Chick's desk. He may have left some kind of record of what he was doing Friday afternoon. He keeps good notes."

Dinah tried to talk her out of it—she didn't like the thought of going into a dark empty office with killers on the loose, and Coleman half-sick—but Coleman was adamant, and Dinah gave the driver *ArtSmart*'s address.

The snow was accumulating on the sidewalks and streets. Traffic had all but vanished, as drivers headed for home before the roads became too hazardous to drive. The car crept through the silent night the few blocks to *ArtSmart*'s offices. The night elevator man took them upstairs, where Coleman unlocked a series of doors, turned on lights, and led Dinah into the conference room. She kicked off her high-heeled shoes, and in her stocking feet filled and started the coffee maker. She handed Dinah a pad and pencil before heading down the hall to Chick's office.

She came back almost immediately, holding a desk diary open at Friday's page. "These notes must be related to what he was doing Friday, but they'll have to be deciphered. His writing is totally illegible—he always typed everything. I think there are a couple of phone numbers here, but I can't read them."

"Let me try. I'm used to artists' handwriting." Dinah frowned over the notes, while Coleman filled two coffee mugs, handed one to Dinah, and sat down at the conference table across from her.

Coleman, holding her mug in two hands for warmth, said, "I haven't been able to reach David, Chick's partner. I want to tell him how sorry I am. If I hadn't insisted, Chick wouldn't have been investigating La Grange's death, and this wouldn't have happened."

Dinah looked up. "Tell me again everything Clancy said. I can listen and do this at the same time."

"The cops claim they saw Chick making the rounds at gay bars in Greenwich Village early Friday evening. They insist he was cruising. They say he picked up the gorillas they couldn't find after Jimmy died, and that he met Jimmy's fate. I *know* Chick was in the Village trying to discover something about Jimmy's murder, but Clancy says the police won't care why he was hanging around gay bars. He was there, and he left with those guys, and they killed him."

"You're positive about why Chick was in the Village at those bars? He wasn't just playing mouse while the cat was away?" Dinah said.

Coleman shook her head. "No way! Chick and David have lived together since college, and they never went out with anyone else, never went to gay bars. I have Chick's notes from before Christmas, including a list of the bars he planned to visit. He checked some of them out in November, but he got the flu and then he went to California, and didn't cover them all. He must have planned to finish the list Friday."

Coleman crossed to the coffeemaker again. She raised her eyebrows at Dinah, who shook her head.

Coleman refilled her own mug and sat down. "I insisted that La Grange's death was connected to the Print Museum story. If I hadn't been such a know-it-all, Chick would be alive today. Even the *New York Times* gave up on the story. They couldn't connect his death to the art world, and they have access to sources I don't. Damn it all, why didn't I keep *ArtSmart* out of it?"

Dinah knew better than to argue. "I think I've figured out Chick's notes. This says 'Dürers too perfect, no stamps, why?' And this one says 'Rembrandt? Restrike?' And under that, three names: Strauss, Valentine, and Parker. Chick is questioning why those Dürers were in such pristine condition. Good question. They tend to get a little banged up after five hundred years of handling, and it's unusual to find sixteenth-century prints without a collector's mark."

"I know what 'Rembrandt restrike' means—he thinks someone got hold of one of Rembrandt's etching plates and made a print with it. Is that possible?" Coleman asked.

"There were Rembrandt restrikes in the nineteenth century, but as I recall, they were a mess. Bain's *Sleeping Kitten* isn't one of those. According to the press, it's a superb impression. A lot of Rembrandt's plates still exist, and maybe you could still make prints from them, if they were accessible. But I think they're in a museum."

Coleman ran her fingers through her rumpled hair. "If somebody got the plate, the right paper, and all that, and made an acceptable-looking restrike, how much would it be worth?"

Dinah shook her head. "Not much, if it was *identified* as a contemporary restrike. What makes a print an original work of art—and valuable—is that the artist was involved in making it. If somebody used Rembrandt's plate to produce impressions hundreds of years after Rembrandt died, they'd have little value, no matter how good they looked. *Sleeping Kitten* fetched a big price. If it's a restrike, Bain was cheated. Tomorrow I'll find out if the plate for *Sleeping Kitten* still exists, and where it is."

"Suppose we learn that the plate for *Sleeping Kitten* does exist? If there's been a recent restrike, the plate has to be missing, right? Someone had to remove it from wherever it's supposed to be to make a print. That means it's been stolen, and would be evidence of an art crime that can be firmly tied to Jimmy La Grange."

Dinah shook her head. "Even if the plate is missing, we'd have to prove *Sleeping Kitten* was made recently. That would require analysis of the paper and ink."

"Okay, but a missing plate would be like finding a trout in the milk. Why do you suppose Chick thought it was a restrike?"

"Maybe because *Sleeping Kitten* is so rare? And it's odd that it was sold in an unknown auction house in Boston. It fetched nearly a million dollars, but I'm sure it would have sold for more at a major auction house in New York or London," Dinah said.

"Chick thought selling these rare prints in offbeat locations was strange, too. Let's go back to the phone numbers. Can you make them out?"

"Yes, I'll read them to you, and you dial them. Let's assume they're 212 area codes. The first number is 744-1600," Dinah said.

Coleman put the phone on speaker, punched nine for an outside line, and the number. "Carlyle Hotel," a voice answered.

"Sorry, wrong number," Coleman said, and terminated the call. "That's where Simon lives. I *know* he's involved. What's the other number?"

"477-3600."

She punched in the numbers and a gruff male voice said, "Blackbeard's."

"Is this a restaurant?"

"No, girlie, it's a bar. You got the wrong number."

Coleman hung up, and grabbed the Manhattan telephone directory from the book shelves. "Blackbeard's is on Christopher Street. I bet it's one of the bars Chick visited. Maybe it's where he met his killer. But it's not on the list of bars he gave me."

"Maybe he didn't learn about Blackbeard's till he was in the Village," Dinah said.

Coleman shook her head. "No, he knew about it when he left the office, or the number wouldn't have been on his calendar. How did he hear about it? Maybe from someone on the phone? And what about the names in Chick's notes? Do they mean anything to you?"

"Strauss is probably the Rembrandt scholar, Walter Strauss. I'll try to find out who the others are when I can get to my art books tomorrow. 'Valentine' isn't familiar, but if 'Strauss' is the person I think he is, the other names probably have something to do with Rembrandt, too," Dinah said.

Coleman cocked her head, and cupped her hand behind her ear. "Did you hear that?" she whispered.

Dinah looked up. "What?"

Coleman put her finger to her lips. "Shh. The elevator. It stopped on this floor. Nobody should be coming here this time of night."

"One of the staff? A cleaning crew?"

Coleman shook her head. "On Sunday night? I've never seen anyone cleaning here on a Sunday during the day, let alone at night. The guard downstairs knows we're here. He should have called me to tell me someone was coming up. The switchboard's off, but security has my cell phone number. Whoever it is must have sneaked past the guard. But why didn't the elevator man stop him? I don't want to scare you, but it must be somebody up to no good. I'll turn off the lights. If it's a burglar—or worse—I'd rather he not know we're here. Take your things, and get under the table. I'll lock the door to the conference room."

Dinah did as she was told. Coleman switched off the conference room lights, locked the door to the hall, and crawled under the table to join Dinah. Dinah reached for Coleman's hand.

"Listen," Coleman whispered. "Whoever it is just opened the door from the elevator corridor into the reception room. He has a key card or the access code."

Footsteps approached the conference room and the door handle rattled. They froze at the sound of someone entering the code that unlocked the conference room door. The overhead lights came on. All Dinah could see was a pair of black-trousered legs, and feet in highly polished black shoes. Oh, my God, she knew those feet and legs.

Dinah shot out from under the table. "Jonathan? What in heaven's n-name are you d-doing here? You scared me half to d-death."

Coleman crawled out, her green velvet pantsuit rumpled and covered with carpet lint, her cheeks red, her eyes glittering. "What the hell are you doing here? How'd you get in? What happened to the guard downstairs?"

Jonathan, immaculate in his tuxedo, looked down his nose. "Why are you under the table? You look like escapees from an insane asylum. I came to find you, Dinah. The guard told me you were here. I tried to call but couldn't get through to *ArtSmart*, and your cell phone doesn't answer. And Coleman, I've always had keys and codes to get in here. I'm one of your emergency contacts, remember?"

Dinah enunciated each word, "Jonathan, I do not want you following me around. You're—you're nothing but a stalker."

Coleman rubbed her forehead. "If I knew you had access, I'd forgotten it. I'm headed for the ladies' room to wash up, and cool off. Right now I could bite nails, I'm so furious. You two go ahead and fight it out. Don't bother about me—I just work here."

Jonathan paced the floor. "I heard about Chick's death, and I knew Coleman would poke her nose into it. Listen to me, Dinah: it's dangerous involving yourself in a murder investigation. I insist you stay out of this."

"You listen to *me*, Jonathan. I *will* help Coleman, and if *you* don't help her, I'll never speak to you again. Coleman's involved because Chick worked for her, and I am *not* going to desert her. And stop telling me what to do. I'm not a half-witted child. You may be my husband, but you are *not* the boss of me. And I've left you. Remember?"

The muscle in his cheek twitched. "I'll help you both, if just to keep you from getting killed. But don't blame me if you're unhappy with the outcome of my investigations. I am confident that your beloved Bain is behind all this."

Coleman returned from the ladies' room, her hair combed, and the lint brushed off her suit. Ignoring Jonathan, she sat down and doodled on the pad in front of her. "I've always thought La Grange was someone's tool, and Simon is the most obvious person to have used him," she mused.

Dinah nodded. "But even if La Grange were fronting for Simon when he sold the prints, I don't see how Simon's role can be proved. He bought the prints publicly and legally. I guess La Grange could have been forced to testify against him, but with La Grange dead—"

"Exactly," Coleman said. "With La Grange dead, we may never know what happened to him, or what Simon's relationship with him was. I think Simon made sure of that. But maybe we can find out what happened to Chick."

"Well, we can't do it tonight. I'm exhausted," Dinah said. "Let's get out of here. I can hardly wait to get to my quiet little room at the Creedmore Club."

"Tom's waiting downstairs with the car. I'll take you home, Coleman, and you to the Creedmore if that's where you insist on going, Dinah," Jonathan said.

"No need," Dinah said, not looking at him. "I hired a limo. It's waiting downstairs."

"No, it isn't. I let it go. You know I don't like you riding around in strange cars with strange drivers," Jonathan said.

Dinah closed her eyes. "Dear God, give me strength," she said through clenched teeth.

Coleman sighed, collected the dirty coffee mugs, and put them on the tray by the coffeemaker. They could wait till she was next in the office. She turned out the lights, and followed Dinah and Jonathan to the elevator.

After they dropped off Coleman and were crawling up Park Avenue, Dinah said, "Who was the sexy blonde in the red dress you were talking to at the Print Museum?"

"Judy."

"Your ex-wife?" Dinah stared at him. "What was she doing there?"

"She said she was Bain's date. She also said she's a free-lance writer writing a story on the opening."

"You never told me she was so beautiful." Dinah had always been curious about Judy. She was much more attractive than Dinah had imagined.

"I don't want to discuss Judy," Jonathan said, his tone curt.

He was angry again. Fine. So was she. She was silent during the rest of the drive.

Coleman was unlocking her apartment door when the telephone rang. She groaned. Would this day never end? Before she ran to answer the phone, she scooped up Dolly and hugged the little dog to her chest. Dolly licked her face.

Zeke didn't bother to say hello. "Is it true? I heard at the opening tonight that Chick was killed?"

"Yes, it's true. He's dead. They think the people who killed Jimmy did it. If he was the leak to the *Artful Californian*, it's over. Whatever he did, he didn't deserve to die."

"I wouldn't be too sure it's over, Coleman. Maybe it's the spy bit that got Chick killed. Remember how we calculated how much money an unethical person could make if they could take over *ArtSmart?*"

Coleman rolled her eyes. "Nonsense, that's ridiculous. *ArtSmart* is my whole life, but I wouldn't kill for it. Even if we're right about why it's happening—that it's about money—no one would do anything so drastic. I'm sure Chick was killed because he discovered something about Jimmy's death."

"Yes, but we still don't know why Jimmy was killed. This all could be tied together," Zeke said.

"A conspiracy theory? Please!"

"Coleman, John Buchan wrote that *civilization* is a conspiracy. Conspiracies are not all that uncommon. How about humoring me: give Chick's partner a call, and ask him about Chick's relationship with the *Artful Californian.*"

"Oh, for God's sake, Zeke, I can't do that. Chick has been murdered, and I'm responsible. You want me to call David and ask him if Chick was spying? Right this minute, I don't give a damn. I'm interested in who killed Chick."

"But don't you see, Chick's death may be linked to the leak. It might be dangerous to ignore that possibility," Zeke argued.

Coleman rubbed her forehead. She *had* to get off the phone. "I'm too tired to talk. I'll think about it tomorrow. I'll call when I can. Good night, Zeke."

She took a hot shower, put on a flannel nightgown, and crawled into bed. But her head ached and she couldn't sleep, so she got up, swallowed a Tylenol PM, made herself a cup of diet cocoa, and gave Dolly a Milkbone. She tried to reach David again, but he still didn't answer. She didn't go back to bed, but lay on the sofa with a blanket over her, and Dolly snuggled by her side. She fell asleep with the television droning in the background.

—— Twenty-Five ——

Monday
London

Rachel, in a violet wool suit and pearls, was ready to leave when George Quincy arrived. Her mink coat and alligator carryall were lying on the bench in the entryway, and a hired Jaguar waited. The driver knew her destination, and the car pulled away from the curb as soon as they were settled in the back seat.

"We are going to visit the Baldorean Collection. Do you know it?"

"It sounds familiar, but I can't place it."

"It is in a house near Oxford, not far from Le Manoir aux Quat' Saisons, the restaurant and inn. The house and the collection belong to the Greshams. An ancestor of the present Lord Gresham assembled the *objets*. One sees the collection by appointment. The collection is generously endowed, and in an unbreakable trust. Nothing can be sold."

Even in her fur coat, and with the car heater on high, Rachel felt chilly. She wished she had brought a thermos of coffee. They'd be offered it at the Baldorean, but it would be undrinkable. "There is a curator, a well-known scholar. He is in his late eighties. He was a friend of Professor Ransome's."

Quincy wiped the perspiration from his forehead. "And it's here that you think we'll find the evidence that Simon stole?"

"The evidence will be that the Dürers—which Heyward Bain recently bought in the United States—are missing," Rachel said.

In less than two hours they pulled into the courtyard of an unpretentious gray stone house. Rachel rang a bell. After a long wait, an untidy-looking middle-aged woman in a mud-colored twinset, rumpled tweed skirt, and sagging heavy stockings, appeared.

"Good morning, Mrs. Ketcham. Mr. Yeats is expecting us."

"Yes, indeed, Mrs. Ransome, come in."

She led them through a dark hallway into an equally dark and cluttered library, as hot and stuffy as the hall was cold and drafty. The room smelled of wood smoke and ancient paper. A shrunken old man sat behind a massive desk, a shawl around his shoulders. He rose as they came in, but he tottered, and leaned against the desk for balance.

"Sit down, please, Mr. Yeats. We will sit, too," Rachel said. "Mr. Yeats, Mr. Quincy."

"Good morning, good morning," Yeats said, and lowered himself back into his chair. "Come close to the fire, it's chilly in here." He rubbed his shriveled hands together. "What about coffee, eh? Too early for sherry, I think. I never drink sherry before one o'clock."

Mrs. Ketcham returned, carrying a tray. She served tepid instant coffee, passed a plate of limp-looking biscuits, and left.

"What brings you here, Mrs. Ransome?" Yeats asked, his mouth full of biscuit, crumbs spraying over the papers on the desk.

"I should like to show Mr. Quincy the Dürers. I have told him of their exceptional condition," Rachel said.

"Of course, of course, I'll get them." He rose again, and selected a large folio from a stack of similar folios on a nearby table. He placed it on his desk, dangerously near his half full coffee cup.

Rachel rose, removed the cup and the biscuit plate, and put them on another table. She remained standing near Yeats while he opened the folio.

It was empty, except for the tissue paper that should have separated the prints. The old man looked at Rachel. "They're not here," he whispered, his face gray.

"I was afraid of that. I suspect they have been stolen, and sold in New York. But calm yourself, we will get them back."

Yeats opened his mouth, but nothing came out. Quincy helped the old man sit down, and replaced the shawl around his shoulders. He picked up a lap robe that lay on the floor and spread it over Yeats's knees.

"We should have this folio fingerprinted. It is probably useless, but one should never overlook the obvious," Rachel said.

She pulled an old-fashioned bell cord, and Mrs. Ketcham reappeared.

"Mrs. Ketcham, the Baldorean has suffered a theft. Will you please bring me a case for this folio? I want to take it to London to be checked for fingerprints. And will you bring me your ledger? And the photographs?" She turned to Quincy. "When I first moved to England, I visited this collection. I could see that it would be easy for an unscrupulous person to steal objects. Visitors sit at the table in the alcove out of sight of Mr. Yeats's desk. Mr. Yeats is usually concentrating on his reading or his writing. But most of the works are stamped with the Baldorean stamp. It looks like this."

She selected a book from a nearby shelf, and handed it, open, to Quincy. The inside of the back cover had been stamped with a seal. "Stamps like this are not easy to remove, and nothing in the Baldorean Collection has ever been sold. Removing the stamp would require great effort, and it would be impossible to disguise its removal. This is a deterrent to theft. But the missing Dürers were not identified in any way as being a part of the Baldorean Collection."

Yeats nodded, shuffling papers on his desk. "It was my folly, my folly. I could not bear to mark them. Everyone said I should, but I simply could not, could not do it," he said, his voice barely audible, his hands trembling.

"Yes, it was folly, but understandable. Never mind, I am sure they will be returned. But not unmarked, I fear," Rachel said in a quiet aside to Quincy. "I suspect the new 'owner' will have stamped them."

Mrs. Ketcham returned with a large suitcase, a pair of gray suede gloves, and a tapestry carryall. She donned the gloves, put the folio in the suitcase, and set the suitcase by the door. She opened the tapestry bag.

"The ledger and the pictures are in here. Here is the latest picture." She handed a Polaroid to Rachel, who held it out to Quincy.

He stared at it. "It's you and me. Where was it taken? The window above the door?"

"Yes. Mrs. Ketcham took the photograph before she opened the door. It is part of the security system she and I devised for the Baldorean. Mrs. Ketcham keeps a guest list with all the names of those who visit here, the dates, how long they are here, what they asked to see. Each guest must sign a register. But as it is easy to use a false name and produce false identification, she also photographs visitors.

"We shall look at the photos of everyone who was here in the last year," she said, accepting a small stack of Polaroids from Mrs. Ketcham and running quickly through them. "Thank you. Yes, here is Simon," she said to Quincy, passing a photo to him. "Disguised, but clearly recognizable if you know what to look for." The bearded figure in the photograph wore horn-rimmed glasses, and long dark hair partly obscured his face.

Quincy shook his head. "I'd never have known that was Simon. In fact, I don't recognize him even now that you've identified him," he said.

They looked at the name written on the back of the photo: "Ravenscroft" in Mrs. Ketcham's writing. "I took the name from the register, of course," she said.

"The shape of that long boney head is unmistakable," Rachel said.

"Well, I suppose the use of the name Ravenscroft settles it. Very few people know that was your name," Quincy said.

"I noticed the name when he signed the register, but I didn't recognize him," Mrs. Ketcham said. "He wore jeans, an American sort of pullover, and a cap. He spoke with an American accent. I only saw Simon twice, and his clothes were so splendid, one hardly noticed anything else, except his fair hair, his beautiful teeth, and his Oxbridge accent."

Rachel turned the pages of the guest register. "I am sure he did not expect anyone to notice for a long time that the Dürers were missing. He tried to implicate me by using my name: he signed the register 'R. Ravenscroft.' Is there anything else can you tell us, Mrs. Ketcham? He did ask to see the Dürers?"

"He did, and no one has asked to see them since he was here. He," she spoke softly now, and nodded toward the old man, "said he'd checked them when he put the portfolio away. I photographed 'Ravenscroft's' car and the registration plate, as I always do." Mrs. Ketcham handed another Polaroid to Rachel.

"It is a rental car—look at the plates. Perhaps he rented it at Heathrow—it is the logical place. He may have rented it in his own name, even charged it to the gallery. He would have been confident no one would check. That should be easy to determine," Rachel said. She turned to Quincy. "Will you handle whatever needs to be done to prosecute him? Get in touch with the authorities? And Lord Gresham? Someone will have to call this man Bain. Will you do that as well?"

"Certainly. I think we should start back to London now, don't you? We have quite a lot to do."

—— Twenty-Six ——

JONATHAN'S FIRST CALL of the day was to the Hath-away law firm in New York. He spoke to one of the young lawyers assigned to look after his family's inter-ests, and outlined the facts as he knew them: the deaths of Jimmy La Grange and Chick O'Reilly; the notes Coleman had found in Chick's office; the possibility that Chick's murder might have been related to his investi-gation for *ArtSmart,* a magazine owned and run by his wife's cousin. He added that Jimmy La Grange might be connected to a possible art fraud involving a Rembrandt print bought for the Print Museum. "What should we do? Tell the police? And if so, which police?"

"As I understand it, you have no proof that this Rem-brandt is not what it's supposed to be?" the lawyer said.

"No, we're trying to get more information, but we don't have anything yet."

"I'm not sure you have anything that will interest the police, and they might resent your interference. I think you should talk to Robert Mondelli, an attorney who specializes in art crime. Why don't I telephone him, and tell him who you are, and that you'll be calling him?"

"I don't understand why I should talk to this Mondelli. Explain how he can help us."

"He can evaluate what you and your wife and her cousin have discovered and tell you the likely police response to your information. He'll know what you'd need to build a stronger case and he can help find missing information, if that's what you want. He can be your liaison with the police—find out what they're doing, what they think. And he'll be able to provide the three of you with protection around any legal issue, should that become necessary. The situation sounds as if it could get nasty. I'd advise you to try to avoid becoming directly—or publicly—involved."

"I agree with *that*. Okay, call Mondelli, and tell him I'll be in touch later today or tomorrow."

It was time for Jonathan's daily call on the researcher working on the Bain question. She was a bespectacled waif-like little creature, and one of the best fact-finders he'd ever met. When he walked into the library, she looked up and smiled. "I was just going to phone you. I've checked everywhere, done everything I can think of, but this is all I can find. It's not much." She handed him a flimsy piece of paper covered in faded print.

"What does it say?" he asked, squinting at it.

"It's a copy made from microfilm of an article in an education magazine about child prodigies who studied at MIT about thirty years ago. One of the children mentioned is a Heyward Bain. I can't be sure this is your man, but the age is right and it's an uncommon name. The professor cited in the article is a Dr. William Laramie. He's still at MIT, and probably worth talking to."

"Great! You may have uncovered the only thing in print about Bain." Jonathan rushed off, resolving to send the researcher flowers, and to write Human Resources a note about her good work.

A few minutes later, he spoke to a Hathaway lawyer in Boston, explaining that he wanted an appointment with Laramie today. "Make up a reason if you have to. I don't care what you say, but don't take 'no' for an answer. We'll pay for his time. Call me back as soon as it's arranged."

Jonathan leaned back in his chair and smiled. At last, a clue to Heyward Bain's past. Jonathan was certain that Bain and his activities lay at the heart of everything wrong that had happened in the print world since October. Even his marital problems began with Dinah's attitude towards Bain. If he could unmask Bain, all of the other pieces of the puzzle would fall into place, and Dinah would come home, and be herself again.

The phone rang, and Jonathan grabbed it. "Yes?"

"You have an appointment with Professor Laramie at four o'clock this afternoon, Mr. Hathaway. No excuse was necessary, nor any compensation. Laramie is a garrulous chap. He'll talk your ear off. The Hathaway name is well known in Boston. He sounded flattered that you want to meet with him."

Dinah, digging away in the little library in the apartment on Cornelia Street, had learned that many of Rembrandt's plates survived, and Rembrandt restrikes had been published as early as 1785, a hundred years or so after the artist's death. The quality of the impressions was poor.

In 1957, a Rembrandt expert, W. R. Valentiner—not Valentine, as she'd thought—had examined all of the surviving plates he could locate, but the plates that interested Dinah weren't among them. A 1983 article by Walter Strauss declared that only about a third of Rembrandt's plates had been accounted for.

Finally, in a piece written by Dr. Jane Parker, chief curator at the Harnett College Museum in Myrtle, Virginia, Dinah struck gold. Parker described the discovery of a group of previously lost plates by Rembrandt, including not only the plate *Sleeping Kitten*, but also *Shells* and *Winter Landscape*, the other two Rembrandt prints on Simon's list. The plates, a recent legacy to the Harnett, were in excellent condition.

Dinah phoned Coleman to bring her up to date. "Do you think I should call the Harnett, and ask if the plate is where it should be?"

"We'll go there," Coleman decided. "I'm afraid we won't learn anything if we try to do it by phone. If the plate is missing, they might not admit it. I'll call Dr. Parker, and we'll fly down tomorrow, if she'll see us. I'll make the plane reservations and call you back as soon as we're set."

When Dinah went downstairs to the gallery, Bethany gave her a message from Jonathan: he'd gone to Boston, and would phone her tonight, but probably not until eight or later. Good. Maybe she and Coleman could have dinner without Jonathan turning up, and scaring them half to death. She was still furious with him. She needed more time to cool off.

— Twenty-Seven —

MONDAY AFTERNOON

ZEKE AND BETHANY peered through the window of the Spy Shop on West Fourth Street. The space was small, and the glass cabinets were crammed with unfamiliar-looking equipment. A short gray-haired man, red-faced and fat, stood behind the counter, looking at catalogs.

A bell rang when Zeke opened the door, and they could see themselves on a television set on the wall. Zeke thought the security seemed excessive, until he looked at the price tags. Wow. Expensive.

"We're interested in checking an office for listening devices," he said to the fat man, who wore a "My name is Pete" tag.

"I can do that for you," Pete said. "My minimum fee is twenty-five hundred dollars."

"We were thinkin' of doin' it ourselves," Bethany said.

"Who d'ya think is bugging you? The Feds or the state?"

"Uh—private," Zeke said.

Pete shook his head. "I wouldn't advise doing it yourself. To get the job done right, you need a pro."

"Can we rent equipment?" Bethany asked.

"No, ma'am, we don't rent. The equipment's valuable, and people would ruin it."

"How much is the cheapest device?" Zeke asked.

"The best one is seven fifty. It vibrates so you can tell when someone you're talking to is wearing a wire without him knowing it."

"I just want to check an office," Zeke repeated.

"We got something here for five hundred," Pete said. He took an instrument that looked like a cell phone out of the case. "It don't vibrate—lights up when you get near a bug. It'll do okay, but I don't advise it."

"I'll take it," Zeke said, and pulled out his wallet. He could hardly wait to get out of the place. The Spy Shop was hot and claustrophobic, and Pete reeked of alcohol. Maybe being a spy or spy detector drove a person to drink. Zeke was pretty sure today's spying would be a one-time thing, thank goodness.

—— Twenty-Eight ——

MONDAY AFTERNOON
Boston

J ONATHAN, SEETHING, SAT in a chair by Laramie's cluttered desk. Laramie was a talker and while he talked, he chain-smoked. The window was closed, and the air was nearly unbreathable. Jonathan had rarely been so uncomfortable. Worse, he couldn't get the man to focus on Heyward Bain. Laramie had told him in great detail a lot about child prodigies, but nothing about Bain. Finally, Jonathan interrupted, speaking loudly. Laramie was forced to either shut up, or shout.

"That's fascinating, Dr. Laramie, but I have to get back to New York," Jonathan, said, looking at his watch. "I want to hear about Heyward Bain. He *was* a student of yours, wasn't he?"

"Oh, yes, he certainly was." Laramie lit another cigarette, and stared at the papers on his desk. Now that the topic that interested Jonathan had been broached, the man had nothing to say.

"What can you tell me about him?" Jonathan asked.

"He was one of the most brilliant kids I've ever encountered, but he didn't remain in the program long." Laramie stared at his cigarette, tapping it against the side of the overflowing ashtray on his desk.

Getting information out of Laramie was like pulling teeth. "Why was that?"

"As you see, I'm a smoker, and Heyward Bain was phobic on the topic of smoking. He said he couldn't stay around anyone who smoked the way I did."

"Oh, I see," Jonathan said. He could identify with that. He was suffocating after less than an hour in Laramie's company. Now he knew why Laramie was so unforthcoming about Bain: his addiction to tobacco had cost MIT a promising student. "What else can you tell me about him?"

"None of us knew what his real name was. He might have been an orphan—at least, when he came here, he didn't come with his parents, or any relative. He's white, as you probably know, but he lived with an African American couple. The man drove him here every day, and I exchanged a few words with him. I saw the woman from a distance. The man told someone they'd been living in Washington—"

Jonathan leaned forward. Maybe this was it. Washington was a cesspool. The roots of almost everything wrong in the USA were in Washington. "Washington, DC?"

"Yes, but I never believed it. Bain had an English accent, but when I asked about it, he said he'd had an English tutor. The black driver came from the deep South. The way he spoke was unmistakable."

Jonathan leaned back, frowning. "Didn't Bain have to fill in applications of some kind? Didn't they tell you anything?" Surely a student at MIT had left a paper trail.

Laramie shook his head, and took another drag on his cigarette. Ash fell on his chest, and sparks added two burn marks to the old ones on his ancient gray sweater. "I thought he might be a mafia child or something of the kind, given the total blackout on his family. But then I learned that his application came in through Daniel Winthrop."

Jonathan eyes widened. "*Daniel* Winthrop?" Daniel Winthrop, one of the most prominent men in Boston, and one of the city's greatest philanthropists, attached to all the city's great institutions as a trustee or advisor. Revered by all who knew him. Could Winthrop, like Dinah, have been deceived by Bain?

"Exactly. Winthrop's name was all Admissions needed, especially after seeing Bain's test scores—they ran off the charts. If there were applications or other papers with the facts in them, I never saw them." Laramie put out his cigarette, and emptied the ashtray in the wastebasket by his desk. "After he left we never heard any more about him, but someone said Bain turned up in New York recently. Is that right?"

Jonathan was staring at the wastebasket, hoping it wouldn't catch fire. He forced his attention back to Laramie. "Yes. He's supposed to be extremely well off. Do you know where his money came from?"

Laramie nodded. "Oh, yes, he was already rich when he got here. Inherited wealth, and by the time he was twelve, he'd invented a number of anti-smoking devices—super-sensitive smoke detectors, anti-nicotine chemicals to put in gum or lozenges to help people quit smoking. An ashtray that sucked up smoke. Filters that clean the air. I'm telling you, he was obsessed with smoking, or rather *not* smoking. He'd already donated millions to groups working to strengthen the anti-smoking laws. In fact, I was told one of the reasons he lived in such secrecy was threats from smokers' rights groups, and there was a rumor Big Tobacco had him on a hit list. Guards accompanied him everywhere."

"Are you kidding? That sounds fantastic." Everything about Bain sounded like a fairy tale. Could Laramie be jerking his chain?

Laramie lit another cigarette. "Not so fantastic. Did you see that film *The Insider* about Jeffrey Wigand, a former Brown & Williamson employee? He tried to go on TV and expose some of the stuff his employers were doing. According to the film, the tobacco people pulled out all the stops to get Wigand, and people I talked to said they'd do worse to get Bain. I'm surprised he's surfaced."

Jonathan frowned. "Did he ever explain why he was so anti-tobacco?"

Laramie shook his head. "He wouldn't talk about his inventions or about why he hated smoking, but when he told me why he was leaving the program, he said his grandfather and mother had both died of lung cancer."

—— Twenty-Nine ——

Greenwich Village

The Mexican Garden was warm, dark, and at this early hour, deserted. The room smelled of coriander and chilis, onions and garlic. Dinah's mouth watered. "What'll we have?" she said, looking at the menu.

"Lots of comforting fat and cholesterol," Coleman said. "How about cheese enchiladas and bean burritos, with some greasy nachos while we wait?"

"Sounds good. Me, too. I'll have a frozen margarita with salt," she said to the hovering waiter.

"Make mine a Diet Pepsi," Coleman said.

"Well," Dinah began, and at the same time Coleman said, "Dinah, I—" They both laughed. "You go first," Dinah said.

Coleman took a deep breath. "I've kept secrets from you, and I feel really bad about it. The first one has to do with the magazine. A few months ago I became convinced one of the writers was selling my ideas to the *Artful Californian*."

Dinah's eyes widened. "No! I can't believe it. All your staff love you and *ArtSmart*."

The waiter brought their drinks, the nachos, chips and salsa. Coleman gulped her Diet Pepsi. "I didn't want to believe it, either, but there was no other explanation. So I asked Zeke to help me figure out who it was. We'd narrowed it down to Chick, although it seemed impossible, and then Chick was killed. I guess I'll never know now if he did it."

"Why didn't you tell me?" Dinah said, picking at a piece of cheese on a nacho.

Coleman twisted a paper napkin in her fingers, and tore a bit off the corner. "I have this financial agreement with Jonathan—he can take over the magazine if profits fall, and while they haven't fallen much yet, they could. The leaks have hurt the magazine—the numbers are a little off for the first time. I thought he might want to take over, and I didn't want him to know I was having problems."

"I see," Dinah said, sipping her margarita. She was furious with Jonathan, but she couldn't believe he'd take Coleman's magazine away from her. If he had any such idea—well, it would never happen. She wouldn't let it.

Coleman looked up from the shreds of her napkin. "I didn't want to ask you not to tell him. I thought I'd be putting you on the spot."

"Let's forget about it for now. What else is bothering you?"

The waiter came with their food, and Coleman was silent while he served. Then, "I'm embarrassed to tell you what else. I had this crush on Heyward Bain, mostly because he's so good-looking, but I also think he's interesting, and, I don't know, the mystery of him appeals to me, and—I can't explain it—I hardly know him. Anyway, at first I didn't tell you because I was so humiliated when he didn't call me. And when I realized he liked you—"

Dinah looked up from her enchiladas. "Hold on. What do you mean 'he liked me'?"

"I heard him ask you out to lunch at the Rist opening. He said he wanted to see you alone. You didn't tell me about the lunch, so I thought you liked him, too. You don't have to tell me about it—why are you laughing?"

"Because—" Dinah sputtered, choking on her margarita. When she could speak, she said, "He invited me to lunch to talk about you. He asked me all kinds of questions about you. He knows a lot about us, Coleman. About when we were children—things I didn't think anybody knew. But this is the really astonishing part: he knows about what happened to you at Duke with Maxwell Arnold and his homeboys."

Coleman's eyes widened. "How could he know? Nobody knows. I've never told anybody but you."

"Neither have I—not even Jonathan. Bain told me he heard it 'indirectly' from one of the boys," Dinah said.

Coleman leaned forward, frowning. "Wait a minute. Dinah, are you saying he likes *me*? Did he *tell* you he likes me?"

Dinah smiled. "Well, he didn't come out and say 'I'm in love with Coleman,' but he must be. He's so curious about you, and when he talks about you, he's intense. There's no other explanation. I pressed him as to why he hasn't asked you out, but he was evasive. He wouldn't answer any of *my* questions, but he sure asked plenty."

"I had the same experience with him—he doesn't give away a thing. But why didn't you tell me? What else did he say?"

"I meant to talk to you about it, but the moment never seemed right. We haven't had any private time, and I've been away, and I've been so worried about Jonathan and the gallery. I'm sorry, Coleman. I'm not going to let anything get in the way of talking to you again."

"Me, either," Coleman said.

After short silence, Dinah said, "Did you know Judy, Jonathan's ex-wife, was at the opening last night?"

"No! Did you see her?"

"Yes, she's gorgeous. I'm going to have another margarita." Dinah signaled the waiter.

"Speaking of Judy, what do you know about Jonathan's marriage to her?" Coleman asked.

"Nothing. He won't talk about her. I don't even know why they split up."

"Well, at the Rist opening, Marise told me that Judy trapped Jonathan into marrying her. She'd lied, said she was pregnant. And then he caught her in bed with somebody, and that's why they got divorced."

"No! Why didn't you tell me? Why didn't Marise tell me?"

"As you said, there hasn't been much time, and I haven't seen you alone. And Marise wasn't sure you'd want to know," Coleman said.

Dinah sighed. "I guess that explains Jonathan's jealousy and possessiveness, but knowing *why* he's the way he is doesn't make him any easier to live with."

"What else did Bain say?"

"He offered to put me in business in a bigger gallery—to finance me. He thought the reason I'm in a small off-beat space is lack of capital—"

"No! Doesn't he know Jonathan is rich?"

"Apparently not. I explained that Jonathan is my backer, and that I wanted to move and expand. I said that if Jonathan doesn't finance me, I'd be in touch. But as you know, I got the loan from Zeke."

Coleman frowned. "I think Jonathan would have an apoplectic fit if you took Bain's money."

"I agree. But Jonathan and I might not be together. He's too controlling. I can't stand it anymore. This baby thing was the final straw. If we can't straighten things out, I'm going to divorce him. I'll give it another try on the phone tonight—lay it out for him, tell him about everything, including my lunch with Bain, and Bain's offer, and that I borrowed money from Zeke. If I can't make him see sense, I'll hire a lawyer."

Dinah looked at her watch, and groaned. "It's nearly nine o'clock, and we have an early start to Virginia tomorrow. I'll probably be up half the night talking to Jonathan—he said he'd call when he gets back from Boston." She called for the check.

A few minutes later, outside on the sidewalk, Coleman said, "Why don't we take a look at Blackbeard's? It's around the corner. It's a gay bar. We should be safe."

Dinah looked at her watch again, and sighed. "Oh, all right. In for a penny, in for a pound."

The exterior of Blackbeard's was undistinguished. The name was painted in small letters on a dark glass window, and they couldn't see inside.

"Let's go in," Coleman said. "We won't ask about Jimmy or Chick, but let's see what it's like."

"Jonathan would be furious. He told us not to do anything like this. But—oh, all right! Let's do it, as long as we're here."

The nearly empty bar stank of stale beer and cigarette smoke and a dirty men's room. Two men in business suits sat in a booth at the back, and a young man in jeans nursed a beer at the bar. The bartender was maybe six five, and his black sleeveless tank top revealed huge tattooed biceps. His shaved head looked like polished mahogany. All four men glared at the women.

"You're in the wrong place, girlies," the bartender said. "Why don't you run along before you get in trouble?"

"I'm with a magazine," Coleman improvised, "and I'm looking for a couple of good body types—twins if possible—to pose for some pictures. I heard this was the place to come."

"Somebody'll call you," the bartender said. "It'll be after midnight. Write your number here." He handed her a pad and the stub of a pencil, and Coleman scribbled her home number.

When they were outside again, Dinah said, "Coleman, you're crazy! What if they call?"

"I hope they will. I'm going home to change the message on my answering machine. I'm sure that bartender didn't believe I was with a magazine. I bet he thinks I want them for a date—can you imagine? Yuck. I bet that's how you book the hulks, through that bar. Maybe Chick came here and asked about them just like I did, and their connection with La Grange, and that's all it took to get him killed. I'm going to nail these creeps, I swear I am." Coleman signaled a passing taxi. "Let's go. I have to get ready for their call."

MONDAY EVENING
Boston

It was after five when Jonathan left Laramie's office. Could he be totally wrong about Bain? The source of his wealth was definitely not from money laundering or drug transactions as Jonathan had suspected. Unless Bain had used his original fortune to expand into less righteous activities.

He wished he knew Daniel Winthrop, a friend of his parents, well enough to call him. He was thinking how to approach Winthrop when his cell phone rang.

It was his secretary in New York. Daniel Winthrop had called, knew Jonathan was in Boston, wanted to see Jonathan right away, and made it clear Jonathan's convenience didn't concern him. Jonathan was to come to Winthrop's house on Beacon Hill immediately.

What in Heaven's name—? How did Winthrop know he was in Boston? What could he want? Jonathan sighed. He was tired, and he wanted to go home. But a summons from Daniel Winthrop could not be ignored. And Jonathan would have a chance to ask him about Bain.

In the mahogany-paneled library at Winthrop House on Beacon Hill, Daniel Winthrop gave Jonathan a scotch on the rocks, seated him in a chair opposite his desk, and sat back down behind it. His normally friendly face was angry.

"I've known your family all my life, went to school with your father, and I attended your Christening. I've followed your career with interest, and I used to think you were pretty smart, but you've made a fool of yourself with your suspicions of Heyward Bain. Our lawyers told me you were inquiring about Bain, and I instructed them not to give you any information. Bain's background is none of your business. But you stumbled on the MIT connection, and I let the lawyers set up that appointment, since I'm convinced you won't give up.

"Because you're obsessed with Bain, I'm going to tell you a little of his history. My information comes through The Firm. The Firm administers Heyward's trust funds, and we've known him since he was a child. I'm one of his trustees."

The Firm. Winthrop, Winthrop and Cabot, the prestigious law firm where generations of Winthrops had worked. "The Firm" was always mentioned as if it were capitalized, and as if everyone should know which firm was meant. Most people did. To invoke The Firm's name on the side of an issue or as the source of information was to settle the matter.

"Bain never knew his mother, and his father despised him. He inherited enormous wealth from his grandfather, but he was banished as a small child to a remote estate he'd inherited from his maternal grandparents, with only servants and lawyers to take care of him.

"He was a prodigy with wide interests, and he was given every kind of tutor, book, learning device, hobby kit, and lesson known to man. But he had no playmates, no friends, no social associations of any kind. He did nothing but work and study, although his physical needs, including riding, tennis, swimming lessons, trainers and the like, were provided."

Winthrop walked to the fireplace, and stood with his back to the fire, his hands clasped behind him. "The name of the owners of the estate where he grew up was different from his name, which, incidentally, is not the name you know him by. And the name his tutors knew him by is different from the name of any relative or connection of his. His fortune, which is far larger than the press has suggested, is managed through trusts, and his many inventions—which have paid him far more than his inherited fortune—have been patented in corporate names. The Firm became involved with him through the estate in South Carolina he inherited. I share his hatred for tobacco, and I became interested in his inventions, his activities, and his future.

"As you've learned, when he was twelve he spent some time at MIT, but he was unhappy there, and in any case I thought Boston might be dangerous for him. He has many enemies, all connected to the tobacco industry. Since he came of age, he's lived in states where other recluses have hidden. He's had everything in the world that money can buy, but he's the loneliest person I've ever met. He's generous—he's given major gifts to colleges, including Harvard, where he had no connection except that he knew me. He has never wanted recognition. His gifts are always anonymous."

Winthrop paced the area in front of the fireplace. "I was astonished when I heard he'd become a public figure in New York. He must have a compelling reason to emerge from his anonymity, and he must believe it's less risky than it once was. I haven't talked to him in the last year or two, but you have my word that in all the time I've known him, he's never done anything illegal or dishonorable." Winthrop sat down at his desk again.

Jonathan was speechless, stunned by Daniel Winthrop's anger, and even more by what he'd said about Heyward Bain. That settled that, if all of this were true.

And how could it be otherwise, given that the source of the information was Winthrop, Winthrop and Cabot, and that Daniel Winthrop vouched for Bain? Jonathan didn't like being wrong, and he'd had enough lecturing and disapproval for one day. He thanked Winthrop, put down his glass, and stood up. He excused himself, and Winthrop rang the butler to show him out.

Jonathan felt as low as he'd ever been, even during the months before and after his divorce. He had plenty of time to think about his behavior on the way back to New York: the drive to Logan Airport, the wait for the shuttle, the plane ride, and the seemingly interminable trip to Greenwich Village.

He'd made a terrible mistake in his assessment of Heyward Bain. He'd clung to the idea that Bain was evil when he'd had absolutely no evidence to back up his opinion. He'd been blinded by prejudice and jealousy. The prejudice was an infamous Hathaway characteristic. The jealousy he'd developed on his own, a result of his experience with Judy.

He'd thought that if he could prove to Dinah that he was right about Bain, she'd see that he was right about other things, too. She'd stop trying to be so independent, and stop—stop what? Stop moving away from him. That's what was at the heart of his insistence that the Greene Gallery remain small and non-competitive, that it be an annex to their home: he didn't want Dinah to be a successful businesswoman. He wanted all of her attention focused on Jonathan Hathaway.

Jonathan didn't like the picture of himself that Winthrop had forced him to see. He was acting like his father, or worse. Less than seven months had passed since his and Dinah's wedding, and he'd made a mess of the marriage. He didn't know what he'd do if he lost Dinah.

When the driver pulled up in front of the house he shared with Dinah, the dark windows made Jonathan's heart sink. She hadn't come back, as, for no good reason, he'd thought she might.

He'd eat crow on the topics of Heyward Bain and the gallery. He'd make amends. He'd start by sending flowers to her at the Creedmore Club, with a letter saying how sorry he was he'd hurt her, and that he was behind her new gallery one hundred percent. He'd tell her she was absolutely right about Heyward Bain. He only hoped it wasn't too late.

— Thirty —

MONDAY NIGHT
New York

COLEMAN GOT OUT of the taxi at the corner of Fifty-Fifth and First Avenue. She scooped Dolly out of her pouch, and put her down on the sidewalk. "Okay, Dolly, time for a last stroll, and then bed."

They walked towards Second Avenue, passing the door to her building, where she waved to Ralph, the night doorman. But a few doors west of the entrance, Dolly sat down. She looked up at Coleman, her dark eyes beseeching, and refused to budge. "What is it, Dolly? C'mon, I'm tired. Let's walk to Second Avenue and back."

Coleman tugged at Dolly's leash, but the little dog held firm. Coleman tugged again, and Dolly rose, turned, and pulled Coleman towards First Avenue. "Oh, Dolly, no. It's so dark near the river." She leaned down, picked up Dolly, and headed back towards Second Avenue. A few doors later, Coleman put her down, and this time Dolly reluctantly followed.

Despite Chick's death and her feelings of grief and guilt, Coleman was happier than she had been for some time. She no longer had secrets from Dinah. Heyward Bain was not in love with Dinah, Dinah was not in love with Heyward Bain, and Heyward Bain was interested in Coleman Greene. Whatever Bain's problem was— why he didn't call her, why he didn't ask her out—she was sure she could fix it.

She felt like whistling, singing, skipping. When had she last skipped? A shadow emerged from a doorway, and before she could react, strong arms grabbed her from behind. Her assailant clamped a hand over her mouth and nose, and held an arm tightly around her throat. She had an impression of hair and scratchiness— a beard, a rough tweed coat, wool gloves, and then she couldn't breathe, couldn't scream, couldn't move. Blackness closed in. She fell to the pavement. She heard Dolly's shrill bark, and someone shouting. "Ms. Greene! Ms. Greene!" Then nothing.

When consciousness returned, she was lying on her back on the icy sidewalk. Faces stared down at her, and Dolly was licking her cheek. Her back and legs were numb with cold, and her neck hurt. She struggled to sit up, and recognized Ralph, the doorman, leaning over her. A uniformed policeman knelt beside her. "Are you okay, miss?"

She put her hand on her throat. "I think so," she whispered. "My neck hurts, and my throat's sore, but I don't think anything is broken. What happened?"

"You were mugged, Ms. Greene." Ralph was speaking so fast she could barely understand him. "I saw you walk by with the dog, and the dog barked—this dog never barks," he said to the policeman, whose expression suggested it was not the first time he'd heard Ralph's story— "so I went to see why she was making all that noise. A guy had a hold of you, and I yelled, and ran toward you. The perp took off, and this cop came running."

"Did he take anything, miss?" the policeman asked, helping her up.

"I don't know—no, here's my bag—it's okay, Dolly," she said, picking up the dog, and putting her in her pouch. "I can't thank you enough, Ralph—you and Dolly saved my life. You, too, officer."

"Oh, no, miss, just your purse," the policeman said, his tone reproving. "Muggers want your money. You must've struggled with him. You shouldn't of done that. You shoulda given it to him. It's not worth getting hurt." He looked as if he'd like to shake his finger at her.

"I promise you, officer, I didn't have a chance to give him anything," Coleman whispered. "He just jumped me, and tried to strangle me. I'd like to go inside—I'm freezing. That is, if we're through here?"

"Can you describe the mugger, miss?"

"Long hair and beard, and a rough, scratchy coat. That's all I saw, or felt. But I have a feeling there was something else, something I should remember and can't." She rubbed her forehead.

"You get some rest, miss," the policeman said. "You can make a report tomorrow. Maybe you should see a doctor, too."

Coleman fed Dolly, took an Aleve, and heated some apple juice to soothe her throat. She was trembling with shock and cold, but she had to change the message on her answering machine. She hoped her hoarse voice sounded sexy, and not as if she'd just been strangled.

"Hi there! I'm a pussycat looking for fun. Pictures would be delicious, and when I'm a bad little kitten, I need punishment. My favorite playmates come in pairs. Want to play?" She prayed no one in her professional life called while the new message was in operation. God forbid Clancy should hear it; there'd be no end to the ribbing.

She took a hot shower, keeping an ear peeled for the phone, and put on the green cashmere robe Dinah had given her for Christmas a year ago, and fleece-lined slippers. She lay down on the sofa, with Dolly, a furry hot-water bottle, snuggled beside her. She'd check some galleys, and she wouldn't think about the mugging.

A little after midnight the phone rang, and her message played. A gruff voice said, "Hi there, Pussy Cat. We're the Apemen, and we're ready and willing. But you gotta put your money where your mouth is if you want photos, and you gotta pay to play rough. You tell us where and when, and we'll be there. Cash up front, we get two hundred an hour apiece, two-hour minimum, so eight hundred before playing or pictures. Leave a message at Blackbeard's."

"Got 'em," she whispered to Dolly. "These guys must be idiots. I bet they could get in trouble for that little message alone." She removed the tape from the machine, and replaced it with a new one, but she was too tired and too hoarse to record a new message. She turned the machine off, and put the tape with the Apeman's message on her bedside table. She fell asleep almost as soon as her head touched the pillow.

—— Thirty-One ——

W HEN THE ALARM went off Coleman leaped out of bed before she realized how sore she was. She was a wreck. Groaning, she limped into the bathroom, and examined herself in the mirror. She'd have to cover her bruised neck with a turtleneck and a scarf.

She felt better after another hot shower and two cups of coffee. The thought of Chick's death hovered at the back of her mind, but sad as she was about poor Chick, she was happier than she'd been in months. A few of the clouds hanging over her seemed to be floating away.

She chose a lightweight gray pantsuit—it should be warmer in Virginia, and anyway, they'd be inside—and a white silk turtleneck. She tied a gray-and-blue-paisley silk scarf over the turtleneck, and checked her image in the mirror again. No one would know she'd been injured.

"Listen, Dolly," she said huskily—her throat was still sore, and she was hoarse—"You'll have to stay here. I'm flying to Virginia, and as much as I hate to say it, you can't come."

Dolly stood on her hind legs and stared at Coleman, her eyes pleading.

Coleman melted. "Oh, all right," Coleman said, "but make so much as a squeak when we're in that museum, and we'll probably go to jail. We'll take a short walk, and then you have to stay in your pouch till we land in Virginia. I'll call the airline and make your reservation."

The plane was halfway to its destination before Coleman could tell Dinah about the Apemen or her mugging. Dinah was bubbling over about a letter from Jonathan dropping his opposition to the gallery's move to midtown, and Coleman wasn't able to get a word in.

"He thinks we should live in midtown, too, so I won't have to travel back and forth from home to the gallery. He's being incredibly considerate," Dinah said, her face glowing.

Coleman doubted that Jonathan could make such a dramatic change so quickly, and she was sure that Dinah would encounter the overbearing, unreasonable Jonathan again. Still, since this particular issue was resolved at least temporarily, Coleman wouldn't say anything to bring Dinah down. Let her enjoy life with Dr. Jekyll while she could.

She smiled at Dinah. "That's terrific. I'm really happy for you. Can I tell you my news?"

"Oh, sure. Did Bain call?"

"No, but an Apeman did." Coleman told her what he'd said, and added, "I left the message tape with my doorman, with the telephone pad from Chick's desk in an envelope addressed to Jonathan. That pad's the link that led us to Blackbeard's and the Apemen. If we can persuade the police to think of Chick's death as an art-related murder, they might want it. I asked one of the assistants at *ArtSmart* to have the package picked up and delivered to Jonathan to put in his office safe."

Coleman pulled the turtleneck aside to show Dinah her bruises. "More news: I was mugged last night. At least, that's what the police think. But I'm sure it was Simon. I think he tried to kill me."

Dinah paled. "Are you okay? Why do you think it was Simon?"

"My neck's sore, but I'm fine. The mugger definitely wasn't a bum: he didn't have BO, he didn't smell unwashed, or like booze or tobacco. He didn't try to steal my bag or my jewelry. He just choked me. It had to be Simon. Who else could it have been?"

"But why would Simon want to kill you?"

"He must know we're investigating his connection to La Grange. I'd swear on the Bible it was Simon, but I haven't got a shred of evidence, and I know nobody will believe me."

Dinah said nothing, but Coleman knew her cousin didn't think Simon had been the attacker. Coleman was not surprised. Simon was revolting, but he was too effete to come across as a mugger.

"Do you remember that professor at MIT Marise told you about—the one who taught a child genius whose name was Heyward Bain?" Dinah said.

Coleman made a face. "Sure, my big lead—a dead end."

"A researcher at Jonathan's office came up with the same story and Jonathan used Hathaway pull to get in to see him yesterday. It *was* our Heyward, and when he was a kid he invented all this anti-smoking, anti-tobacco stuff—that's where his money came from."

Coleman took out her notebook. "Funny how confidentiality goes out the window when a Hathaway calls. May I use that in my story about Bain for the magazine?"

"Jonathan didn't say it was a secret, but you better ask him. The other thing he told me was that Heyward had to have all that security because of threats from the tobacco kings. He's given a lot of money to anti-smoking causes, as well as inventing the stop-smoking stuff. They see him as an enemy."

Coleman frowned. "Good Lord! Given his problems with security, I wonder why he wanted all that publicity at Christmas? Why did he come to New York and hire Debbi? Or start the Print Museum? That doesn't jibe with being threatened or in fear for his life. Nothing about that man makes any sense."

At the little regional airport that served Harnett College, Dinah dealt with Hertz while Coleman walked Dolly in a nearby grassy area. The weather was clear and balmy, the temperature in the high fifties. Chick's murder, the Apemen, and Simon seemed much further away than the few hundred miles they'd flown from snowy New York.

Still, this part of the country had its own special dangers: it was Arnold territory. The family plantation was less than twenty miles from the airport, and the headquarters of Arnold Tobacco even closer.

As if thinking of him had summoned him, like an evil genie, Maxwell Arnold appeared.

"How's Miss Ida's granddaughter, the iceberg? I always knew you'd come back to Dixie to get what you always wanted."

Dolly, who'd been sniffing the grass and enjoying the unfamiliar smells, bared her sharp little teeth and growled. Arnold looked down at the little dog. "Shut that bitch up, or I'll kill her," he said, tensing as if to kick Dolly.

Coleman's residual anger about the attack of the night before surged up and joined a tidal wave of fury at Arnold. How dare this monster threaten Dolly?

She leaned over and grabbed the dog. "Help!" she shouted at the top of her lungs, ignoring the pain in her throat. "Help! Help! Help!" Dolly, for the second time in less than twenty-four hours, loosed her glass-shattering bark. Everyone in the car rental area looked their way, and rushed across the grass to assist her, Dinah among them.

"I'm coming, Coleman!" Dinah yelled.

A uniformed security guard idling on the sidewalk outside the arrival area trotted towards them, pulling his gun out of its holster. Arnold saw the guard, shook his fist at Coleman, and sprinted for the car park.

Coleman, surrounded by worried faces, cuddled and stroked Dolly. The little dog was trembling with fright and anger. Coleman wished the security guard had shot Maxwell Arnold, but she remembered she was back in the South and a ladylike reaction would be expected of her. She glanced at Dinah, and whispered huskily in a heavy Southern accent to the group who gathered around her, "I'm so sorry for makin' such a fuss. He scared me. He was so big, and he said—he said—he'd kill my dog." She covered her eyes with one hand, holding Dolly close with her other arm.

The crowd buzzed like a swarm of angry yellow jackets. Threatening that little blonde girl and that precious little dog. What was the world coming to?

"Anyone recognize him?" the guard asked.

"I certainly did," said a well-dressed portly gentleman. "It was Maxwell Arnold. That vicious cad should be in jail. This isn't the first time he's threatened a young lady. It's time someone did something about him. I'm going to call the governor."

"This is my cousin," Dinah told the guard and the crowd. "I'll take care of her. Thank y'all so much for your help. I don't know what we'd have done without you." Dinah sounded even more Southern than Coleman. She put her arm around Coleman, and led her towards the car. The crowd dispersed, but the security guard followed them.

"Did he touch you, miss?" he asked.

"No, no, just scared me," Coleman whispered.

"I wish we could charge him with something," the guard said. "He's a real bad guy."

"I know you'll do everything you can," Coleman whispered. "We surely thank you, suh."

In the car at last, with Dinah driving rapidly towards Myrtle, Virginia, Coleman was quick to snap back from the encounter with her old enemy, but she was feeling the strain of her shouting, and sucked one of the peppermint lozenges she'd taken from Chick's office. The familiar scent, so evocative of Chick's presence, nearly brought tears to her eyes. She sat up straight and turned to Dinah. "Maxwell was waiting for us. How did he know we'd be here? Someone at the Harnett Museum must have told him."

"Or someone at *ArtSmart?*" Dinah said.

"No one at the office knows where I am. I left word I'd be out all day, reachable on my cell phone. I'd think

Maxwell Arnold was my New York mugger, if I weren't so sure it was Simon. God, I can't believe I've been threatened twice in less than twenty-four hours. It's hard to believe *two* people hate me that much."

"I started to suggest that the mugger could be Maxwell Arnold, but you seemed so sure it was Simon—"

"Maxwell was scary today. Maybe I should carry mace or hairspray or something. I feel like I'm surrounded by nuts." She looked out the window at the passing landscape, mostly pine trees, and took out her cell phone. "I can't sit here doing nothing. I'm going to call Clancy.

"Clancy? Coleman here. I have some information for you. I'm pretty sure the killers the police are looking for call themselves the Apemen and hang out at Blackbeard's on Christopher Street."

"Thanks, Coleman. I'll pass it on to the police and to the right people here. I owe you," Clancy said.

"Let me know how it comes out. I'm out of town today. Leave a message for me at the office, or e-mail me. If you get a story out of it, you can take me out to dinner, and I get to pick the restaurant."

"You got it. Thanks again."

"That should do it," Coleman said. "With the *New York Times* on the case, the police will have to check out the Apemen. If they arrest them for killing La Grange, they'll get them for Chick's death, too."

"Do you think Simon's involved with the Apemen?"

Coleman nodded. "I'm sure of it, but if I can't prove it, he's going to get away with everything. Right now it looks as if we can prove he did anything—and that's doubtful—it'll be some kind of art fraud. But even Simon's not as bad as Maxwell Arnold. He pollutes this whole area by living here. I'll be glad to get away from this part of the world."

"He comes to New York, too, and he doesn't 'pollute' it. He can't ruin New York or the South for me. If I could persuade Jonathan, I'd buy a house near Wilmington."

"Go right ahead. But I'm not coming to visit," Coleman said.

Dinah laughed. "You may have to. Since I'm your boss, I might decide to make you come south for a meeting."

Coleman scowled at her. "What do you mean? Just when did you get to be my boss?

"Well, after I got his letter last night, I called Jonathan, and asked him about the ownership of *ArtSmart*. I didn't mention your spy, of course. He says *I'm* the owner of our interest in your magazine. He put it in my name when we married. Apparently I signed all the papers. He said you and I knew all about it. I don't think he told us—he probably didn't think it was that important—but we wouldn't have forgotten. He says the agreement is standard, and investors hardly ever intervene in the management of a company unless the manager gets arrested, or something. You don't have to worry about that any more, unless you plan to go to jail. And even then, *I* wouldn't take *ArtSmart* away from you."

Coleman took a deep breath, and let it out. "Well, that's one problem I can forget about. I wish I'd had the gumption to ask Jonathan about it a long time ago—I'd have saved myself some worries. When I think how I've stewed over the spy, scared to death of losing *ArtSmart*. Poor, poor Chick. I feel worse than ever about him. That reminds me, I owe Zeke a call."

She picked up her cell phone again. "Hey, Zeke, how are you?"

"Coleman, I know you won't want to do this, but I think you ought to have the *ArtSmart* offices checked for bugs," he said.

Coleman rolled her eyes. "Hold on, I want to put you on speaker. Dinah's with me. She'll want to hear this. Now start over."

"Hi, Dinah! Well, it was Bethany really. I told her about your leak and she suggested maybe *ArtSmart's* office is bugged. We talked about it before Christmas, but I kept thinking the problem might get resolved. Then the holidays shut everything down, and Chick died. If there's a bug in the office, it would clear him. So we were thinking of checking the office for listening devices. What do you say?"

"Don't you think it will upset the staff?"

"After Chick's murder, why should a little thing like having somebody sweep for bugs bother anybody? We thought you'd want to prove Chick wasn't the spy. You've always said it couldn't be him. Maybe you're right. As Reginald Hill wrote, 'Elimination is the better part of detection.'"

"Would it be very expensive?"

"Well, I'm kind of interested in the process, and the truth is, Bethany and I'd like to do it so it won't cost anything," Zeke said.

"I suspect it's a waste of your time and money, but go ahead if you want to. I can see you're well on your way to becoming a detective," Coleman said.

"Don't laugh. I'm so bored with the newsletter, I *might* become a detective. We'll get on it right away."

After Coleman hung up, Dinah said, "The office being bugged would never have occurred to me."

"Me either. But I'd never have dreamed Chick would be killed. I'll do everything I can to learn what's going on, no matter how ridiculous it seems."

They passed through two stone pillars to reach the grassy, tree-lined Harnett College campus. The museum, not far from the campus entrance, was a modern one-story red brick building. When Coleman told the guard at the desk in the lobby that Dr. Parker expected them, he spoke briefly on the telephone, and a tall, fortyish woman in a dark blue dress, her fair hair pulled back at the nape of her neck, came out to greet them.

"I'm Jane Parker. Welcome to the Harnett College Museum. Come on in, I'll get the Rembrandt plates out. We keep them locked up, of course."

Dr. Parker left them in a study room to wait while she fetched the plates, but when the door opened a few minutes later, a different woman appeared. She looked to be in her early twenties, and was extremely pretty, with shiny brown hair and big brown eyes. Coleman couldn't believe the powder pink twinset and skirt, the perfectly matching lipstick and nail polish. The girl was a 1950s throwback.

"I'm Delia Swain," she said. "I handle press and public relations for the college and the museum. Which one of you is Coleman Greene?"

Coleman raised her eyebrows: the pink magnolia's words were innocuous, but despite her syrupy Southern accent, her tone and manner were rude,

"I'm Coleman, and this is my cousin, Dinah Greene."

Delia sat down at the table, and ignoring Dinah, stared at Coleman. "Are you writing about the plates?"

"No, not necessarily," Coleman said. "*ArtSmart* is doing an article about the Print Museum, and the museum recently acquired an impression of *Sleeping Kitten*. We thought it would be interesting to see the plate for the print."

Ms. Swain raised her eyebrows. "Really? The two of you flew all the way down here just for that?"

She sounded skeptical. Coleman didn't blame her. She wished she'd thought of a better explanation for their visit, but she wasn't expecting an inquisition. She was relieved when Dr. Parker, carrying a metal box, returned.

"Y'all have met, I see," Dr. Parker said. She unlocked the box, and opened it. It was lined with fabric, and the plates were in individual brown envelopes, labeled with the name of the print made from the plate.

"We're especially interested in the plate for *Sleeping Kitten*," Coleman said. "As I explained on the phone, and as I told Ms. Swain, I'm working on a story about the Print Museum in New York. As you know, they recently bought an impression of that print."

Dr. Parker was sorting through the plates. "Oh, my God, it's not here. And look, two more are missing— there should be seven envelopes, and there are only four—oh, no!"

"Which are the other two that are missing?" Coleman asked.

Dr. Parker checked. "*Shells* and *Winter Landscape*," she said, staring at the empty envelopes.

Coleman and Dinah exchanged glances. "Do you have records of the people who've come to look at them?" Coleman said.

Dr. Parker, her face pale, clutched the envelopes containing the four remaining plates, her eyes fixed on the empty box as if she expected the others to materialize. "We invited a bunch of curators to look at them when we first got them a year ago, and since then a few press people have been here. But only one recent visitor came specifically to examine the plates, a Rembrandt scholar from Holland. He had a red beard, and spoke with a heavy Dutch accent. I don't see how anyone else could have taken them, but I showed him the plates myself, and I'd have sworn they were here when he left."

Coleman was sure the bearded visitor was Simon, but she had a horrible feeling the curator wouldn't be able to identify him. Not in the disguise she'd described.

"Don't you think you ought to tell someone? The dean? The police? You'll have to report it to the police if you want to claim insurance," Dinah said.

"Yes, you *would* think of that," Delia Swain said. "Have you had experience with theft, and the police? Are you a reporter, too, Ms. Greene?"

"No, I'm an art historian," Dinah said. "I've worked most of my career with prints, but one doesn't have to be a reporter—or even very intelligent—to know that one should call the police when there's been a theft."

"And you both live in New York?"

Coleman thought Swain pronounced "New York" with distaste, as though the city were populated exclusively with pederasts. She seemed an unlikely type to be in public relations: being pleasant was part of the job. Coleman would have snapped her nasty little head off, but Dinah got there first.

"Yes, we do. But we're from Slocumb County, North Carolina, near Wilmington, a place called Slocumb Corners. The name of our house was Four Oaks. If you're from the South, you should have heard of the town, and the house. But perhaps you're a newcomer to Virginia? You seem unfamiliar with Southern manners. We both went to Miss Dabney's in Raleigh. Our undergraduate degrees are from Duke, our graduate degrees are from Columbia and NYU. Maybe you'd like our résumés?"

Coleman nearly laughed. Dinah rarely snubbed anyone, but when she did, her put-downs were effective.

Delia tossed her hair, emitting a sickening aroma of cigarette smoke and hairspray, but she didn't reply. It was just as well. Coleman ached to slap her.

"Well, there's no help for it. I'll call the dean," said Dr. Parker, apparently so preoccupied she hadn't heard Swain's rudeness or Dinah's response.

When they'd said goodbye to Dr. Parker and were in the parking area, Dinah took out her cell phone. "I'm going to call Jonathan and tell him what's happened, and see what's going on in New York," she said.

"Don't tell him about Maxwell Arnold. You can tell him when we're back in New York, but not now. He'll have a fit unless he can see you're safe," Coleman said.

Dinah punched Jonathan's recall button. When he answered, she said, "It's just as we thought, the plates are missing. There's only one suspect, a Dutch guy with a beard. We think it must have been Simon in disguise." Dinah filled him in on Coleman's call from the Apemen, and explained how Coleman had sicced the *New York Times* on them. "The police might have already picked up the Apemen. Maybe it's time to call the man your lawyer suggested. What's his name? Mondelli?" Dinah said.

Coleman interrupted. "Is Jonathan going to call that jerk Robert Mondelli? Oh, no, say it isn't so."

Dinah stared at Coleman. "Hold on a minute, Jonathan. Coleman, you *know* Robert Mondelli?"

"Unfortunately." Coleman reminded her that Mondelli had interviewed her about Jimmy La Grange, and had been sure that art had nothing to do with La Grange's death. "I hoped I'd never see that know-it-all-know-nothing again."

"I don't think you told me his name," Dinah said. "Anyway, we ought to at least talk to him once—he comes so highly recommended. Maybe your experience with him was an aberration. Let's meet with him, and if you still think he's an idiot, we'll find someone else."

"All right, but if he'd listened to me about the La Grange murder, Chick might not have been killed," Coleman said.

"Mr. Mondelli? This is Jonathan Hathaway. I think you may have heard from my attorney. I hope he told you why I'm calling."

"Yes, he said you had information about what appear to be art-related crimes, and that two people who may have been connected with these crimes have been murdered. Why don't you tell me the whole story?" Mondelli said.

Jonathan told him everything he knew, finishing with the story of the Harnett Museum's missing Rembrandt plates, including the plate for *Kitten*, a print Bain had bought. "I guess that covers it, through fifteen minutes ago."

"And no one in the police force sees any art links to the murders? I looked into the La Grange killing in October, and that was their position then. Has anything changed?" Mondelli asked.

"The police were convinced that no art crimes were involved. But the Harnett Museum must have reported the missing plates, so by now they know about at least *one* art crime, which is almost certainly connected to the Print Museum. None of us has met with anyone investigating either of the two deaths, so we don't know who's on the case, or what they think, except through third-hand sources. I believe you interviewed my wife's cousin?" Jonathan said.

"That meeting didn't go so well, as she probably told you. What would you like me to do?"

"I'd like to retain you on behalf of myself, my wife, and her cousin Coleman. We want you to listen to what Coleman and Dinah have to say, and to tell us how the police see things. After that, maybe we could discuss what we should do next. My attorney thought we might have information helpful to the police, but advised us to stay away from the front lines," Jonathan said. "One thing I didn't tell you: Coleman was attacked last night, and she thinks it was connected to all this, although the policeman at the scene thought it was a random mugging. She wasn't hurt, and nothing was taken."

"Okay, I'll check that out, too. Why don't you wire me a $20,000 retainer? Ask your assistant to call mine about where to send it. We'll messenger you standard agreements—they'll enable me to represent you officially with the police or anyone else, if necessary. I'll get on it right away, and I should have some preliminary information by late afternoon. Could you meet around six? We could get together at my office on West Forty-Seventh, if you like." Mondelli said.

"Could we meet at our apartment in Greenwich Village? I'll alert Dinah and Coleman. They'll both want to be there," Jonathan said.

—— Thirty-Two ——

"MRS. RANSOME, MR. QUINCY is on the line," Miss Manning said.

She picked up the receiver. "Mr. Quincy?"

"Mrs. Ransome, the police have checked the Baldorean portfolio. As you suspected, the only fingerprints on it are those of Mr. Yeats. The car that Mrs. Ketcham photographed was rented at Heathrow by an American woman, one of a tour group that stayed at the Randolph Hotel in Oxford for three days, including the day the bearded man visited the Baldorean. She and all of her party have alibis, and the police think someone must have 'borrowed' her car. They haven't found any evidence that Simon has been in the Oxford area, or at the Baldorean, apart from the photograph."

"I see."

"The police are concerned about your identification of the man in the photograph as Simon," Quincy continued. "Because you have so much money involved, they think you may be the victim of wishful thinking. They think that when the photograph is enlarged and enhanced, it will be clear that it isn't Simon. They've asked the New York police to check on Simon's whereabouts on the day the bearded man was at the Baldorean. If he was in the United States, he couldn't have been at the Baldorean, or responsible for the theft of the Dürers."

"I see. Please let me know what they learn."

Rachel was certain that the man in the photograph was Simon. She'd seen the false hair in the Mount Street flat, and the shape of Simon's long bony face was unmistakable. But two hours later, Quincy reported that Simon had an impeccable US alibi for the day the Dürers disappeared. He hesitated, then added, "There's a group in New York investigating what may be a series of crimes involving the Print Museum. They share your suspicions of Simon. I'm faxing you all I know about the people, in case you want to speak with them."

Rachel had no intention of dealing with strangers. She would continue her investigations, and, sooner or later, she would get rid of Simon.

TUESDAY AFTERNOON
New York

Coleman, stiff and sore and with the beginnings of a headache, planned to go straight from the airport to her apartment and soak in a hot tub. But as soon as she got off the plane, her cell phone rang: it was Jane Parker from the Harnett Museum.

"The Dutch police have interviewed the red-bearded Dutch scholar I suspected. He told the police that he saw me put the plates back in the box, and lock the box. The dean says he's well-known and respected, and the police think it's unlikely that he took the plates."

Coleman frowned. "Then how could it have been done? Didn't you say he was the only visitor?"

"I must be mistaken. Someone must have come when I wasn't around. We're checking everything and everybody. The window of opportunity is narrow, since the theft had to take place after the Dutchman was here. But thank the Lord he swears he saw me put the plates back—at least I'm clear through his visit. I'll let you know if I hear anything else."

Jonathan had sent his car and driver to meet them, and on the way into Manhattan, Dinah told Coleman about the meeting with Mondelli. "You'll come, won't you?"

Coleman groaned, partly from her aches, and partly at the thought of Mondelli. "I guess so, although I can't imagine what that idiot will say. But first I'm heading home for a bath and a painkiller."

While she waited for the tub to fill, Coleman checked her e-mail. Clancy reported that the police had picked up the Apemen. The *Times* would run a little story, the *News* and *Post* would probably run bigger ones.

Coleman smiled. A victory at last. But her smile faded when she read her second message. David, Chick's partner, wrote that a memorial service for Chick would be held two weeks from Friday. He'd included the details, and hoped Coleman would be there.

She felt again the reality of her friend's death. The warm water in the tub soothed her muscular aches, but only time would diminish the pain of her loss.

—— Thirty-Three ——

DINAH LIKED ROB Mondelli's looks, even if he were a little too jockish. Despite his bulk, she found him cozy. It was too bad Coleman had taken against him; Coleman's first impressions were usually fixed in concrete.

After introductions, and Jonathan had served drinks, Jonathan asked Rob for an update.

Rob pulled a folder out of his briefcase and glanced at the papers in it. "I've spoken to the people who interviewed the Apemen—they're brothers. They talked their heads off after they learned their fingerprints were all over everything at La Grange's, and that witnesses had seen them leaving his building. They say Raven left a message at Blackbeard's to set up a date for them with La Grange. Raven was at La Grange's apartment when they got there. He paid them in cash, and left. They've identified a photo of Simon Fanshawe-Davies as Raven."

Coleman and Dinah exchanged glances. "I knew he had to be involved," Coleman said.

Rob looked at his notes again. "They said the date was routine. There was no rape involved. Sex was consensual. When they left him, La Grange was alive, and not complaining. They insist they didn't touch La Grange with anything but their fists, and they didn't hit him in the face or on the head—they never do, their clients don't want visible injuries. But according to the autopsy, blows from a blunt instrument to his head killed La Grange. The Apemen were insulted about the blunt instrument accusation. They said it's against their principles to use a weapon," he added, rolling his brown eyes.

"A man who lives in La Grange's building saw the Apemen leave around one AM, about an hour and a half before La Grange died. The estimate of the time of death is pretty good, because La Grange and Fanshawe-Davies had a sandwich together right before the Apemen arrived, and of course, the body was found fairly soon after death occurred. The witness said the Apemen weren't carrying a weapon of any kind, or anything where they could have concealed a weapon. The police initially thought maybe the Apemen came back later, and finished La Grange off. But half a dozen witnesses at Blackbeard's say they were there until four AM when the place closed. Then they had breakfast at the Village Diner. Again, plenty of witnesses."

"What about Chick?" Coleman said.

"The Apemen say O'Reilly came snooping around Blackbeard's, looking for them. A telephone call from Raven warned them he was coming. They admit they beat Chick up, but they swear he wasn't seriously hurt.

Like Jimmy, O'Reilly died from blows with a blunt instrument—which, again, they insist they never use. The time of O'Reilly's death is less certain because the body wasn't discovered for nearly forty-eight hours, but they think it occurred the same Friday night the Apemen beat him up. The murder weapon appears to have been the one used on La Grange, some kind of club or bat."

Dinah frowned. "Are these men saying someone else came along after they'd beaten Jimmy and Chick? And that person killed them?"

"Unlikely as it sounds, that's what they claim. Back to O'Reilly: unlike La Grange's death, there was no sex involved, although the police initially assumed there was because of the other similarities. The police have verified the Apemen's alibi for late Friday night, and they're looking for others who were out and around. The Village is so active all night on weekends, they're optimistic they'll find people who saw something or someone."

"I'm glad Chick wasn't raped," Coleman said, almost inaudibly.

Rob looked at her, and nodded. "The Apemen claim they left O'Reilly lying in the open and conscious. They say they didn't push him behind that dumpster. These guys aren't rocket scientists. They didn't think about fingerprints, or other trace evidence, or even witnesses. I guess they've been beating up people for money for years, and there have never been any repercussions. As far as I can tell, they don't feel guilt, and I don't think they have the brains to make anything up."

"What does Simon have to say?" Coleman asked.

"Fanshawe-Davies confirms everything the Apemen said, although he puts a different spin on it. He says he called the Apemen at La Grange's request, and stayed to pay them because La Grange asked him to—Jimmy was shy, never had done anything like that before. Fanshawe-Davies's previous association with La Grange was all about prints, and he says he met the Apemen for the first time at La Grange's apartment. La Grange had heard about them, and knew how to reach them."

Jonathan refilled Rob's glass with red wine. "What about his fake name, 'Raven'?"

"Fanshawe-Davies says he uses the name Robert Raven or Robert Ravenscroft to deal with what he calls 'the lower orders.' He didn't want his association with people like the Apemen to hurt his 'reputation.' He picked the name because his employer, whom he apparently hates, and who calls herself Ransome, was known as Rachel Ravenscroft when Simon first met her."

"How did Simon explain warning the Apemen about Chick?" Coleman asked.

"He claims that Chick telephoned him, and said he'd heard about the Apemen, and wanted to talk to them about La Grange. He asked Simon to set up a meeting for him. Fanshawe-Davies said Chick pretended he wanted to interview them for *ArtSmart*, but he thought Chick was interested in them for other reasons—he implied Chick's interest was sexual. Incidentally, Fanshawe-Davies voluntarily told the police about both calls to the Apemen. He claims he didn't know the police were looking for them for La Grange's death. He said they were so easy to find, he assumed they'd been cleared. And Fanshawe-Davies has alibis for both murders," Mondelli said.

Coleman shook her head. "He's disgusting. He knows damn well Chick wasn't interested in those guys sexually.

I don't believe Chick called him for an introduction to them, either. It just doesn't sound like Chick. But are you saying the police learned about the Apemen when Jimmy was killed?"

"Yes, I'm afraid so. But remember, the police thought Jimmy's death was an accident, consensual sex gone bad, and that sort of case doesn't get much attention. Now that they've got the Apemen, and it's looking like both La Grange's and O'Reilly's deaths might be murder, the cases are high priority."

Coleman sighed. "How depressing. If they'd arrested the Apemen for Jimmy's death, Chick would still be alive. That reminds me: do you remember my telling you that Simon looked angry when he heard Jimmy was dead, and you said the police knew all about it? What was that about?"

"Fanshawe-Davies told the police that Jimmy was very talented—he'd spotted Homer's *Skating Girl*, and knew it for what it was, while most people would have missed it. He said it was a shame La Grange was killed. It was a waste of that 'rare instinct for recognizing quality.'"

"Yeah, right," Coleman said.

"I bet they can't pin the theft of the Rembrandt plates on Simon, either," Dinah said.

Rob nodded. "I was coming to that. After you left the museum, they had a staff meeting to make sure the plates weren't in the museum, misplaced somehow. But they didn't turn up. The people at the Harnett Museum don't know when or how the plates were stolen. There's no record of Simon flying to Virginia or renting a car since the museum acquired the plates, and he never telephoned the museum on his cell phone or from the Carlyle."

Coleman scowled. "I still think he used the Apemen to kill La Grange, and set Chick up to be killed by them. You don't have to have an alibi if you pay someone else to do the dirty work. But when he mugged me, I'm sure he did it himself."

"So far we haven't been able to place the Apemen at either of the murder scenes at the right time, or with weapons at any time, and there's no evidence that Fanshawe-Davies was involved, other than what he's told us. And I have to advise you to be careful about what you're saying, Ms. Greene. As I'm sure you know, you could be sued—"

Coleman interrupted. "Oh, I know. I know nobody believes me, either."

Dinah started to speak, but Mondelli beat her to it. "Tell me why you're so sure Fanshawe-Davies mugged you."

"I *know* it was Simon, but I can't explain why. It's almost as if I recognized him somehow," Coleman said. "Oh God, the policeman I saw last night said I should make a report today, and I forgot about it. I was in Virginia."

"I'll take care of it," Rob said.

After a moment of silence, Jonathan changed the subject. "Does anybody believe that the Apemen are telling the truth—that they didn't kill La Grange or O'Reilly? That they didn't use some kind of weapon? As Dinah said, that implies someone else came along after the Apemen and struck the killing blows after the Apemen had beaten La Grange and O'Reilly—which, frankly, seems fantastic."

"I agree, it seems improbable, but there's no getting around the fact that no weapon has been found or seen. Also, the Apemen are known to the Vice Squad, and they confirmed that the brothers don't use weapons," Rob said.

Coleman leaned forward, her green eyes bright. "Bethany's doctor," she said.

"Of course!" Dinah said.

"What doctor?" Rob said.

Dinah turned to Rob. "Bethany, who works with me at the gallery, saw a doctor on Charles Street the night Jimmy La Grange was killed. She knows exactly when he was there, and she can describe him. She doesn't know if he was in Jimmy's building, but he went in one of the brownstones in Jimmy's row. It was long after one, when you say the Apemen left."

Mondelli didn't move, but Dinah thought he seemed more alert, like a bird dog that had picked up a scent. "Did she tell the police?"

"No, they never questioned Bethany. Anyway, she didn't know where La Grange lived until right before Christmas," Dinah said.

"And I told my friend with the *Times*, who passed it on to the cops, but they weren't interested," Coleman added.

"About the doctor: how can Bethany remember exactly when it was? That was a couple of months ago," Mondelli said.

"She kept a diary—she was playing detective—reading a book about how to be a detective. Why don't I have her call you? You should get the story directly from her," Dinah said. Mondelli nodded, and made a note in his notebook.

"I'll tell you somebody else you ought to talk to," Coleman said. "That weirdo what's-her-name at the Harnett Museum."

"Goodness yes, Delia Swain. She *is* strange! She treated us as if we were Martian invaders. I don't think

I've ever met anybody who detested both Coleman and me on sight and didn't bother to hide it," Dinah said.

Mondelli looked up. "She acted suspiciously?"

"We don't know. We never laid eyes on the woman before. Maybe she's always rude and obnoxious," Coleman said. "She works at the museum. She came uninvited into our meeting with Dr. Parker and jumped on us like a lion on a zebra. Maybe she had something to do with the disappearance of those plates, and was angry that we drew attention to their absence. If it hadn't been for us, they might not have been missed for months."

"Okay. I'll look into that, too," Mondelli said.

After the door closed behind Mondelli, Coleman stood up, assuming she and Dinah would share a taxi uptown. But Jonathan said, "Coleman, I wonder if you'd excuse Dinah and me? We have some things to discuss."

Coleman looked at Dinah, and raised her eyebrows. Dinah nodded, and walked Coleman to the door. "Thanks for everything, cuz. I'll talk to you tomorrow," Dinah said, smiling.

In the taxi, Coleman thought about Dinah and Jonathan. The lamb had returned to the fold, which was probably good news. Only time would tell. Dinah's problems with Jonathan were a reminder—not that Coleman needed one—of why Coleman would never marry.

— Thirty-Four —

COLEMAN OVERSLEPT, AND awoke aching even more than she had the day before. She raced through her shower and pulled on a black knit turtleneck and matching slacks. The bruises showed above the turtleneck. She knotted a red and black silk scarf around her throat, making sure the marks were covered. She fed Dolly, gulped a cup of coffee, ate some lemon yogurt from the carton, and set off at a fast clip for the office, Dolly bouncing ahead of her.

Coleman usually arrived around six but it was nearly seven thirty when she stepped off the elevator near the door to *ArtSmart's* office. Her absence the day before meant she'd find lots of problems waiting, and she had to finish the piece she was writing about poor Chick for the March *ArtSmart*. The copy deadline was Friday. It would be a busy day.

She was not pleased to find Zeke and Bethany sitting on the floor in the corridor outside the locked door to the *ArtSmart* reception area. They were drinking coffee from cardboard cups, reading newspapers, and looked very much at home.

"What in the world—" she began.

"We're here to check the office for bugs," Zeke said. He stood up, and pulled Bethany to her feet.

Coleman scowled. "Why so early? And why didn't you call first?"

"I tried to call you last night, but your machine wasn't on. We're here early because Bethany has to be at the gallery by ten. Anyway, you were worried about bothering the staff, so we thought early was better."

"Sorry, Coleman. Should we come back another day?" Bethany said.

Coleman was too busy for this foolishness. But now that they were here, she couldn't send them away. "No, go ahead, but try and not disturb anyone."

"We'll work as fast as we can. But remember, you've cleared everyone who works here, right? The only possibility remaining was Chick, and he's dead. If Chick didn't do it—and you keep saying you don't think he did—it has to be someone who *doesn't* work here. If so, there's only one way it could be done: with a listening device. I know it sounds strange, but as Sherlock said, 'When you've eliminated the impossible, whatever remains, however improbable, must be the truth.'"

"All right, all right," Coleman said. "Let's get it over with." She unlocked the outer doors and headed towards her office, talking over her shoulder. "Do me a favor, will you? No progress reports. If you find a bug—and I can't believe you will—tell me. If you finish checking and find nothing, tell me. But no blow-by-blows, okay? I've got an enormous amount to do today." She went in her office and started to close the door, thankful that not many of the staff were in yet. Most of them rarely turned up before nine.

"Wait," Zeke said. "We'll check your office first, and we won't have to bother you later."

"Oh, my God! I'll be in the conference room." She grabbed a pile of papers from her desk and disappeared down the hall.

A few minutes later Zeke appeared in the conference room door. "Your office is clean," he said.

Coleman sighed. Zeke was having a wonderful time playing detective. Bethany should have more sense than to fool around with this business, but she looked excited, too. Maybe they did have a future, despite their disparate backgrounds. They could open a detective agency together. Or write detective fiction.

She returned to her office, and closed the door behind her. She soon finished her short, sad article on Chick's career and his contributions to *ArtSmart*, and had started through the piles of mail and manuscripts on her desk, when her door crashed open.

"How dare you bring Zeke Tolmach and his slut in here to spy on me?" Tammy shouted. "I'm quitting, but not before I tell you how despicable I think you are. You and your damned sneaks can go to hell."

"For heaven's sake, don't make so much noise," Coleman said, covering her ears. "Come in, and close the door. They'll hear you in Queens. Zeke isn't spying on you—"

Tammy's face was beet red. "You're lying. You can't deny you've been checking up on people here."

"Yes, to some extent I have," she said. "I didn't like having to do it, but—"

Tammy interrupted again, still at the top of her lungs. "And you found out I was leaving, didn't you? And you pretended not to know, you sly bitch. You're jealous. Some of us can have marriage *and* a career—I don't have to be an old maid like you. You think you're so terrific. Well, when I'm gone, you'll see just how much of this magazine I've been carrying." Her voice shook with rage.

"You told me you wanted to keep writing for *ArtSmart* from Chicago," Coleman said, struggling to keep her voice level. "I gather that you *don't* wish to continue writing for *ArtSmart*?" She didn't like being shouted at, and she was appalled by Tammy's rage. What had she done to incur Tammy's wrath? She began to recite *If* in her head. "If you can keep your head when all about you—" It was one of her best calming tricks, but it wasn't working. She was going to lose it, if she could get a word in.

"You're damn right! I told you that to buy a little time! I was going to wait another month to tell you to fuck off, but I can't stand it any longer. I'm leaving today. And, for your information, I'm going to be Senior Editor of the *Artful Californian*."

Coleman gave up trying to keep a lid on her anger, and stood up. "Ah! All is explained. You won your new job with my ideas. How long do you think you'll keep it when your employer learns you don't have ideas of your own? You haven't had an original thought since I met you."

"Oh, really? Ellen Carswell thinks I have good ideas— and with Ellen and me running the *Artful Californian*, we'll bury *ArtSmart*." Tammy stormed out.

Coleman picked up Dolly and sat down with the little dog in her lap. So Tammy was the spy, and Ellen Carswell the spy mistress. Ellen had certainly fooled Coleman. Coleman was irritated with herself for not seeing through Carswell's nice girl act, but her strongest emotion was relief. She'd thought from the beginning that Tammy was the most likely person to be the spy, and now that Tammy had confessed, she had one less problem. But Coleman was sad, too. She'd never dreamed that Tammy hated her so much. This, after the attacks by Maxwell Arnold and Simon the mugger. Why was this happening?

Well, she could tell Zeke to drop the de-bugging operation. She was about to go in search of him when he appeared in her office door, Bethany at his side. They were both beaming. Could hearing Tammy's confession have brought that glow to their cheeks? More likely they'd been canoodling in an empty office.

"Holmes and Watson, I presume," Coleman said. "Did you hear two-timing Tammy scream her confession? She admitted she's the leak, and she's leaving, so the bug detection team can retire."

Bethany's smile broadened, and Zeke laughed. "We heard Tammy—who could help it? But we were on our way to tell you: the conference room *is* bugged," he said.

Coleman stood up. "You've got to be kidding! Tammy admits she was the leak to the *Artful Californian*. And now you're telling me there's a bug besides? Why would the *Artful* crowd have installed a bug when they had Tammy on their payroll?"

Zeke shrugged. "Maybe there's another spy."

"*Two* spies? I can hardly believe in *one*. Who else could possibly be interested?"

"Why don't I ask Tammy?" Zeke said. "After I've questioned her, I'll escort her out, and get her keys to the office. She shouldn't be allowed to take anything. If she'd steal your ideas, she'd steal your property, too."

"Oh no, I don't want you and Bethany involved in this. It's all too ugly, maybe dangerous. Two people are dead, and now this. I'm going to call Mondelli, the guy Jonathan hired to investigate Chick's death and everything else that's been going on. He's a pro, has a police background, he'll know what to do. Meanwhile, I guess you should keep checking—if there's one bug in the place, we might have more."

She called the number Rob had given her the night before. "Rob, it's Coleman Greene. Could you possibly come to the *ArtSmart* office right away? One of the staff has gone as crazy as a peach orchard pig. She's leaving, and could be stealing *ArtSmart* property, and her departure involves Ellen Carswell. What's happening here might be a piece of the mess you're investigating."

Mondelli arrived in less than twenty minutes. By then Coleman had calmed down, and wished she hadn't called him. She should have been able to deal with this herself. She hated having to ask others for help.

Coleman introduced Bethany and Zeke to Rob, and explained what had just happened.

Rob smiled. "I'm sure you have work to do. Why don't you go in your office, close the door, and let me handle this?" His voice was gentle, soothing and comforting.

Coleman looked at Mondelli, and, as if hypnotized, went into her office. The door closed quietly behind her. Before it closed, she heard Zeke speak. "Wow," he said. "That was awesome. How'd you do that?"

Coleman was as surprised as Zeke was. Why had she followed Mondelli's instructions without arguing? She didn't like bossy men, and usually rebelled when they started ordering her around. Mondelli certainly had a way with him. Anyway, he was right. She had work to do.

Rob turned to Zeke. "Is this the device you're using? Nice equipment, keep at it. Leave anything you find in place, and I'll look at it later. But before you go back to work, what's the name of the woman who admits being the leak, and where is she?"

Zeke explained who Tammy was, and pointed out the closed door of her office. Mondelli entered without knocking. "Ms. Isaacs, I'm Robert Mondelli, an attorney representing Coleman Greene and *ArtSmart*. I'll escort you downstairs. Don't take anything but your purse. If you leave any personal belongings here, we'll deliver them to you."

Tammy, surrounded by piles of paper, Bloomingdales bags, and file folders, glared at him. "You can't do this."

"Watch me. I'm going to empty your purse on the desk. I'll take your *ArtSmart* keys and your key card. Do you keep all your ID in your billfold?"

She stared at the floor, and didn't answer.

"I'm taking your *ArtSmart* ID, your business cards, this *ArtSmart* American Express card, and your cell phone," Rob said. "If the phone turns out to be yours, not the company's, I'll return it. Put your other things in your purse, get your coat, and let's go."

In the hall outside her office, he locked the door behind them. "Within a few days, you'll receive a termination agreement from Ms. Greene and *ArtSmart*. Sign it and return it promptly.

"Your response to my next few questions will influence how we'll treat your offense. How long have you been giving the *Artful Californian* ideas? You were giving them, not selling, I assume?"

She nodded.

"For how long?"

"More than a year, since before the *Artful Californian* started publishing." Her voice was barely audible.

"Who approached you about working for the *Artful Californian?*"

"Ellen Carswell."

"Do you still claim they were your ideas? Remember, we can interview the other writers who were at the meetings when Ms. Greene presented them."

"No, they were Coleman Greene's ideas," she said. "So what? I have plenty of ideas—she just wasn't interested in any but her own. And Ellen wanted stuff that had already been assigned to *ArtSmart* writers."

"Did you bug the place?"

Tammy shook her head. "No, I don't know anything about any bugs, and I don't believe there are any. Zeke and his crazy bitch probably made it up. Why would anyone bug the place? The *Artful Californian* didn't do it. They were getting everything they wanted from me."

They rode down in the elevator in silence, and left the building together. He hailed a taxi, and opened the door for her. When she was inside he said, "Ms. Isaacs, I urge you to get a lawyer. I taped our conversation," he held up a pocket recorder, "and, in any case, I'm told you shrieked your confession loud enough for the entire office—maybe the entire building—to hear. Ms. Greene may decide to take legal action against you.

"One more thing: you should be very careful. Two people involved with the Print Museum, where Ellen Carswell worked until recently, have been killed."

—— Thirty-Five ——

SIMON SLEPT LATE, and called room service for crois-sants and coffee. He'd breakfast in bed. The luxuri-ous suite at the Carlyle had been home for months, and he would soon be giving it up. He already felt nostalgic about it. Fortunately, Ellen had tons of money, and he'd make sure she arranged comparable living space for him. And, he had much to look forward to.

After breakfast, pleased with life and with himself, he took a cab to 110th Street and Broadway.

She was waiting for him in the back of the coffee shop on the corner in what they'd come to think of as their booth. She was gorgeous, delicious, fabulous. He sat down opposite her. "Black coffee," he said to the waiter, and turned back to her with a smile.

"Did Ellen get off all right?" she asked.

He added sugar to his coffee, and took a sip. "Oh, yes. We've spoken on the phone several times, and all is well with Ellen."

"I'm going to be here a week," she said, and puckered her lips, as if for a kiss.

"I know, my dear Kestrel. What would you like to do tonight?" He smiled, longing to touch her hand, her hair, to kiss her, but that was against the rules. He could do none of those things in public. He stepped out of a Gucci loafer, and rubbed his stockinged foot against her leg.

"You know exactly what I'd like to do." Her voice was low and throaty, and her eyes widened as his foot moved up her leg. "I can't get enough of you. Every time I'm near you, I want you."

"Where, then? Not at the Carlyle, of course." It was important that he and Kestrel avoid being seen together.

"I took a room in Soho. It's the kind of place you like—very decadent. Here's the address." She handed him a card. "Why don't you bring food and drink? We don't want to go out, do we?" Under the table, she rubbed her foot against his.

"Not at all. And we don't want to talk business tonight. Bring me up to date." He continued the movement of his silk-covered toes. He'd never met anyone who enjoyed sex as much as Kestrel.

"Well, for a while we stopped getting much out of *ArtSmart*—Ms. Greene has been holding her cards very close to her chest—but I've made some alternative arrangements. Taking over *ArtSmart* is essential to our plans. But best you know nothing, dear one. Did you hear Her Highness Coleman Greene was mugged?" She was crumbling her blueberry muffin into tiny pieces.

Her breathing had quickened and her lips were parted. She was hot, but he could tell that she was also excited about Coleman's injuries. Kestrel hated Coleman and her cousin Dinah.

"Good God, no! When? How? Was she badly hurt?"

"I don't know the details. It happened Monday night. I don't think it was serious. Are you worried about her?" He could see that she was annoyed that her news hadn't thrilled him. She was jealous of Coleman Greene. He'd leave her now. He wanted her on edge, hungry.

"Of course not. Just curious. I'll see you tonight, Kestrel. Unless there's anything else?" He slipped his foot back in his loafer, and smiled at her.

"I look forward to our meeting," she said.

Simon took a taxi to the Metropolitan Museum at Eighty-Third and Fifth, and walked the few blocks south to the Carlyle, enjoying the clear crisp day, the bright blue sky. He'd miss Manhattan when he was living in California, but he'd be back often. He'd never give up the joys of New York, no matter how many attractions California offered.

He stopped at the desk to collect his mail and messages. Manning, Rachel's pet poodle, was trying to reach him—probably to nag him about money. He'd like to ignore the call, but Rachel could always cut off his allowance, and pathetic as it was, he couldn't do without it. But he'd postpone calling Manning. He had a more important call to make. He was ready to invoke the criminal clause in his agreement with Rachel. Ransome's would soon be his.

In his suite, he dropped his mail on the desk and glanced at his watch. It was late afternoon in Paris, a perfect time to reach the person he wanted. He sat down at the desk and placed the call.

"Good evening, Madame Jardin," he said in his rich, plummy voice. "I understand that you recently sold a Lautrec poster, *The Midget*, to the Ransome Gallery for $30,000. Did you know Ransome's sold it at auction in the United States for more than a million dollars? You were cheated out of a great deal of money."

"You are misinformed, monsieur," she said, her beautiful voice icy. "I asked the Ransome Gallery to dispose of the poster for me, and I received the full amount of the sale. Good evening." She hung up.

Simon, four thousand miles away, was stunned. Why was this woman lying? No one knew better than he that she wasn't telling the truth. Should he question Rachel? Raising the topic of the Lautrec with Rachel would be no joy. She'd been furious when she'd heard how he'd sold it, and at what price. He'd managed to shut her up by telling her that Yvonne Jardin would blame Rachel—of course! That was it! Rachel had reimbursed Jardin. Damn, damn, damn! She'd managed to wriggle out of the trap he'd set.

He'd better call the gallery. He punched in the familiar Ransome Gallery number, and asked for Miss Manning.

When she answered, he was deliberately rude. "What do you want?" he demanded.

"Mrs. Ransome has asked me to inform you that it has been necessary to cut expenses. The country house, the cars, the horses are being sold. And the flat. All staff who don't work for her or for the gallery have been dismissed."

She'd hung up before he could respond. This was terrible. Rachel had every legal right to dispose of the properties, of course. They were all owned or leased by the Ransome Gallery, and she was the majority owner of the gallery. But Rachel had always consulted him about such decisions, and after all, everything she was selling, he used. He was angry, but he was also frightened.

He dialed Rachel's private number.

"Rachel, what's this I hear? How dare you sell—?"

"Do not say another word," she interrupted. "I know about the Dürers. I have proof that you stole them. Our partnership is ended. I am invoking the criminal clause, and you are—or soon will be—wanted by the police." She hung up.

Beads of sweat dampened Simon's forehead. She was bluffing. She couldn't have proof. That was impossible. But she must have something. By now, Rachel would have gone through his flat. Oh, hell, she'd have found his copy of *The Record*. Why hadn't he brought it with him? He had a duplicate in California, but he'd rather she hadn't learned that he'd copied it. He had plans for *The Record*, and she might interfere. Still, she wasn't likely to anticipate what he had in mind. She never took her head out of her books.

He had to calm down. He took a Xanax and drank a hefty slug of scotch. Within minutes, he felt in control again. How much money had he? He began to calculate. Luckily most of his money was in Ellen's name, where Rachel couldn't find it. The company was safe—it, too, was in Ellen's name. He even had a little money tucked away for his secret pleasures. Not even Ellen knew about that nest egg.

The more he thought about it, the more certain he was that Rachel couldn't have evidence against him— nothing solid, nothing that would give her the ability to invoke the criminal clause. He'd planned for every contingency.

He poured himself another drink and sat down. He should call his lawyer, but more important, he needed to come up with another way to get rid of Rachel: that should be at the top of his to-do list. He leaned back in his chair, and closed his eyes, considering possibilities.

—— Thirty-Six ——

WEDNESDAY EVENING
London

RACHEL STOOD UP, her hand gripping the receiver so tightly her knuckles were white. "Please repeat that, Mr. Quincy. I cannot have understood you properly."

"Well, as I explained, Lord Gresham—he owns the Baldorean collection, after all—thinks—and he spoke to others—very important people, all concerned with museums—who agree with him—that the Baldorean situation should be handled quietly. It's Lord Gresham's hope that Heyward Bain will return the Dürers to the Baldorean, and that Bain will try to get his money back from Fanshawe-Davies privately, without attracting the attention of the press. I told Lord Gresham that Fanshawe-Davies had not deposited the money in the gallery accounts, and that we'll cooperate with Bain in his—uh—endeavors. He hopes that Bain will not prosecute. Lord Gresham will not."

"How do you know Bain is not involved? And are you saying that Simon will walk away from this unpunished?" Rachel said.

"There's no reason to think that Bain knew the Dürers were stolen, or that he was a party to the theft. As for Fanshawe-Davies, if we can prove that he stole the Dürers, he will lose a great deal," Quincy said.

"If no one will prosecute Simon, how can I invoke the criminal clause in the partnership?"

"If we have sufficient proof of his criminal activity—evidence that would stand up in court *if* presented—we'll be able to invoke the criminal clause. But those who could prosecute him will not do so. Publicity about this kind of theft inevitably attracts imitators. We could have a rash of thefts in private museums and country houses all over England. Remember, it would mean bad publicity for Ransome's, too."

"I would risk the publicity. Simon should not be allowed to walk away from this. I want him in prison," Rachel said.

"Oh, but Mrs. Ransome, you want vengeance, and that's not what the law is about."

"Nor is it about justice," she said. She hung up the telephone and began to consider her options. She was determined to rid herself of Simon. He had become a major liability.

WEDNESDAY AFTERNOON
New York

From: Rob Mondelli
To: Coleman Greene, Dinah Greene,
and Jonathan Hathaway
Subject: Simon's Alibis

Simon has an alibi for Monday night, and couldn't have been your mugger, Coleman. He was on Heyward Bain's plane returning from Santa Fe, and arrived at Teterboro airport around two AM Tuesday. The police questioned Bethany. Her sighting on the night La Grange died was between 2:20 and 2:40, so the doctor could have been the person who struck the fatal blows. Simon has an alibi for that night, too. He claims he spent the night with Ms. Carswell, and she has confirmed it.

Coleman was re-reading the e-mail when Dinah telephoned. "Can you believe it? They're lovers after all. I never thought they were. It still seems incredible," Dinah said.

"I'm not as astonished about that as I am that he has an alibi for my mugging. I was positive he did it," Coleman said.

"Since it couldn't have been Simon, something about the mugger must have been Simon-like, or reminded you of Simon," Dinah said.

Coleman slapped the desk in front of her. "Yes! That's it! It was that weird scent of his—the mugger *reeked* of it! I'm going to call Rob right away."

"I remember that horrible scent. It's unmistakable. I can see why you thought it was Simon, but some other idiot must wear it. Rob wants to meet again this evening. Are you free at six? Can you come to Cornelia Street?"

"Yes, sure. Are you permanently back in residence?"

Dinah laughed. "So far, so good. We're still working out the details, but I think it's going to be okay."

Coleman remained skeptical—she had known a number of Jonathan-types, and none of them were capable of learning new tricks—but it was Dinah's business. "Whatever you say, dear heart. See you tonight."

Coleman punched in Rob's number. "Rob? Thank you for this morning. It's a relief to have that woman out of here."

"I was pleased to be of service," he said.

"I've remembered why I was so sure Simon mugged me: he wears this peculiar perfume, maybe an aftershave, and my mugger wore it, too."

"Do you know anything about the scent? The name or where he gets it?"

"Not a thing, except I don't like it. It smells like dead grass or hay, or something like that."

"Okay. I'll look into it. Will I see you later on Cornelia Street?"

"Oh sure, I'll be there," Coleman said.

"Would you like to have dinner afterwards?"

Coleman was speechless for a moment. Then, "Oh— uh—sure, that'd be great," she said.

"Do you know Leopard? Where Café des Artistes used to be?" Rob said.

"I haven't been there, but I've heard it's great."

"Okay, we'll go there. See you at six. But if you have any problems between now and then, call me. I can be in your office in half an hour or less," Rob said.

His invitation had caught Coleman by surprise. She hadn't thought of going out with Rob. But why not? He was intelligent, not bad looking. She'd disliked him initially, but he'd acted okay since they'd met again. And just because she was interested in someone else didn't mean she couldn't have dinner with Mondelli, especially when that someone else had never even called her, never mind asked her out.

But dinner was hours away. She stared at the piles of paper on her desk, wondering how she was going to cope. She was killing herself trying to keep up. She should have hired another writer long ago. Now she was short two writers, not counting the one she'd planned to hire before Chick died and Tammy left.

Bethany had a cousin in North Carolina who sounded good, and was interested in the job, but she wouldn't be available for a couple of months. Coleman would just have to keep looking, and meanwhile use freelancers. She sighed, and began to sort through the papers on her desk.

Her cell phone rang. It was Zeke, asking if they could get together.

Coleman groaned. "Is this about the bug? I thought we were through with that."

Zeke laughed. "No, nothing to do with the bug. I want to talk about *ArtSmart*, but I'd rather do it in person."

She'd have liked to put him off, but Zeke had listened to her problems when she needed him, even though *he'd* been busy. "Would you mind coming here? I'm swamped. I'm up against deadlines. But I can always take a coffee break. If this won't take too long?"

"No, not long. When should I come?"

"Now, if you like."

Coleman looked again at the stacks of paper on her desk. Fifteen minutes with Zeke wouldn't matter. She'd be here all night anyway.

She'd read only two pages when the receptionist announced Zeke's arrival. She went out to greet him, Dolly at her heels.

Zeke sat down in her guest chair and passed her a cardboard Starbucks cup. "Cheers," he said. "I'm here on business. I'd like to work for you."

"My stars! Doing what?"

"I'd merge *Print News* into *ArtSmart*. You'd get a mailing list and me and a couple of clerical people—we could let them go if you don't need them. I'd write all your print stories, and any other assignments you give me, plus a monthly piece, or at least an occasional story, on art scams. I'd like to work closely with IFAR—the International Foundation for Art Research—as you know they track art thefts—their stuff is interesting, and no one is covering it. Anyway, I think I have a lot to offer," he concluded.

Coleman considered him. Zeke's proposal seemed too good to be true. But she probably couldn't afford him, and she didn't want to buy *Print News*, if that's what he had in mind. "What would you expect to make?" Coleman asked.

"To begin with, whatever you paid Chick, and I'd like to buy stock in the magazine, if you're willing to sell."

Glorious heavens, he wanted to put capital in *ArtSmart*, and he'd work for much less than she'd expected. Zeke was turning into the Greene family banker. "I think that sounds like a good deal for me, but not so great for you. Why do you want to do it?"

"I'm bored and restless. I'm tired of *Print News*. I need a change and a challenge. I've watched what you've accomplished here, and I'd like to be a part of it. You've made *ArtSmart* the best art magazine in town, fun and exciting." He paused, looking sheepish, and added, "I've been in a rut for a long time, and carrying a lot of old baggage. But I've developed new interests, and I feel like a new person."

Coleman smiled. "I've noticed one new interest. What does Bethany think about your working here?"

"It was her idea. I wouldn't have thought of it—just not smart enough, I guess. But I leaped into action when she suggested it. She knows how bored I've been, and she's a great fan of yours," Zeke said.

"Frankly, Zeke, you're the answer to my prayers. I was feeling at the end of my tether. There's so much to do, and I'm so far behind. When could you start?"

Zeke looked at the piles of paper on her desk, and grinned. "How about now?"

"You've got a deal. I'll show you to Chick's office. His partner came in yesterday and cleaned it out. It's all yours. Here's a stack of manuscripts to go over—they've been edited, but they need a final look by an educated eye. That's you. I'll get the lawyers working on the agreement, and tell Jonathan you'll be in touch to set up an appointment to talk about stock."

Coleman escorted him to Chick's office, which had been stripped of his belongings and personality. It was just an empty room, but it still smelled faintly of peppermint.

"Did you ever find out what was on Chick's mind?" Zeke asked.

Coleman sighed. "Yes. David told me when he came in to clear out Chick's office. David wanted to move to California—his family's there, and he thought his career prospects would be better. Chick thought it was disloyal to me to even consider it."

"He was a good friend to the end. You can count on me, too," Zeke said.

She smiled. "I know I can. Thanks, Zeke."

—— Thirty-Seven ——

"WELL," ROB SAID, "we started off with the hypothesis that Simon Fanshawe-Davies might be a thief, could have been involved in two murders, and was probably a mugger. But he's alibied by Ms. Carswell for La Grange's murder, Bain alibis him for Coleman's mugging, and he was clubbing with a large group when O'Reilly was killed. We can't tie him to the theft of the Rembrandt plates—we have no clues as to how or when they were taken—and there's nothing to suggest Simon has ever been anywhere near the Harnett Museum."

Coleman, seated opposite Rob, groaned to herself. Simon Fanshawe-Davies was slippery as a water moccasin.

"The London police have told the New York police that the Dürers Bain bought for the Print Museum were almost certainly stolen from the Baldorean, a country-house museum near Oxford. The Baldorean Dürers— the same four images, unstamped, and in superb condition—are missing. There's no way of proving they're the ones Bain bought, but it seems probable. Once again, an unidentified bearded man is the suspect. They have a Polaroid of him, and he used the name Ravenscroft at the museum," Rob said.

Coleman's eyes widened. The Dürer thief *had* to be Simon.

"Rachel Ransome, formerly Ravenscroft, identified Simon from the photo, but no one agrees with her identification. They're checking to see if he has an alibi," Rob said.

Coleman was the first to speak. "Could you get me a copy of the photo of the guy at the Baldorean? If Rachel Ransome thinks the guy is Simon, she must have a good reason."

"Sure." Rob made a note.

"What do we do now?" Dinah said.

"I think we should talk to Heyward Bain. He has a lot at risk. The public embarrassment and the financial losses are his, and he brought both Simon and Ellen Carswell into this."

"I agree," Coleman said.

"Me, too," Dinah said.

"It's okay with me," Jonathan said.

"I suggest I make an appointment to see him as soon as possible," Rob said.

"I want to go with you," Coleman said.

Rob looked at Jonathan and Dinah.

"If Coleman wants to go, I think she should," Dinah said.

"I think so, too," Jonathan said.

"Okay, it's the two of us," Rob told Coleman. "On another topic, I called Ellen Carswell about Ms. Isaacs as soon as I got back to my office. I taped the conversation. Want to hear it?"

"Absolutely!" Coleman said, just as Dinah said, "Oh yes," and Jonathan said, "I wouldn't miss it."

He turned on the tape recorder, and they heard Rob's voice:

"Ms. Carswell, did you make a job offer to Tammy Isaacs?"

"Yes. She approached me when she heard I was launching the magazine. She told me she'd like to join me, and we agreed on terms. She's to start here after her marriage in April, working out of Chicago."

"Did you ask her to steal Coleman Greene's article ideas and give them to you?"

"Of course not. Tammy made a few suggestions for articles, but the ideas were hers."

"Ms. Isaacs admits that she has been stealing ideas from Ms. Greene, and she says it was at your request."

"Oh, I can't believe that. Why would she say such a thing? I must speak to her, and put a stop to this nonsense."

He turned off the tape recorder and was about to speak when his cell phone rang. "Excuse me," he said, and withdrew to the kitchen.

"I think we should get in touch with Rachel Ransome," Dinah said.

"Why? Do you have something specific you want to ask her?" Coleman said.

"No, but like Bain, she has a lot to lose. Rachel Ransome believes Simon stole the Dürers. We should join forces."

"That's a good idea," Rob said, who'd come back in the room. "Why don't you call her, Dinah? Meanwhile, does anyone here think Simon is not guilty on all charges?"

"Absolutely not," Coleman said.

"I think he's guilty of something. I just don't know what," Dinah said.

"I'll go along with Dinah and Coleman. I don't know him, but they do, and that's enough for me," Jonathan said.

"Well, whatever he's guilty of, it isn't the theft of the Dürers. He was in New York when the beard was at the Baldorean. The call I just took was to give me that information," Rob said.

Coleman raised her eyebrows. "With Carswell again? Anybody think she might be lying?"

"When the Dürers were stolen, he was with a group of print dealers," Rob said.

"I guess that's that, although I still can't believe it," Coleman said. "Is it definite that Carswell is the owner of the *Artful Californian*? Because if so, she's the person trying to ruin *ArtSmart*."

"She owns the magazine and several other businesses, but I don't agree that anyone is necessarily out to ruin your magazine. Don't you think it's possible Carswell just took advantage of a situation that presented itself when Ms. Isaacs approached her? But talking of the *Artful Californian* reminds me that I told Zeke and Bethany to leave the bug at *ArtSmart* in place. I have some ideas about how to use it. We'll talk about that at our next meeting.

"But you'll have to excuse me. Coleman and I have a dinner reservation. Coleman, are you ready to go?" Rob stood up, and held out his hand to Coleman. Moments later, they were gone.

"Well, I never!" Dinah said when the door had closed behind them. "Coleman detested Rob! She didn't want to hire him. I wonder why she didn't tell me she'd changed her mind?"

Jonathan laughed. "She probably hasn't had time. It sounds like she had a busy day at the office. Can you imagine it—Zeke and Bethany playing detective, and Ms. Isaacs having a fit? And Zeke joining *ArtSmart*. Too bad Coleman doesn't drink. This would be a night to tie one on. Speaking of that, I'm going to have another glass of wine. Is dinner nearly ready? Something smells good."

"Roast chicken keeping warm in the oven. Would you carve it, and toss the salad? I want to send Rachel Ransome an e-mail."

He smiled at her. "Sure. Let's make an early night of it, why don't we? Why should Rob and Coleman have all the fun?"

To: Rachel Ransome
From: Dinah Greene
Subject: Print Crimes

Dear Mrs. Ransome,

My friends and I are investigating a series of crimes in the NY print world. We've heard about the Lautrec and the Dürers. Would you call me at your convenience to see if we can help each other?

———～———

"Have you recovered from this morning?" Rob asked, after they'd ordered. He couldn't take his eyes off Coleman. She looked like a daffodil in a lime green jacket and skirt and a pale yellow silk blouse.

She smiled, her blonde curls gleaming in the candle-light. "Oh, yes. By the end of the day I could even see how funny the debugging was. I won't get over the loss of Chick for a long time, but I'm feeling a little better about that, too."

Rob toasted her with his wineglass. "I'm glad. I know that the problems at your office have been deeply troubling you. The idea I wanted to try out on you: how about using the bug in the conference room for disinformation? Maybe get revenge on whoever is listening?"

"Oh, what fun! I'd love it!" Coleman laughed, and several heads turned to look at her. Her laugh wasn't loud, but nearby diners smiled when they heard it.

The patrons of Leopard apparently found Coleman as irresistible as Rob did, and he was smitten. Even the playful nymphs in the Howard Chandler Christy murals decorating the walls of the restaurant seemed to smile on Coleman. Rob wished he and she hadn't gotten off to such a bad start. He hoped he could make it up to her.

"Good! We can have a lot of fun with it. We might even be able to find out if you're right about *Artful* trying to ruin *ArtSmart*."

"I'm pretty sure I'm right about that, even if I've been wrong about Simon—and I still can't believe *that*. I've wasted time getting angry, but I've decided that if I can figure out how to do it, I'm going to get even with the *Artful Californian* crowd. I hadn't thought of using the bug—that's ingenious."

Rob looked into her eyes, his face serious. "Coleman, I can't tell you how much I regret not getting it right about Jimmy La Grange's murder. You tried to tell me, and I wouldn't listen. I apologize."

Coleman, who'd called him an ass and worse, and had said she never wanted to see him again, dropped her eyes and flushed. "It's okay," she said.

"Not okay, but I hope to make it up to you. Tell me about yourself. Mind you, I've read all about you in articles. I know you grew up in North Carolina, and came north to graduate school after Duke. Then what?"

"I wrote for several art magazines, some freelancing, but mostly on staff. Along the way I read a lot and I took courses trying to learn how to manage or run a magazine. My last job before buying *ArtSmart* was as editor of a small magazine, and by then, I thought I could do it all." She laughed. "Maybe that doesn't surprise you?"

He smiled. "Then what?"

"I looked for a magazine in trouble, but with potential. When I found *ArtSmart*, I bought it with borrowed money—Jonathan helped me finance it." She shrugged. "That's my story. What about yours?"

He told her about being a cop, studying law, and the interest in art crime that led him to open his own business. "My parents are dead, I'm divorced, no kids, and my wife remarried and moved upstate."

"I've never married, never lived with anyone, never been engaged," Coleman said.

He raised his eyebrows. "You don't like men?"

She smiled. "I do, but in small doses. I have flings, and that's all I want. I love living alone. I love my work."

"Are you warning me off?"

"If you're shopping for a wife, or even a roommate, I am. I have a dog and she's the only live-in companion I can imagine."

"Where *is* the famous Dolly?"

"In my pouch under the table."

"I'd never have guessed. She's very well-behaved."

"She's also a good friend. She thinks I'm perfect, listens to my every word, and doesn't talk back."

He smiled. "Back to your flings: when can I see you again?"

—— Thirty-Eight ——

THURSDAY MORNING
New York

COLEMAN AWOKE IN a good mood. She'd had fun with Rob, and she was glad that Tammy had confessed and left. She was relieved that Chick had been cleared, although sad about his death. She no longer had to worry about the leak, or Jonathan taking over the magazine. Zeke was on board to help her at *ArtSmart*. She'd promised herself not to think about Heyward Bain; she was far too busy. Anyway, his image, which had dominated her consciousness for months, had dimmed. She had a meeting with him and Rob coming up—the first time she'd have spoken to Bain in months—and she wasn't even excited. Strange. Bain was the fling that never happened.

"Dinah, Mrs. Ransome is on the phone."

"Mrs. Ransome, thank you so much for calling."

"It is good to speak with you, Ms. Greene, but I regret that we are speaking in such unhappy circumstances. How may I help you?"

Dinah told her everything that had happened in the New York print world since October. "A bearded man keeps turning up, and we all thought it was Simon in disguise, but Simon always has an alibi. We hoped you could help us. We're up against a stone wall."

"I had not heard about the two deaths, nor the attack on your cousin, nor the Rembrandt plates. I am so very sorry. As for Simon, I believe he is capable of anything. I was certain it was he who stole the Dürers. I am still certain he planned the theft." She paused.

Dinah thought she had finished speaking and was about to reply, but Rachel continued, her voice harder. "There is much I should tell you about Simon, but I do not think it should be on the telephone. Will you come to London? I urge you to come immediately. The attack on your cousin concerns me. It is possible that she remains in danger."

Dinah frowned. Why did Rachel think that Coleman might be in danger? After Simon was cleared of Coleman's mugging, Dinah had dismissed it as attempted theft. When Coleman had identified Simon's scent as the source of her certainty that Simon was the attacker, Dinah had assumed that others wore it. She'd mentioned the attack on Coleman to Rachel only because Coleman was so certain it was connected to the print crimes, not because Dinah, or anyone else, agreed. Was Rachel suggesting Simon *was* involved? How was that possible?

"I'll talk to my husband and Coleman and I'll get back to you later today," she said. When she reached Coleman, she repeated Rachel's warning.

"I can't get away," Coleman said. "I'm short of staff and swamped."

"Come on, Coleman, don't miss a trip to London because of work. It's only a weekend. Suppose she's right? If your mugging is connected with the art crimes, you could be in danger."

"I'm in danger of having a nervous breakdown if I don't get caught up," Coleman said.

Heyward Bain had agreed to see Coleman and Rob at his house on East Sixty-Fifth Street. When they arrived on his doorstep, a grizzled and slightly stooped African American man in a white jacket led them to a small room, where Bain sat writing at a black lacquered table. Crammed bookcases covered the walls. No art, no *objets*, no photographs, nothing personal in sight. The desktop was bare except for Bain's writing pad.

He greeted Coleman with a friendly smile. She introduced Rob, explaining why Jonathan had retained him. Bain seated them in chairs grouped around a low table and joined them. The man in the white jacket—Bain introduced him as Horace—served coffee. Coleman noticed that the furniture had been subtly scaled down to accommodate its owner, but it was not uncomfortable even for someone as large as Rob.

"Mr. Bain—" Rob began.

"Heyward, please."

"Thanks, call me Rob. You probably know most of what I'm going to tell you about what we think is a series of related art crimes." Rob summarized everything he knew, careful not to criticize Simon Fanshawe-Davies, who, after all, was Bain's business associate. "The only way to tell for sure whether the Rembrandt is a restrike is technical analysis. The Metropolitan Museum can tell you where to have it done, maybe even do it for you," Rob concluded.

Bain sighed. "I'd better call my lawyer again. He'll have his hands full with the Dürers, and now this. And I'll have someone take the Rembrandt to the Metropolitan Museum right away."

"What are you going to do about the Dürers?" Rob said.

"I'll return them. They can't prove the prints I bought are the Baldorean Dürers, but it seems obvious that they are. It's a good thing I wouldn't allow them to be stamped. I'm sorry to lose them, but it can't be helped."

Every time she'd seen Bain, Coleman had had a sense of familiarity, and she felt it again today. But that was all she felt—no excitement, thrill, or attraction. He seemed like a decent man—his attitude towards the Dürers was evidence of that—but the spark was out. She was glad. "That's very generous of you," she said.

"Let me tell you why we're here," Rob said. "The Dürers, Rembrandt's *Sleeping Kitten*, Lautrec's *Midget*, and Homer's *Skating Girl*, which Simon Fanshawe-Davies bought for you at auction, were all sold by Jimmy La Grange. As you know, La Grange and Chick O'Reilly, an *ArtSmart* writer who was trying to learn more about La Grange's role in all this, have been killed. As Coleman said, I was retained to find out what's going on, and if possible, bring those responsible to justice. We hope you might like to help."

"What do you have in mind?" Bain said.

"Well, initially all of us thought that Simon must be involved. But he seems to be clear on everything—he has good alibis, including one you gave him." Rob smiled at Heyward, whose face remained impassive.

Coleman's cell phone rang. She took it out of her bag and glanced at it. "I'm sorry. It's Dinah. I'll step out to take the call, if you'll excuse me."

"Certainly—Ellen will—oh, I keep forgetting—Ellen's gone back to Chicago. I'll take you to another room." He showed her into a much larger and more colorful sitting room, and left her.

Dinah, sounding as excited as a child, told Coleman that she and Jonathan were taking the eight PM British Airways flight to London. "Jonathan wants to know if Rob and Heyward want to come."

"I'll ask them. Talk to you later."

When she reentered Bain's office, the two men looked at her, expecting a report. "I'll tell you later. You still have the floor, Rob," she said.

"Well, on the topic of Ellen Carswell, one of Simon's alibis was that he was spending the night with her, and she confirmed it. Did you know they were lovers?"

Bain flushed. "No, and I don't believe it. I never saw a sign of it."

Rob shrugged. "They both say they were together. Meanwhile, we've learned a lot about her. You probably know she owns Computer Art Research Services, and she also owns a magazine, the *Artful Californian*. Ms. Carswell has been—uh—there's no polite way to say this—stealing article ideas from Coleman. She hired one of Coleman's writers. While still working for *ArtSmart*, the writer became a spy for Carswell."

"You astonish me. I knew she owned Computer Art Research Services—she worked for me in that capacity—

but I didn't know she owned a magazine, and I find it hard to believe that she'd do anything unethical," Bain said.

"Back to Simon," he continued. "I can see that suspicion might have fallen on him because he's done so much for the Print Museum, but he has my total confidence. He's been vital to the success of the museum, and I can vouch for his honesty and integrity."

"Well, that's good to know. On another topic: Have you heard about Coleman's mugging?" Rob said.

Bain frowned, and turned to Coleman. "Were you hurt?"

"No, just bruised. I thought it was Simon because the mugger smelled of that scent he wears, but Simon has an alibi."

Bain nodded. "Yes, his scent—quite distinctive. I can see why you'd think it was he. I can't imagine anyone else wearing it, but there must be someone who does. Simon would never physically hurt anyone. I'm certain of that."

"Simon was with you, Heyward, coming back from Santa Fe, when Coleman was attacked," Rob said, watching Bain.

Bain smiled. "Oh, so that's why the police asked about that trip. Yes, he *was* with me—the crew saw him, and so did the driver who met us at Teterboro airport. I'm not alone in giving him an alibi." He turned back to Coleman. "But Coleman, you couldn't be wrong about that scent. It's unmistakable and—uh—regrettable, although he loves it—says it's very 'New Age.' I think someone in California makes it for him. Maybe the maker has sold it to someone else, even though Simon think it's his exclusively."

"We'll look into it," Rob said. "There's another question: where's the money? You bought at auction—with Simon bidding for you—the Dürers, the Rembrandt, the Lautrec, and the Homer. The checks for the Homer and the Lautrec hadn't been sent out when Jimmy was killed, so they've been held up. But the other auction houses mailed the checks to box numbers rented in Jimmy's name. They've also been endorsed in Jimmy's name—forgeries, of course—and the checks have been cashed. So someone has the money. But who? Obviously, you can't recover the money you paid for the Dürers and the Rembrandt unless they can find it."

Coleman leaned forward. "There are lots of unanswered questions, but we may be about to get some answers. Dinah and Jonathan are going to London tonight. Rachel Ransome wants to talk to them about Simon, and she warned Dinah that she thought I could still be in danger."

Rob frowned. "Did she explain why?"

"She wouldn't say anything on the phone." Coleman turned to Bain. "I can't go to London—I have too much work to do—but Dinah and Jonathan wanted to know whether you and Rob will join them."

Rob shook his head. "If you're not going, I'll stick around. I think you need me here."

"I'll go with Jonathan and Dinah," Heyward said.

Coleman smiled to herself. Heyward Bain certainly didn't act as if he were in love with her, never mind what Dinah said. Rob, on the other hand . . . but maybe Rob saw guarding her as part of his job? No matter, it was comforting having someone thinking about her safety. The mugging, the encounter with Maxwell, Tammy's furious attack, and Chick's death had shaken her more than she would admit to anyone, even Dinah. Having Rob around was like having a big warm St. Bernard watching her back.

~

Coleman and Zeke shared an early Chinese take-out lunch in Coleman's office, while they plotted how to use the bug to trap The Listener.

"I have a lot of ideas I can never use because they're too way out, too dangerous, and they'd make us too many enemies," Coleman said. "I thought we might pass them on as stories we've decided to run. If it's the *Artful* crowd listening in, maybe they'll be dumb enough to use them."

"You think the bug was installed by the *Artful Californian* people?" Zeke asked.

"Yes. I think they put it in when I stopped telling the staff my ideas, and Tammy wasn't coming up with anything they could use."

"Wouldn't they have told Tammy about the bug?"

"Who'd tell her? Never trust a traitor," Coleman said.

She stacked the empty food cartons, and put the used plates and plastic utensils in the wastebasket. She tossed Dolly—who had watched her every bite—a piece of raw carrot she'd brought from home. Dolly retreated to her basket to gnaw her treat.

"What stories should you and I discuss in the conference room?" Zeke asked.

Coleman grinned. "We'll do an 'Arts Climb,' the worst examples we've encountered of social climbing in the art world. We'll talk about them as truly imaginative steps, as if we admire these people. I'll tell you some, you take notes and organize the material, and then we'll go through it again for the tape. We'll work out a little script." She leaned back in her chair.

"Let's see. The funeral as social event. A Wall Street mogul—let's call him the Squeaking Head—whose art collecting activities opened a lot of doors to him, but not as many as he'd expected, was leaving his office to attend the funeral of a member of a prominent family, when a business associate said to him, 'I didn't know you knew the Engleharts.'

" 'I don't,' said he, 'but it's an important funeral at which to be seen. Rockefellers will be there.' "

Zeke was wide-eyed. "No, not really! Can you imagine pushing your way into the funeral of somebody you don't know?"

"Wait: the most unattractive couple in New York—I call them Tank and Dank—take turns promoting each other. He approached the president of a New York college and offered to buy Tank an honorary degree. He opened the bid at $50,000 and kept raising it. The president—someone I know well, he's a honey and top drawer—told me he practically had to shove Dank out of his office."

"Wow!"

"And there's the place card shuffle. There are two women in art circles who are notorious for that—let's call them Missy and Prissy—they go to parties early, and sneak into the dining room to rearrange the seating, making sure they're in the best places . . ."

Zeke was laughing. His laughter was so infectious that Coleman joined in, despite herself. She'd never found these people amusing—more like disgusting— but Zeke was right to laugh at them. People kept telling her to lighten up. Maybe Zeke—and Rob?—would help make it happen.

"Wait, wait," Zeke sputtered. "What will we call these people? We won't use their real names, will we? Or the names you just gave them?"

"We'll give them thinly disguised names, so even the *Artful* dopes will know who they are. If they're the idiots I think they are, they'll use the names we give them, or even their real names. If Tammy is a sample of their brain power, I'm sure they'll take the bait. Carswell's smart, but she must turn the magazine over to morons while she concentrates on the Chicago company."

—— Thirty-Nine ——

S IMON SLEPT UNTIL nearly two, but even so, he woke feeling jaded. Kestrel was a ferocious and demanding lover. He'd been up until nearly three satisfying her rapacious appetite. He didn't know how he'd manage without Viagra. And now there was this other pill—the one that advised you to call a doctor if you kept an erection for four hours. Not a chance: he'd call Kestrel.

He ordered breakfast and glanced through his messages while he waited for room service. Ellen. He'd call her as soon as he'd had his coffee. It was important to keep her happy. And my God—a message from Owl, from a 212 number. What was he going to do with her in New York when Kestrel was here? He wasn't sure he had the stamina to deal with both of them.

There'd be hell to pay if Ellen found out about his relationships with Owl and Kestrel. He shuddered at the thought. He was going to have to marry Ellen, and probably soon, too. Marriage was the only way he could protect himself financially. Ellen had her own special sexual tastes and inclinations. They were a part of his hold over her. But her sexual desires were so much less athletic than those of Kestrel and Owl. Sex with Ellen was downright restful.

Kestrel had taken her sexual model from *The Story of O*. He'd never heard of the book until she gave it to him—it had been published in the 1950s, well before his time. Because of it, Kestrel had a hankering for being whipped, which he found too tedious for words. But he liked some of the other tricks she'd picked up from the book. She'd abandoned tights, girdles, bras and panties. She said it made her "accessible." Provocative, too. Like Sharon Stone in *Basic Instinct*.

He'd been only mildly interested in the activities described in the book until the end, with its descriptions of the animal and bird masks made of feathers and fur. Those masks sounded more appealing than those stupid leather things some of the sadomasochist crowd wore. They were ugly, uncomfortable, hot, and stiff. Anyway, that group was ridiculous. Imagine excluding females: why eliminate half the available sex from one's games? He'd found a like-minded crowd, more attractive, more eclectic, and definitely higher class than the Apemen and their zoo-mates.

In the book, O's animal name was Owl, but Kestrel didn't want to be called Owl. She'd chosen Kestrel because she liked its picture in Peterson's *Eastern Birds*. So Simon had given his latest bird the name Owl. She was up for everything; she was a game little owl, and very useful, too, although not as wise as her name suggested, and certainly not as wise as she thought she was.

He and Kestrel had a lot in common. For one thing, she liked both female and male lovers. He longed to arrange a threesome with Owl and Kestrel, but he'd have to move gradually, and make a ménage à trois seem glamorous, especially to Owl. She was, after all, very young. Tonight he'd see Owl early, and meet Kestrel later. Too exhausting. But needs must when the Devil drives.

A tap on the door. Room service had arrived. He'd postpone his phone calls until after breakfast.

The waiter also brought him a package, and Simon opened it right away. It was a duplicate of his California copy of *The Record*, sent him by Ellen. He'd use it to set another trap for Rachel. The bloody bitch had threatened him, but his lawyer said she could do nothing. Simon still owned twenty percent of Ransome's, and she couldn't take it away, not for anything he'd done that *she* could know about. One day Ransome's would be his.

———— ～ ————

Coleman and Zeke, scripts in hand, walked noisily into the conference room, rattling papers and coffee cups, and speaking loudly to alert the bug. When Coleman signaled, Zeke said, "Coleman, I really appreciate your letting me write this story. I know how important it is, and I promise to have it finished tomorrow to make the March copy deadline. But I'd like to go over a few details with you, just to make sure I've got it right."

"Sure. Fire away."

"Well, this is the introduction of a new monthly feature, 'ArtsClimb.' We'll use it to talk about people skillfully using the arts as an entry to social life in New York, and discuss some of the very imaginative ways they've moved up the social ladder?"

Coleman smiled. "That's right. How are you doing on the story?"

"This is my lead sentence. . . ."

—— Forty ——

DINAH WAS TOO excited to sleep. She wanted to talk to Jonathan, but he put his "Do not disturb" sign on the back of the seat in front of him, reclined his seat, covered himself with a blanket, turned out his light, put on his sleep mask, and blew her a kiss. "Sleep tight," he said.

She leaned across the aisle to chat with Heyward, saying how sorry she was that Coleman hadn't been able to come. She thought he wouldn't be able to resist discussing Coleman, but he smiled, and kept reading.

She wracked her brain for a way to engage him, and came up with the vacancy Carswell had left in his life. "I guess you'll be needing to replace Ms. Carswell," she said. He looked up, and asked if she knew anyone.

"Bethany Byrd, my assistant, could find you one of her cousins. I bet she could have someone there by next week," she said.

He stared at her, an odd expression on his face. "Good idea. I'll look into it when we get back to New York. Now, if you'll excuse me, I think I'll try to get some sleep." He put his book aside, switched off his reading lamp, and turned away.

Dinah was left alone with her thoughts and Agatha Christie's *At Bertram's Hotel*, which she was rereading to get in an English frame of mind. But she couldn't concentrate, and she, too, fell asleep.

FRIDAY MORNING
London

After the travelers checked into Claridge's and cleaned up, they took a long walk. London was warmer than New York, and the sun was shining. Brilliantly colored flowers filled the window boxes, pedestrians jammed the sidewalks, and the shop windows displayed so many beautiful things, Dinah hardly knew where to look. Just as she was beginning to feel tired, Jonathan led them into Fortnum & Mason's, and downstairs to the food and wine department.

Dinah craned her neck, trying to see everything at once. She was nearly overcome by the aromas—Stilton, lilies, fruit cake, Madeira, coffee. The counters were crammed with tea and coffee; jams and jelly and honey; chocolates; fruits, fresh and dried; bottles and bottles of wine; and boxes and tins of cookies, or biscuits, as they were called here. Refrigerated glass cases displayed meat and cheese and other perishables. She longed to go over to the cases to look more closely—the cook in her was nearly bursting with excitement and curiosity—but Jonathan herded her and Heyward back upstairs, and to the back of the street level floor, past candies and baked goods, and down some steps into a bright dining room, full of small tables.

Jonathan's office had made a reservation, and they were seated immediately and given menus. Dinah's head was whirling, and she felt a little dizzy and disoriented, but she *was* hungry. She asked Jonathan to order for her; she felt too confused to choose. He ordered Welsh rarebits and small salads for them both, and Heyward chose fish and chips. She and Jonathan ate every bite, but Heyward barely made a dent in his meal, which looked big enough to serve a family of eight.

Although Fortnum & Mason's was a short walk from Claridge's, Dinah begged to take one of the big black London cabs, so different from New York's cramped yellow taxis, back to the hotel. To Dinah's delight the driver said "Where to, guv?" just as they did in the movies.

When they were in their room, Jonathan insisted she rest. She was still protesting that she wasn't tired when she fell deeply asleep. She didn't wake until she heard the insistent ring of the telephone.

"Wake up call," Jonathan said. "The bathroom's yours." He leaned over and kissed her, and handed her a huge terry robe. When she put it on, tall as she was, it came nearly to her ankles.

Dinah longed for a soak in the big tub, but she didn't have time. She showered and put on her blue velvet pantsuit and the sapphires that went with it, remembering what Marise had said about how elegantly Rachel dressed. She piled her hair up and pinned it in place. Jonathan beamed at her, and told her she was beautiful.

Rachel was waiting for them in a room full of treasures. The pictures, the furniture, the rugs—everything was exquisite, including Rachel. She wore a plum-colored suit with an ankle-length skirt and matching suede shoes. The tailored jacket fit perfectly—Dinah was sure it had been made for her. It closed—how? Maybe with an invisible zipper. The collar rose up around her throat and was stiffened so it stood away from her neck. On her lapel, Rachel wore an ancient-looking spiral-shaped gold brooch, and smaller spirals in her earlobes.

Rachel introduced George Quincy, her solicitor, and explained that he was helping her deal with the problem of Simon.

A maid in a black uniform and white ruffled apron served drinks and passed cheese biscuits. When she'd left the room, Rachel said, "Even Mr. Quincy has not heard what I am about to tell you." She paused, and began again, as she had when she spoke to Dinah on the telephone.

"It is very difficult for me to talk about my personal life, but I feel that I must tell you the whole story if you are to see what we face." She paused again, and seemed to gather her strength. "I may be the only person alive who knows who Simon really is—I'm not even sure *he* knows anymore. And I believe these problems—crimes—center on Simon."

She told them of meeting Jock McLeod when he was a student at Harvard, after she'd worked for Ransome for about ten years. She described his poverty, his horrible teeth, his unpopularity and inability to fit in at Harvard, her pity of him, their involvement, the fact that he was younger than she.

"It was briefly a physical relationship, but mostly I needed a friend, especially after Ransome died. I also needed someone to help with the gallery I planned to open. I thought Jock would go on for further study in art history, but in the end, he was not interested. First he had his teeth fixed—they were a great handicap, a disfigurement—and then he took acting lessons. I agreed to the expenses. I thought the lessons would give him poise and confidence, and those teeth definitely needed work."

She took a sip of her sherry, and continued. "He took to acting. Perhaps he should have been an actor. He said he wanted to stay in New York to learn more about art dealing. I did not object, as I was busy here. I did not see him for nearly two years, and when he arrived in London, he was Simon Fanshawe-Davies."

Quincy gasped, and Jonathan and Heyward Bain looked surprised. But Dinah had anticipated the bombshell. She now understood why Simon made her think of Shakespeare's plays. He was always acting. He was self-created. He had been reborn when he was in his early twenties.

Rachel continued. "I was astonished, but he was unwilling to discuss the new Simon. He wanted me to pretend that the past we shared had not taken place. It seemed harmless, so I acceded to his wishes. It was as if Jock McLeod had never existed." She took a deep breath before continuing.

"In retrospect, that was a mistake. I believe he hates me because I remember him as he was when we met. At first he was useful in the gallery—he bid at auctions, he did most of the traveling and all the customer wining and dining. He can be a good salesman. Over time, I gave him twenty percent of the gallery. I thought he had earned it." Rachel paused again. "More recently he has spent far more than he brings in."

"Didn't—uh—Jock—ever refer to his former life, his past?" Jonathan asked.

Rachel shook her head. "Never." She reached for a sheet of paper lying on the table beside her. "I found this in his flat. The original is in my safe. I may be the only person in the world who knows that Jock McLeod and Simon Fanshawe-Davies are the same person, and if he were to 'Get rid of Rachel,' as this list suggests, no one alive would know. Perhaps that is one reason he wishes me gone. But now the four of you know."

Jonathan took the paper from her hand, and read aloud, "'To-Do's—Get rid of Rachel.' I'll see that copies of this are put in the right hands in the United States. I assume that's been done here?" He looked at Quincy, who nodded. "Tell me again what his name was—Jock McLeod? Born on Long Island? Went to Harvard? We'll see what we can learn about him." Jonathan made a note on the paper, folded it, and put it in his inside breast pocket.

"What about his family? His friends? Do you know any of his associates?" Dinah said.

"No, I do not know if his parents are alive, nor do I know any of his friends. But there have always been women. As I did not care, I never raised the topic with him."

"How do things stand between you now?" Jonathan said.

"When I believed he had stolen the Dürers from the Baldorean—I never doubted that you would return them, Mr. Bain—I was relieved. I thought I could 'Get rid of Simon,' and I confronted him. You see, if I can prove he is guilty of a crime, I can oust him from our partnership. If I cannot, he remains my partner, and is entitled to twenty percent of the gallery's profits, whether he works at the gallery or not. But so far, my efforts to prove him guilty of any crime have failed."

Heyward was frowning. "But Mrs. Ransome, 'Get rid of Rachel' doesn't necessarily mean that—that Simon would do anything to physically harm you. Perhaps he thinks that *you've* been guilty of something, and wants to use whatever it is to get *you* out of the partnership. Perhaps you've wronged him in some way."

Rachel's eyes flashed. "No one thinks that I would do anything criminal, least of all Simon. If you doubt me, perhaps you should investigate: my reputation is unblemished. However, he recently attempted to make it appear that I had done something unethical, and once again, it involved a purchase for you, Mr. Bain." She told the story of *The Midget*, and how, at considerable expense, she had blocked Simon's efforts to blacken her reputation, and that of the gallery. "I have hired special auditors. They are now going over the books. A great deal of money is missing from the gallery's accounts. It must be returned." Her face looked as if it were carved from stone.

Dinah felt the hair on the back of her neck stand up. Rachel would be a formidable enemy. Just as Marise had said, she *was* Medici-like.

Quincy nodded. "The gallery has not received any of the money it should have for sales in the US." He glared at Bain, who refused to meet his glance.

"Have the police identified the bearded man who seems to have been the person who stole the Dürers?" Jonathan said.

"No, I'm afraid not," Quincy said. "The car he drove turned out to have been rented by an American woman—"

"What's her name?" Dinah interrupted.

Quincy looked annoyed at the interruption. "I'm not sure I was told, but she was never anywhere near the Baldorean. She was out with a tour group that day. The police checked her alibi thoroughly."

"Could you find out her name?" Dinah said.

Quincy raised his eyebrows and stared at her. "I suppose so, although I cannot imagine why you want to know it, Mrs. Hathaway. Mrs. Ransome, may I use the telephone in your study?"

Rachel nodded. "Of course," she said.

Dinah forced herself to smile at Quincy. (What a stuffy old crab he was. She might have known he wouldn't own a cell phone.) "I'd appreciate it."

Bain was still frowning. "There's nothing illegal about what Simon did—improving his looks and changing his name. I don't understand why that's an issue," he said.

"No, people do it all the time. But there's something about Simon that makes us all uneasy," Dinah said.

"Yes, and rightly so," Rachel said.

Bain glared at Rachel. "Mrs. Ransome, what Simon did with *The Midget* was sharp business practice, but that goes on all the time. There are those who would say the seller was a fool, and deserved to be cheated. That you, the senior partner in the gallery, were criminally careless. In any case, what he did was not illegal. I can't understand why you're so determined to force him out of the gallery that has been his life's work."

"You do not think it was unethical for him to have the gallery buy *The Midget*, and ask La Grange to pretend to be its owner to sell it for him, and then bid it up to get money from you?" Rachel asked.

"Can you prove that he did that?" Bain said.

"It is obvious to all who choose to see. How else could La Grange sell it, when the Ransome Gallery owned it?"

Before Bain could reply, Quincy returned. The maid who'd admitted them followed him in. "Mr. Hathaway is wanted on the telephone," she said.

Jonathan left the room, and Quincy said, "The woman's name is Delia Swain."

"Finally, a link!" Dinah said. "She's the unpleasant young woman Coleman and I met in Virginia."

"You know this woman? How very improbable," Quincy said, his bushy eyebrows almost touching his receding hairline.

"We met her at the Harnett Museum, where the Rembrandt plates were stolen," Dinah said.

"But as I told you, she couldn't have stolen the Dürers—" Quincy said.

"No, I understand that," Dinah said, "but—"

Jonathan came back, his face ashen. Dinah stood up. "What is it? Has something happened to Coleman?"

"No, but someone poisoned Baker—my dog," he explained to the others. "Dinah, he may die. He's a very old dog, and the vet says he probably won't make it."

"How did it happen? Who called?" Dinah said, tears rolling down her face.

"The office. They said the dog sitter called them from the vet's office."

Dinah sat down again, and Jonathan sat on the sofa beside her. He handed her his handkerchief. "I'm so sorry," she said, wiping her eyes. "Baker is such a good dog."

"Who would do such a terrible thing?" Rachel said.

"Who indeed? They were walking in Washington Square Park, and the sitter didn't see anyone feed

Baker—but he got violently sick, and the vet said he had eaten poisoned meat. We tried to train him not to take food from strangers, but Baker is very trusting. He's a golden retriever, maybe you know the breed, and how friendly they are."

Heyward Bain fidgeted in his chair. "Surely this has nothing to do with the Print Museum and its problems," he said. "Can we get back to business?"

Jonathan looked at him. "Of course not. It's just a sad coincidence."

Dinah knew that Jonathan was as surprised as she was at Bain's rudeness and indifference to their grief. Bain was beginning to annoy her. He had an inhuman quality. He didn't react normally, or see events as others did.

"Do not be too sure of that," Rachel said. "I don't believe in coincidences. When a series of evil events take place, they are usually connected. Simon hates dogs," she added, "and they hate him. I always wanted one, but when he was here, that was impossible. Perhaps I will buy one now."

"Oh, *really*," Bain said. He turned to Quincy. "Can we get back to Ms.—what's her name again?"

"Delia Swain," Quincy said. "She was the American woman staying at the Randolph when the Baldorean was robbed. It was her rented car the thief drove."

Bain frowned. "Could her presence be a coincidence?"

Dinah shook her head. "I think she's a part of all this. Coleman and I both thought she acted suspiciously."

"She has an alibi," Quincy said for the third time.

Dinah grimaced. Quincy was annoying her even more than Bain. She must be jet-lagged. "So you've said, several times. She obviously had an accomplice. Her role was to rent the car, and to make sure it was available."

Jonathan looked at Dinah, and then at his watch. "It's nearly eight o'clock. We should leave you in peace, Mrs. Ransome, and I should feed Dinah—she's scarcely eaten a bite in the last twenty-four hours."

Dinah stood. He was lying. It was a white lie, but still, unusual for him. She knew he was worried about Baker, uncomfortable with Heyward's behavior, and distressed by her impatience with Rachel's solicitor, whom Dinah had mentally christened Quincy the Thick.

"How shall we proceed?" Rachel said.

"We'll discuss all this over dinner, and I'll call Rob Mondelli, the detective who's working on this for us. I wish he could have come with us, but he thought he should stay in New York to protect Coleman," Jonathan said.

"Quite right, too," Rachel said. "I'm worried about that young woman."

"Can you explain why you're worried about her?" Dinah asked.

"It is as I said: I do not believe in coincidences. I am a student of history. During the past, when a series of events like these have occurred, they have been connected. Your cousin was attacked. She has offended someone, or she is in someone's way. She should be very careful."

Bain looked as if he were going to say something unpleasant, but Jonathan intervened. "We'll telephone you tomorrow. Thank you so much."

Dinah took Rachel's hand and kissed her on the cheek. "Thank you, dear Mrs. Ransome. We're all after the same thing—the truth, and punishment for whoever's responsible for these terrible things—murders, spying, theft . . . it must be stopped."

Coleman looked at the clock on the wall of her office. It was nearly one o'clock—five hours later in London—and the group must have assembled at the Ransome Gallery. If she'd gone with them, she'd have met the fabled Rachel Ransome. And she might have had an opportunity to ask Bain why he'd quizzed Dinah about her private affairs.

She no longer had any interest in Bain, except to find out why he was asking questions about her, and how he'd come by personal information about her. She didn't believe he'd heard of her near-rape from one of the participants. They'd never have talked about it. On the other hand, if not from one of them, how *could* he have learned about it?

The phone rang. "Coleman, a huge bunch of red roses just arrived for you, and there are some packages with it. Is it your birthday?" The receptionist sounded breathless with excitement.

"No, it's not my birthday, nor any other special occasion. I'll be right out."

She counted the roses: four dozen, and what a delicious scent. Most hothouse roses had no fragrance at all—they might as well be lettuce. Someone had spent a bundle. "Gorgeous," Coleman said, and looked at the card: "'From your secret admirer.' Well, that's nice. I wonder who it can be? I'll take the packages to my office. I'll come back for the flowers."

Zeke appeared in the reception area, and picked up the vase of roses. "I'll bring them. Who're they from?"

Coleman handed him the card, and in her office, tore the wrappings off the packages. "Lots of doggie goodies for you, Dolly—and for me—wow! Coffee truffles, and chocolate-covered coffee liqueurs. Somebody knows I'm addicted to caffeine and chocolate."

"Coleman, don't eat any of that stuff. Don't give any of it to Dolly, either," Zeke said, setting the vase of roses on Coleman's desk. "Do you have a shopping bag? I'm going to pack everything up."

Coleman frowned at him. "Who're you—the food police? I wasn't planning to pig out," she said, and leaned over to pick up Dolly, who was standing on her hind legs, begging, "but I think Dolly and I could each have one treat. I'll have a truffle, and Dolly—"

Zeke held up his hand. "No, Coleman! Don't touch it. I'm taking all this stuff to my office, and we'll ask Rob to come get it. If he says it's okay, fine."

"Are you saying there's something wrong with the food?" Coleman and Dolly were still staring at the boxes. Dolly was licking her chops, and Coleman could taste the chocolate.

"Rob asked me to be on the lookout for threats to you, and I don't like anonymous gifts. Will you call Rob, or shall I?" He poured the candies into the shopping bag, careful not to touch them. A Doggie Treat—Dolly's favorite brand—fell to the floor, and bounced across the room. Dolly scurried over to pick it up before Zeke could reach it. He watched, helpless, terrified that it might harm her.

But Dolly stopped short several inches away from the treat, sniffed at it, growled, and backed away. Zeke sighed with relief. Coleman shrugged. "She usually loves those things, but they've been near the candy, and she doesn't like chocolate or caffeine." Zeke grabbed a piece of paper from the nearby wastebasket, used it to pick up the treat, and dropped it into the shopping bag. Coleman was on the telephone with Rob, explaining why she had called.

Rob agreed with Zeke. "I'll be there right away," he told Coleman. "We'll get everything checked, but it's good you didn't taste or touch anything. Would you like to have a late lunch? I'll spring for a gooey dessert as consolation for your not being able to eat the candy."

Coleman smiled. "Absolutely! Could we go to Swifty's? If I can't have chocolate, I'll settle for a cheese soufflé."

Coleman didn't believe anything was wrong with the candy. She thought the presents were from Heyward Bain. He could afford roses like that. But she shouldn't eat the candy anyway, and sometimes paranoid people were right. After all, she would never have believed that Chick would be murdered, or that someone had bugged *ArtSmart*.

—— Forty-One ——

When the maid had closed the door behind Dinah and her escorts, Quincy said, "Mr. Bain is offensive. Why do you suppose he's so determined to defend Simon?"

"Two reasons, I think. The first is that Heyward Bain has, like Simon, recreated himself. He empathizes with Simon. He is uncomfortable about my unmasking of Simon, since he lives in fear of being unmasked."

"And the second?"

"I shall keep the second reason to myself for a while, but it, too, has to do with secrecy and exposure. Would you like another drink?"

He looked at his watch. "No, thank you, I'm expected at my sister's for dinner. I must leave or I'll be late. But may I telephone you tomorrow to learn what Mrs. Hathaway has to say, and what you plan to do next?"

Rachel was amused at Quincy's insistence on calling Dinah Greene by her married name. He was a traditionalist, and as slow as Dinah had found him. But she trusted him. "Of course. I will expect your call."

~

In their booth at Richmond's on Duke Street, Dinah sipped Chablis while she waited for her grilled Dover sole. But she was seething, and decided to have it out with Bain. "Why did you come with us?" she asked.

Bain looked at her, surprised. "It's mostly my problem, and if Mrs. Ransome had anything helpful to say, I wanted to hear it. But all we learned was that Simon had been poor and unattractive, that she'd picked him up when he was just a kid, that he helped her establish the gallery—but she's tired of him, and would like to be rid of him."

Dinah couldn't believe her ears. "And *The Midget?*"

Bain shrugged. "A misunderstanding, and as I said, sharp business practice."

"His going through her things, and using *The Record?*" Dinah said.

He shrugged again. "They were partners. It was his right to look at documents important to the gallery's future."

"And Ellen Carswell, and her theft of Coleman's ideas?"

"Silly of Ellen, but not serious. No permanent damage was done, was it? In any case, there's no reason to believe that Simon knew about it."

Dinah's blue eyes glittered. "I cannot believe I'm hearing you right. You'll excuse and forgive Simon anything, won't you? *Of course* he knew about Ellen's stealing from Coleman. They're lovers. Did you never hear of pillow talk?"

Bain flushed. "I don't believe they *are* lovers. Maybe he spent a night with her, but that's hardly being 'lovers.'"

"Does Simon have something on you?"

"Dinah!" Jonathan said.

Bain folded his napkin, pushed back his chair and stood up. "I won't sit here and be insulted," he said.

"Aren't you worried about Coleman? I thought you were in love with her."

He glared at her. "I never said that, you did. Since you're wrong about my feelings for Coleman, don't you think you could be wrong about other things? You shouldn't leap to conclusions. Excuse me." He stalked out, his back stiff, his head held high.

Dinah covered her eyes with her hands, and groaned. "Oh God, what have I done?"

"Well, you were pretty rude, but I'm sure if you apologize, he'll get over it," Jonathan said.

"Apologize! Never! He's horrible, and he can go to hell. I don't give a damn about him. But I t-told Coleman he was in love with her, I was sure h-he was. She was so h-happy when I t-told her. Now I h-have to tell her I was wrong."

"There, Dinah, please don't cry—Oh God, here's the waiter with the fish," he said.

Dinah was sobbing, barely coherent. "I can't eat. I want to go to home—I mean to the hotel—I wish I were in New York—poor Baker."

Jonathan's cell phone rang, and several diners glared at him.

"Dinah, calm down. Let the man serve the fish, wait here—I've got to take this—it's Rob. I'll step outside."

He was back in less than a minute, his face pale. "Dinah, brace yourself: someone tried to poison Coleman. No, no, she's fine, don't get hysterical. But when I told Rob about Baker, he said the person who tried to kill Coleman was probably practicing on the dog. Practicing on poor Baker, damn the evil bastard! Anyway, what with Coleman, and Baker, and this unpleasantness with Bain, I thought you'd want to go home as soon as possible. Is that right?"

"Oh, oh, oh, yes." Tears were pouring down Dinah's face, and she was choking down sobs. He called for the check.

"We'll be at Claridge's in minutes, and we'll take the first available flight to New York tomorrow," he promised.

Dinah controlled her sobs, and wiped her face with her napkin. "You were right about Bain. He's a terrible person. How could I have been so wrong about him?"

—— Forty-Two ——

THE CROWD AT Swifty's had thinned, and Coleman was finishing her soufflé when Rob said, "Coleman, this business gets worse and worse. I think there's a nut involved. I don't know why someone wants to harm you, but someone does."

Coleman made a face at him. "Oh, Rob, we don't know there's anything wrong with that candy."

"Yes, we do. I examined a few of the chocolates before I sent everything to the lab, and there were tiny holes in the soft pieces, the kind a hypodermic needle would make. That candy has definitely been doctored. We're waiting to learn what was in it. Maybe it's just stuff to make you sick, but Jonathan's dog was poisoned this morning. I think someone was testing the poison to see if it worked, and you were the intended victim."

"My God. I've been mugged and threatened, and someone who worked for me was killed, and another person who worked for me betrayed me, and told me she hates me. Now someone wants to kill me? I can't believe it." She put down her fork. "Baker is dead? Oh, God, that's my fault, too."

"The dog isn't dead yet, but they don't think he'll make it. It isn't your fault, but we have to take it seriously. I think it's time for amateurs to leave this business to me and the police and stop taking risks."

His voice was warm and gentle, and his eyes were kind, but his words were annoying, patronizing.

Coleman had to struggle to control her temper. She had to find a way to make him see how wrong he was. "Did you ever hear of *The Women's Murder Club* series?"

"No. Why? Are you trying to change the subject?"

"No. The books are about four women—a homicide detective, a medical examiner, an assistant district attorney and a newspaper writer—who join forces to solve crimes."

He groaned. "Coleman, that's fiction. We're talking real-life murder here. Amateurs just get in the way in a situation like this."

Coleman was unpleasantly reminded of her first meeting with Rob. She hoped he wasn't going to turn into a know-it-all bully again.

She forced herself to speak calmly. "Now hear me out, Rob. I don't take kindly to being interrupted. We're in a good-versus-evil battle. There's an evil person involved, maybe more than one. Two people are dead, and you say someone's trying to kill me. So far, the police have done a terrible job. I rarely say 'I told you so' but a while back you and the police were sure none of this had anything to do with art. Don't forget, Chick and Dinah and I found Blackbeard's, and with Clancy's help, forced the police to arrest the Apemen. Using Chick's lead, Dinah and I discovered that the Rembrandt plates were missing. Rachel uncovered *The Midget* scam, and found out the Dürers were stolen. None of that would have come out but for us amateurs."

Rob winced. "Okay, you have a point, but I'm terrified you're going to be hurt. Your friend Chick was investigating this, and he was killed. The same thing could happen to you."

She smiled. "But you're going to prevent that, aren't you? Look at how we've discovered clues in the case: we've needed art historians, amateur de-buggers, and my friend at the *New York Times*."

Rob nodded. "Granted, this is an unusual situation, and it hasn't been susceptible so far to traditional police methods. Maybe that's the way it's going to be. But please, Coleman, be very, very careful."

Dinah, still teary, called Coleman from Claridge's. Coleman reassured her that she was fine, and Jonathan grabbed the phone to suggest that Coleman and Rob meet them at Cornelia Street. "Our plane gets to Kennedy at eleven thirty, and we should be at the apartment before one. We have a lot to tell you," he said.

Dinah reached for the phone again. "Rachel Ransome's a darling, and she'll do all she can to help. She thinks Simon would kill her if he could get away with it—she found a note with 'Get rid of Rachel' on it. But Heyward Bain is a rat. I've never been so deceived by anybody in my whole life. I hate him, partly because he's made me feel like such a fool. I stood up for him when Jonathan insisted he was a crook. I hope this doesn't make you feel bad, but he says he's not in love with you. I was wrong about that, too. I'm so sorry I misled you."

Coleman laughed. "I'm not surprised. He sure hasn't acted like he's in love with me. When we're not talking transatlantic, you'll have to tell me why you've taken against him. I hope it's not because he isn't in love with me. Lots of people aren't, and you can't dislike them all."

Dinah had been sure that Coleman would be upset when she learned about Bain. What was going on? But Coleman was right. This wasn't the time to discuss it. "Don't hang up—I have to tell you a few more things." She recounted Rachel's story about *The Midget*, and Bain's reaction to it. "Some ethics, right? But the most interesting thing we've learned is that Delia Swain—that snippy little twit at the Harnett—was the woman in Oxford whose rental car was 'borrowed' and photographed at the Baldorean."

"No! A link at last!" Coleman said.

"That's exactly what I said. How can we get her?"

"We'll talk about it when you're home. Fly safely—I'll see you tomorrow."

Coleman paced her office and thought about Delia Swain. Jane Parker should know Swain's background. The Harnett Museum must have files on anyone working there. When Jane answered her phone, Coleman asked about new developments.

"Nothing. I'm afraid we'll never find the missing Rembrandt plates. I feel terrible."

"Don't give up yet. We're checking some leads. In that regard, what can you tell me about Delia Swain?"

Jane hesitated. Then, "Why do you ask?"

Maybe Jane *liked* Delia. Coleman would have to be careful. "Well, she was so bitchy to us when we were down there. I've had her on my mind ever since. I couldn't figure out what she had against Dinah and me."

"Oh, that's just Delia. She's the only child of rich parents. They moved down here from New Jersey when she was a baby. They don't pretend to be Southern, but she acts like the reincarnation of Scarlett O'Hara. She's a volunteer here. She calls herself our public relations person, but she just hangs around the museum and bothers people. Her father's chairman of the board of the museum, and on the board of the college, so she can do whatever she pleases."

"Where'd she go to school?"

Jane said Swain had attended a finishing school in Switzerland, having failed to get into a college that met her social standards. She'd interned with a public relations firm, and considered herself a PR expert. "As you saw, she doesn't exactly make friends for the museum," Jane concluded.

"Could you fax me her résumé, if you have one? If not, could you patch together whatever you can find, and fax that? Confidentially, her name has cropped up again in our investigations, and I'd like to check her background for connections to other people."

"Do you think she could have had something to do with the missing plates?"

"It's possible," Coleman said. "But I don't think you ought to tell anybody. It might cost you your job if you even hint she's a suspect. Send me anything you can without getting into trouble."

"I'll see what I can do. It would be a great relief if the theft were solved and the plates returned without hurting any of the employees—which she isn't. I've always wished she'd find another playpen. Uh—no one questioned Delia about the plates. They wouldn't have dared, given who her father is."

"I understand. And Jane? One more thing. Bain took *Sleeping Kitten* to the Metropolitan Museum yesterday to find out if it's a restrike. I bet they already have an answer. Do you think they'll talk to you?"

Jane laughed. "I'm sure they will. They know we have—had, I should say—the plate. I'll let you know."

"Thanks, Jane."

—— Forty-Three ——

QUINCY CALLED RACHEL early Saturday morning. "Your American friends telephoned me last night—it was late, and they didn't want to disturb you but they wanted you to know they're leaving this morning. They may have already left," he said.

Rachel frowned. "Did something happen?"

When Quincy described the gift meant to harm— perhaps kill—Coleman and her dog, Rachel was horrified, but not surprised. She had been sure Coleman was in danger. "How dreadful! Thank God no one was hurt."

"Yes, quite. I gather the group also quarreled. Mrs. Hathaway was unhappy about some of the things Heyward Bain said earlier in the evening, and she criticized his behavior. As she should have, in my opinion. The Hathaways expect to be in New York by lunchtime."

"I'm concerned about Coleman Greene. I hope they're protecting her. On another topic, I have devised a scheme to prevent Simon from repeating his Lautrec trick. I will fax you material to your office today. Could you telephone me on Monday, and let me know what you think?"

After her guests left, Rachel had combed *The Record*, and had identified twenty-six people who owned prints that Simon might attempt to acquire at low prices, and sell for multiples of what he'd paid. He would try to implicate her and the gallery, of that she was sure. She would block his efforts.

Miss Manning, who did not usually work on Saturdays, had come in at Rachel's request to type letters to the people she thought he'd approach, and to help Rachel reach the experts to estimate values for the works Simon might try to buy. When Rachel had done all she could, she asked Miss Manning to fax Quincy a copy of the letter to a woman who owned many valuable prints, including three by Degas and one by Mary Cassatt.

Rachel's letter explained that the prints' values had increased greatly in the last few years, and included an evaluation for each. The letter warned the recipient that she might be offered very low prices for the prints, ostensibly on behalf of the Ransome Gallery, and ended by saying that she, Rachel, was the only person authorized to acquire prints or any other art objects on behalf of the gallery. Rachel advised her to refuse any offers for less than the evaluation.

SATURDAY
New York

Coleman fed and walked Dolly, drank two cups of coffee and checked her e-mails. She read Rob's first.

> I enjoyed Wednesday night. And despite the circumstances, I had a great time yesterday at lunch. I still owe you that gooey dessert.
>
> Here's the Baldorean photo you wanted.

Coleman smiled, and turned to the e-mail from Jane Parker:

> I made some calls, and got a few details about Delia's background. After school in Geneva, she worked in Los Angeles at a PR firm for a couple of months. She spent another month or two in LA interning at a magazine, then worked for some kind of research outfit in Chicago before returning to Virginia. *Sleeping Kitten* is a very contemporary restrike. Let me know if I can do anything else.

Chicago and Los Angeles were the two cities where Ellen's companies were located. Could Ms. Swain have worked at the *Artful Californian,* or at Computer Art Research Services? Or both? Coleman couldn't follow up on most of the information in Jane's letter until Monday, but there was one thing she *could* do.

She dialed Clancy at home. "Clancy? Do you know anyone at the major newspaper in Richmond?"

"The *Times-Dispatch?* I do know someone. Why?"

"I'm investigating a woman whose name has come up a couple of times in connection with art thefts. Would you call your friend and check her out for me?"

"Sure, fax me her name and anything else you've got on her, and I'll get back to you. If this is a story, we'll share, right?"

"You bet. Thanks, Clancy."

Coleman leaned back in her chair and thought about everything that had happened in the art world since the October auction at Killington's. Dinah had predicted it: Heyward Bain's money had unleashed greed, and some person—or persons—had come up with a number of ways to get Bain's money. If she listed all the print-related and other art-related cons, scams, and crimes that she knew or suspected had occurred, maybe she could detect a pattern.

A. Print crimes directly related to the Print Museum and Heyward Bain:

- Theft of the Dürers.
- Theft of three Rembrandt plates.
- Restrike from stolen plate (Rembrandt's *Sleeping Kitten*) sold, and not identified as a restrike.
- Cheating owners—persuading them to sell low—so that the resale would be *very* profitable (*The Midget*).
- Conspiracy at the auction houses? "Ring" practices—a partner "bidding up" works to an agreed price level. (The underbidder always on the telephone; record prices, always above expectations.)

- Falsely identifying the owner of prints to the auction houses that sold them—Illegal? Or unethical? (Jimmy La Grange consigned prints owned by someone else).
- Overpricing of the prints sold to Bain—selling prints to him at way above the market. (No evidence, but again, logical.)

B. Art world illegal practices not necessarily connected to the Print Museum, or Bain:

- Espionage at *ArtSmart*: part of a plan designed to take over *ArtSmart*?
- Simon's attempt to damage Rachel's reputation: part of a plan to take over the Ransome Gallery?
- Coleman's mugging, and the attempt to kill her, or to make her sick. (Dolly? Baker?) Was this to facilitate taking over *ArtSmart*? Or was there some other motive?

C. Two murders: Chick's connected to La Grange's, but La Grange's still unexplained. Was it art connected? Or . . . ?

Coleman tapped her pencil on the desk. She had no way to prove or disprove that anyone had sold overpriced objects to Heyward Bain. They probably had, but if they had, it wasn't a crime. It was caveat emptor, and Bain apparently didn't care. She crossed it off her list.

Cheating owners, persuading them to sell too low, as Simon had done with *The Midget*. Sharp practice, but not illegal. Caveat *venditor*. She crossed that off, too.

The false seller issue was an auction house problem. The rule that the seller must swear he or she owned the work was to provide the auction houses with recourse if the work turned out to be problematic. It wasn't a big deal to anyone else. Of course, Jimmy's "selling" all those important works when he obviously didn't have the money or the contacts to have bought them—and at off-beat auction houses—raised red flags. But the victims were the auction houses and Bain, and Jimmy was dead. She crossed that off, too.

The theft of the Dürers and the theft of the Rembrandt plates were crimes. Selling the contemporary restrike without identifying it was stealing, too, or, at least, selling it under false pretenses. If exposed, the seller would have to refund the money to the buyer. Same with the Dürers; jail was a possibility, too. But the value of the stolen objects, while huge to the likes of Coleman, was small as art thefts went. They were surely *too* small to be associated with murder? If one dared pun over something as serious as murder, the murders were "overkill." But if the killings *weren't* associated with the print thefts, what was the motive for them? Was it possible, as the police had thought from the beginning, that La Grange's death was not connected to the art world? And that poor Chick was killed because he stumbled on La Grange's killers?

Taking over the Ransome Gallery ("Get rid of Rachel") could involve real money: The Ransome Gallery had to be very lucrative. And if the espionage at *ArtSmart* was part of a plan to take *it* over ("Get rid of Coleman"?) for the reasons she and Zeke had concluded, that could produce big money, too. But were the amounts large enough to inspire murder? Murder didn't come easily to most people, thank God.

Forgetting alibis, who had the ability to do all these things? Simon? Coleman didn't think he was smart enough. Bain? Bain had the brains, and his recent behavior was suspicious. Suppose he turned out to be a crook after all, as Dinah now believed, and Jonathan had thought all along? Ellen? She had the ability, but the print stuff seemed too petty to interest someone as successful as Ellen. That went for Bain, too, in spades. Why would a billionaire involve himself with penny-ante crime?

Rachel Ransome? She had the ability, but no motive. She might be a little too eager to identify Simon as the culprit—but then, so was Coleman. That reminded her of the Baldorean photo. Why had Rachel been so sure it was Simon?

She printed out the jpeg and put the picture of the bearded man on her desk, tilting her desk lamp so the image was brightly lit. She laid beside it a photo of a grinning Simon—the *ArtSmart* photographer had caught him at his moment of triumph when he'd bought *The Midget*—from the Print Museum file. The two figures were about the same height. The face of the Baldorean figure was so covered with hair it was difficult to compare the two, but the heads were about the same size, and both figures had long horsy faces. But that was as far as she could go.

Coleman threw her pencil on the desk and stretched her arms over her head. God, what a mess! She felt as if she were comparing apples and oranges. The items on her list were incongruous, from the grand designs— the plans to take over the magazine and the gallery—to the petty print crimes. And the vicious killings and her mugging and attempted poisoning were another kind of crime entirely. There must be a motive behind the violent crimes she hadn't considered.

Oh hell, her head was splitting, and she hadn't come up with anything new. She stood up and grabbed her coat, and Dolly's pouch. "C'mon, it's time to go to Cornelia Street."

~

Dinah and Jonathan arrived at their apartment a little before one, and were greeted by Coleman and Rob, who had bought a dozen pots of daffodils to bring a touch of spring to the empty apartment. A fire burned brightly in the fireplace and Rob had made spaghetti sauce, redolent with garlic, basil, and tomatoes. Under his direction, Coleman had put together a salad. Best of all, the vet had called, and Baker was better—not out of the woods yet, but definitely better. He could have visitors tomorrow.

Rob and Coleman served lunch, while Dinah and Jonathan described the trip to London, including Rachel's revelations, Heyward Bain's reactions, and the unpleasant scene at Richmond's.

"To me, the oddest thing you've told us is Heyward Bain's behavior. I can't understand it," Rob said.

"Bain's behavior was peculiar, but *I* think the most interesting information you turned up is the fact that Delia Swain rented the car that was driven to the Baldorean. I've started making inquiries about her. I wish I'd trusted my instincts and done it earlier. I've learned a few things already," Coleman said, and repeated everything Jane had told her.

"I bet she works for Ellen Carswell, and if so, she's part of the Fanshawe-Carswell alliance. Wouldn't it be great if we could get Delia for the missing Rembrandt plates, and tie the theft to Carswell?" Coleman looked at Rob. "Rob,

Jane Parker says the police haven't questioned Delia about the plates because of who her father is. What can we do?"

"If necessary, I'll go to Virginia and question her myself. But first I'll talk to the police here, and see if they have any ideas," Rob said.

"You'd better warn them not to let the Virginia police know someone's going to interview her. They'll tell her father, and she'll be gone in a flash, probably out of the country," Dinah said.

"Right." Rob was making notes, and didn't look up. "On the topic of loose ends, we found the man who made Simon's aftershave lotion, and he swears it's unique. The scent maker is very proud of it, says it's the latest, with emphasis on grasses and herbs—not flowers. So masculine....Which, of course, doesn't get us anywhere, as Simon couldn't have faked his alibi for your mugging, Coleman."

"I think the information about the scent *does* get us somewhere. It's a link to Simon. He must have shared that stuff with someone," Coleman said.

"Simon must have an accomplice—the phone bidder," Dinah said.

"The telephone underbidder would have used a false name, so that doesn't take us much further," Coleman said.

"I'd like to put a tail on Simon, and see if we can catch him at something. But it would be expensive, and we might not learn anything," Rob said.

"Hire anyone you like," Jonathan said. "I want to do everything possible to get this thing resolved—and a killer locked up."

Rob got up. "Okay. If you'll excuse me, I'll go arrange that tail. I know a guy who can probably get on the job immediately."

Late that afternoon, Coleman listened to a message from Clancy on her apartment answering machine.

> My friend says Delia Swain gets almost as much press in Virginia as the Duchess of Cornwall. She was Debutante of the Year when she came out, and goes to social events all over the state. He's faxing clippings. I'll get them to you.

A few minutes later, Coleman had copies of the newspaper clippings—parties, benefits, gatherings of all kinds. A gala ball at the Harnett—wait, was that Maxwell Arnold in the background?

Coleman picked up the phone and called Jane Parker. "Jane? Does the Arnold family have any connection to the Harnett?"

"Oh, yes. The Arnolds are patrons of all the Virginia museums. An Arnold in-law is on our board."

Coleman thanked her and hung up. How could she have missed something so obvious? The Harnett Museum wasn't far from Richmond, the social center of Virginia. Naturally the Arnolds would be involved. That link explained how Maxwell could have known she and Dinah were coming to the Harnett—Maxwell could easily have heard it from any number of people connected to the museum. All of his family would know how much he hated her. He'd never made a secret of it. But she still didn't think he was her mugger. He couldn't have access to Simon's scent, could he?

Early Saturday evening, after a much-needed rest, Simon strolled over to Ellen's apartment on East Seventy-Sixth Street, the only place where he could be sure of total privacy. No one had the address or her unlisted telephone number except Heyward and Simon himself.

He detested the apartment. It was bland and beige, but adequate for their present needs. They'd do better in time. He would insist on a decent New York apartment.

He leaned back on the sofa and thought about what he wanted Ellen to do. She had to call the print owners he'd found in *The Record* and persuade them to sell the prints to him way below their value, as he'd managed with the Lautrec. If they were as ignorant as Yvonne Jardin, they'd leap at the chance. Ellen wouldn't want to make the calls, and in the end, she'd probably assign it to one of her minions. But he'd start with her. He enjoyed bullying Ellen, perhaps because Rachel was so bossy.

Rachel thought she was so smart. Little did she know. He'd deceived her from the very beginning. He'd known who she was when he sat beside her at Ransome's lecture at Harvard and initiated a conversation with her: she was his ticket to enter the circle around the revered Ransome, a circle he could never otherwise have penetrated, especially since he wasn't enrolled at Harvard.

He'd enjoyed the act he put on for Rachel that first spring. She hadn't let him anywhere near Ransome, but he'd learned enough from her about the old man to convince others that he'd known him. Ransome's name was a good one to drop, and Rachel had been ripe for the plucking. His relationship with her had been *very* lucrative. He'd cheated her in every conceivable way—money, art, lovers.

He'd begun to appreciate the thrill of secrets as a child on the Long Island estate where he grew up. He'd lived in the servants' quarters, far from the big house. His mother, a housemaid, made him hide if a member of The Family approached: The Family must not be annoyed by his presence. Crouching behind the rhododendrons, he'd enjoyed eavesdropping and spying.

He valued secrets even more after he discovered *The Record*. He'd wondered what was on the fourth floor of Ransome's house on Ware Street, and why Rachel wanted him out of the way when, after Ransome's death, she went through the house. He'd sneaked back to Boston and while she was out, made his own inventory. He was quick to see the value of the descriptions, locations, and valuations of the treasures Ransome had encountered all over Europe. He'd waited until Rachel completed her summary pages, and photocopied them.

He'd loved his acting classes in New York. He'd adored learning dialects and accents, and role-playing. Creating Simon Fanshawe-Davies was easy when he could afford the right clothes, the right barber, and to associate with the right people. He'd also discovered the pleasures of costumes and masks, and acting out sexual fantasies.

Rachel had been obsessed with him, and it had never occurred to her that he didn't feel the same way about her. She'd assumed in him a gratitude he'd never felt. He thought he more than earned what she doled out to him; it was ridiculous that he should have only twenty percent of Ransome's. He was confident that he was responsible for the gallery's success. Anyone could read books, but sell? That required talent.

As the years rolled by, Rachel turned more and more to her studies. Her scholarly interests bored him, and he let it show. Their sexual relationship lasted less than a year, and after that, she treated him as if he were an indulged nephew to whom she gave treats: cars, a country house, the London flat. But he wanted far more than he was getting from the business, and he and Rachel quarreled frequently over money.

Even more than money, he wanted Rachel out of his life. She'd known him at twenty, and he could not forgive her for that. He'd long since discarded everyone else who'd known Jock McLeod. For years, he'd dreamed about getting rid of Rachel, but felt no sense of urgency until he met Ellen Carswell.

He'd found Ellen attractive in a chilly sort of way, but she'd never encouraged him, and he had plenty of other women. But one evening, while they were having dinner in his suite at the out-of-the-way hotel in Chicago where he always stayed, he had a fantasy about her. She was dressed in a nanny's crisp white uniform, and bathing a naked little boy. She caressed the slippery little body, and he knew what Ellen wanted.

"Nanny, hug Simon, p'se," he said, kneeling at her side, burying his face in her lap, and running a hand under her skirt and up her thigh. Her response to his caresses was as violent as Rachel's had been many years earlier. He smiled. He had a flair for discovering weaknesses in women.

Later, when she lay next to him sipping champagne, she said, "How did you know, Simon?"

He'd turned on his side to look at her. Her glorious red hair was dark with sweat, and her normally theatrically made-up face was naked and damp. She looked younger and vulnerable. Her nude body was magnificent—all opulent curves and white, white skin.

"I didn't, precisely. But there was something. And I've known others like you." He touched her breast lightly with his fingertip. Her skin was almost transparent. He'd have to buy her some decent lingerie. That plain white cotton stuff didn't do her justice.

"I've never told anyone, it's not the kind of secret one is likely to confide." She put her hand over his to stop his caresses. She wanted to talk. He sighed inwardly. They always wanted to talk.

"Tell me about it."

Ellen Carswell had been the sexual toy of an uncle when she was young. His attentions had ceased by the time she was ten, but she'd never been able to respond sexually to adult men. To her, they were all reflections of that shadowy, disgusting old man who'd made her childhood a nightmare.

Before she'd discovered her taste for little boys, she'd taught nursery school. She hadn't known why the occupation appealed to her until she'd nearly succumbed to her desires. She said she'd never given in to her passion—he wondered if that were true—but had resigned her job, and stayed as far as possible from children. She'd learned computer skills, and earned an MBA at the University of Chicago. With inherited money—ironically, from the uncle who'd abused her—she started Computer Art Research Services.

She was successful, but her social—and sexual—life had been non-existent until she met Simon. All of her repressed emotions were released into their relationship. He satisfied her desires without harm to anyone. He'd extended her fantasies in ways she'd never thought possible. When she pretended he was her child, she could forget that he was an adult.

Ellen Carswell was beautiful and intelligent. She was avidly enthusiastic about their sexual games, and the partner of his dreams, both in business and in bed. She loved dressing up and role playing, especially the Nanny games. Best of all, she looked up to Simon in every way. After years of Rachel's superior attitude, he delighted in Ellen's humility, her dependence. At even a hint of Simon's disapproval, she crumbled.

And joy of joys, Ellen had a remarkable knack for making money. She'd seen the possibilities of owning an art magazine, researched the field, and had selected *ArtSmart* as a takeover target. She'd buy *ArtSmart* for chickenfeed—a slam dunk after the *Artful Californian* had taken over all of Coleman Greene's advertisers—and merge the two magazines. She'd turn the new *ArtSmart* into a money machine.

As part of Ellen's research on *ArtSmart*, she'd put together dossiers on Coleman, Jonathan Hathaway, who'd financed the magazine, and on the *ArtSmart* writers. One writer, Tammy Isaacs—jealous, resentful and unattractive—had been an obvious target, and seen the benefits of switching sides. Ellen had also discovered Judy Nelson, Jonathan's gorgeous and ambitious ex-wife, who always needed money, and disliked her ex-husband and his lovely wife intensely. Judy—Ellen's loyal lieutenant—would run the new *ArtSmart*.

When Ellen had read about the Harnett Museum's inheritance of the Rembrandt plates, and seen their money-making possibilities, she'd assembled her usual dossiers, looking for anyone connected to the Harnett who might be receptive to her approaches. Delia Swain had been in a bit of trouble—alcohol, drugs, a touch of shoplifting, an affair with a teacher (male) before she was sent away to school in Switzerland, where an affair with a teacher (female) had resulted in her abrupt return to Virginia. She was exactly what Ellen was looking for.

Delia had fancied a career in public relations, and Ellen had arranged for the PR people who represented Computer Art Research Services to offer the little idiot an internship in their Los Angeles office, followed by a stint at the *Artful Californian*. Delia became, if not a lieutenant—she wasn't nearly bright enough—a loyal foot soldier in Ellen's organization.

Delia's greatest value was as an information source. She knew lots of people, talked constantly, and said whatever came into her feathery little head. She'd told Ellen all about the Arnold family scandal—how there was a secret oldest son, born illegitimate, but adopted.

Who was this mysterious heir—this "FitzArnold?" Delia didn't know. His identity was a closely guarded secret. Delia had heard the Arnolds were embarrassed by him. Maybe he was locked up in an attic. Ellen had encouraged Delia to learn more. Delia had fancied playing Mata Hari and had picked up lots of scraps of information, including the fact that most of the adopted brother's affairs were run by the famously impregnable and incorruptible law firm, the Boston-based Winthrop, Winthrop and Cabot.

That might have been the end of it, but Judy had pumped Jonathan Hathaway's bitch of a sister, and identified a weak link at The Firm—a doddering old fool, senile and susceptible to a pretty face, retired from Winthrop, Winthrop and Cabot. He had a long memory, and with a few drinks and a little sex, Judy literally screwed what they needed out of him. The old man nearly failed to survive Judy, but they learned that "FitzArnold" lived in Big Sur. His name was Heyward Bain.

Bain was a recluse, but a gossipy neighbor hinted that, given a chance, "FitzArnold" might be more interested in boys than girls. Ellen had planned to send Judy to Big Sur, but sent Simon instead. The relationship with Bain had led to a major shift in Simon's plans.

Judy and Delia had helped with the print project, and for a while, everything had gone well. Most of the works Simon had sold Heyward had been obtained legitimately—Heyward turned a blind eye to the exceptions—although, of course, everyone in the print world had raised prices when they saw Heyward throwing money around. A fool and his money were soon parted, and it was the fool's own fault if he were cheated. Heyward didn't care. He had so much money, no one could make a dent in it.

But La Grange got greedy and needed to be taught a lesson. Simon had told the police the truth: Jimmy asked Simon to call the Apemen for him, after Simon described the delights they were said to confer. He didn't know them, but they were infamous and it was easy to make them sound exciting to naïve and inexperienced Jimmy. When Simon called them, he'd exaggerated the amount of roughness Jimmy wanted, but Jimmy wasn't supposed to die, for God's sake. His death was a considerable inconvenience. Why, thought Simon, did the police think someone else had delivered the fatal blows that killed Jimmy and Chick? Surely the police didn't believe those lunatics' story of another, later killer? Who came and went in a UFO, perhaps?

The nosy Greene women had interfered again and again. They found out that Jimmy was the "seller" of *Skating Girl* and *The Midget*, depriving Simon of a hefty sum. That money could never be recovered; Jimmy's family would get it all. Simon would never forgive the Greene cousins. Revenge would be better than sweet.

Simon desperately needed to replace Jimmy. Judy had been the telephone bidder on his earlier transactions, but she was always looking for an angle, and it was Judy first, all the way. He didn't trust her around money. And Delia didn't follow orders. Delia wasn't supposed to introduce herself to the Greenes, but she couldn't resist showing off. She was jealous of Coleman, and she had to get in the act. Well, brains weren't her strong suit.

Chick's death was Coleman Greene's fault. She'd sent him sneaking around, peering into things that weren't anyone's business. If only people would tend to their knitting. Simon hated blood. He wouldn't harm a soul unless that soul got in his way.

Simon sat up. He had things to do, and places to go. He must call Ellen, and get on with the evening ahead. "Hello, Nanny, dear."

"Simon, darling."

He explained what he wanted—the calls to the print owners, the low offers for their prints, and the need for a trustworthy seller.

"It's riskier now that Rachel knows you have *The Record*. Won't she anticipate your doing this?"

Simon laughed. "Absolutely not. Her head's in the past. She might learn about it later, by reading about the sales in the art press. But if she finds out afterwards, who cares?"

"I'll get Judy to make the calls," she said.

"I want *you* to do it, Nanny dear," Simon said, in the pouting child voice he used when they were alone.

Her voice softened. "I'd like to do it for you, darling Simon, but I'm swamped. Moving all these bloody computers to Los Angeles is a nightmare. But the move is what you want, my love, and you shall have it."

Simon couldn't argue with that. He hated Chicago, and loved Los Angeles. In many ways, LA was even better than New York.

"All right. I'll fax the details to you. Can Judy start making calls on Monday?"

"Of course. What would you think about my using Tammy, too? After she shot off her mouth to Ms. Greene, she lost her value to me, and she's constantly after me to give her work," Ellen said.

"Will she do it?"

Ellen laughed. "Oh, yes. She hates Coleman Greene, and she'll do anything to hurt her."

Simon yawned. "Well, dear Nanny, if you think she's up to it, it's all right with me. As long as I don't have to look at her. She's repulsive."

"She is, isn't she? Poor thing," Ellen said, a smile in her voice.

Simon smiled, too. Ellen liked him to criticize other women, especially their looks. About Tammy, he didn't even have to lie.

Over supper in Rob's apartment, Coleman said, "Rob, I have something to tell you. It's not about the Print Museum, or Chick. At least, I don't think it is."

He took her hands in his. "Tell me."

She described the long-ago episode in Durham with Maxwell Arnold and his friends, and Bain's asking Dinah about it. She told him about Dinah's running into Maxwell at the Four Seasons, and her own encounter with Maxwell in Virginia, and learning today about the Arnold family's connection to the Harnett. "I don't know what to make of it all," she concluded. "It's like a spider's web."

Rob nodded. "I'll sort this out. Don't worry, Coleman."

SUNDAY
London

Rachel had been thinking about Coleman's mugger, and Simon's ghastly scent. She decided to go to Simon's flat to pick up a few of his clothes. She wanted to know whether Simon's scent clung to them after they were removed from Simon's environment, and if so, for how long.

She'd thought that the odor in his flat might have dissipated, but the scent seemed even stronger. It permeated the place, and radiated from the clothing in his closets and drawers. Perhaps she should remove all his clothes and donate them to Oxfam? That would have to wait for another day. She packed a couple of his sweaters and a jacket in the case she'd brought with her. She took the nurse's uniform, still on its hanger, out of the closet, and noticed that it had obscured a cupboard door she'd missed on her previous visit.

Inside it, a pile of starched aprons and caps lay on a shelf; next to them, baby powder, baby shampoo, baby oil, and diapers or nappies, as they called them here. Who had a baby? One of his women, she supposed. Surely these diapers were too large? A canvas bag. Inside, a thermometer, a stethoscope, cotton balls, swabs, Vaseline, milk of magnesia, rectal suppositories, enema equipment. She packed the baby things, including a diaper, the canvas bag, the nurse's uniform, and one of the giant-sized women's suits she'd noticed on her first visit.

When she was back in her office, she e-mailed Dinah that all of Simon's clothes had picked up the scent of his aftershave, and that she'd seen a huge bottle of it, labeled "Only Simon" in the bathroom. She listed everything she'd found in his closet, starring the items she was sending to Dinah. Maybe Dinah and her associates could make sense of it. Miss Manning would have the case couriered to New York for next day delivery.

NEW YORK

The detective following Simon phoned Sunday afternoon to urge Rob to add another person to the watch. "This guy stays up half the night, and is all over town," the detective complained. "He left the Carlyle around seven Saturday night, and went to an apartment on East Seventy-Sixth Street. The doorman said the apartment belongs to a big sexy redhead, Elizabeth Carroll. The doorman thinks she's away. Mean anything to you?"

"Ellen Carswell: the description fits, and she's using her own initials. We know they're lovers. How long was he there?"

"About an hour. Then he went to the Suffolk House on West Twelfth Street. He called Room 346 on the house phone, and took the elevator to the third floor. The room is in the name of D. Swain. The house clerk said she's a pretty little thing with brown hair and a Southern accent. Know her?"

"Yes, indeed," Rob said. Coleman's pink magnolia.

"They had room service, and he left just after midnight. He took a cab to a seedy Soho hotel, the Rudolph, and left around four in the morning for the Carlyle. Oh, yeah, on the way to the Rudolph he stopped to buy food, and pick up a bottle of wine."

"Who'd he visit at the Rudolph?"

"A Judy Nelson. The desk clerk said she's a stunner, a blonde glamour girl. This guy is something else. Two good-looking women in hotels waiting for him, and you say he's screwing Carswell, too? What's he got I haven't got?"

"Amazing, isn't it?"

"Security guys at the Carlyle say the subject has never had a woman in his suite, and most mornings he sleeps late. Hell, I can't stay up all night, and hang around the Carlyle all day waiting for him to get up. You gotta get somebody else on days, so I can catch some sleep."

"Do you have someone in mind?"

"I've got a friend who'd do it. I spoke to him yesterday, and he's free. Want me to call him?"

"Go ahead. Where's Fanshawe-Davies now?"

The detective yawned. "In his room, probably asleep, the lucky bastard."

Rob was still thinking about Fanshawe-Davies's womanizing when the lab, working on overtime at his request, called.

"The poison in the meat the dog ate, and in the candy, is nicotine."

"Jesus! Where did it come from?" Rob had never worked on a nicotine poisoning case, although he'd read about it. Filthy deadly stuff.

"It's a home brew: somebody soaked tobacco—probably chewing tobacco—in water, till they had some powerful juice. They injected it in the candy, the dog treats, and the meat. Coffee-flavored candy covered with bitter chocolate was a smart choice to put it in, the flavors would have helped mask the nicotine. Nicotine's readily available for the killer who's willing to mess with it, but cooking this stuff up is dangerous. It can kill you just by getting on your skin," the lab technician said.

"Well, thanks for your help, and for the fast turnaround. Would you fax me a written report? I'll send a copy to the police."

Did the type of poison have significance? Or was it used because it was easily available? You didn't have to know Coleman well to know that she loved caffeine and chocolate, and hated tobacco. But so what? Information was pouring in, but as far as he could tell, it didn't lead anywhere. All he could do was try to get more facts, and hope something would fall in place.

He'd better get on to the NYPD, and figure out how to make sure someone interviewed the Swain woman. He'd see that Maxwell Arnold was questioned, too. He didn't think Maxwell was involved in stealing the missing Rembrandt plates, but he'd like to see him shaken up.

His phone rang again. "Mr. Mondelli, this is Tammy Isaacs."

"I'm surprised to hear from you, Ms. Isaacs." Why was that revolting woman calling him? Only four days had passed since he'd evicted her from the *ArtSmart* office, and he'd made it clear what he thought of her.

"Something awful has happened, something you'll want to know about."

Any information was welcome, no matter how unattractive the source. "Do you want to come here? I can see you now, if you'd like," Rob said.

Less than half an hour later, Tammy faced him from the chair opposite his desk. Her hair was dirty and unkempt, and she had dark circles under her eyes.

"I made a terrible mistake betraying Coleman," she said. "As soon as Ellen found out I'd been caught, she told me I couldn't write for the *Artful Californian*. She said the job she'd offered me was no longer available—my reputation was ruined."

Rob started to speak, but Tammy hadn't finished. "Yes, I know, it serves me right. But last night Ellen offered me another job. She thinks I'm so desperate, I'll do anything. She got the desperate part right. I've messed up my career, and I hadn't planned to stop working—I have debts I need to clear up before my wedding—but I'm not doing what she told me to do. You said I should be careful, and reminded me two people have been killed, so I got scared. I took a chance you'd be in your office, and called you."

Ellen wanted Tammy to consign to auction houses prints Simon obtained, using a fake name, and when the prints came up at auction, to bid against Simon on the phone using still another name, making sure that the prices rose to an agreed level. "She's set up two false identities for me. She said she'd have the documents delivered to my apartment Monday."

"Ms. Isaacs, I'm taping you. You must have known I would. Will you testify, if all this goes to court?"

"Will Coleman give me back my job?"

Was the woman insane? After everything she'd said to Coleman? "I doubt it. You made it clear you hated her.

Anyway, she's hired two writers. I don't think she has any more openings."

Tammy looked surprised. "I heard she'd hired somebody from North Carolina who's coming in a few months. Who's the other writer?"

Rob made a mental note to identify her source at *ArtSmart.* "Zeke Tolmach," he said.

Tammy scowled. "I might have known. Well, he's got what he always wanted. I guess he's earned it. He did everything in the world to get it," she said.

"What do you mean?"

"He's always been wild about Coleman, and always trying to get closer to her. Now he's managed to get rid of two of her best writers. She's making him the senior person at the magazine, right?"

Maybe she *was* crazy. "What do you mean 'managed to get rid of' two senior writers? You and Chick? What had Zeke to do with your departure or Chick's death?"

"If Coleman had treated me better, paid me more, I wouldn't have gone to work for Ellen. I deserved better, but Zeke poisoned Coleman against me. And this ridiculous bug story: do you really believe there was a bug at *ArtSmart?* I don't. If there *was* a bug, it wasn't the *Artful Californian's*—if they'd put a bug there, I'd know it. If there *was* a bug, Zeke put it there himself to make him look like a hero when he found it. As for Chick, didn't Zeke try to persuade Coleman that Chick was untrustworthy? Coleman probably would have fired Chick if he hadn't been killed. It seems like Zeke's always around, advising her, interfering, being a busybody. Now he's rid of both of us, and he has the job that should have been mine."

Rob stared at her. He'd seen the bug at *ArtSmart*, but he had no proof that it had been installed by the *Artful Californian*. Could Tammy be right? Could Zeke be a part of a plan to take over *ArtSmart*? Had they all been duped? If Zeke turned out to be a bad guy, Coleman would be terribly hurt.

When she arrived at the office at noon, Coleman found several more faxed articles and a note from Clancy summarizing all he could find on Delia. There it was: she had worked for both the *Artful Californian* and Computer Art Research Services. She called Rob, and told him the news.

"We now have Delia linked to Ellen, but still nothing on the bearded guy. Could it be Maxwell Arnold? He's evil enough to do anything. Theft wouldn't bother him, he'd enjoy mugging me, and he's tall. Has anyone checked his alibis for the Dürer theft?"

Rob promised to get right on it. He wouldn't tell Coleman about Tammy's accusation of Zeke; he'd wait till he had more information one way or the other. Why would Tammy say it wasn't the *Artful Californian*'s bug if it was, given that she'd broken with Ellen? And why this attack on Zeke, unless what she said was true? Zeke would have to wait. Delia Swain had priority.

Rob mulled the problem of the well-connected Ms. Swain, and called a few of his NYPD friends. He needed a good Virginia cop, one with the juice as well as the guts to make sure Delia was questioned, despite her family's pull. The consensus: a retired Richmond cop who worked behind the scenes to make sure the good guys won. His identity was a closely-held secret. Plenty of people, law and criminals, would like to put a stop to his activities. He was known as The Voice, and he could be contacted on a special cell phone. Sunday was a good time to call him.

A few minutes later, Rob was explaining the problem of Delia Swain. "We think there's a good chance she stole the Rembrandt plates from the Harnett Museum, or set up the theft. She rented the car used by the person who robbed the Baldorean in England of four Dürer prints, although we don't know who that person was. Another suspect, Maxwell Arnold, is also in your area. He's stalking two women here," Rob said.

"I know him. He's a nasty piece of work," the Voice said.

"You may know Ms. Swain, too. We have some petty stuff on her, but I'd guess there's more that never made the police records or the press. She's having an affair with a New York man, who's linked to art fraud, and maybe murder, although we haven't been able to prove it."

"You're sure no one has interviewed Delia Swain about the Harnett Museum thefts?"

"Positive. Not even superficial questions. No one has talked to Maxwell Arnold, either. I don't know if he's involved in any of this, but I'd like to find out for sure. I need to know if he has alibis for two killings, and an attempted mugging."

"We'll have to surprise Ms. Swain. She'll be in the wind if she hears we're coming. But don't worry. We'll talk to her, and him, too. I'll enjoy arranging to have his cage rattled," the Voice said. "Give me the times you want checked out."

Rob hung up, satisfied that the Virginia end of the case was in good hands.

Around six, when Coleman was thinking of heading home, Clancy called. "You're a fast worker. My friend at the *Times Dispatch* just told me that an exposé program on local TV announced that the Virginia police had failed to interview some prominent Harnett Museum people about the theft of the Rembrandt plates—Delia Swain was at the top of the list. Apparently she showed the plates to various press people, and the commentator questioned whether the plates have been seen since."

Coleman laughed. "Great news!"

"That's not all. The family that donated the plates heard the program and called the Governor. They're a First Family of Virginia, and my pal says they have more clout in Virginia than the Arnolds and the Swains put together. The Governor called the editor of the *Times Dispatch* to ask if anyone at the paper knew anything, and somebody noticed my pal's name listed as having been in the files yesterday researching Delia, and asked him why. He told his coworkers that a *New York Times* reporter tipped him that Delia was connected to art fraud and theft. How are we doing?"

Coleman stood up, and raised a fist in the air. "Yes!" she yelled. Dolly startled, woke up and pushed against her legs. Coleman leaned down to pick her up.

"I'm sure it's good, but will you tell me what's going on?" Clancy said, his voice plaintive. "I need to be on top of this story, and I have to let my buddy in Richmond know what's happening."

Coleman brought him up to date, concluding, ". . . so we think Delia's an accomplice in the theft of the Rembrandt plates. If she's stolen those plates and let others take the blame, she deserves jail time."

"Do you have anything I can use immediately?" Clancy said.

"You have everything I have on the Print Museum, and on the two deaths. The only thing you don't have is the story about the thefts of the Dürers from the Baldorean." She filled him in, and added, "Apparently some of the big deals in England don't want the story published. I say to hell with them. They'll let a murderer escape so they won't be embarrassed about their bad security. If you want on-the-record confirmation, call Rachel Ransome at the Ransome Gallery in London, and use my name."

"My piece will be in Tuesday's paper," Clancy said. "I'll get the story about the Dürers in for sure. I'm with you about the Baldorean: it's CYA time, and I'll fix that. Thanks, Coleman."

—— Forty-Four ——

JANE PARKER CALLED Coleman early Monday morning. "Some Richmond detectives are on the way here to interview me and Delia. And reporters are calling. They want a list of every journalist who saw the plates since that Dutch scholar was here. There's only one I don't know: a reporter from the *Artful Californian*, Jennifer Norris."

"Blonde, brunette or redhead? They've got at least one of each at *Artful*," Coleman said.

"A gorgeous blonde, I'm told," Jane said.

"Judy Nelson. That's two of the *Artful* crowd who've kept their own initials when they use fake names. What dopes. I'll see if I can find a picture of her, make a jpeg, and e-mail it to you, so we can be sure. Okay?"

"Yes, but who is she?" Jane said.

341

"She used to be married to Jonathan Hathaway, who's now my cousin Dinah's husband."

"Why would she do this?"

"For the money. She's a big spender," Coleman said.

As soon as she hung up, Coleman called Debbi Diamondstein. "Debbi? Do you have any pictures of Bain's date from the Print Museum opening?"

"Jennifer Norris? The blonde with the exposed breasts? Yes, indeed, but it wasn't a date. I set it up as an interview. She said she was a freelance writer specializing in the arts."

"She's really Judy Nelson, who is: (a) Jonathan's former wife, (b) one of Simon's girlfriends, (c) a serf for Ellen Carswell, and (d) probably a thief."

"God, Coleman, how do you know all this stuff? Sounds like I threw Heyward to a lioness." Her friend was joking, but Coleman could tell that Debbi was worried.

"Yeah, afraid so. Jonathan hired a detective to follow Simon, and he had girls stashed in two hotels over the weekend, one of whom was the gorgeous Judy. We know she's Jonathan's former wife because Jonathan says so, and we think she works for Ellen because we're pretty sure she visited the Harnett Museum for the *Artful Californian* as Jennifer Norris. I want the pictures to send to the museum. If it's Judy, she's almost certainly a thief," Coleman said.

"Oh, rats. I'll messenger the pictures."

"No, I'll come to you. I'd like to get out of here for a while."

"Your news has left me faint. I'm going to have some cool clear Evian, and maybe dampen a cloth to put on my forehead. See you soon," Debbi said.

Half an hour later, Coleman sat on the white sofa in Debbi's bright red office going through photographs. Debbi lounged in the chair behind her white lacquered desk, watching Coleman.

"She *is* fabulous looking," Coleman said.

"Oh, yes, she certainly is. Coleman, what the hell is going on? Is it true someone tried to kill you? After I spoke to you, a friend called, said someone sent you poisoned candy."

"It's true. Poisoned goodies for Dolly, too. It was nicotine, I'm told. Ironic, given how I hate the stuff."

"Good grief! Are the police looking into it?"

"Yes, but they're on the wrong track. They think the poisoner's a crank, trying to get at me because of something we've printed in the magazine. They can't come up with any other possible motive—no rejected lover, no jealous wife, whatever. But I know someone tried to kill me before—you remember my mugging? I was sure it was Simon, because whoever it was wore his ghastly aftershave, but he has an alibi."

"I've always thought Simon was a creep, and I hate his aftershave, but I don't think he'd hurt you physically. He's a wimp," Debbi said.

"I still can't believe he's making love to three women simultaneously—the two in the hotels and Ellen Carswell. What in the world do they see in him?"

Debbi gaped. "Wait, wait, you lost me when you mentioned three women, including Ellen. Are you telling me that she and Simon are an item? Are you sure?"

"She alibied Simon for La Grange's murder. They were sleeping together."

"Well, you could knock me over with a feather. I thought Simon was gay. He and Heyward Bain are at it constantly, but Simon is obviously very bisexual. Three women and Heyward—you've got to hand it to him," Debbi said.

Coleman put the photographs down, and stared at Debbi. "Simon and Heyward are lovers?"

"You didn't know? Heyward's crazy about Simon. That's how Simon's managed to get so much out of the Print Museum. Simon is why I had to set Heyward up with all those models and socialites at Christmas. People were talking, and Heyward wanted to try to squelch the rumors. He's a very private man, and didn't want to see his sex life discussed in the tabloids."

"I feel like a fool, and not for the first time since all this mess started. I kept asking myself why Simon was doing so much business with the Print Museum, but it never occurred to me that he and Bain were lovers, or even that Bain is gay. I had a crush on Bain for a while," Coleman admitted.

"Heyward's gorgeous, but I don't think he swings both ways, so if I were you, I'd put that crush permanently to rest. Anyway, would you want to make love to anyone, no matter how handsome, who'd been with Simon? Ugh!"

Coleman stood up. "Perish the thought. I might get sick if I think too much about that. May I borrow these?" She held up four of the photographs.

"Sure. But tell me: is this going to be bad for Heyward and the museum? As you may recall, I *am* their PR person. I should be trying to figure out what I should do, if anything," Debbi said.

"Well, if someone who's part of Heyward's little circle gets arrested, and I'd guess one or two of them might, he's not going to look good. And if someone in that little circle is trying to kill me, that's not going to be great press for him either. But I don't think we've identified the key figure yet. We need a guy with a beard who's close to Simon, or to Ellen. Don't worry, it isn't Heyward—he's way too short. The guy we want is maybe six feet tall."

Coleman paused in the door of Debbi's office. "Debbi? If you mention any of this to Bain, and he tells Simon— well, it could mean trouble for you. Someone might think you're involved, and you might even be accused of obstruction of justice. You're my friend, and I'd like to see you out of the firing line, and definitely out of jail."

Debbi stared at Coleman, her eyes even bigger than usual. "Amen."

When Coleman left, Rob was waiting for Coleman in the elevator lobby of Debbi's building. "What a nice surprise," Coleman said.

Rob kissed her on the cheek. "May I walk you back to your office? Do you have time to stop for coffee?"

"Sure! Let's go to the Starbucks in my building."

He settled her at the table farthest away from other people, and stood in line for their coffee. When he sat down and handed her a cup, Coleman said, "Did you know Heyward Bain is gay, and having a thing with Simon?"

Rob stared at her. "I certainly did not. I don't see how Simon has time for everyone he's sleeping with."

"I know, it's astonishing. What did you have to tell me?"

"First, tell me how you feel about Bain and Simon?" Rob asked.

"Oh, when Bain first came to town, I had a crush on him, and when he didn't pay any attention to me, I convinced myself I was in love with him. If a man ignores me, I tend to fixate on him—just immature, I guess. Well, after a bit, I lost interest in Bain, and the truth is, I never knew him. I've hardly talked to him." Coleman shrugged.

He took her hand. "Well, as long as you aren't unhappy?"

She smiled. "Oh, no, I'm definitely not unhappy."

"I've been thinking about Simon and his lady friends, and wondering how much they know about each other. We might be able to stir things up by arranging a conversation about Simon's affairs for the bug," Rob said.

"Great idea! Let me see if I can come up with a good storyline. Hey, take a look at these pictures. 'Jennifer Norris' was at the Print Museum opening. Jonathan saw her there, and Judy Nelson and Jennifer Norris are one and the same. I need to get one of these photos off to Jane Parker. Someone calling herself 'Jennifer Norris,' claiming to be with *Artful*, visited the museum. She could be the thief."

"Good-looking woman. Can't imagine why she's interested in Simon. So, will you and Zeke work out a script for The Listener?" Rob prayed Zeke wasn't the traitor Tammy had painted.

"Absolutely. I'll keep you posted."

Debbi called as soon as Coleman was back in her office.

"Coleman? You know this *Beaux Arts* ball tomorrow night? Simon just asked me to get him three tickets. Do you suppose he's taking those two women he's got stashed in hotels?"

"I wouldn't be surprised. I'd forgotten about that ball. Are you going?"

"Oh yes, and you should, too. Do you want tickets?"

"Absolutely. Get me two, will you?"

"Sure. Keep in touch."

Coleman hung up, and thought about the ball. She'd read about it—guests would wear costumes. Maybe it was the opportunity she needed.

—— Forty-Five ——

MONDAY
London

Quincy called Rachel Monday to tell her he approved of her plan and the sample letter. After they'd discussed the letter, Rachel said, "Mr. Quincy, can you get a list of the Americans staying at the Randolph when the Swain woman was there?"

"I expect so, but why?" Quincy asked.

"Dinah said that Ms. Swain had an accomplice in the Dürer theft. The accomplice might have stayed at the same hotel. Americans would have to produce their passports, so we should be able to get a list of those who were at the Randolph. Dinah or that detective they've hired might recognize a name."

"An excellent idea. I'll get it for you right away."

"I also recall a cheap hotel not far from the Randolph? Is that correct?"

"Yes, Pendleton's, a shabby little place."

"Will you ask the police for a list of the Americans staying there when Ms. Swain was at the Randolph? Just in case the accomplice was there?"

"Of course. I'll fax both lists to you."

Rachel glanced at the lists, and asked Miss Manning to fax them to Dinah. A few minutes later, Dinah examined the sheets. "Well, for goodness sake!" she said to Bethany. "Delia was with a tour group at the Randolph, and Ellen Carswell was at a hotel nearby. Delia is Ellen's protégé. I wonder why they didn't stay at the same hotel?"

MONDAY

New York

Simon, sleeping soundly at the Carlyle, was wakened by the telephone. He'd asked the hotel to hold calls, but had forgotten to shut off his mobile.

It was Ellen, in a rage. "Well, you were wrong about Rachel. She's blocked you on the prints you wanted. Judy called four of the people on your list, and all of them said the same thing: the prices were too low, and Rachel had warned them that someone might try to cheat them. There's no point in calling the others."

Simon sat up. "Goddamn Rachel. I could kill that woman."

"It's over, Simon. Forget selling anything to the Print Museum," Ellen said.

"What about—?"

Ellen cut him off. "Don't say anything else on the phone. I'm at the airport, and I'll catch the first available flight to New York. Grab everything you've got on the

Print Museum—every scrap of paper—and take it all to the apartment. I'll meet you there."

———～———

When Heyward Bain telephoned Jonathan early Monday morning and asked if he could come to see him, Jonathan assumed Bain wanted to apologize for his behavior in London. But he raised a very different topic.

"How much do you know about Coleman's parents?" Bain asked.

Why in heaven's name did the man want to talk about Coleman's family? "Not much. Dinah told me her father and Coleman's were brothers, but Coleman's father was a black sheep, drank too much, maybe drugged. Coleman turned up at Slocumb Corners when she was about five, an orphan, although I don't know that I ever heard anything about her mother, nor do I know how her father died," Jonathan said.

Bain took a deep breath and expelled it. "I wouldn't be telling you anything about it, but the past is intruding on the present. Coleman's father, Andrew Greene, had a childhood sweetheart, Angela Fairgrove, who lived on the plantation next to the Greene's. She was a tiny blonde, a fairy princess, and they were together constantly. Everyone assumed they'd get married and live happily ever after.

"But the serpent entered paradise the summer Angela was fifteen." Bain cleared his throat. "May I have some water, please?"

Jonathan poured him a glass from the pitcher on his credenza. Bain took a sip, then continued. "Angela was picking wildflowers on the road that passes the drive to her home one July day, when a man stopped to ask directions. He was only a little younger than her father, and she was probably disarmed by his age—she'd been taught to be polite to her elders." Bain took out his hand-kerchief and wiped the sweat from his forehead.

"He made friends with Angela, gave her her first drink, her first cigarette, her first marijuana, and her first cocaine. In a few weeks, he'd seduced her, and before school started in September, he'd abandoned her. When she learned she was pregnant, she telephoned him. He came and got her, and he told her they'd put the baby up for adoption. But the child was a boy, and he needed an heir. He'd been mar-ried for many years and had no children.

"Angela's seducer tired of her before the baby was a month old. He kept the baby—that is, he kept me—but delivered Angela, my mother, to her parents' door late one night. She'd been missing for months, and her fam-ily hadn't heard a word from her. They were frantic with worry. They'd called the police, but the Fairgroves didn't know the identity of her seducer, hadn't even known of his existence until after she disappeared, when they learned she'd been seen with a stranger, an older man."

Heyward took another sip of water. "The girl who returned was not the girl who'd left. Angela, at sixteen, drank, smoked cigarettes, and smoked dope when she could get it. She'd also acquired some sophisticated sex-ual tastes. But she still looked like a fairy princess, and Andrew still adored her. He already had a great thirst for alcohol, but it might not have become the dominating force in his life, if he hadn't married Angela two years later.

"When her parents or Andrew asked about the time she was away, she said she'd been kidnapped and imprisoned, and had managed to escape. She claimed she didn't know the identity of her kidnapper—he called himself 'John Smith.' She never told anyone she'd had a child. Coleman was born a little over a year after their wedding, when Angela was nineteen." He wiped his forehead again. "May I have some more water, please?"

"Of course." Jonathan refilled his glass. "Does Coleman know all this?"

"I doubt if she knows any of it," Bain said.

"What happened next?"

"Angela died shortly before Coleman's second birthday. She had lung cancer, but before it could kill her, she drowned in the river near her house—maybe an accident, maybe suicide. I don't know much about Coleman's life after that—her father took her away, and as you know, she reappeared at Slocumb Corners when she was five."

Jonathan frowned. "Why are you telling me all this?"

Heyward looked at him, an odd expression on his face. "I'm Angela Fairgrove's first child."

Jonathan stood up, and began to pace. "Are you saying you're Coleman's half-brother? Same mother, different father?"

"Oh yes, but it's more complicated than that. My father—he's dead now—was also the father of Maxwell Arnold, who plotted to have Coleman gang-raped when she was at Duke. Maxwell's my half-brother."

Jonathan said, stunned. "Dinah never told me anything about a gang rape. Was Coleman hurt? Did Maxwell Arnold know who she was? Her relationship to you, I mean?"

"She wasn't hurt, at least not physically. Maxwell *did* know who she was. My half brothers hate me, especially

Maxwell. Because of me, Maxwell's not the eldest son. My father adopted me and gave me his name. I was christened Jefferson Davis Arnold.

"After my adoption, my father's first wife died, he immediately remarried, and sired three legitimate sons, all football-types like him. When he realized I was going to be small, he regretted having adopted me. Coleman and I inherited our mother's frame—she was small, like we are. In my father's eyes, I was a freak. But it was too late to get rid of me. All of his legitimate children inherited money from a trust fund set up by his father, my grandfather, and as the eldest, I got the lion's share. My father hated the sight of me, and he arranged for me to live with an African American couple in South Carolina, Heyward family servants. They were the only parents I ever knew. I started calling myself Heyward Bain when I was ten, and when I was twenty-one, I changed my name legally. Heyward was my father's mother's maiden name, and I'm the bane of the Arnolds."

"The black family you lived with were Byrds?"

Bain smiled for the first time since he'd walked into Jonathan's office. "Yes, Horace—you met him—worked for the Heywards. They lived on a plantation west of Charleston, and when the Heywards died out, I inherited the place. That's where I lived as a child. Long before I was born, Horace married Irene, a North Carolina Byrd, and took the Byrd name. The Byrd telegraph is the source of some of my information about Coleman, and her mother."

Jonathan sat down, and stared at his visitor. "I repeat: Why are you telling *me*? And why now?"

Bain sighed. "I had some enemies because of anti-tobacco activities, but when they lost interest in me, I decided to come to New York to introduce myself to Coleman. I'm not much older than she is, and I thought we might be friends. I decided to do something in the art world because of Coleman and Dinah—Dinah and I are not related, but since she and Coleman are like sisters, I wanted to get to know her, too. When Carswell's outfit came up with the idea of a print museum, I was delighted. It meshed with Dinah's interest in prints, and I thought it would make it easy for me to get to know her. I planned to tell Dinah about my relationship with Coleman, and to ask her to talk to Coleman. I tried to tell Dinah the story in December, but somehow Dinah became convinced that I was in love with Coleman, and I—well, I guess I lost it—I didn't know what to say or do, and I retreated. I hope you'll tell Dinah and Coleman," Bain said.

"I'll certainly tell Dinah. But don't you think *you* should tell Coleman?"

"I feel too awkward, too guilty. I should have done something for Coleman as soon as I knew about her. I should have at least helped her financially. I haven't had much practice with relationships, and I didn't know how to approach her. I'm sure Coleman doesn't even know I exist. I didn't know *she* existed until a couple of years ago. I got access to the family papers when I was twenty-one, but I didn't rush to look at them. I knew the Arnolds despised me, and my mother didn't want me, so the papers weren't likely to make pleasant reading. It was a mistake not to look at them. After Coleman's experience with Maxwell, I hated to tell her that Maxwell's my half-brother, and that I think he targeted her at Duke because she's my sister."

Jonathan considered him. It was irresponsible of Bain to ignore the family papers. And Bain's excuses for not helping Coleman sounded lame. Given his great wealth and the extreme poverty Coleman—and Dinah—had endured, Bain should be ashamed.

But Jonathan kept his opinion to himself. Heyward had been in his office for more than an hour, and it seemed an eternity. Jonathan wanted him to finish his story and leave. He needed to talk to Dinah, and to figure out how to tell Coleman this incredible story.

"So once again, why are you telling me now?"

Bain hesitated; then, "Is it true someone tried to poison Coleman with nicotine?"

"Yes."

"I've wondered if Maxwell could be involved."

Jonathan frowned. "Why would he do such a thing?"

"He despises me. He hates Coleman, too. He thinks Coleman made a fool of him in college, and anyway, she's my sister. I'm sure he knows that I've made over all the Arnold money I inherited to Coleman. It's in trust, but she can collect the income immediately. You probably know the Arnold money came from tobacco, which I've fought my entire life. Nicotine is the kind of thing Maxwell would use to kill, especially someone close to me."

Jonathan paced. "Is the money you're giving Coleman a large amount?"

"Oh yes, quite a lot. I've made a great deal of money, mostly from anti-smoking inventions, and I don't need or want the Arnold money. The Arnolds harmed Coleman, her mother, and her grandparents. I consider their money reparation, restitution, amends—whatever you want to call it. But because I inherited money Maxwell might have inherited, and he knows it's now Coleman's, Maxwell probably hates her even more. I'm sure he thinks the money should be his."

"But if Coleman died, the money wouldn't go to Maxwell Arnold, would it?" Jonathan asked, frowning. Could Coleman's mugging have something to do with this inheritance?

Bain shook his head. "No, of course not. As things stand now, if something happened to Coleman, Dinah would inherit, but Coleman can make a will and dispose of it however she wants. But Maxwell is stupid and irrational, he wouldn't think about it analytically. I suppose you know Maxwell accosted Dinah in November at the Four Seasons? And he threatened Coleman in Virginia the other day? I've wondered if he were Coleman's mugger and attempted poisoner."

Jonathan glared at Bain. Damn the man. He and his family were nothing but trouble, a threat to both Dinah and Coleman. "No, I knew none of that. If Coleman or Dinah had told me, I'd have arranged security for them, and reported Maxwell Arnold to the police. If he comes near either of them again, I promise you he'll go to jail. But Coleman thinks her mugging and the poison attempts are linked to your museum, and that Simon Fanshawe-Davies is involved."

Heyward stiffened. "Simon had nothing to do with it. I cannot understand why you are all so down on Simon."

"Bain, I'm out of patience with you on the topic of Simon. He's a cad. Last weekend he had two women who don't know about each other stashed away in two New York hotels—he was running back and forth between them like a rooster servicing hens. He's sleeping with Ellen Carswell, who doesn't know about the other women. He's cheating Ellen. He's cheated his partner and benefactor, Rachel Ransome—"

Bain stood up, his face red. "That's enough. Why are you telling these lies?"

Jonathan reached for a folder on his desk. "Look, Bain, Daniel Winthrop vouches for you, and he'll vouch for me, too, if you ask him about me. I don't lie. Here are the reports of the detective who followed Fanshawe-Davies all weekend." He handed Bain the folder.

Heyward skimmed through the papers. "I grant you these two women, but not Ellen Carswell. I've asked him about her, and I assure you it isn't true. As for Rachel Ransome, Simon was an inheritor under Ransome's will, and helped build the Ransome Gallery, and now Ms. Ransome wants to take away what's rightfully Simon's."

"Don't be absurd. Ms. Ransome was Ransome's housekeeper and assistant for many years. Simon never even met Ransome. He was *not* in Ransome's will. Ransome left Rachel his entire fortune, and she used part of it to pay for everything for Simon, or Jock, as he was then—his teeth, his clothes, acting lessons—because she felt sorry for him. I can prove it: look at Ransome's will. I have a copy—I got it when Simon's name and that of the Ransome Gallery started cropping up."

Heyward slapped the papers down on Jonathan's desk. "I've heard enough of this defamation. I want no part of your attempts to destroy an innocent man." He stormed out of the office and slammed the door behind him.

Jonathan shrugged. Bain was crazed on the topic of Simon Fanshawe-Davies. He wanted to speak to Dinah, but she was out, and her cellphone was off. Jonathan left word with Bethany to have Dinah call him, and asked his assistant to make a copy of Ransome's will, and have it hand delivered, faxed and emailed to Bain. He'd stuff the truth down Bain's throat, whether he wanted to learn it or not.

Unable to reach Dinah, he called Rob. He described his conversation with Bain, and concluded, "Heyward's crazy. What is it with him and Simon?"

"He's in love," Rob said.

"What? I don't understand."

"Heyward won't believe anything bad about Simon, because they're lovers—he's in love with Simon. Simon is using him, of course, but Heyward Bain can't see it."

"Oh, my God. That damn Simon would—would— fornicate with a goat. Is there anyone in New York he isn't having sex with—present company excepted?"

Rob laughed. "Debbi Diamondstein told Coleman this morning about Simon and Heyward. I haven't heard anything about a goat, but the day's young."

Jonathan wasn't amused. "Is there anything we should do about Bain's relationship with Coleman? How do you think Coleman will take it?"

"Who knows? We'll have to leave that up to her, and get on with our investigation. We should meet tonight, if you're free."

"What about eight at Cornelia Street? Dinah and I'll arrange for some sandwiches or something."

～

Dinah made Jonathan repeat Heyward's story three times. She didn't know how Coleman would react, but she had to be the one to tell her, and as soon as possible. She wouldn't call ahead. She'd appear at Coleman's office.

Coleman hated being interrupted at work, but that was too bad. This was an emergency.

Dinah started talking as soon as she entered Coleman's office.

"Coleman, you remember when Heyward Bain took me to lunch before Christmas? He'd planned to tell me something, and it wasn't that he was in love with you."

"I know. You told me. Stop worrying about that. I don't give a hoot about Heyward Bain. I can't imagine why I was ever interested in him," Coleman said.

"Brace yourself: Heyward is your half-brother, born to your mother, but by a different father."

Coleman stared at Dinah. "Are you out of your mind? I don't have a brother—you know that."

"You *do* have a brother. Your mother had a child before you, and it was Heyward. That makes him your half-brother," Dinah said.

Coleman shrugged. "I suppose anything is possible. Given my parents' alcohol and drug history, I might have several half-brothers or -sisters. Where does Heyward fit in?"

Dinah repeated the story Bain had told Jonathan about the Arnold connection, including Bain's relationship to the Arnolds, especially the awful Maxwell.

Coleman looked thoughtful. "Even if it's true, I'm not sure it matters, except it may explain Maxwell's coming after me. I wonder if he'll turn out to be my mugger? If so, how'd he get Simon's scent?

"But Coleman—you have a *brother*."

"So what? I hardly know him, let alone feel sisterly love for him. I've never understood about loving people just because they're kin. Kids who're separated from their mothers at birth don't love some woman who comes out of nowhere when they're grown up and claims to be their 'birth mother.' Kids love the women who raised them—took care of them, fed them, cuddled them. When I came to live with you and Miss Ida and Aunt Polly, no one had ever loved me, and I'd never loved anybody. Most adults hadn't treated me well, and I didn't trust them. It took a while for me to recognize Miss Ida and Aunt Polly as family. Even longer to love them. It was different with you—quicker, because you were a child."

Dinah nodded. She remembered the filthy five-year-old: precocious, stubborn, independent. Coleman had eventually learned to love Dinah and their grandmother and great-aunt, but she had formed few other intimate attachments.

"You and Miss Ida and Aunt Polly and the Byrds became my family, the only family I ever had, and it's been enough," Coleman said.

"You can't turn your back on Heyward Bain. Don't you want to get to know him? And don't you feel terrible about the story of your parents?"

"I'm sad about my parents. I wish fate had been kinder to them. But I was around my father long enough to understand that he was an alcoholic and an addict—and after I moved to North Carolina, I learned how my mother died, and about *her* drinking. As for Bain—it would have meant a lot when we were so poor and alone after Miss Ida and Aunt Polly died, to have had a loving—and rich—older brother. But after all these years? Where was he when I needed him? I'm not going to cut him dead or anything. I'll be polite when we meet, and maybe if I get to know him someday, it'll be different, but right now, I just don't care."

"Are you angry with him?" Dinah asked.

"No, not a bit. When I'm not so busy, I'll try to figure out how I feel, and what I think. I'll try to make an effort to get to know him, and look for common interests, like hating the Arnolds and tobacco, and being interested in art. Maybe we can be friends." She paused. "Can I change the subject? Rob and the troops and I have been busy. We're close to getting these creeps. Wait till you hear what I've planned."

Dinah stared at Coleman. She'd expected anger, resentment, sadness, but not lack of interest. Still, why should Coleman be interested in Bain, just because he was a relative? He was a stranger. Everything would have been different if he'd appeared earlier in their lives.

She interrupted Coleman. "We can't leave the topic of Heyward Bain yet. You may not care about having a new half-brother, but how about this: you, Coleman Greene, are unbelievably rich."

Coleman eyes widened. "Now I know you're crazy."

Dinah explained about the trust that Bain had set up for her. "It's guilt money, partly because of how the Arnolds treated your mother, and how Maxwell treated you, and probably because Heyward's so rich, and you've always had to worry about money. Please don't say you're going to reject it."

Coleman laughed. "Reject it? Are you kidding? No way! I'm going to love having money. How rich am I?"

Dinah smiled. "You'll have to ask Bain. Or maybe Jonathan can find out."

Simon had a splitting headache. Rachel had blocked him getting the prints he'd staked out in *The Record*, and even worse, Ellen was on her way to New York. She was going to pull the plug on the Print Museum project. He'd fight it, but he knew she'd made up her mind. Anyway, he couldn't come up with an argument for staying with it. She was right; there was no money in it. He could get the money from Heyward, but not enough to buy a gallery. Anyway, he didn't want any gallery. He wanted Ransome's. Most of all, he wanted Rachel out of his life. Damn, damn, damn.

Ellen was acting so bossy. All that bossiness reminded him of Rachel. He could understand Ellen's ending the print project, but he needed space. How could he have a private life, if he couldn't get to New York? He couldn't bear living in Ellen's pocket.

Her timing couldn't be worse, either. Kestrel and Owl were psyched for the ball, and he'd hinted at what he had in mind for afterward. He was sure they both knew what was up. He'd rented a suite at the St. Regis; everything was set. What would he tell Ellen? He had to think of a story about where he had to be Tuesday night. Since he'd be in costume, and so would Kestrel and Owl, even if people saw him at the ball, no one would know who he was. What Ellen didn't know wouldn't hurt her, or him, for that matter. But he wished she'd stayed in Chicago.

CORNELIA STREET
Monday Night

"So much information is pouring in, I thought we ought to get together," Rob said. "But there's no good news. Delia

Swain has been interviewed by a capable detective, and she swears she was with Jennifer Norris—aka Judy Nelson—every minute Judy was at the Harnett Museum, and that the plates were there when Judy left. Nobody believes Swain, but that's her story, and she's sticking to it. Nelson's story is the same, and she says that Jennifer Norris is her *nom de plume*. There was no intent to deceive."

"So, we can't get either of them for the missing plates?" Jonathan said.

"No, and they're not going to break—they're two tough cookies. That's not all. Swain was interviewed again about the trip to Oxford. She was with her tour group the whole time she was in Oxford. The group backs her," Rob said.

"Ellen Carswell says she visited Oxford to investigate it as a possible site for a Computer Art Research Services office. She stayed at Pendleton's to avoid Swain and her friends; she had work to do, and didn't want to be distracted. She was in London shopping the day the Dürers were stolen—went up the night before with a car and driver, stayed overnight at Brown's Hotel, came back to Oxford late the next day with the driver. Brown's and the driver confirm everything she says. Maxwell Arnold has an alibi for the time of the theft at the Baldorean. He was in Virginia with other people all day. He also has alibis for both La Grange's and Chick's deaths, and he was dining with a big group at the Virginia Country Club the night you were mugged, Coleman. He's apparently not a part of any of this," Rob continued.

"We traced Jock McLeod back to his childhood, and during the years he spent in Boston. He didn't go to Harvard using that name either. In fact, he didn't go to Harvard at all. When he was in Cambridge, he worked odd jobs, and wandered around pretending to be a student. He has no criminal record. He's a phony, but doesn't seem guilty of any crime. His family stopped hearing from him long ago, and they think he must have died."

The group was silent. Finally, Coleman spoke. "Your idea about stirring the crowd up, putting the cat among the pigeons, is our only hope. Ellen seems to be in love with Simon. I think she'll go wild when she hears about his other women, especially since they work for her. Maybe she'll turn on the women, and even on Simon. If we can split the gang up, maybe one of them will talk. Zeke and I are going to stage a show in the conference room early tomorrow morning, and talk about the *Beaux Arts* ball for the bug. We'll say we've heard Simon will be there with both of his cuties."

"Have we heard that?" Dinah asked.

"Debbi thinks he's taking them—he asked her for three tickets. Debbi's going to the ball, and I'm going, too. If there are fireworks, I don't want to miss them," Coleman said.

"Does anyone know where Ellen is?" Jonathan asked.

"Debbi says Ellen's on her way to New York, or maybe already here. She told Debbi she might stay till Friday," Coleman said.

"Does Ellen know about the ball?" Dinah wanted to know.

"If she does, she hasn't mentioned it to Debbi," Coleman said.

"If Simon's taking those two to the ball, he's not telling Ellen. The first she'll hear about them will be through you tomorrow, and she's sure to react—maybe at the ball.

I don't think you should go, Coleman. It could be dangerous," Rob said.

Coleman smiled at him. "I'm taking my guard dog, and you, too, if you'll come." She stroked Dolly, lying in her lap.

"On the topic of Simon, what do he and Ellen get up to?" Dinah said. "Since Rachel wrote about the stuff in his apartment, I'm dying to know what goes on between them."

"I'd like to know, too," Coleman said. "Crossdressing, but there's more to it than that, isn't there?" She looked at Rob.

"It's a fairly unusual perversion. Jerry Springer stuff. She's the nanny, and Simon's the baby, hence the over-sized diapers. She does to him what a nanny would do for a baby: bathes him, changes him. That fires them up, and nature takes its course," Rob said.

"Yuck," Coleman said. "If Ellen is Simon's only alibi for the night of Jimmy's death, isn't it likely that she's lying? If she's in love with him, she'd give him a false alibi."

"Maybe so, but again, if they both stick to the story, there's nothing we can do," Rob said. "The police don't have any evidence against Fanshawe-Davies, so they can't get a search warrant. That means there's no chance we'll turn up the Rembrandt plates, even if he has them. If the doctor is his accomplice, Fanshawe-Davies may have hidden the weapon used to kill Jimmy and Chick, but we can't get at that either. I don't think Simon would keep anything incriminating at the Carlyle. Too many people have access to a hotel room."

"Where would he keep stuff? Her apartment?" Coleman said.

Rob shrugged. "Who knows?"

"Has anyone investigated her background? I've always wondered if Carswell is her real name. Computer Art Research Services owned by someone whose name starts off Cars is too good to be true," Coleman said.

"It is her name, though—she's exactly who she says she is, complete with a widowed mother in Chicago," Rob said.

"Oh, well," Coleman said, "I guess it's up to the *ArtSmart* Acting Company. Now, how many tickets for the ball do we need?"

"Six," Dinah said. "The four of us, and Zeke and Bethany."

"Good plan," Coleman said. "We need all the help we can get. They'll be a big crowd at the ball, and all of us need to be alert and looking around us. With everyone in costume, it would be easy to miss someone or something."

—— Forty-Six ——

TUESDAY

COLEMAN WAS UP at five thirty, and had finished her second cup of coffee when she heard the *New York Times* hit the doormat in the hall outside her apartment. She grabbed it and turned to the arts section.

Hurray for Clancy! He reported that Bain was returning the Dürers to the Baldorean, and that Simon had bought them for the Print Museum. He wrote that Coleman and Dinah had discovered that the Rembrandt plates were missing from the Harnett Library, and that *Sleeping Kitten*, bought by Simon for the Print Museum, was thought to be a restrike, made from one of the stolen plates. He mentioned Jane's and Delia's names as receiving the people who'd come to see the plates, and that Jane had been exonerated by a visiting Dutch scholar. He didn't say anything bad about Delia, he just didn't cite a witness who'd cleared her. A perfect job.

Coleman turned to her computer. The *Artful Californian Online* had taken the bait: the rats had devoted the entire issue to the art climbers she and Zeke had discussed. The writer hadn't used real names, but the descriptions and nicknames were so explicit that few readers would fail to recognize the climbers. The newsletter was going to infuriate a number of people—some of them pretty influential—but more important, there was no longer any doubt: The bug belonged to the *Artful Californian*, replacing Tammy the Spy. Could anything happen at that organization without Ellen's knowledge and involvement? Not likely. Ellen *must* be the mastermind behind the plot to steal Coleman's ideas, and damage *ArtSmart*. She'd probably expected Coleman's backers to have ousted her by now. But her plan had been thwarted, and tonight could lead to her total defeat.

"Are you ready?" Coleman whispered to Zeke in the hall outside the conference room. He nodded. When they were seated at the big table, Coleman said, "Let's talk about the *Beaux Arts* Ball at the Sorcerer's Club tonight. You'll be there, won't you?"

"I wouldn't miss it," Zeke said.

"Keep your eyes open for anything we can use in the magazine. We'll have a photographer there, but if people keep their masks on, we won't necessarily recognize anyone. Try to spot celebrities." Coleman's instructions were not just window dressing; the ball would be featured in *ArtSmart*. If she hadn't been so preoccupied, she'd have long ago arranged to have it covered.

"Do you know what anyone is wearing?" Zeke said.

"I heard Simon Fanshawe-Davies is going as a raven." Coleman held her hand up so he could see her crossed fingers. "And we know he'll have both his secret loves with him."

"Why would he want both of them there?" Zeke said. "Sounds like a ticklish situation to me."

"Oh, he's showing off. Now that we know he's the unattractive Jock McLeod from Long Island, who didn't go to Harvard or a top-notch English boarding school, it's easy to understand why he needs all the signs of sexual prowess he can get. He has to reinforce his pathetic self-image," Coleman said.

"I feel sorry for Ellen and Rachel. Rachel Ransome supports him, pays to have his teeth fixed, pays for acting school, and he cheats her every chance he gets. Ellen Carswell finances him, does who knows what for him, and he cheats her with her friends and employees," Zeke said.

"I wonder if Judy and Delia would find Simon attractive if they knew he wore diapers so Ellen can put on her nanny outfit and change him? Wait—I have an idea. You know that guy who does caricatures, the Al Hirschfeld wannabe? Let's get him to make cartoons of Simon and Ellen as a baby and nanny for the magazine. Wouldn't that be a hoot? We won't explain that we're making fun of their sex life. People will think it's the obvious—he's a mama's boy, and she takes care of him."

"Simon's sex life could take up an entire issue. Now that we know that he and Heyward are lovers, are you going to use it in the Print Museum story?" Zeke asked.

Coleman shook her head. "I can't see why it would be relevant, or even news. Debbi says Bain's sexual preference is widely known, thanks to Simon's big mouth. Apparently *ArtSmart*—yours truly—was the last to know. I didn't understand until she explained that all that publicity Debbi arranged at Christmas was a cover-up for Bain's being gay—he prefers privacy, but didn't know Simon would brag about their relationship. I'm not usually that dense, but I had a lot on my mind.

"Okay, I think that's everything. I'm due at another meeting in a few minutes. Is there anything else we need to talk about before the ball tonight? No? Okay, see you later." Coleman was longing to bring Rob up to date on *Artful Online*, and to let him know that there was no longer any doubt about who placed the bug. So much that had happened remained inexplicable, it was good to have proof of a solid fact.

———～———

Simon, exhausted after a night of wrangling with Ellen, dragged himself back to his suite at the Carlyle. She had, as he'd expected, shut down the print project. Worse, she'd *ordered* Simon to come to Chicago to help with the move to Los Angeles. Well, Ellen could go to hell. He'd tell her so, too, if she weren't holding all the money. He was even more financially dependent on her than he'd been on Rachel. He wished he hadn't let it happen, but for the moment, he couldn't figure out what to do about it.

At least he'd escape from her tonight. He'd told Ellen he was spending the evening with Bain and a print dealer. He had to make sure Heyward would confirm his story. He lay down on the bed and picked up the phone. When Horace put him through to Bain, he said, "Heyward, love, Ellen is after me to do some truly tedious things tonight."

"Like fucking her?" Bain said. His voice had an unfamiliar edge.

"Of course not. Why do you say that? I've told you there's nothing sexual between Ellen and me. Why do you keep bringing it up?" Heyward was a jealous and possessive bore, but Simon had to keep him sweet.

"Everyone says you're lovers, and that you both admit it."

"Heyward, you *know* Ellen gave me an alibi for the night La Grange was killed. She told the police we spent the night together—but as you very well know, I spent that night with you. You didn't want people to know that, remember?" Simon was constantly having to say he was someplace he hadn't been. Pretty soon he wasn't going to remember where he was supposed to have been, or when he was supposed to have been there, never mind with whom.

"Oh, is *that* the night they meant? I thought—well, never mind Ellen. What about the two women you've been visiting in their hotel rooms? Weren't you with them either?"

Heyward was far too well-informed about Simon's activities. Where was he getting his information? "Business, all business," Simon said. "Both of the women are Ellen's employees and they've helped get prints for you. You know a great deal about my tedious little life. Have you had someone following me?" His tone was deliberately arch to mask his fury.

"No, the Greene crowd has," Heyward said.

"*They've* had someone following me? Whatever for?" What could they have learned? They'd have discovered Kestrel and Owl, but he wasn't hiding them from anyone but Ellen and Heyward. Ellen still didn't know; if she did, she'd sure as hell have brought it up last night. Fortunately, Heyward would believe anything Simon told him. The fool was besotted.

Simon was proud of his seduction of Heyward. Until he met Simon, the poor idiot hadn't admitted, even to himself, that he was attracted to men. Heyward was in love with Simon, which was handy for getting money, but Bain wanted to be with Simon all the time, and that was a drag. He acted like a teenaged girl. On the other hand Ellen, insanely jealous of other women, was tolerant of his relationship with Heyward. She saw it as a "boys will be boys" kind of thing, and chalked it up as a leftover from the English boarding school Simon had told her he'd attended.

"They're sure you're up to something, and they're trying to find out what. *Are* you guilty of anything?" Heyward said.

Simon sighed. "Good Lord, no. Well, let them follow me. All they're doing is wasting their money. But back to why I called: I told Ellen I'd be with you tonight. Will you back me up?"

"Do you mean we can spend the evening together? Shall we go out to dinner? Where would you like to go?"

Heyward was so thrilled at the prospect of an evening with Simon, it was a shame to have to deflate him. "No, no, you misunderstand me. I have another commitment. I'm investigating the possibility of some outstanding prints for you."

"Why would Ellen object to that? I don't see why you don't tell her the truth."

Simon took a deep breath and exhaled. "She *does* object. I'm a part-owner of her business, and she wants me to work on projects that are important to *her*. She says there's not enough money in your project to justify the time." At least that part was true.

"Shall I speak to her? There could be much more money in it, if you can find the right prints."

"No, no, leave it for the moment. Let's have dinner tomorrow night. It's been too long since we've had private time together. We can talk about it then." Making a date with Heyward would keep him quiet for a few hours, and Simon wanted nothing to ruin the evening ahead.

———✦———

"Debbi, it's Coleman. I need four more tickets for the ball. Dinah and Jonathan and Bethany and Zeke want to go. Possible?"

"Sure. Anything else?"

"Yes, would you offer a ticket to Bain? Tell him Simon will be there with two guests. And offer a ticket to Ellen, too. Tell her the same story."

"Blood might flow," Debbi warned.

"I kind of hope it does. I'd like to see this thing blown wide open, and have it over."

Rob was relieved to get Coleman's message about the *Artful Californian Online*, but furious with Ms. Isaacs. What the devil was the woman playing at? Zeke must know why she'd lie about him. He dialed Zeke's number. "Zeke, why would Tammy Isaacs try to incriminate you?"

"Oh God, is she still bad-mouthing me? Rob, this is so embarrassing—"

"Never mind that. What's going on?"

"A while back she decided I was a good matrimonial prospect, and pursued me like a man-eating tiger," Zeke said. "I took her out a couple of times just to be polite, and I told her we could be friends, but there was nothing else going. She wouldn't listen, so I leveled with her:

I told her I was in love with Coleman. She went crazy. She's hardly spoken to me since."

"Aha. A woman scorned. I suppose that's why she hates Coleman?"

"Part of it, maybe. But I think she's always detested Coleman. She's jealous of Coleman's talent, her success, her attractiveness," Zeke said.

"Okay. Got it. Thanks."

"Wait. What did she do? What did she say I did?"

"Another time. See you later." Rob hung up and dialed Isaacs's number."Ms. Isaacs? We have proof that the listening device at *ArtSmart* belongs to your erstwhile employer, and has nothing to do with Zeke Tolmach. Don't call me again, or anyone connected with Coleman Greene, or *ArtSmart*. If you do, I'll come after you for harassment. And I've told that idiot receptionist at *ArtSmart* if she talks to you again, she's out of a job. Have a good life—ideally in some other country!" Rob slammed down the phone. He rarely allowed himself the luxury of that kind of explosion, but if anyone deserved it, that woman did.

Coleman was going to the ball as Bo Peep, with Dolly as her sheep. Rob, annoyed because Coleman wouldn't stay away from the ball, had reluctantly agreed to attend as a New York City cop, wearing his old uniform.

Bethany was Cleopatra, in a slinky cloth of gold outfit she'd made herself, with a fake asp around her neck. Zeke was Mark Antony in a toga and wreath. Dinah was a swan, in a slim white evening dress with a swansdown jacket, and a swan half-mask. Jonathan was wearing a matching black swan's mask, with black tie. They hired two cars with drivers—parking would be a nightmare—and planned to arrive about ten.

———— ∼ ————

Simon picked up the nestlings at their hotels in a stretch limo. They were wearing the costumes and masks he'd ordered, and they looked exactly as he'd fantasized. He'd asked that neither of them speak in the car, because he didn't want them to reveal their identities to each other until later. They knew each other, but they were unrecognizable in their costumes, and he was sure they didn't know that he was involved with both of them.

Kestrel didn't mind being quiet, and she loved being told what to do. But Owl was sulking. That woman loved to talk. Well, she could shut up or ship out. He had to put up with Ellen, but not Owl. When she'd argued with him, he'd told her if she said one more word, he'd shove her out of the car, and she could find her own way to wherever she wanted to go. Ellen had exhausted his patience, and although he was looking forward to his late night activities with the nestlings, until then they'd better mind their p's and q's. He'd cancel the entire evening before he took any more backtalk from a woman.

———— ∼ ————

"My goodness, what a mob," Dinah said.

"Debbi says they sold over a thousand tickets. The Sorcerer's Club can handle the crowd because they have three ballrooms. One of them is set up with tables for supper, and another is reserved for under-thirties with less expensive tickets. But this one, where Peter Duchin is playing, is where the people who interest us will turn up." Coleman was already taking notes.

The vast room was alive with floating red, yellow, blue, and green balloons, and the ceiling was draped in sails and banners in the same colors. The orchestra played at one end, and the dance floor swirled with vividly dressed figures. Bars, manned by bartenders in clown costumes in the colors of the decorations, were set up at intervals along the walls.

"How will we find anyone in this crowd?" Zeke asked.

"If Simon comes as a raven, he'll be conspicuous," Coleman said. "I can't imagine anyone else wanting to wear an ugly black costume. Everyone's wearing bright colors."

"I see a raven," Jonathan said, who was looking towards the ballroom entrance.

They peered through the crowd at the tall figure dressed as a black bird, with a big black beak and huge feathered wings. He was accompanied by two smaller figures, costumed as a white owl and a hawk.

"We should split up and take turns following them," Coleman said. "I can't get too near them. If Simon sees me up close he'll know me. I should have worn a mask." She glanced down at her blue and white flounces, at the beribboned basket holding Dolly, and at her shepherdess's crook. She'd tried to think of something less girly, but it was hard to design a great costume for a person of her height. In the end, she'd run out of time, and had remade an old evening dress. Her huge white hat with trailing blue ribbons over a wig with long dark curls disguised her, at least from a distance.

"It would help if you told us what you thought was going to happen," Dinah said.

Coleman shrugged. "I don't know. We just have to watch the cast of characters, and see what they do. Look for Heyward Bain. I expect he'll wear a costume that plays to his size, since he can't disguise it." Coleman said.

"Like what?" Zeke asked.

"A toy soldier? Tom Thumb? He might get angry when he sees Simon with his lady friends, but he's too controlled to make a scene. But I think Ellen will crack. By now she's heard the tapes." Coleman was scanning the room, trying to spot celebrities for the magazine, keeping an eye on Simon and his companions, hoping to see Bain and Ellen.

"Will Ellen wear a nanny costume?" Dinah said.

"What do you think, Rob? You haven't said a word."

"I don't like any of this, and I don't think you should be here. I think you're in danger. We should leave," Rob said.

"Well, stay close to me. That's not so awful, is it?"

"Why don't you and Dinah and Bethany go home? I'll stay here with Jonathan and Zeke to see if anything happens," Rob said.

"Not a chance," Coleman said.

"Coleman, look at Debbi," Dinah said.

Debbi was magnificent as a dragon. She wore a strapless green bodysuit covered in glitter, and spangled tights. She held a green sequined tail draped over one arm, and her half-mask had giraffe-like eyelashes.

"Did the fish bite?" Coleman said, after she'd complimented Debbi's costume.

"Hook, line, and sinker. I took some papers to Heyward's, and Ellen stopped by while I was there. I told them that Simon was going to the ball, and that he'd taken three tickets. I thought Heyward was going to pass out. As for Ellen—God, I'd sooner face a gorgon. They each took a ticket. I'm sure they'll come, and I plan to avoid them." Debbi pretended to shiver, and shed a few sequins.

"Any idea what either of them will be wearing?" Coleman said.

"Not a clue," Debbi said.

"Let's spread out, and look for Bain and Ellen," Coleman said. "Jonathan, why don't you and Dinah head directly opposite where we are? Over there, by that bar."

Jonathan, with Dinah on his arm, was barely out of sight when Bethany called out, "Coleman, look! There's a doctor! It's my doctor! Look at the beard!" She was standing on tiptoe, jumping up and down, pointing across the room.

"Zeke, you and Bethany try to get near that doctor. See if you can find out who he is, or at least how much of that beard and hair is a disguise," Coleman said. Zeke and Bethany pushed their way through the throngs of costumed figures towards the tall figure in white standing near the entrance.

"Damn it, I can't see a thing. I *hate* being short," Coleman said to Debbi. Setting Dolly's basket on the bar, Coleman used her crook to help her climb up on it. From her new vantage point she had a great view of the ballroom. She ignored the staring bartenders, who were probably going to tell her to get down.

A disturbance at the door distracted them. The doctor had forced his way through the crowd towards the raven. When he closed in on the big black figure, he pulled a club from the bag he carried, and without warning, smashed it into the feathered head.

The raven's mask disintegrated, leaving Simon's blond head and startled face visible. The doctor struck Simon repeatedly. As if paralyzed, none of the shocked bystanders attempted to stop him. Blood covered Simon's face and his hair and spattered all over costumed guests standing nearby. Simon staggered and collapsed to the floor, vanishing from view. The crowd struggled to get as far from the doctor and his blood-covered weapon as possible. Men shouted and women screamed for the police, for security, for help.

The doctor apparently noticed the owl and the hawk for the first time, both covered in blood, both staring down at the floor where Simon must lie. The doctor struck out at them, and when they collapsed, he turned and tried to force his way through the crowd towards the entrance.

Rob looked up at Coleman. "Get down. I'll take you home."

"No way," she shouted, struggling to make herself heard above the din. "I'm okay. The danger's near the door. Catch the doctor if you can."

"Go on," Debbi yelled. "I'll stay with Coleman."

Rob hesitated, then, holding his courtesy police badge above his head, he bellowed, "Security. Coming through." The crowd parted, and he disappeared into the swarm of people struggling to get away from the assailant and his victims.

The doctor was making little headway. New arrivals, unaware of the attacks, pushed their way into the room. The doctor was trying to move against the tide. Those who'd seen the white-clad figure's vicious attack struggled to reach an exit. A fire alarm clamored, and sirens shrieked in the street below.

Coleman began to fear a crowd catastrophe where people were crushed, even killed, trying to escape. But so far, costumed guests were exiting freely through three of the four formal exits, and the crowd was shrinking. Only the main entrance remained blocked with people. No one had tried the two emergency exits.

Heyward Bain appeared, dressed as Lautrec's *Midget*— top hat, white tie, and tails. He climbed up on the bar beside Coleman. She nodded, but didn't turn her head to look at him. She was concentrating on the group clustered around the area where Simon had fallen.

"Who are the people in the bird costumes with Simon?" Bain asked.

"Judy Nelson and Delia Swain. We think they're both involved with Ellen and Simon in the schemes to cheat you," Coleman said, still staring at the spot where Simon and his companions had fallen to the floor. The noise level had dropped, as the crowd diminished. It was no longer necessary to shout.

"Did you see it from the beginning? What happened"

"The doctor—there, near the entrance door, in the whites, with the black beard—came up and started hitting Simon with a club. The first blow got him in the mouth. It was horrible—teeth and blood flew everywhere—and the doctor kept hitting him till Simon fell down. Then the doctor struck out at the women—the birds—and they fell, too, but I don't think they were hurt. They probably realized it was the only way to escape the blows."

A group of uniformed police, followed by a cluster of medical technicians, shoved their way into the ballroom. Seeing them, the doctor changed direction, and headed toward the rear exit. Coleman couldn't make out his features—he wore a black stocking cap, black hair fell to his shoulders and covered his brow, and a heavy beard disguised his mouth and chin.

"Who do you think it is?" Bain said.

"I don't know. We never found a tall man connected to Simon. Could it be Maxwell Arnold?"

"Maxwell's tall enough, and rotten through and through, but I can't see him making a public attack like this. He'd creep up behind his victim in a dark alley. I'm going to see how badly Simon's hurt, and where they're taking him." Bain signaled with his hand, and one of his musclemen appeared. Bain jumped down from the bar, and the two of them pushed through the crowd, the huge guard forcing an opening.

Debbi looked up at Coleman. "You're safe here—the action's across the room. I'd better go with Heyward. I'm going to have work to do." She followed in their wake.

The figure in bloodstained white continued to force his way through the crowd. The shrinking crowd, frightened or repelled, struggled to keep their distance from him. The doctor twisted and turned, moving like an eel, until, as if by magic, he disappeared. Coleman stared at the spot where she'd last seen the white coat. The doctor had covered the bloody white jacket that drew every eye with a long black raincoat—an incredible feat of trompe l'oeil. His pursuers, bewildered, looked around them. Their quarry had inexplicably disappeared. Coleman tried to catch Rob's eye, but he, as puzzled as the others, scanned the room for the white coat.

Oh God, the doctor was coming straight towards her. The bartenders who'd been on duty at the bar where she stood had deserted their posts, and she couldn't see anyone she knew. If the doctor attacked her, how would she protect herself? The shepherdess's crook was a toy, and would break instantly. Maybe a bottle?

Coleman grabbed a bottle of red wine, prepared to make a stand. But the figure in the black raincoat ignored her, and veered towards the emergency exit behind Coleman's perch. In seconds, he'd be out of the ballroom and down the stairs. "Speak, Dolly," she commanded.

Dolly jumped out of her basket and began to bark at the top of her lungs. Faces turned toward Dolly and Coleman, and should have spotted the doctor, but the black coat was like Harry Potter's cloak of invisibility. No one recognized the figure as Simon's attacker.

It was up to her. Given their relative size, Coleman felt like Dolly attacking a Weimaraner, but she had no choice. She took a deep breath and launched herself into the air, tackling the tall black-coated figure, who tumbled to the floor beneath her.

Coleman was on top, but her right side hit the hard wood of the ballroom. The little dog jumped to the floor, and followed Coleman, still barking shrilly. The wine bottle lay in shards around Coleman, and red wine stained her ruffles and Dolly's white fur.

Coleman was in agony. She was sure she'd broken her shoulder. Her right arm was useless, and she'd hit her head. She felt dizzy and faint, but the killer was struggling to turn over and grab her. If she were going to be killed, she'd damned well see her killer. She pulled at the beard with her good left hand, but the whiskers wouldn't come off. She grabbed at the stocking cap, and it came away, bringing with it the black wig. A mass of red curls tumbled out.

Good God, the doctor was Ellen Carswell.

Ellen managed to turn, making a horrible hissing noise as she reached for Coleman, but Dolly sunk her sharp little teeth into the arm that was trying to snake itself around Coleman's neck. Ellen screamed, and the crowd closed in. Coleman heard Dinah say something she couldn't understand, and Rob's voice shouting, "Out of the way! Police!" He pulled Coleman to her feet, and she nearly fainted with pain. Someone picked up Dolly and held her out to Coleman.

Coleman, holding the dog with her left arm, watched Rob handcuff Ellen Carswell.

Ellen was almost unrecognizable. Her eyes bulged, and the black beard covered her mouth and chin. She was still making that horrible hissing noise.

"Get Coleman out of here," Rob told someone. "She'll have to talk to the police, but not tonight. I'll deal with that. She should see a doctor. Maybe one of the emergency people can help." His voice faded, and the room went dark.

—— Forty-Seven ——

COLEMAN, FRUSTRATED, HELPLESS, and fuzzy-headed with painkillers, sat in Dinah and Jonathan's living room in front of a blazing fire. Her right shoulder was broken, and her useless arm was in a sling. Despite all the pills, she felt excruciating pain. She had three cracked ribs—her sides hurt every time she breathed—and she was black and blue all over. Her head ached from a slight concussion, and with her two black eyes, she looked like a bedraggled panda.

When she'd spent a night and a day in the hospital, and the doctor had said she could leave, she'd planned to go to her own apartment. But when she realized she couldn't hook her bras, or pull on tights, or wash her hair, or even hold a pencil, let alone walk and feed Dolly, she'd agreed to stay in Dinah's guestroom until she was better able to take care of herself and her dog.

Dolly, who'd been to the groomer to have the blood and red wine washed away, was sparkling white, and snuggled beside her on the sofa. Coleman envied Dolly her clean fur. Her own hair was a rat's nest of blood, tangles, wine, who knew what.

"Tell me everything," she commanded Rob, who'd come by to cheer her up.

"You know everything I know," Rob said. "Try to get your mind on something else. You shouldn't keep dwelling on Tuesday night."

Coleman groaned. Bossy and patronizing again. "Rob, I've had so many painkillers I hardly know my own name. Pretend I know nothing, and talk. I can't remember much since the ball, except pain and doctors. I'll never see a white coat again without feeling nauseated."

Rob nodded. "All right, here goes: Ellen was the master criminal. She says she killed Jimmy because he was threatening Simon, wanted more money, and said he'd talk if he didn't get it. She was your mugger, and your would-be poisoner. She tried to kill Baker and Dolly. She says Simon doesn't like ugly dogs. They're 'nasty and they bite,' and 'Nanny didn't want little Simon hurt.' She says you're nosy, and you 'chased after Simon.' Chick was nosy, too, and like Jimmy, you both threatened Simon.

"She used the club she was carrying Tuesday night to kill both Jimmy and Chick. She wore the doctor outfit when she killed Jimmy, and was a bearded man in jeans and a sweatshirt when she killed Chick. She says she did it all without Simon's knowledge. Simon never did anything 'bad.' By giving Simon a false alibi for La Grange's death, she alibied herself, but I don't think anyone ever suspected her of the violent crimes. I certainly didn't."

"And the thefts?" Coleman said.

"She stole the Dürers, and she borrowed Delia's car to do it. Delia knew Ellen took her car, but Ellen says Delia didn't know how it was being used until later. Ellen went to London with a driver when she said she did, but she came back to Oxford in a rental car, parked it outside of town, and took a taxi to the Randolph. She drove to the Baldorean and back to the Randolph in Delia's car, returned to London in her rental car, and finally came back to Oxford with the driver. Ellen planned the Rembrandt plate theft, Delia set it up, Judy took them, and Ellen managed the restrike. She said an ordinary commercial printer in Chicago made it, on paper she obtained from an antique book dealer. She isn't naming names, but I'm not sure any crime was committed until the print was sold."

"Is Ellen insane?" Coleman asked.

"Maybe she is now. Who knows? But I don't think she was crazy during most of her criminal activities. It was more about money and power than she's admitting."

"How about Simon's girlfriends? How are they?" Coleman asked.

"Neither Delia nor Judy was hurt at the ball. They had the presence of mind to fall to the floor as soon as the doctor took a swing at them. They say the theft of the Rembrandt plates was a 'prank,' they 'borrowed' the plates, and Delia planned to return them before they were missed, but they were missed sooner than they expected. They swear they knew nothing about any restrikes. The police have searched Ellen's apartment, and the plates were there, with two more restrikes of *Kitten*. The plates will go back to the museum, and the restrikes will be destroyed."

"What about Maxwell? Did he have any part in this?" Coleman said.

"None. His harassment of you and Dinah is totally unconnected to Ellen's activities. He's been warned, and I don't think he'll bother you again."

"And Simon isn't guilty of anything?"

"I'm sure he knew about the theft of the Rembrandt plates, and he must have set up the theft of the Dürers—he was the only one who knew about them—but he won't admit anything, and Ellen won't testify against him. The British won't prosecute him, and neither will Bain. I doubt if the Harnett Museum will prosecute anyone, not with Chairman Daddy's little Delia involved, and the plates back where they belong.

"I'm guessing Delia and Judy will have their hands slapped, but as far as I can tell, the police have absolutely nothing on Simon. He'll walk away with a pretty new face and beautiful new teeth, courtesy of Heyward Bain. Bain's been at the hospital with Simon, dealing with police and bad publicity, lawyers and who knows what—but Dinah says Bain found the time to send you flowers?"

"Yes," Coleman said. "Nice of him, especially with all he had going on. But since we can't prove Simon guilty of anything, does that mean poor Rachel is stuck with him?"

"Afraid so, but Simon is co-owner of everything Ellen owned. She's going to be out of the picture for a long time. When everything's settled, Simon could end up rich. He might lose interest in Rachel."

"I doubt it. He's tied to the past and to Rachel by hate and envy," Coleman said.

"If you had it to do over, would you still put on the act for the bug and set them all up?" Rob asked. "I can't forget

I suggested it, but I didn't expect Ellen to try to kill Simon right in front of us."

Coleman shuddered. "I've been thinking about that ever since I saw Ellen bash Simon in the face. It was horrifying. But I'd do it again. Someone who'd killed twice wasn't going to stop, and I was on the hit list. Self-preservation was part of my motivation, I'm sure. I didn't enjoy throwing myself off that bar and tackling her, but I'd do that again, too. Someone had to stop her.

"But there won't be a next time. You were right—detecting is too dangerous." She stroked Dolly, who snuggled closer and licked her hand.

"I hope you never run into anything like this again," Rob said.

"I'm sure I won't. I'm going to be too busy. As soon as I'm able to get around, I'm going to buy another magazine. I've always wanted to run more than one, and now I have the money."

He stared. "Not the *Artful Californian?*"

Coleman laughed. "Oh, no. Something in an entirely different field—the art world can be soooo quiet and boring. I need a little excitement."

Acknowledgements

MY THANKS FOR the support, encouragement and assistance of Marilyn Breslow, Susan Cheever, Kenny Cook, Bert Fields, Amanda Foreman, Barbara Guggenheim, Susan Kinsolving, Susan Larkin, Elisabeth Norton, Mollie and John Julius Norwich, Alexandra Penney, Betty Richards and Noreen Tomassi. A very special thank you to Emma Sweeney, my wonderful agent, and above all, thanks to Dave.

EXCERPTS FROM

Fatal Impressions
Coleman and Dinah Greene Mystery No. 2

——— Chapter One ———

T HIS MONDAY IN March was the happiest day of Coleman Greene's life.

The people she liked best had gathered to celebrate with her. Long before she bought *ArtSmart*, her first magazine, she'd dreamed of owning a family of publications—perhaps ten, or even more. Today, with the acquisition of *First Home*, she—Coleman Greene, thirty-three years old, with financial help from her brother—was a step closer to making that dream come true. In the five years she'd owned *ArtSmart*, she'd changed it from a dowdy flop into the most successful art magazine in New York. She'd do even better with *First Home*. And then on to the next one.

Coleman looked around at the glittering crowd. So New York: artists, actors, antique dealers, landscape gardeners, architects. People Coleman had written about in

ArtSmart. People she hoped to persuade to write for *First Home*. Her cousin, Dinah, ravishing in a lavender-blue silk suit Coleman had designed and made, with her husband, Jonathan Hathaway. Debbi Diamondstein, not only a friend but Coleman's publicist, who had arranged the lunch at the hot new restaurant on Central Park South. The immense windows allowed guests to see almost to the north end of the park—a spectacular view. A pianist played music from *South Pacific, Phantom, Les Misérables* and other Broadway hits in a corner of the room. A buffet enticed the guests with delicious odors: smoked salmon, miniature crab cakes, tiny toasted cheese sandwiches, garlicky lamb on skewers. Huge vases of forsythia and pussy willow, and smaller bowls of yellow tulips and daffodils decorated every surface, their delicate scent heralding the approach of spring. The perfect party.

Uh, oh. Not quite perfect: a man she knew and detested, greasy black hair hanging to his shoulders and in his face, black tee shirt and torn jeans, was mingling in the crowd. Trying to act invited. As if.

Debbi appeared at her side. "What's the matter, Sunshine? You were glowing, and now you look like a thundercloud. Cheer up, Madame Media Mogul, this is your big day! And you look great. That satin suit is exactly the shade of the daffodils and your hair—clever choice."

"Two magazines don't a mogul make, but just wait, someday I will be one. Meanwhile, I just spotted that no-talent photorealist who calls himself Crawdaddy. He never stops badgering me to write an article about him. He calls me all the time, and turns up in places where he knows he'll see me. He's close to being a stalker. How in heaven's name did *he* get in?"

Debbi shrugged. "A few crashers always make it through the cracks no matter how tight the security. I can have him thrown out, but he'll make a scene."

"No, I'll ignore him. I won't let him get anywhere near me."

But a few minutes later when she and Dinah were standing by the piano listening to "Some Enchanted Evening," Crawdaddy shoved his way between them, threw his long simian arms over their shoulders, and shouted "Photo op." A flashbulb went off in their faces.

Within seconds, Jonathan had appeared, froze Crawdaddy with what Debbi called the Hathaway Sneer, developed during several centuries of being THE Hathaways, rich and in the top echelons in Boston, and rescued Dinah. Coleman, holding her breath against the stench of Crawdaddy's body odor, struggled to remove the heavy arm wrapped around her. She was thinking of kicking the creep when Rob Mondelli appeared. Rob had been a New York City policeman and played college football, and looked it, though many years had passed since he'd scored a touchdown, or arrested a mugger. His business today, specializing in art-related crime, rarely brought him into contact with violence, but lots of gym time kept him fighting fit.

"Come have some lunch," he said. He removed Crawdaddy's arm as if it were weightless, and whisked her away from the interloper.

Good old Rob—protective, warm, kind. Always there when she needed him and a lot of the time when she didn't. He was nagging her to marry him, and she hadn't been able to convince him that wasn't going to happen. She sighed. She had to do something about Rob. But not today. She wanted today to be perfect, unmarred by unpleasant conversation. Rob remained at her side until the last guest left, and walked her and Dolly, the tiny Maltese who accompanied Coleman everywhere, to her office. In the building lobby, he kissed her lightly, and said, "I wish you'd come with me to Europe. I'm seeing a number of clients about security issues, but I won't be working all the time—and wouldn't you like to meet some of these museum people? Collectors? Anyway, I won't have to work all the time, and we could have a lot of fun."

"Goodness, Rob, I couldn't leave now even if I wanted to. And I can't think of anything more fun than my new magazine. But you have a good time." She looked at her watch. "You better go, or you'll miss your plane." She tried to hide her impatience to get to work, but he looked like a spanked puppy, and she knew she'd failed. Well, too bad. She was glad he was going out of town. She didn't have time for him right now, and the fact that he didn't understand the importance of *First Home* and her joy in it showed how little he understood her.

It was after four when she arrived at her *ArtSmart* office. She groaned when she saw the stack of messages. She flipped through them. Mostly congratulations, and calls from reporters responding to the morning press release announcing the acquisition. Hmm, here was something different: a hand delivered letter from Sweeney & Kaufman, investment bankers. She ripped it open.

Dear Ms. Greene:

On behalf of my client, a major publicly held media company, I am pleased to present this offer to acquire CG Holdings, LLC.

My client, who prefers to remain anonymous at this time, is prepared to pay twice your current rate of annual revenues, subject, of course, to normal due diligence procedures. Furthermore, my client wishes you to remain as chief executive officer of CG Holdings, LLC, and editor in chief of *ArtSmart* and *First Home* for a period of no less than two years, during which time your annual compensation will be $250,000 per year, or twenty-five percent of the annual pre-tax, pre-incentive compensation income of CG Holdings, LLC, whichever is greater.

Very truly yours,
Richard C. Sweeney

She frowned. News of the acquisition of *First Home* couldn't have reached the writer much before noon. The letter had arrived less than six hours later. Fast work, and presumptuous. Why did these people think she'd want to sell? *ArtSmart* was her beloved creation. *First Home* was her new baby. Not a very attractive enfant at the moment, but with potential. What was going on?

When she called Jonathan, who was her business manager as well as Dinah's husband, he explained that maybe they didn't necessarily think she wanted to sell. "Could be their client hoped to buy *First Home*, and you got there first. Or maybe they wanted *ArtSmart* and you, even before you acquired *First Home*. I know Rick Sweeney. Do you want me to talk to him?"

"Would you? Tell him I won't sell at any price."

Jonathan laughed. "I can tell him, but he won't believe it. He'll say everything is available at a price."

She twisted a curl around her forefinger. "Well, can you tell him I don't need money?"

"No, I'll tell him you appreciate his offer, but aren't interested—that the magazines are your true love as well as your livelihood. But the buyer might keep trying."

Coleman swallowed, trying to make the dryness in her mouth go away. "They can't make me sell, can they?" she asked.

"They won't want to. I'm sure they want *you*. A forced sale wouldn't make you a happy employee."

When she'd thanked him and hung up, she selected a message slip, and punched in the number of *Publishing News*. She tried to forget about the letter, but the thought of it prickled like a tiny splinter, invisible, but a constant source of discomfort. The golden glow of the happiest day of her life hadn't vanished, but it had dimmed. She wished the letter hadn't come today of all days. She couldn't think about it now; she had work to do.

—— Chapter Two ——

DINAH LOOKED AT her watch. 11:25. She'd been in this uncomfortable reception room for two hours. If she sat in this torturous chair much longer, she wouldn't be able to stand. She needed to move around, and she should let Bethany know she'd be late getting back to the gallery. She'd call from the elevator corridor, where she wouldn't be overheard and the receptionist could see her.

"Greene Gallery."

"Hi, it's me," Dinah said.

"Thank goodness you called—I've been goin' crazy. Did we get the contract?" Bethany asked.

"Would you believe I haven't seen the wretched man? I arrived at nine thirty to make sure I was on time for my ten o'clock appointment, and he still hasn't turned up. We must have lost out. Why would he make me wait for good news?"

"Oh, don't say that," Bethany protested. "His tardiness probably doesn't have anything to do with us. His train from Greenwich, or wherever he lives, may have been late."

"Maybe you're right, but if we weren't desperate, I'd leave this minute. And it's my fault we have to put up with being jerked around like this," Dinah said.

"Hush that talk. No matter what, the move uptown was the right thing to do. We were barely surviving on Cornelia Street. We'd have been out of business by summer if we hadn't moved," Bethany said.

Dinah sighed. "We may be out of business by summer anyway. I better go. I'll call you when I know something."

Back in the reception room, Dinah considered shifting to another chair, but they were all designed to cripple—icy steel bent in every way except to fit the human form, scratchy upholstery the same shade of gray as the carpet. The austere reception room declared the hand of one of Manhattan's best-known designers, but it looked and felt frigid. It was also empty of people and this was an ordinary Tuesday, a workday. Where were the workers? The clients? She sighed, and tried again to find a comfortable position.

She wished she could think of anything but the probable failure of the Greene Gallery. When she'd leased the Fifty-Seventh Street gallery in January, she'd counted on the better location to attract new artists, more customers, bigger sales. But March was halfway over, business was terrible, and the midtown Manhattan rent was murderous. In Greenwich Village she'd run her pocket-sized gallery with one assistant in a building her husband owned. The new space was much larger, and she'd been forced to hire another full-time person and two part-timers. They were graduate students, less costly than experienced gallery staff, but expenses were up, and the bottom line was red.

Today she'd learn whether she'd won the contract to select, buy and hang art in the New York office of the management consultants Davidson, Douglas, Danbury & Weeks—DDD&W to nearly everyone. She'd been introduced to Theodore Douglas by Coleman, who'd known him from way back. He was not only one of the Ds in DDD&W, he also chaired the firm's art committee. He could make her or break her. Well, not break her exactly, but he could save the Greene Gallery. The fee for the job would support the gallery for a year. If Theodore Douglas ever deigned to see her.

To continue reading *Fatal Impressions*,
please email us at artsmart@delosfiction.com.